FLICKERS

FLICKERS

A NOVEL BY

PHILLIP ROCK

DODD, MEAD & COMPANY · NEW YORK

Copyright © 1977 by Phillip Rock
All rights reserved
No part of this book may be reproduced in any form
without permission in writing from the publisher
Printed in the United States of America
by The Haddon Craftsmen, Inc., Scranton, Penna.

1 2 3 4 5 6 7 8 9 10

Library of Congress Cataloging in Publication Data

Rock, Phillip, date
  Flickers : a novel.

  I. Title.
PZ4.R68Fl   [PS3568.033]   813'.5'4   77–22577
ISBN 0–396–07506–1

To my wife Bettye and Kevin, my son,
who kept me writing with love and threats

REEL ONE

ORPHANS OF THE STORM

The rains came unexpectedly that August, drenching the cotton lands and turning the dirt streets of the river towns into stinking quagmires. The levees were breaking all along the Yazoo as the warm rain from the Gulf poured unceasingly onto the black earth. The Vicksburg papers reported that whole towns were moving out, with the residents seeking the high ground, taking their belongings with them, and there was talk of calling out the National Guard to prevent looting of abandoned homes and farms. The rain ceased before the emergency got out of hand, but the roads between Vicksburg and Yazoo City remained impassable for weeks. One of the casualties of the flood was Doc Klickspiel's carnival, although the distress of the little group was not deemed worthy of newspaper space. It was a shabby carnival and its nonappearance in such places as Waltersville, Ballground, Eldorado and Bentonia would not be greatly missed, except by Doc of course, who saw his profits for the season running off like the stinking water. Doc had been in trouble even before the rains came. The war had given him a false sense of his carnival's importance and he had bought some Reo trucks and a new tent in Biloxi in September 1918, but the Armistice had played havoc with the Gulf Coast economy. Doc wouldn't have put it quite that way had he been asked a direct question on the subject. Doc would have grunted and said that the rubes were holding on to their money, which was as good an analysis of conditions as any. The war factories were closed, the soldiers had all been paid off and jobs were scarce. There was more to do with a dollar than spend it seeing a pinhead, a fat lady or an alligator boy. Doc Klickspiel was in trouble and he knew it. There was a man from a collection agency in Biloxi

1

looking for the trucks and when he got them Doc would be through. He was not surprised to see a sheriff and two deputies coming down the road, sloshing ankle deep through the mud and then knee deep as they reached the mired convoy of three nearly new trucks and five battered old cars. Doc sat on the tailgate of one of the Reo's, which was axle deep in semiliquid Mississippi dirt. Doc wore a yellow rain slicker and he was smoking a rum-soaked cheroot.

"'Morning, Sheriff." He wondered why he had never seen a thin sheriff in Mississippi, or a small deputy. The three men seemed to block out the light like towering pines.

"Where is he?" the sheriff asked.

"Where's who?" Doc said.

The sheriff spat a stream of tobacco juice into a rain puddle.

"What's-his-name . . . the big, redheaded bo."

"Earl?" Doc said.

"I'm askin' *you.* I don't know the bastard's name."

Doc sucked on the cheroot and wrinkled his brow as though thinking deeply. He had a face like a toothless yellow monkey and the sheriff glared at it with distaste and annoyance.

"You know the bo," the sheriff snarled.

"Earl," Doc said, nodding. "That's the only redheaded guy I know of—except for the pinhead. He's got a fringe of red hair."

The sheriff shifted his awesome bulk from one mud-caked leg to the other and jammed his thumbs into a broad, black belt from which dangled a holster containing a Smith & Wesson six shooter, the handle shiny from much use.

"I ain't lookin' for no pinhead. I'm lookin' for this Earl what's-his-name."

"Donovan," Doc said wearily. "Earl Donovan. What do you want him for?"

"Sellin' bibles," the sheriff said.

Doc shook his head sadly. "The country's sure going to the dogs when a man gets in trouble for selling the good book."

"They ain't *good books,*" the sheriff said grimly. "Ten pages an' the rest blank. An' the genu-wine morocco leather covers are nothin' but *cardboard!*"

Klickspiel made a gutteral sound deep in his throat, a rattle of phlegm that could have been taken for a note of understanding for the sheriff's position. Actually, he was silently cursing Earl Donovan for being such a damn fool as to try and sell his bibles while the carnival was rooted in the mud like so many tree stumps.

2

"The books ain't worth five cents in the crapper," the big lawman went on, his already angry face becoming more clouded, "an' that sonofabitch is sellin' 'em for *five* dollars! Folks had the fear o' God put in 'em because of the storm an' all and that flim-flammer's just takin' advantage of 'em, especially the *old* folk. The bastard even sold one to my own *mother* . . . a sweet, God fearin, people-trustin' old lady who can't hardly see her hand if it was in front of her nose!"

Klickspiel winced. He removed the cheroot from his bloodless, flesh-less lips and rolled it slowly between fingers stained mahogany from nicotine.

"I'm sure he'll make restitution."

"Horse turds!" the sheriff said. "He'll sure as hell make restitution. I'll put him on the chain gang repairin' the levees. An' you can bet on that, bo!"

"I believe you," Doc said. "Chances are he's gone across the river, but if he shows up here, which ain't likely on account of he owes me money, I'll call you right off an' you can come an' get him. He ain't no pal of mine."

"Double horse turds," the sheriff said. "You carnie bastards are thick as thieves."

Klickspiel sighed. The cheroot had become tasteless and he tossed it away. He felt a twinge of sympathy for Donovan. Selling one of them Hong Kong bibles to the sheriff's *mother!* Well, how was the mick to know?

"I always cooperate with the law," he said bleakly. The sheriff wasn't listening, he was staring at something past the truck with an expression of mingled awe and discomfort.

"Is that the alligator boy?"

Doc peered around the side of the truck. Little Joe was standing between the Reo and Doc's Ford. He was naked except for a dirty yellow blanket that he had wrapped loosely around his body. He looked horrible in the hard light of day. The scales that covered three-fourths of his emaciated body were a dull grayish brown, tinted here and there with the green watercolor solution that he painted on them before a show. The kind was nineteen and he had been with Doc for seven years. He had run away from his home in Coldfield, Alabama, where his parents had kept him locked in an attic room since the time he'd been able to walk. They had viewed his terrible affliction as a curse from God. He suffered from elephantine psoriasis for which there was no known cure—not that Doc had tried to find one. Alligator boys were a popular attraction. A man could get a pinhead from any loony bin,

3

but a good alligator boy was hard to find.

"Yes," Doc said. "That's him."

"Je-sus," the sheriff said, letting his breath out slowly. "Ugly sonofabitch, ain't he?"

"Well, he ain't pretty," Doc said. He felt uneasy seeing Little Joe standing there. There were many things that the kid hated—crowds, staring people, pointed fingers, open mouths—but the one thing on earth that he hated the most was Earl Donovan. Doc was not certain of the reason for this hatred, but he thought it might have been triggered by the kid's infatuation with Stella Dole, the show's "Little Egypt." Stella was a whore from Mobile. Her pimp had hit her across the head with a bottle one night and when she had left the hospital after a week a good deal of her mental powers had stayed behind. But her body was first class and Doc had hired her. He knew that just about every male except pinheads and geeks who had been with the carnival during the past three years had pumped away at her, himself included, but Little Joe had not (because even though she was not bright she was not insane) and Earl had not because Earl felt sorry for her. He bought her candies or flowers on her birthday and a bottle of perfume once at Christmas when they were working Tampa. Maybe Little Joe hated Earl because Stella was so fond of him. If you were an alligator boy, it wasn't hard to find someone to hate.

"Go back to the truck, Joe," Doc said. "Go put some pants on."

"I don't need no pants," the scaly kid said. "I know what they're here for. They're lookin' for that asshole Earl."

"You seen him?" The sheriff moved his right hand and rested it on the butt of his pistol.

"No," the kid said, "but I know he'll be here sooner or later. He's out hawkin' his phony bibles to get some scratch, but he gotta come back for his gear. He's movin' out. Got his bag packed an' all."

"That's a lie and you know it, Joe," Doc said. There was no conviction in his tone.

"Jus' stick aroun'," the kid said. "Shoot his balls off."

The sheriff cleared his throat and spat at his feet. There was something frightening about the reptilian creature, an aura of hate that he found ominous. Hell, he thought, I might be doing this Earl Donovan a favor by locking him up. A vision flashed through his mind. He could see a man sleeping peacefully, not realizing that a naked boy with green scales was crawling through a window and reaching for his throat with crusted, bony hands. He shuddered.

"Nobody's goin' to shoot nobody. Jus' got a warrant is all."

4

"I'd shoot him," the kid hissed. His eyes were wild and a string of saliva hung from the corner of his ruined mouth. "I'd put a slug in his belly an' then blow his cock off."

"Now, Joe," Doc sighed. So Donovan was planning to cut out. He couldn't blame the man, only marvel that he had stuck around as long as he had. There had been a few good seasons, but this hadn't been one of them. Captain Kroner had left the show in New Orleans taking his cats with him, and Logan and his ferris wheel never had shown up. But Donovan had stuck, doing the work of ten men for less than one man's pay. He had no gripes. "Listen," he said to the sheriff, "there's a telephone down the road in Belmont. If Donovan turns up here I swear to God I'll call you. He don't have an automobile or anything. He can't get far hoofin' through this muck carryin' a suitcase."

"Horse turds," the sheriff said. "I'm out for that Bo an' I ain't leavin' here without him."

And then the younger of the deputies cocked his head to one side as he heard the distant pop-pop-popping of an automobile engine. There was a cluster of backfires and then someone must have adjusted the spark because the backfiring ceased.

"That's the Dodge!" the deputy cried.

The sheriff, cursing, moving very quickly for such a big man, climbed up on the tailgate of the Reo. He could see the canvas top of the Dodge where they had parked it beyond the cottonwoods at the top of the rise. The car was moving—slowly, crabbing sideways on the mud slick road. A tall, redhaired man was behind the wheel.

STOP, GODDAMN YOU, STOP! The sheriff tugged his hogleg pistol from the holster and fired a shot in the air. The sound rocketed back and forth in the hollow, booming off the rain dark trees and the sodden slopes of the hill.

The alligator boy screamed, a ferret's shriek, and clambered up on the tailgate, dropping his dirty yellow blanket. He hurled his naked lizard body against the sheriff and grabbed for the pistol.

SHOOT HIM-SHOOT HIM-SHOOT HIM.

The sheriff recoiled in horror as the boy pawed at his arm. He struck out at him with the pistol the way he would have struck at a rattlesnake if one had dropped on him from a rock. The alligator boy clutched the barrel of the pistol with both hands and tried to wrestle it away from the sheriff. The gun went off, blowing a hole in the boy's chest big enough to stick an apple in.

MA!

and then he was dead, falling backward into the mud.

5

That was in Warren County, Mississippi, in the late summer of 1920. They buried the alligator boy in a pine box in the town of Belmont near the swollen bank of the Yazoo River. The sheriff paid for the burial. A team of men from the collection agency in Biloxi arrived the day after the funeral and drove the Reos away after dumping everything that was in them beside the road. That was the official end of Doc Klickspiel's carnival. Madame Tauras, nee Klopf, the gypsy fortune teller, went back to Tampa with her husband, Fred; Stella Dole went down to Baton Rouge and entered a house there; the sword swallower and the India rubber man and the fat lady and etcetera and etcetera drifted off to join carnivals or circuses in Des Moines, St. Louis, Omaha and etcetera, and Doc took the pinhead to the Mississippi State Mental Hospital in Jackson and had him committed. He then drove his Model T Ford to Knoxville, Tennessee, and moved in with a widowed sister. He died there in the spring of 1933.

BANG.
Earl Donovan had been shot at before and he knew the difference between a gun fired in the air and one fired at his head. He did not panic as the sheriff's car went into a slide, but kept his foot off the brake and turned the wheel in the direction of the skid while teasing the engine with a little gas.
BANG.
The second shot sounded muffled. Donovan was out of range anyway, coasting down the backslope of the low hill, with the car gliding from one side of the narrow road to the other like a cow on ice. Then the tires bit through the mud and he was able to steer the car and give it more gas. It was a good feeling.

> *Old Fogerty had a motor car*
> *the finest ever seen*
> *Forty mile an hour the boyo went*
> *on the road to Innisfree*

"Damn!" Earl said, spitting out the word as he glared at the road. He had suddenly thought of his suitcase in the back of Fred Klopf's car and his momentary euphoria was replaced by black Irish gloom. There wasn't a whole lot in the suitcase—he was wearing his only suit and best shirt—but at the bottom, below the underwear, the soiled shirts, the

6

socks, the white trousers and blue blazer, the blue felt cap and bow ties lay an envelope. There was a hundred dollars in that envelope, his ace-in-the-hole money, his cutting out money, and now he was cutting out and he didn't have it. All that he had in his pocket was fifteen dollars from the sale of three bibles. There were ten unsold bibles in a canvas sack on the seat beside him, but there was no chance of his selling any of them, at least not in Mississippi. He had to cross the river and get into Louisiana. But the immediate problem was getting as far as possible down the road to Vicksburg before someone spotted him driving the sheriff's car and tipped off the State Police or took matters into their own hands and blew his head off with a shotgun—as the man standing in the middle of the road looked like he might be on the point of doing. Donovan braked slowly so as not to skid and the man walked up to the side of the car—but not too close—the ugly barrels raised and pointed at the door of the car.

"Who are you?" the man said. He had a long, heavily weathered face and small, suspicious eyes.

"Are you Bannister?" Donovan said.

"I ain't never heard of no Bannister."

"U. S. marshal from Vicksburg."

The shotgun began a wavering descent from the horizontal.

"U. S. marshal?"

Donovan nodded quickly. "Right. The sheriff sent me looking for him. All hell's broke loose in Belmont. Water knee deep in the streets and folks looting . . . running wild."

"Niggers?"

"What do you think?"

"I'd better get up there," the man said darkly. "Can you give me a lift?"

"No," Donovan said, putting the car into gear. "Gotta get that marshal or the sheriff'll skin me alive."

"Hold on a minute," the man said, stepping closer to the car.

"No dice, buddy. I'm in a big hurry." He stomped the gas pedal and the car bucketed forward before the man could put his foot on the runningboard.

Luck, Donovan thought. Jesus, what if the man had said "Who the hell you tryin' to fool, mister? There ain't no U. S. marshal in Vicksburg. What the hell you doin' in the sheriff's auto-mobile? Git outa there or I'll blow your guts to gravy!"

Could have happened. Could still happen. Donovan drove grimly on. He had to put miles between himself and the sheriff, but he also had to ditch the car before he ran into any more people. He spotted a side road that cut through deep woods toward the river and turned down it, not getting more than a mile before the road ended in a sea of mud. He plowed through it in low gear, muddy water over the wheels, over the runningboard, reached high ground and then the engine coughed and died.

And that was that. Earl Donovan took the sack of bibles from the front seat and started walking—in the dismal land between the rivers (between the Yazoo and the Mississippi) with the mud up to his knees and then, as the evening slipped across the gray sky, the rains came again and tried to beat him into the earth.

"I'll make it," he kept repeating to himself as he sloshed along toward a black, tree-gloomed horizon. "I'll make it. I really hit the pits this time, but I'll make it . . . I'll make it . . ."

It was raining and flooding in Louisiana too, and there were sheriffs on the roads. None of them paid much attention to a tall white man with red hair walking the highways with a sack over his shoulder, but their glances worried Donovan. The Law was The Law. They were a fraternity and they passed on their bits of information from one to another. This man wanted . . . that man wanted. Please hold for the sheriff of . . . kindly detain and phone collect. . . . He flagged a truck heading north into Arkansas and the driver shared a meatball sandwich with him and lukewarm coffee from a fruit jar. Donovan got out in Pine Bluff which was as far as the truck was going with its dark brown sacks of Louisiana rice. He had fifteen dollars in his pocket and the bibles and the sun was shining.

"I'm going to be okay."

He was mud to his ass. His shoes were ruined. He had a stubble of beard and was tired as a dog. If he went any deeper into Arkansas someone would arrest him for sure as a public eyesore. He went to a bath house and sent his suit out to be cleaned. A negro kid took his shoe size and a five dollar bill and bought him a pair of shoes. There was thirty cents change which he gave to the boy. He spent that day and the night in Pine Bluff and it cost him the lion's share of his money— the bath, a shave, the shoes, the cleaning of the suit, a meal and a few drinks and a hotel room. He felt pretty good in the morning after twelves hours sleep in a clean bed, but his wallet was light. He thought about trying to sell a few bibles, but there was one road into Pine Bluff and one road out of it and he didn't know the country. He figured that southern Arkansas would be a rotten place to get arrested in. After

8

breakfast in a hash joint around the corner from the hotel, he walked to the bus station to find out how far four dollars and eighty-five cents would take him. As he stood on the corner of Main and Elm a truck pulled up and the driver blipped the horn to attract his attention. It was the same man who had given him the lift from Louisiana and he was now on his way to Joplin, Missouri, with a stopover at Fort Smith to pick up a quarter ton of cement.

The driver, whose name was Randall Glins, was grateful for the company. He had once driven a truck for the Ringling Bros. and he liked carny people. When the truck had a flat tire thirty miles out of Little Rock, Donovan took his bibles out of the sack and placed them in the sun to bake the moisture out of them. The bibles were in cardboard boxes wrapped in heavy waxed paper. Only the selling sample had been ruined by the rain and Donovan tossed it into the bushes beside the road, but not before Randall Glins had thumbed through it.

"You mean, you can really sell these things?"

"Sure," Donovan said. "For whatever the traffic will bear. Five, even ten bucks, some times."

"People must be crazy," the driver said, turning the cheap newsprint pages. "How the hell do you do it?"

"Well, it takes practice. You gotta have good hands."

He took the book from the driver and flipped through it rapidly, stopping five or six times. Each double page spread that he stopped at was beautifully printed on vellum paper. He flipped back through the book, this time stopping at a faultlessly engraved illustration. He never glanced at the book as he did this. His fingers were like eyes.

"I'd sure hate to play poker with you, mister."

"Yeah," Donovan said gravely. "That would be a mistake."

Poker.

Poker was his way out. A good game in a good place. Some place where men had money and played recklessly with it. Kansas City was such a place. Topeka was good, and Tulsa, and the oil towns of East Texas. But he'd need a stake. He couldn't buy many chips with four dollars and eighty-five cents. If he sold the bibles he could make fifty, and he could run fifty up to five hundred pretty quick playing with Kansas City stockyard rubes, then cut out with the half grand and play with the big boys. Life can be simple if you have a plan.

Joplin was not K.C., but it *was* the gateway to the southwest and a lot of fancy cars were parked at the new motor courts; Appersons and Jordans, Mercers and Studebakers, Standards and Knight Sixes, their owners resting after the long drive from points east. Heading west. To

New Mexico and Arizona and then on to California. A lot of people sure had money, Donovan was thinking as he strolled through the town in the early afternoon. He felt like a damn fool lugging a gunny sack. The sack had been okay with the good folks in Mississippi, but what he should have for the pitch was a decent suitcase, a salesman's sample case of simulated leather. He wondered dully if there was any chance of buying one for a couple of bucks. But he didn't hustle around looking. He just dragged his feet down one street and up another, moving in a kind of daze. It was easily ninety degrees in the town, but he felt chilled to the bone and lightheaded. He had a temperature of 102.8° and it was rising.

"I feel lousy."

What he needed was a belt of rye and he looked around for a likely place to buy one, a barber shop or a pool hall. Bootleggers seemed to favor barber shops and pool halls, but he was certainly in the wrong part of town. He was halfway down a street lined with big frame houses that were set back from the sidewalk amid clipped lawns and shade trees. A gramophone was playing somewhere, the melody drifting through the rustling leaves. He was mesmerized by the sound and thought of a summer night in Baltimore . . . a beer garden down by the Potomac . . . Japanese lanterns glowing in the dusk. He wore a white suit and was dancing with a girl in a green dress . . .

> . . . *poor butterfly* . . .
> *Poor butterfly*

The chill was leaving him, burned away by the fever that was now an even 103°. He felt consumed, as if a fire raged in his skull. He stepped out of the sun, staggered across a lawn and flopped on his back in the dappled shade of a chestnut tree.

"You get out of here or I'll call a policeman."

The words came to him as though from an immense distance. He opened his eyes, but could see nothing but hard shafts of sunlight filtering through the canopy of leaves above him.

"Do you hear me? Now you just get off my lawn!"

He struggled to raise himself on his elbows. A woman was standing at the edge of the shade. She was a large blonde, wearing a pink silk dress. Donovan judged her age as forty, not that he really gave a damn.

"Sorry, ma'am. Just . . . resting."

"Well, you go sleep off your drunk someplace else."

10

Earl Donovan was not and never had been nor ever would be drunk under a tree in Joplin, Missouri. He felt outraged. The fever honed his pride.

"Lady . . . you are . . . seriously mistaken."

He stood up with great effort, then bent down again and dumped his sack of bibles on the grass. He picked one up, tore off the waxed paper wrapping and took the book from its cardboard box.

"I have here . . . for the ridiculous price . . . five dollars . . . a mere . . . pittance for . . . a masterpiece of . . . printer's art . . . genuine morocco leather . . . vellum . . . etchings of the masters . . . Jacob. Saul. Solomon and Sheba . . ." His strong hands gripped the book. His sure fingers rippled through the pages. "All here. Every blessed word—'Set me as a seal upon thine heart, as a seal upon thine arm . . .' Solomon. Judges. Samuel. Psalms. 'Blessed is he that considereth the poor' . . ."

He brought the book to her and placed it in her hands. She did not run from his approach. She studied him curiously, seeing neither madman nor drunk, but a sturdy, handsome man of about thirty with a feverish look in his eyes, eyes that were hazel, set in a strong, lean-jawed face. His hair fascinated her. It was thick and wavy, a deep, shiny chestnut red. Her late husband had been hairless as an egg, the result of typhoid fever in his youth.

"Well, I don't know."

"Feel it, ma'am. This is morocco leather. . . . The finest . . . money can . . ."

"Why, land sakes," she said, turning the book every which way. "It's nothing but brown cardboard. If there's one thing I know it's leather!"

"That is *Chinese* cardboard," Donovan whispered conspiratorially, leaning toward her, placing a hand on the woman's upper arm—a solid arm, fat and white. "Don't tell anybody. Made in Canton, China, by Chinese people. Not a *Hong Kong* bible like they call 'em. A *Canton, China* bible. Buy 'em for fifty cents and I weep to think what they pay those poor bastards to make 'em."

His fever had now peaked at 104.5° and he was as far out of his head as anyone is ever likely to be.

"Poor butterfly," he whispered.

The woman dropped the book and placed the palm of one hand on Donovan's brow.

"My Lord, you're just burning up! Why, you're sick!"

"Lady," Donovan said, "I'm dead."

And then the ground roared up at him and slapped him into oblivion.

11

REEL TWO

HEARTS OF THE WORLD

The Katz Rialto theater in Cleveland, Ohio, was a good booking. Abe Katz, who owned the theater with his brother-in-law, Milton Feinberg, was not afraid to spend money for good acts. Mabel Wilson was headlining, followed in importance by Jimmy Pepper and his Komedy Klub; Lindsay and Hammond; Vesper and Morgan; Toledo Laine and his wonder dog, Yukon; the Dove Sisters and the Vespini family. The house was nearly two-thirds full, not bad for a Saturday matinee in August, and the evening performances were sold out thanks to a convention of Elks. Abe stepped out of his little office just off the mezzanine, lured by the throaty, belting tones of the one and only, if aging, Mabel Wilson.

> *You're just playing a game*
> *with me, baby . . .*
> *an' it sure is a cryin' shame.*
> *You're playing a game with me, baby,*
> *but I don't know the name of the*
> *game.*
> *You walk in at any old hour . . .*
> *you walk in then walk out again.*
> *Oh, I know you're just playing a*
> *game with my heart, but*
> *I don't know the name of the game!*

The audience picked up the last stanza at her urgings and she walked off stage to the roaring chorus of the crowd singing what had become her trademark since introducing the song in 1915. She took three curtain calls, blew kisses and made her final exit to a thunder of applause. Getting Mabel Wilson down from Chicago had cost plenty, but she was worth every nickel. Listening to the ovation gave Abe Katz a warm glow in the pit of his stomach, a little balm for the ulcer. The pain returned a few minutes later, gnawing at him like a rat's tooth.

The Pepper Komedy Klub were on. Fat Billy Wells, Joe Rhine, Mike Dale and Jimmy Pepper's wife, Mae. No Jimmy Pepper. Some punk understudy playing the waiter . . . coming on stage like a husband sneaking into the house at two in the morning. Joe Rhine almost pushing him—Mae leading him by the hand. Abe chewed at the hard ridges of flesh that had once been fingernails and glared at the spotlit stage. There should be laughter by now. Jimmy Pepper could draw laughs just by walking across the stage, his tall, thin, stoop shouldered body; his horse face and mocking eyes. He could break up a house with one glance. No laughs now, people sitting back, waiting for something to happen. The understudy walked to the table at stage center, a restaurant table set for one diner. The understudy flicked it with his napkin, rearranged the vinegar and oil cruets, moved the knife and fork a fraction of an inch. Nothing funny in that, but Jimmy Pepper would have *made* it funny, would have started the laughs rolling to break with a roar when fat Billy wandered on stage and handed his overcoat and hat to Mae, the hatcheck girl. It was what Pepper called the laughter of anticipation. There was no laughter, just a snicker or two as Billy came on, moving with surprising grace for such a fat man.

"I hope I can get a good meal here," Billy said.

"I hope so, too," the waiter said.

He missed the wink, Abe Katz thought furiously. The stupid clod. Missed the damn wink to the audience that let them in on it, telling them that this fat rube was about to have a meal he'd never forget. No wink. No laughter of anticipation.

"What kind of soup do you have?"

"Oyster," the understudy said. "And clam . . . chicken . . . corn chowder . . . pea . . . ham bone and mulligatawny."

Abe stifled a groan. The words should have come out in a rush: oysterclamchickencornchowderpeahambone and mulligatawny. That was a dead cert laugh when Pepper said it, stressing mulligatawny, making it sound like a dog's howl.

"I'll take the pea."

"You can take it, but we ain't got it."

13

"Then I'll try the chicken."

"Try tomorrow."

Pepper would have been leaning insolently against the table, studying his fingernails. The understudy was just standing there, sweating, trying to remember his lines. Abe had had enough, more than enough, his ulcer was trying to jump up his throat. He went back into his office and closed the door. Later, when Vesper and Morgan were doing their Gallagher and Shean imitation, Abe went backstage and up to Mae Pepper's dressing room. He knocked on the door and then entered before she had a chance to say anything. He knew that he wouldn't be welcome. He knew also that she would be expecting him. She was still in her makeup, seated in front of the mirror, smoking a Murad. The small, cramped, airless room was hazy with the pungent Turkish smoke.

"I'm sorry, Abe. I shoulda told you." She did not turn to speak to him. Her eyes were rooted on her own image in the mirror. Jesus, what a beauty, Abe thought as he pulled up a chair and sat down. He felt sorry for her, but business was business and his business was the Rialto.

"Sick, huh?"

"Yea," she said. "Sick." Her tone was hollow.

"What is it this time?"

"Spanish influenza." She took a drag on the cigarette and then stuffed it into a china saucer that was filled with butts and ash.

"Don't give me no banana oil, kiddo. Is he back on the booze?"

She shook her head and reached for another cigarette. "No. I swear it, Abe. He hasn't touched a drop in a year. Just sick. I swear to God. I told him to stay in bed. If you wanna blame anyone, blame me."

"I'm not blamin', Mae. But I know Jimmy. Know him better than you do. We've been good pals and I'd cut off my right arm for the guy if it'd do any good. But, you know, I got a house to run. I pay for Jimmy Pepper an' I want Jimmy Pepper on the stage an' not some punk who's still wet behind the ears."

Mae Pepper kept her eyes fixed on the mirror. It was like looking at a stranger.

"Dan's a good kid," she said dully.

Abe snorted. "He's got four left feet. You shoulda let Joe or Mike do the part, at least they know the routine."

"He knows it. He just wilted under fire."

"Fine. I feel sorry for the rube, but I ain't billing the show as no amateur night. You tell Jimmy to get his butt off the deathbed."

14

"He'll be here."

"He better be." He tried to make it sound like a threat, but it came out like a plea. "We got every Elk in Ohio comin' in tonight."

"We won't let you down, Abe."

"I know *you* won't." He stood up and looked at the dark-haired, slender woman for a moment and then touched the back of her neck, his fingers lingering on the smooth, cool flesh. An avuncular caress.

"You look lower than a snake's patoot. If you ever feel like talkin' things out, you know where my office is."

"Thanks, Abe. But everything's going to be okay."

"Oh, hell yes," Abe said, starting toward the door. "Things always work out."

She wasn't so sure. She wasn't sure of anything all of a sudden. Today was her birthday. She was twenty-four years old and yet the woman who stared back at her from the mirror seemed ageless. Ageless but not wise. She examined her image minutely, as though searching for flaws. She could find none. The mouth a little too wide, perhaps. The nose a trifle too thin. Were the cheekbones too prominent? She didn't think so. It gave her face a vaguely Oriental cast. The eyes, too. Dark brown and almond shaped. She accentuated the Oriental slant by careful application of mascara and shadow pencil. She wore her black hair parted in the middle and then rolled into tight buns behind the ears. When she wore the silk lounging pajamas that Jimmy had bought for her in San Francisco she looked Chinese. Perhaps she had some Chinese blood in her, although Indian was more likely. She was French-Canadian and she had asked her mother once if there was any Blackfoot or Sioux blood in her family. Her mother had denied it, too vehemently it seemed to Mae.

Cold and beautiful. No sparkle. No life. The expression blank as a wax doll. She raised a listless hand and reached for another cigarette. Smoking too much. She was going through two packs of Murads a day and her teeth were becoming yellow. She lit the cigarette and looked away from the creature in the mirror. She knew that she had to do something about Jimmy, but she was overcome with a stupefying inertia. It all seemed so pointless. So meaningless. If she helped Jimmy through this it would just start the cycle moving again. It was a circle without end. Round and round and round. She smoked the cigarette down until it began to scorch her fingers, then she snuffed it out in the ashtray and stood up, gave her hair a pat and left the dressing room. The Vespini family were in the hall, all gleaming olive flesh and span-

15

gled tights. They were like sleek, muscular seals and the vibrancy of their bodies and their gaiety of spirit irked her. She stood with her back against the wall until the troop of acrobats had filed noisily down the stairs and into the wings, then she continued along the hall and knocked at a door. Joe Rhine opened it a crack. He was still in blackface and she could smell whisky on his breath.

"Is Billy decent?"

"Yeah, sure," Joe said. He opened the door all the way and stepped aside so that she could enter. The dressing room was even smaller than hers and the stench of cigar smoke, whisky, greasepaint and sweat was almost overpowering. Billy Wells dominated the crowded room. He sat facing one of the two makeup mirrors, wiping the last gelatinous shreds of custard pies from his face and head. Dan Ryan stood nervously in one corner. He was already dressed, but his exit to the door was blocked by the muscular form of Mike Dale. Mae knew that they had been giving Dan the business for missing cues. He would never work out as an understudy for Jimmy and the sooner he realized that the better it would be for him. The boys had probably been telling him that, Billy nicely, the others more bluntly, even brutally. He was looking at her with a kind of pathetic appeal in his eyes, but she avoided his gaze. She had helped him as much as she could because she liked him, even loved him a little, but that was off stage. As a performer he had too much to learn.

"I have to talk to you, Billy," she said.

The fat man nodded and went on wiping his face with a towel.

"You can talk here," Joe said. He took a pint bottle off the top of a wooden locker and pulled the cork. "Like a drink?"

Mae shook her head. "I gotta talk to Billy alone."

The blackfaced comic took a swig of whisky, shuddered slightly and replaced the cork.

"What secrets have we got, for chrissakes?"

She didn't like Joe. He drank too much and never took a bath unless Jimmy screamed at him to clean up.

"*I look like a coon an' stink like a coon.*" That was Joe Rhine's favorite expression. Maybe he hated doing a blackface bit, but no one had forced him into it.

"Alone," she said coldly. "Okay, Billy?"

"Sure, Mae," Billy said in his soft, wistful voice. "I'll only be a few minutes."

"Take your time."

16

As she turned to leave, Dan Ryan bolted away from the corner, ducking under Mike Dale's cannonball biceps.

"Don't go away mad," Mike growled.

The young man slammed the door as he left. His face was flushed. "I should have dropped that big ape."

Mae said nothing. It was a remark of such ludicrous bravado that no comment was required. Ryan trailed her to her dressing room, but she stopped him from following her in.

"No, Dan. Take the cue. Grab a train for Philly. Go home."

"No," he said heatedly. "I'm not taking a powder, not now. No, sir! Nobody ever said Jack Ryan's son couldn't take it." He scowled, but it only made him look petulant. "Take it *and* dish it out, you bet. One more lousy crack from those guys and they'll get a sock in the jaw."

He was very handsome, almost girlish, with pale blue eyes and soft wavy hair. She touched the side of his face and patted his cheek.

"Don't be a silly baby. Go back to Philly. Try for something legit."

He made a long face. "Gee, Mae, let's not go through that again. It's vaudeville for me. Jimmy thinks I'm okay."

"Jimmy doesn't know what he thinks any more. You listen to me. If you can't cut the mustard in Cleveland, you won't cut it anywhere. Your old man has a business, doesn't he? Go down on your knees to him and maybe he'll take you into the firm."

He pressed his body against hers and his arms encircled her waist. "I'll go if you'll come with me. I mean that, Mae."

She shook her head and pushed him away from her. "No."

"Please," he persisted, reaching for her again. "I'm crazy about you, doll."

"So is Jimmy."

"He sure shows it, doesn't he?" he said bitterly. "Always slapping you around . . . leaving you alone nights. Boy, he sure does show it. I bet you could leave and he wouldn't even know you were gone."

"He'd know."

"Well, he sure wouldn't give much of a damn."

"It would kill him," she said quietly.

A door across the hall opened with a bang and a huge white husky bolted out on the end of a heavy chain. A tall, middle-aged man followed, gripping the chain tightly. The man wore a gaudy cowboy outfit complete with woolly chaps and a white ten gallon hat. The dog exploded into a frenzy of tail wagging when it spotted Mae. The cowboy tugged the dog away before it could leap up and lick her face.

17

"He sure barks at your tree, Mae."

"Yeah," she said, holding out her hand for the husky to slobber over. "I got a way with the boys, don't I, Yukon? But they're not all gentlemen like you."

The cowboy winked at her. "Just keep 'em on a short leash an' they'll behave themselves."

"I'll keep that in mind, Toledo."

"You do that," the cowboy said and tugged the dog down the hall toward the stairs.

Ryan was in her dressing room, leaning against her dresser and lighting up one of her Murads. He looked sure of himself, almost smug. It was a look that she detested, the single thing that she found infuriating in all men, that self-satisfied little smile after the night before.

"Out," she said, holding the door open.

"Not till I get an answer."

"I gave you one. Go home to Philly. *Now.*"

He shook his head and tried to blow a smoke ring. "No. I'm not getting out of your life."

"You were never in it," she said coldly.

"You're some kidder," he said.

Her eyes were dead coals. "Am I?"

He forced a laugh. "Yeah . . . sure you are." The way she was looking at him made him uncomfortable. He glanced down at his well cut striped blazer and dark blue pants as though seeking self-assurance. "You know who you're talking to, don't you? This is Dan J. Ryan, the guy who made you coo like a baby last night—and the night before. I'm the guy who . . ."

"Fucked me. So what?"

His face turned crimson to the hairline. He dropped the cigarette on the floor and crushed it out with the toe of his shoe.

"That's not a nice thing to say, Mae."

"It's what you did, isn't it?"

His composure was wilting. "I . . . we . . . made love."

She stared at him in stony silence for a moment. "You fucked me and I cooed. I needed a warm shoulder. That you have, Dan. You also have a warm pecker which I needed too. I don't need it now."

He made an inarticulate sound and tugged at the collar of his shirt. The stud popped and his bow tie fell askew. He rushed past her and into the hall. She thought she heard the word *bitch,* but she couldn't be sure.

18

When Billy Wells knocked gently at the door and came into the room she was lying on the broken-down sofa with one hand over her eyes.

"You okay, Mae?"

"Another week like this and you can drop me off at the booby hatch. I just can't take any more, Billy."

"You have to hang on," he said lamely.

"Oh, gee, Billy, I get so blue."

She was starting to cry, muffling the sobs behind her hand. Billy Wells pulled the chair away from the dressing table and sat down next to the couch. His buttock cheeks bulged over the edge of the seat.

"Everything'll work out. You'll see."

"No, it won't," she sobbed. "I get the willies just thinking about it."

He wanted to reach out and touch her, to stroke her hair and quiet her tears. He sighed deeply and folded his puffy hands in his lap.

"I know where he is."

"He'll be cockeyed."

"Maybe not."

"A hophead."

"I can straighten him out."

"Sure, prop him up until tomorrow."

She turned her face to the back of the couch. Her robe had fallen open and Billy could see the soft curve of one breast. He looked down at his folded hands.

"I'll go and get him."

"Tell him it's my birthday," she whispered.

Billy Wells liked Cleveland. He liked any place that had boats—not sailboats, but ships. Jimmy Pepper called Cleveland the stinking armpit of the world, but Billy didn't see the place that way at all. Sure, it was smoky, and ugly brick factories were clustered along the Cuyahoga dumping their bilge into the winding little river, but the reaches of Lake Erie seemed as vast as the sea and there were ships on it; great iron hulled ore boats and blunt bowed colliers plowing the wind-whipped water. Beyond the horizon lay Canada, also Detroit and the waterway to the great lakes beyond. Cleveland was ships to Billy Wells, and Cleveland was baseball; Tris Speaker leading the Indians to their first pennant. Billy loved ships and had once yearned to captain one. He loved baseball, but had been too fat to play. The fattest kid in Shelbyville, Indiana, where there were no ships and where the young baseball players had been lean as wolves.

19

Billy Wells stepped from the lobby of the Rialto Theater, adjusted his black bowler so that the brim shaded his eyes from the sun, and walked down 12th Street to Euclid. He took a trolley as far as 65th Street and walked over to Carnegie Avenue. He walked as he did on the stage, lightly, on the balls of his feet. The gait appeared awkward, almost perilous, like an elephant on tiptoe, but Billy Wells could, if he were asked to, flip his elephantine body into a back or forward somer-sault, or tap dance on a table, or walk a tight rope forty feet above a circus ring and impart such an illusion of instability and imminent disaster that strong men would gasp and women faint. But walking down a city street, as Billy was now doing on 65th between Euclid and Carnegie in Cleveland, Ohio, his light, almost mincing steps brought only snickers or sneers of contempt. His moon face was sallow, the pallor of those people who spend so much of their lives either on stage or sleeping the day away in theatrical boarding houses. His fat only looked unhealthy, however. At twenty-six, he was in near perfect physi-cal condition. He neither drank liquor nor smoked tobacco and he exercised twice daily, doing a complicated set of calisthenics taught to him by the great Sandow in person. He was not an unhandsome man, either. His dark brown eyes only appeared beady because of the fat that threatened to swallow them. He had a small, but well-proportioned nose and a cupid's mouth; rosebud lips that would have been angelic on a face that supported only one chin. His smile, and he smiled often, was warm and ingratiating. But, it was the sheer wobbling bulk of him that people saw and, contrary to popular legend, all the world does not love a fat man.

The plaster walls of the Chinese restaurant were painted a dull green and the woodwork red. Paper lanterns dangled from the high ceiling and a mural of snowcapped mountains and flying cranes was painted along one wall. There were no diners in the place, it was too late for lunch and too early for dinner. Mr. Wu, who owned the restaurant and the building containing it, was standing behind the cash register count-ing through a small pile of dollar bills. He was a thin, sad-faced man with rice paper skin.
"Good afternoon, Mister Wells."
"Good afternoon, Mister Wu."

Are you positive, Mr. Gallagher?
Absolutely, Mr. Shean.

"You have come for Mister Pepper?"

"If he's still here."

"Yes," Mister Wu said. "He is upstairs with two other unfortunate ones. Companions in misery—Spinoza."

"If you think of them in that way, Mister Wu, why do you continue to sell it to them?"

The elderly Chinese spread his hands outward, palms up, and shrugged his shadow-thin shoulders.

"It is not for me to judge the follies of the flesh, Mister Wells. It is written that powerful indeed is the empire of habit."

"Confucius?"

"I do not believe so, Mister Wells. It was Publilius Syrus who said that. I am addicted, as you know, to the reading of Mister Bartlett's book of quotations which I keep always beside my bed. Conscience chide me not—Dante. I do not make a profit on what I sell. I supply my friends so that their smoke will be pure. No one is injured save by himself—Erasmus."

"I've come to get him."

Mister Wu's smile was arcane. "I would give him an hour more to dream. Have you had your lunch, Mister Wells?"

Billy shook his head. The narrow room was pungent with the mingled odors of fried pork and steamed rice. He forgot about Jimmy, bushwacked by his appetite.

"No," he said faintly.

"We were about to sit for our afternoon meal. I would be honored to have you join us. The guests are met, the feast is set—Coleridge."

There was a long wooden table in one corner of the crowded, steamy kitchen. The cooks, waiters and several members of Mister Wu's family were seated at it. After much laughing and shoving and moving enough room was made for Billy to sit down in comparative comfort, although he was forced to eat with his elbows close to his side to avoid hitting a child at his right side and an aged woman with no teeth on his left. The food was superb. Each dish brought little moans of pleasure and delight from Billy's lips. Mister Wu was proud of his cooking. It was not, he hastened to explain, the fare served to his customers.

"Not chow mein, Mister Wells. Chow mein and chop suey is the cooking of New York. Some say Chicago, others San Francisco, but I know for a fact that they are dishes invented for the occidental palate on Pell Street in the city of New York. I serve both here, of course, for it is expected and it is cheap, but we eat as my ancestors ate. Upon what meat doth Caesar feed?—Shakespeare. As for us, Mister Wells, we shall partake today of *su yeung choy tong,* which is soup of watercress cooked with pork . . . and *tiem shun yu* . . . carp simmered with ginger, cucumber, sweet pickle and cloves, followed by *jar jee guy . . . tiem shun guyon . . . yang chow haan kow . . . tim sun gnow. . . .*"

Later, he felt stuffed and guilty. Surely more than an hour had passed. He managed one last mouthful of thinly sliced red pork in a bed of sweet and sour pea pods.

"I'd better get him back to the theater."

"But of course, Mister Wells. Time and tide wait for no man—a quote that I am unable to pinpoint with certainty. If you will follow me, please."

He led him through a doorway at the back of the kitchen, up dark and narrow stairs to a small room on the second floor. The passageway reeked of cooking and the dim room of another scent—the sickly oily sweetness of opium. Mister Wu held the door open until Billy entered, then he quietly disappeared, his soft slippers making no sound as he descended the stairs.

A shadow stirred on a cot.

"Is that you, fat guy?"

"How are you, Jimmy?" Billy asked.

"Rotten. This stuff doesn't hit me any more. It doesn't do a damn thing."

"Maybe that's a blessing."

"And maybe it isn't. It depends on the viewpoint, see. It depends on how you look at it. To me, personally, it's rotten."

As Billy's eyes became accustomed to the gloom he could see that there were four cots in the otherwise barren room. Jimmy Pepper was sitting on one, his long, horselike head cradled in his hands, and a man and a woman, fully dressed, were lying on another, the narrow canvas bed barely containing their rigid, side by side forms. The woman was staring at the ceiling and singing softly.

" '*Take a whiff on me, take a whiff on me . . . Hi, hi, baby, take a whiff on me . . .*' "

The man next to her stirred, sniffing and whining.

"Shut up with that damn dinge song, will ya? Just shut the hell up."

"You're a sore head," the woman said dreamily. "An old sore head. That's what *you* are."

"Come on back to the theater, Jimmy," Billy said.

The morose man on the cot did not stir. The wind rustled a drawn windowshade and a thin shaft of light fell across him like a stage spot. Five years ago Ziegfeld had called him the funniest man in America. He did not look very funny now.

"You run all of her errands, don't you, fat guy?"

"Now, Jimmy," he admonished.

"Why didn't she send the kid?"

"He didn't work out, Jimmy."

"He worked out with her. He's been screwing her bowlegged."

Billy drew in his breath sharply as though he had been punched in the belly. He knew that Mae had affairs and suspected that Ryan was seeing her, but he hated to hear it put so bluntly.

"Nothing like that," he said tonelessly.

Jimmy Pepper laughed. It sounded like a cough, dry and mirthless.

"You roger her yet, fat guy? Or can't you get it past your gut?"

The woman began to sing again, her voice whispy, touchingly child-like.

" *'Two little niggers lyin' in bed . . . One of 'em sick an' de odder mos' dead . . . Call for de doctor an' de doctor said . . . Feed dem darkies on shortenin' bread.'* "

"Will you for *Christ's sake* shut up!" her companion groaned, tossing fretfully on the cot.

"You old sore head," the woman muttered before collapsing into hophead dreams.

Jimmy Pepper stood up, a gaunt, stoop-shouldered shadow. He had folded his jacket to serve as a pillow and he took it from the cot and draped it over one shoulder like a cape.

"Okay, fat guy. Let's go. Lead me back to Mama Mae. I tried to reach hop heaven, Billy. I didn't get very far today." He twisted his mouth into a sardonic grin. "Better luck tomorrow."

"Ah, Jimmy," Billy said, touching the man's arm. It felt wasted, as though the flesh was melting off the bones. "Lay off that stuff, willya?"

"Sure, fat guy. It's the devil's smoke like the Sally Anns say it is. Booze and hop, right, fat guy? I can see you out there beating the drum. Maybe take Mae along with a tambourine. Boom . . . boom . . . boom for poor old Jimmy's soul."

He was in that kind of a mood, Billy thought dully. Sarcastic and mocking. There was nothing that he could say that wouldn't irritate him. They walked side by side through the fading sunlight. Jimmy Pepper kept his eyes before his feet, glowering at the sidewalk. Billy took his watch from his vest pocket and checked the time. They would

23

have to hurry to make the first evening performance. He looked around for a taxi.

"Nineteen-thirteen," Jimmy Pepper said with quiet intensity. "A circus fat boy . . . hit with a bladder and chased around the ring. You were nothing. A buffoon."

He was still a buffoon, but he lacked the courage to say so, to have it out with him. The skits had been slowly degenerating into mere slapstick routines. The old cleverness, the subtlety of Jimmy Pepper's comedy was a long time gone. Billy could not put his finger on the exact beginnings of the decline. Nineteen-seventeen or early in 1918—it had not happened all at once. The original troupe had drifted away one by one to be replaced by others. Only Billy was left of the group that had taken Broadway by storm in the fall of 1913, the undisputed toast of vaudeville. They had reached their peak in 1916 and it had all been downhill from there. They played the Palace in that year and a split week in Altoona two years later. Getting the Katz booking had been something of a comeback after playing Davenport, Iowa, and a county fair in Nebraska. Jimmy Pepper sensed the decline more strongly than anyone else, but was powerless to stop it. He had missed the brass ring by an inch, for reasons that he could never fathom, and there was no way on God's earth that he would ever have another shot at it. He was forty-two years old and ahead of him stretched an endless string of theaters in Elkhart, Wilkes-Barre, Syracuse, Pontiac, Fort Wayne, Cedar Rapids, Omaha, Lansing. . . . The soul rebelled. The mind cried out to dull the pain.

Had the hop habit an' had it bad,
listen an' I'll tell ya 'bout a dream I had.

"Is he okay?" Mae asked.

Billy Wells took his time replying because he had no idea of the answer.

"I don't know. He's . . . moody." He wanted to tell Mae that he had watched Jimmy Pepper grow old, right before his eyes, somewhere between 65th and 12th on Euclid Avenue in the back seat of a taxi. The man had simply eroded like a statue made of sand, caved in from brow to body; all the juices gone. "He'll snap out of it," he lied. "A couple of drinks and a good night's sleep."

Mae said nothing as she waited tensely in the wings for her cue.

Jimmy had not gone to their dressing room. He had changed into his waiter's costume with the boys, putting on the suit that Dan Ryan had worn for the matinee. Now he was on stage, circling the table, flicking his napkin at the cruets and the silverware as though brushing away flies. The audience was receptive. They were starting to laugh. It was a good pantomime and she felt relieved. Jimmy wasn't just going through the motions, he was putting something into it.

"He'll be okay," she said.

"I hope I can get a good meal here."

"I hope so, too." Jimmy Pepper turned his lugubrious face toward the audience and wiggled his eyebrows. Laughter followed like a storm.

"What kind of soup do you have?"

"Oysterandclamchickencorncchowderhambonepea and . . . MULLI . . . GA . . . TAWNY."

"I'll take the pea."

"Take it . . . but we ain't got it."

"I'll try the chicken."

"Try again tomorrow."

"Give me the oyster."

"I'M GONNA GIVE HIM THE OYSTER."

Mike Dale, in chef's hat and white apron, rushed on stage carrying a bucket that he handed to Pepper.

"You sure you want the oyster," Pepper asked.

"Give me the oyster," Billy said, tucking his napkin into his shirt collar.

"I'M GONNA GIVE HIM THE OYSTER," Jimmy Pepper shouted to the audience as he moved, bucket in hand, toward the waiting diner. The Elks and their wives were a step ahead of the routine and they were howling in anticipation. Abe Katz stood in the darkness of the mezzanine with a smile on his face. Only Billy Wells saw the look of murder in Jimmy's eyes as he came toward him, swinging the galvanized iron bucket like a club. He was supposed to dump the contents—whitewash, oatmeal and a few oyster shells—on his head, but Billy knew that wasn't going to happen. He was going to be brained like a rabbit.

Why?

The question exploded in his skull. He could think about the reason later—if there ever was a later.

Theirs not to reason why—Tennyson

He lunged sideways and ducked, the lethal bucket grazed the top of

25

his head. The sting sent a bolt of fear through his body and he made a desperate lunge to get under the table. Jimmy Pepper hurled the bucket at him and it slammed against his right leg and went ricocheting off across the stage spewing its contents. The audience screamed in delight.

Mike Dale, cursing softly under his breath, started toward Jimmy from stage left. Joe Rhine, who had been waiting in the wings before coming in for the shoeshine bit, dashed in from stage right, brushing past Mae who stood on stage by the hatrack prop. Jimmy Pepper grabbed the chair that Billy had so recently vacated and sent it flying at Mike Dale's head. The big man failed to duck in time and the chair sent him sprawling like a bludgeoned ox.

OYSTERCHICKENCLAMCHOWDERHAMEBONEPEA. MULLI . . . GA . . . TAWNY!

Jimmy was shrieking. His eyes were glazed and a froth of saliva bubbled at his lips. While the audience clapped and shouted their approval he kicked the table to pieces, picked up a broken table leg and tried to beat the crawling fat man as he would have beaten a snake. Billy whimpered in terror as he struggled to get on his feet, but he kept slipping on the oyster soup mixture as blows drummed off his back and shoulders. He felt no pain. The pain of two broken ribs, bruises, contusions and welts would come later, but now he felt nothing. He was numb with the shock of realizing that Jimmy Pepper, whom he loved like brother or father, was trying to kill him. To kill everything. To destroy what he was and the memory of what he had been. He was breaking up the act in the only way that he thought fitting. Billy caught a glimpse of Mae's shocked face and then his feet found a hold and he was up and running.

RUN YOU FAT CLOWN. RUN. RUN.

The curtain was still up, the stagehands paralyzed with indecision. Abe Katz was rooted to his little spot in the darkness of the mezzanine, knowing that something was horribly wrong, but incapable of doing one damn thing about it. The audience was on its feet. They had never seen a routine quite like it. The fat man was clambering off the stage, bulling his way through the orchestra pit, knocking over the musicians, climbing out of the pit and running up the aisle. The waiter was chasing him, whirling the table leg above his head and shouting . . .

RUN . . . RUN.

OUT TAKES

Saturday, August 28, 1920, was the last time that Jimmy Pepper and his Komedy Klub played the Katz Rialto Theater. For that matter, it was Jimmy Pepper's last booking in vaudeville. After Mae brought him home to their small apartment in Brooklyn from a sanitarium near Astoria, New York, in December of that year, Jimmy discovered that he had been blackballed from the major, and even the minor, circuits. Mike Dale's brother was an assistant director with Vardon Bolling's Sterling Pictures in Culver City, California, and Mike took off for the coast where he did very well playing heavies in serials. Joe Rhine joined up with a blackface group but soon drank himself out of the business and disappeared. Mae teamed up with a girl by the name of Anna Marie Shapely and they tried to make a go of it as The Shapely Sisters—Song and Dance. They flopped in Jersey City on their first booking. Jimmy tried a comeback on the subway circuit, playing some of the new clubs that were beginning to spring up all over New York as the speakeasies became more competitive. A bootlegger by the name of Owen Forbes took a liking to him and was planning to star him in a nightclub he had just bought in Havana, Cuba, but Jimmy took an overdose of morphine one night in a Times Square hotel room and died on November 12, 1922.

RUN, CLOWN, RUN.

Billy Wells ran—up the aisle and across the lobby, Jimmy's words striking his ears like bullets.

RUN, YOU FAT CLOWN!

. . . across the lobby and into the street. A hot night. The lake quicksilver under the moon. He ran until there was no breath left in his body and he collapsed on a bench in Public Square, mouth open, gasping like a walrus. Then he vomited—a cascade of Chinese cuisine. Oh God, he thought, starting to weep in his infinite misery, what am I going to do now?

Dry one's eyes and laugh at a fall, and baffled, get up and begin again —Browning.

And a tip of the bowler to you, Mister Wu.

REEL THREE

SALVATION HUNTERS

What did the bitch mean by that? Vardon Bolling puzzled over the article as his chauffeur steered the limousine down the curved driveway and onto Hyacinth Avenue. It was a sunwashed morning in Los Angeles, the palms, hibiscus and rhododendron that flanked the drive glistened after a light rain that had come in the night—like a thief, Mrs. Bolling had said during breakfast. Vardon Bolling had not heard one word his wife said. His position at one end of the fifteen foot mahogany dining table made casual conversation difficult and Mrs. Bolling had a tendency to mumble lately. Anyway, he had been reading at the time —an article by a snot bitch in the society section of the *Los Angeles Times.* Ten days, *ten days* after Vardon Bolling had thrown a party for the crème de la crème of the motion picture world, this Millicent somebody or other had written about it. A mere paragraph wedged in with all the other goings-on about town—all of them current!

"Wallace Reid, Doll Fairbaine, Harold Lloyd, Betty Compson, D. W. Griffith, Cecil De Mille and others cavorting at Vardon Bolling's new one million dollar estate in Los Feliz (where do all these cinema moguls come from!)."

Where *do* they come from! Where do *they* come from! Where do they come *from!* Vardon Bolling wondered how an actor would read that line so as to draw from it every drop of snide venom that Miss Millicent *Wilke* had intended sharing with her high society readers! The damn snob bitch! Mistress of the negative innuendo! Well, Vardon Bolling knew where he had come from even if Miss Millicent Wilke did not. He had come from Bolling Brothers, Inc., Fine Gloves, 1027 East 22nd Street, New York City, New York. *That's* where he had come from and Miss Millicent Wilke could have damn well taken the time and effort

28

to find that out before shooting her mouth off in print. A glove salesman . . . nine months of the year on the road and making good money. Not as much money as he would have liked. Pop had given the business to Fred and Leroy because he, Vardon, had been only seventeen when the old man died. August 2, 1895. Miss Millicent Wilke could have written one hell of a human interest story. An American success story. She could have written how young Vardon had become intrigued with nickelodeons after visiting one in Atlantic City in 1905, how he had later discussed the new multireel motion pictures being made in New York with a fellow glove salesman, Sam Goldfish, and how both of them had agreed that the products being shown could be a great deal better. More exciting . . . more entertaining. Multireel moving pictures could turn out to be just a fad, like the now dead nickelodeons, but the concept was sound. Ah, yes, the *concept* was sound as a dollar. That was in 1912 and the rest, of course, was history. It was now 1921. He had helped build a major industry in a mere nine years. Sam Goldfish had changed his name and gone his separate way, but they had both done all right for themselves. How many people did Miss Millicent Wilke know who had one million dollar homes? (A slightly padded estimate of cost and value, but Vardon Bolling was not one to split hairs.)

Vardon settled back in the steel cocoon of his Italian limousine. His chauffeur sat in front, exposed to the elements. A soundproof glass panel separated them as thoroughly as any medieval moat kept the riffraff from the castle grounds.

The goddamn bitch! The more he thought about it the angrier he became. For a thousand dollars he could hire some men to drug Miss Millicent Wilke one night and ship her off to Shanghai as a white slave. He had a thousand dollars, but he also had too much compassion for the Chinese. He wouldn't wish the bitch on his worst enemy.

Money. That was the hidden meaning to her crack. Old money versus new. Real estate and oil money versus motion picture money. God, but they hated to see it, those smug, long-nosed bastards up in Pasadena and San Marino, or the *better* class of Angelenos with their gingerbread Victorian houses, hated like hell to see the upstarts and, heaven forbid, the *Jews,* coining money out of this new, flashy industry that reeked of derring-do heroics and sex. The blackball and the cold shoulder had been raised to a fine art, cultivated like the orange groves and kept well honed by the likes of Miss Millicent Wilke.

Golf. Why, he couldn't even play golf at the better links because no Jews and no motion picture people were allowed. Zukor had told him not to be upset about it, but then Zukor was a Jew and Jews were used to being blackballed and snubbed. It didn't bother them one bit.

"When you've been snubbed by the Pharoahs, you should care how the Baldwins or the Dohenys treat you."

But he *did* care, because his family had never been snubbed or blackballed by anyone. Good English stock. Late immigrants from Liverpool in the 1850s. Hard working people who had pulled themselves up by their own bootstraps to become welcomed country club members in Westchester County by 1880. But, of course, that didn't mean a pile of dog turd to the landed gentry of Southern California. *His* money had come from moving pictures, from buxom women tied to railroad tracks, from cowboys and train robbers, baggy pants comics and barroom brawls. Two reelers and features. Cliffhanging chapter plays and shorts. Definitely not art. And, oh, the people! Tarts and cowpokes, good looking but semiliterate, making two and three thousand dollars a week. It shot the gorge up in the gentry whose money did not come to them as *salary*. No, no, they were of Puritan stock, in at the beginning, and they had Puritan morals and standards as rigid as the wooden beams of their oil derricks. Well, the Puritans had been moral all right, and stony poor. They had bent that morality a little bit and started to distill rum and run slaves from Africa—not to be sold in the immediate area, of course. Kept their hands clean. Made the rum in Jamaica and sold the slaves below the River James, and the money rolled in. Money from cheap rum and sweaty black bodies. Rum for bodies and bodies for more rum. And so it grew, the Puritan ethic and the golden pyramid. Now their great-great-great grandchildren sat smug and aloof in the purple shadows of the San Gabriel mountains, sniffing the orange perfume of their groves and staring down their blue noses at the antics of the New York Jews and their gaggle of gilded clowns. And *Jew* was no longer an ethnic label to them. If the Pope had picked up a megaphone and shouted for the cameras to roll, he would be a Jew. They would not let the *Pope* play golf at their clubs. They would blackball *God* if he made a picture with Pearl White.

"Fuck them all to Hell!"

"Pardon, monsieur?"

Damn! The voice tube had been open. "Nothing, Gilbert, just thinking out loud."

"But of course, monsieur."

He had a French chauffeur who had been a flying ace in the war . . . a million dollar home (more or less) . . . a full staff of servants including an English butler and an English nanny for the youngest of

30

his three children, seven automobiles and a steam yacht. He was only forty-three years old with the looks of Dustin Farnum and the poise of a Wall Street banker, but he was barred from the best clubs because Miss Millicent Wilke and the people she wrote for had no idea where he *came* from! It was a monstrous absurdity. His wife was of no help. Had he married the daughter of one of the western brahmins he might have been judged at least halfway acceptable, squeezed in the back door as it were, but he had committed another cardinal sin—he had married an actress. A fine, legitimate actress to be sure, a friend of the Drews and the Barrymores, but an actress nonetheless, and everyone knew where *they* came from—if not the gutter, close to it.

He glared at the back of his chauffeur's neck. A strong, deeply tanned neck. Gilbert Rostand had shot down twenty Boche planes in his Spad and he was a peerless driver of motor cars and a master mechanic. His salary was outrageous, but Vardon Bolling did not begrudge a penny of it. If one wanted the best one had to be willing to pay for it. It was an attitude toward life that old Lucky Baldwin would have found most understandable and admirable. That such a man of his taste and panache should be denied entre to a lousy *golf course!* Vardon Bolling choked back the gall. There was no point in brooding about it. Usually he did not. It had been that damn bitch Millicent Wilke's fault. He slipped a platinum cigarette case from the inside pocket of his white linen blazer and lit a Russian cigarette with his initials embossed on the paper in gold. He opened his pigskin briefcase and placed it on the folding walnut table in front of him so that he could peruse the contents in comfort.

The lists of figures from the various Sterling exchanges were more than gratifying. Grosses on film rentals were up, up, up. Nineteen twenty-one would be a banner year, and 1922 would be even better. They would own more of their own theaters by then. By the target date of 1924, Sterling Pictures would be owning and operating their own theaters in every major city in the country, and not musty converted stores with seats as hard as pine boards. No more giving away thirty and forty percent of the take to the owners of sweatbox holes in the wall. The Sterling motion picture houses would be veritable palaces with padded seats and carpets on the floor and every penny that entered the box office would end up in Sterling's coffers.

He glanced at the new advertising proposals from the J. Walter Thompson Company.

IF YOU'RE NOT SHOWING STERLING, YOU'RE NOT SHOWING ANYTHING

31

Not bad.

Very nice indeed. Subdued. Dignified. He liked that one and made a neat little check mark in the upper right-hand corner with a slim gold pencil.

TOM PIPP—SECOND SERIES—GROSS RECEIPTS FROM THE FOLLOWING EXCHANGES:
Albany, N.Y.
Atlanta, Ga.
Boston, Mass.
Charlotte, N.C.

He scanned the right-hand column. The figures were both impressive and depressing. The second series of Tom Pipp two reel comedies were up over one hundred percent from the first series. Close to two hundred percent in Boston. Pipp was catching on in a big way, giving Chaplin a run for his money. Tom Pipp was going to be a big star and it was that thought that Vardon Bolling found depressing.

He was having trouble with Thomas Fanning Pipperal. He was a strange little monkey to handle.

The office was wide and airy with a view on three sides. An English interior decorator had been brought over from London to plan the decor and the result had been exactly to Bolling's taste—the leather-seated, oak-paneled interior of a London club; Boodle's or the Army Navy, or the lounge in the House of Lords. There were eighteenth century framed hunting prints on the walls and two Landseer paintings of rabbits and hares. The battery of ugly black telephones on Bolling's Victorian desk—it had once belonged to Prince Albert—was a regrettable, but necessary, intrusion.

Vardon Bolling stood for a moment by the windows that faced south. He could see the entire studio from that vantage point. His film factory, all abustle like a hive of bees. Stages 8 and 9 were coming along right on schedule, their gaunt wooden ribs a geometric neatness against the sky. Culver City lay beyond them, clusters of stucco bungalows baking in the sun. Through the west-facing windows he could see a line of eucalyptus trees and beyond them rolling stretches of bean fields leading the eye to the dark blue line of the ocean.

He turned almost brusquely to his desk, sat down and flipped the intercom switch.

"Let the day begin, Miss Hanover."

Miss Rose Hanover was in the office like a shot, notepad in hand, two pencils stuck in the iron gray bun of hair at the back of her small, round head.

"Mr. Gilboy has been on the phone from San Francisco, Mr. Bolling. He phoned in at eight-o-five, A.M." She glanced briefly at her notepad although that was hardly necessary. Miss Rose Hanover had a memory like tar. "He left a number where he can be reached and said to tell you that the party has been found. He would like to know how high he is permitted to go."

Bolling sucked his bottom lip and sat down. He tapped the cover of his briefcase with a well-manicured fingernail. A decision had to be reached on this matter while Miss Rose Hanover stood waiting. Mister Thomas Fanning Pipperal was a pain in the ass, but a one hundred and ninety two percent increase in Boston was a one hundred and ninety two percent increase any way one looked at it. Tom Pipp comedies were taking off. He couldn't, much as he had entertained the idea, let the little man drown in his own stupidities.

"Five thousand. Have him go to the Sterling exchange and tell Appleway to call for confirmation. They'll give him the cash. Tell him to make as cheap a deal as possible."

"Yes, Mr. Bolling."

"And then get Tom Mix on the phone, I want to take him to lunch."

Frank Gilboy walked out of the Sterling Film Exchange office on Market Street and took a taxi to the LaMont Hotel on Russian Hill. He had five thousand dollars in large bills in a manila envelope that he carried loosely, almost carelessly, in his left hand. He also carried a .30 caliber Colt automatic pistol in a shoulder holster under his left arm and a black leather sap in the right-hand pocket of his raincoat. If anyone had tried to grab that envelope they would have been either dead or maimed before they could have plucked it from his fingers. He wore a light grey fedora with the brim turned down, a brown trench coat, and heavy black brogues that had "cop" written all over them. "Cop" was written on his large, florid face, too, but his official title was assistant publicity director, Sterling Pictures Corporation.

They were waiting for him in the lobby of the hotel as he had suspected they would be—Turkell of the *Chronicle,* Bishop of the *Examiner* and Hounslow of the *Call.* Like buzzards, they could smell dying meat.

"Well, well, well, if it isn't Gilboy," Turkell said.

"Hello, hello," Gilboy said cheerfully. "What brings you lads out on a rainy morning?"

"You tell us," Hounslow said, nudging a heavy camera case with his foot.

"There's a rumor going around," Bishop said. "Little birds flew into our offices and told us that Tom Pipp took unto himself a wife. Such a rumor did not stop presses, but it did draw me and my respected colleagues out into the rain. Is there anything to it?"

It was still amazing to Gilboy that people actually cared about the private lives of motion picture people. At one time, only the lowest of the newspaper low wrote about what was going on in Hollywood, on or off screen, but now all of the papers had hired top-notch writers to mine every last detail of the comings and goings of film folk. Gilboy remembered when Jack Turkell of the *Chronicle* had been the best police reporter in the business. Now he was running around in the rain to find out if Tom Pipp has lost his cherry!

Gilboy pushed his hat off his forehead, shoved the manila envelope into one of the cavernous pockets of his trench coat, unbuttoned the coat and withdrew a sack of Bull Durham and a packet of wheat brown cigarette papers from the vest pocket of his blue serge suit. He rolled himself a smoke with blunt but sure fingers.

"Well, boys, I'll tell you. There's nothing to it. That's as wild a rumor as ever hit this town."

There was a chorus of protests from the newsmen.

"Don't hand us that malarky," Bishop said.

"Come on," Hounslow whined. "We know he was in Reno with a woman named . . ."

"Theda Carstairs—a phony moniker if I ever heard one," Bishop cut in.

Gilboy gave himself time to think as he carefully licked the edge of the paper. He twisted one end, tapped the cigarette against his thumb and lit it with a match.

"Sure, it's a phony. Listen, I'll level with you guys, give you the straight stuff. No wedding in it, that'll have to wait till Tom finds the right girl, but there's a story all right. Why, it'll touch the heart of everybody who reads it."

"Beeswax!" Turkell snorted. "I got a source who'll swear Pipp took out a license in Reno and married the dame."

Gilboy never had and never would underestimate the ability of Jack Turkell. But of course he had covered that angle and all others. A good

34

reporter could never outsmart a good cop.

"Jack," he said solemnly, looking the reporter square in the eye, "I will personally pay you a hundred dollars . . . no, my salary for the year if you can show me a copy of that license." He inhaled and then blew a thin stream of smoke from the corner of his mouth. "If Tom Pipp was going to get married, do you think he'd *run* off to Reno to do it? Why, we're one big, happy family at Sterling. Mr. Bolling would give Tom the biggest wedding you ever saw. Do you think he'd let Tom spend his honeymoon in a hotel? Hell, no. He'd be on the old man's yacht sailing to Honolulu. Now, you guys know that. You've been given a bum steer."

The three reporters scrutinized Gilboy intently, but they could see nothing in the big man's pale grey eyes that would lead them to suspect him of lying.

"Okay," Turkell said, a note of frustrated resignation in his voice. "So what's the story?"

Gilboy did not sigh with relief, he simply took a drag on his home made and flicked ashes on the lobby's Persian rug.

"I won't tell you the girl's real name, because it wouldn't mean a damn thing to you anyway. She's a sweet little kid and I'd hate to see her name in the papers with any . . . innuendoes attached to it. Let's be truthful, some of you Frisco news hawks think it's open season on film people. Sex orgies and drugs . . . but you guys know that Pipp isn't that kind of guy."

"Just a nice, quiet drunk," Bishop said.

There was a moment of silence. Even Turkell looked vaguely embarrassed.

Gilboy brushed it off with a shrug. "So he's not a saint. I keep forgetting you're a *Bishop.*"

That broke the ice. Bishop grinned and patted Gilboy on the arm. The power that he felt under the cloth awed him.

"Forget that crack, Frank. Hell, I like Pipp—and we drink the same brand."

Gilboy smiled. If a wolf could smile it would have looked like Gilboy. "Don't I know it, Al? Aren't I the one who sends that case of Johnnie Walker Black every Christmas? One hand washes the other. I'm giving you a story."

"Go right ahead," Bishop said.

Gilboy took a final drag and dropped the smoldering butt at his feet. He didn't bother to step on it. "So, okay, he's travelling around with

35

a girl . . . Fresno . . . Stockton . . . Reno . . . Frisco, but it's all on the up an' up, see. She's an old childhood pal from Australia, not even a childhood sweetheart, more like a kid sister."

Gilboy paused for a moment to see how it was going over. Hook, line and sinker. They had their notepads out. Lapping it up. After some of the crap they swallowed from the Metro crowd this was clean, tough prose.

"The guy's in the chips and he never forgets a pal—male or female. He had some tough years down under and he never forgot the people who were good to him. This girl's mother saved his life when he was dying of fever in Queensland. So, when she came up from Australia . . . she won some kind of scholarship, by the way, to one of those fancy Eastern colleges. Vassar, I think. She's a sweet little honey of a girl, innocent as they come. Looks like Mary Pickford or Doll Fairbaine, and just as wholesome. She wanted to see the west . . . the deserts, the mountains . . . the Golden Gate. Boy, it's been a tonic of a trip for Pipp. He's been working like a dog. His second series is cleaning up all over the country and he's got a long, tough grind ahead for the next batch. So, he's been roaming like a vagabond with this marvelous kid, laughing, having a good time. Sure, they stay overnight together in hotels, but always in separate rooms. And if they hold hands a little, why, who's going to throw the first stone. You, Al?"

"Not me," Bishop said quickly.

"Write it up with hearts and flowers—or leave it alone."

"Oh, no," Hounslow of the *Call* said. "It's a good yarn, Frank. Pipp is big here. He outgrossed Chaplin at the Granada last week. I'll give it a play. Did they get to see the redwoods?"

"You bet they did," Gilboy said. "They've seen everything."

Gilboy let himself into Room 714 with a passkey given to him by Mike O'Hara, the house dick. O'Hara had been on the Los Angeles force for ten years, but had quit before a snooping citizens' group could slap him with a subpoena to appear before the grand jury. Gilboy had been a detective-lieutenant at the time and had helped pack O'Hara's bags and had gotten him this job in San Francisco. O'Hara owed him favors for the rest of his life, but he always slipped the guy a C-note when he came across with any worthwhile information. It had been O'Hara who had spotted Pipp behind a phony mustache when he had checked in the night before, signing the register as Mr. and Mrs. Albert Sydney. He had phoned a day or night number in Los Angeles and one of Gilboy's assistants had relayed the message to Gilboy who had followed Pipp's tracks as far as Reno and then had run into a dead end. How the newspapers had gotten wind of Pipp's latest escapade Gilboy had no way of knowing, but he figured that they had their own network of watchers.

The blinds were drawn and the parlor room of the suite was in semidarkness. A room service cart cluttered with platters of stale food and half empty champagne bottles stood in the center of the room. An empty bottle of Scotch with a woman's silk stocking tied around its neck like a noose lay on one of the sofa cushions. The room stank of spilled booze, stale cigarette smoke and cheap perfume. Gilboy moved silently to the partially opened door of the bedroom. Rain seethed against the windows, driven by an offshore wind, but thick velvet drapes muted the sound and shut out the light. It was difficult to make out the lumpy forms in the double bed, but after peering intently for a moment he could see Tom Pipp clearly enough. The little man was lying on top of the bed, a counterpane thrown loosely across his legs. He was fully dressed. The woman was in bed with the blankets drawn up to her chin. Gilboy padded silently up to her and shook her by the shoulder. She awoke with a start and sat up. Her large, naked breasts swayed pendulously and she covered the nipples with her arm.

"Get out of here!" she hissed.

"Put some clothes on, girlie," Gilboy said. He didn't bother to lower his voice. Nothing less than a cannon would have woken Tom Pipp. "The train stops here."

"Go take a leap," the woman said. She had a moon face and a new hairdo, the bleached blonde hair short as a boy's, covering her skull like a brass cap. "If you're the house dick, you're barking up the wrong tree. I'm in bed with my *husband.*"

"I don't care if you're in bed with your pet dog. Put a wrapper on. We got some talking to do."

He turned his back on the woman's filthy expletives and went into the front room. He pulled back the blinds and opened a window. Some rain came in, but a lot of clean air came with it. He sat on the arm of the couch and rolled a cigarette. After about a ten minute wait the woman entered and closed the bedroom door. She was wearing a kimono of Chinese silk that revealed her naked body like a pane of glass. She wasn't the worst looking slut Gilboy had ever seen.

"You haven't got a leg to stand on," the woman crowed. "We got a license in Reno and got married by a justice in Virginia City, so why don't you just peddle your papers down the block!"

Gilboy blew a smoke ring. The woman was sure of herself, but not

37

one hundred percent sure. Gilboy could tell by the way she held her body. A stiff, apprehensive pose. In her world more things went wrong than ever went right.

"Which cathouse did he drag you out of, girlie?" If looks could kill he would have been dead, right there on the arm of the couch. "Okay," Gilboy went on, "let me tell you. Vera Shane's place, Stockton. Vera asked me to say hello and to say that she misses you."

"I hope the bitch rots," the woman said.

"She loves you too, but I didn't come up here to talk shop. You're a business woman. Let's talk business." He withdrew the envelope from his pocket and tapped it gently against his knee. the woman stared at it.

"We're . . . married," she said hollowly.

"Not any more. I got it annulled. Woke up a superior court judge in Reno and raised some kind of hell. Listen, I says, how come one of your justices hitched a two-bit floozie to a guy so drunk he couldn't sign his name? What kind of a cheap mill are you . . ."

"Spare me the details, flatfoot. How much?"

"A thousand dollars."

"No dice. I could get more selling my story to the *Chronicle.*"

"Even the *Chronicle* isn't that low. Listen, girlie, let's put our cards on the table. You got a poor hand, see. All you can do is cause a little trouble and some bad publicity. I can cause a little trouble, too. I got pals all over the state. Pals who wear badges. You get me?"

"I'm not stupid."

"No, I can see that, so let's both play it on the square. What do you say to two grand?" He slapped the envelope against the palm of his hand. "Cash."

"Two grand and a car. If I'm going back to Stockton, I'm going back in style."

"Fifteen hundred and a Ford."

"Fifteen hundred and a yellow Studebaker roadster."

"Done." He opened the envelope and began to count out some bills. The woman leaned against the bedroom door and folded her arms across her breasts as though suddenly aware of her near nakedness.

"Not that it means anything, but I liked the little guy."

"Oh, hell yes," Gilboy said as he continued to count the money. "Everybody likes Pipp."

FLASHBACK

There was primeval darkness when the sun went down, a blanket of night, stifling and impenetrable. It seemed to rise from the earth like a black mist out of the mangrove swamps. It came with humming clouds of mosquitoes and leathery swarms of blood sucking bats. Night was hideous and there was always the terror that the lamps in the house would go out and the screeching, moaning, whining, fluttering darkness would engulf him forever.

Where?

Queensland, Australia. Back-of-beyond. The cattle station of Captain Samuel Thomas Beaumont Pipperal, late of Her Majesty's Horse Guards. A man of imperial vision. An inheritance and a lucky run at cards had prompted him to give up his commission and emigrate to Australia with his young wife, the delicate, genteelly reared daughter of a country vicar.

They arrived in Sydney on the fifteenth of January, 1890. Thomas Fanning Pipperal arrived with them, having been conceived two weeks earlier on a windswept stretch of the Indian Ocean.

Land?

The land lay between a limpid river and a line of red clay hills. A horseman would have been hard pressed to ride around the property in three days. It was an empire vast as a European king's domain and the captain viewed his holdings with an arrogance that his hired stockmen found both foolish and contemptible.

Money?

Money for a house, large and imposing, the lumber carted five hundred miles up from Brisbane. Money for cattle stock and horses. Money for a thousand items, and then more money for a thousand items more. Money was borrowed from banks in faraway Sydney and then borrowed again.

Success?

Dingoes preyed on the calves, yellow packs of them fleeing the sun-withered land beyond the clay hills. One day there would be countless miles of wire fence to keep the wild dogs off the cattle ranges, but now the dingo roamed free and the calves died with their throats torn out and the dogs snarling at the gut. And what the dingoes missed the bats bled white. Rain was capricious. The grass turned to copper wire and the cattle sucked mud from the exhausted river.

Little Thomas Fanning Pipperal was small and delicate like his mother. The cool, dark rooms of the house, shuttered against the heat, became a sanctuary for both of them. Beyond the portico lay dust and death by day and shadowy terror by night. Neither son nor wife rode with the captain as he surveyed his kingdom. The captain cut a dashing figure on a horse, but his stockmen despised him for his English gentry airs and aloof superiority. He was quick to scorn advice and, after a time, none was offered.

Defeated?

By drought, dingo, debt, despair.

The bubble of the captain's dream burst during the summer of 1901. Letters, weeks on the road, arrived from various Sydney banks. The captain solved his financial difficulties with a single stroke, by raising a pistol to his head.

Brisbane?

With what little could be salvaged from the ruin, Ellen Pipperal bought a ramshackle house on River Street and turned it into a boarding house—for artistes and theatrical people. She hired the widow of a soldier slain in the Boer war to do the cooking, and an aborigine woman to do the cleaning. There were few guests and even fewer who could manage to pay their full board and fare. The bill collector and the bailiff were constant visitors. These men brought compassion along with their demands and there was always a roof over the Pipperals' heads and food on their table.

Education?

There is no record of formal schooling. The poorer boys of Brisbane were, by and large, a rowdy bunch of larrikins and Ellen kept her son apart from them. She taught him a love of Shakespeare, Dickens, Goldsmith and Wordsworth. She taught him geography, spelling and penmanship, but her knowledge of arithmetic was sparse and the mysteries of the multiplication tables would elude him for the rest of his life.

Happiness?

Comfort, close to his mother. In the wet season, when the wind drove nails of rain against the clapboard house, the two of them huddled in her bed and she read to him by the flickering light of a kerosene lamp —*Bleak House. David Copperfield. The Vicar of Wakefield.*

Sorrow?

Her death, April 7, 1909.

"Now look, young Pipperal, it don't do no good for you to keep carryin' on about it. She's dead, God rest 'er, but you got to go on livin', an' as far as I can see there ain't nothin' for you here."

The speaker is Victor Blodger, of Blodger, Riley and Pate, acrobats and comedians, knockabout artistes and popular music hall performers. Blodger & Co. stayed at the boarding house whenever they played Brisbane, which had been twice a year since 1904. Ellen had liked them because they always paid their bill. They in turn liked her, and young Thomas. Jocko Pate had taught him how to tap dance and all three men thought him a natural mimic.

"We been talkin' it over, me an' the lads. We'd like to break you into the act. You can do that Harry Lauder mimic and a bit of a funny dance with Jocko. Maybe dress up like a girl with a wig an' all. Don't worry, you'll earn your tucker. 'Course, we 'ave to do somethin' about your moniker. Thomas Fanning Pipperal won't do at all. 'Ow about just Pipp? Tom Pipp . . . short an' sweet."

Debut?

The Victoria Music Hall on Flinders Street in Sydney, July 25, 1909. The dead of winter. A cold, rainy day. Tom Pipp lit up the house. Not a comedian . . . not a clown. A pixie, an elf. He was secretive and withdrawn off stage, but the footlights transported him into another being. Applause and laughter was love washing over him; it was a bright light that drove the pits of fear and loneliness from his frail body. Blodger was quick to note Pipp's appeal to the rough and demanding Sydney audiences. The Australian's compassion for the little man, the underdog, was ingrained into the national character, so Blodger turned Pipp into the misfit, the well-meaning but totally inept character who somehow managed to turn the tables on all those who sought to exploit or mock his innocent naivity. Blodger, Riley and Pate—all big men and superb acrobats—became city toughs and Pipp the bright-eyed country yokel who could be talked into buying a gold brick or a harbor bridge. The tables would be turned at the end of the skit with Pipp emerging triumphant. Blodger, Riley and Pate were hard taskmasters, but good teachers, and they soon had Pipp doing pratfalls, back flips, somersaults and balancing acts. He began to emerge as a unique character on the music hall circuit, a pixilated little fellow who couldn't possibly survive in the rough and tumble world, but who somehow managed to not merely hold his own, but to emerge at the end with his baffled enemies sprawled at his feet.

Success?

Instant. Blodger took the company to London in 1912, enlarging the group there by adding a comedienne and an Irish tenor. It became the key act in the better London music halls until 1915 and then the act broke up. Blodger bought a theater on Shaftesbury Avenue and became an entrepreneur; Pate joined the army and was killed on the Somme; Riley became infatuated with the Irish cause and left for Dublin; and Pipp received an offer from a vaudeville producer in New York and sailed for America.

Triumphant?

Beset by doubts. Driven by ghosts. Rootless. He carried the shadow of his mother's grave about his neck. They had made plans together and now only he had realized them—London . . . the English countryside . . . money and the chance to live gracefully. He had no one with whom to share his success. He was painfully alone except when he drank. The bottle was always in the wings.

Women?

He constantly sought their company. His need was deeply personal.

Friends?

Everybody liked Pipp.

Gilboy held the little man's head under the cold water faucet in the bathroom until he felt some stirring of life—a groggy shake of the head, a low moan. Then he half carried, half dragged Pipp to the toilet and left him kneeling there until he began to retch.

"You'll be okay," Gilboy said. He went back into the bedroom and phoned for room service. He ordered a pot of coffee, two fresh eggs, raw, and a bottle of Worcestershire sauce.

"Did I do anything silly, Gilboy?"

"No."

"There was a woman . . . I think. Where did she go, Gilboy?"

"She had a house to keep up. She went home."

Pipp raised a cup of coffee to his lips, holding the cup with both hands.

"She was . . . nice to me. Very nice."

"Seemed like a good egg," Gilboy said, rolling a cigarette.

"Is Vardon angry at me?"

"Nobody's angry at you, Tom."

"I . . . I took a bit of a holiday, that's all." He was staring past the rim of the cup at the windows where the rain still drummed. "We stayed in bed mostly," he whispered. "And had a lovely time."

Gilboy cleaned up the bedroom and packed Pipp's suitcase. He found a leatherbound volume under the woman's pillow and skimmed through the pages. *The Vicar of Wakefield.* It didn't look like a smut book to Gilboy and he wondered why the whore had been reading it.

WINDS OF CHANCE

It seemed that winter would never leave. It was late March and the gutters of New York City were still piled high with mounds of gray ice and snow. It was warm in his room at the Clarendon Hotel on 44th and Tenth Avenue and Billy Wells spent most of his time there. The Clarendon was an old theatrical hotel and the rooms were large and airy. Billy's had a fine view of the Hudson and the Jersey Palisades. It contained a Murphy bed, which Billy never bothered to push up into the wall, and a smaller bed that also served as a couch. He shared the room with a midget by the name of Ambrose Pike who was booked on the Keith–Albee circuit as part of a comedy adagio act called the Sky Highs and Runty. The "Sky Highs" were two enormous Hungarians and their sister. Ambrose made good money with the act, but it was rough on him since the Hungarians tossed him around like an Indian club at the finale. They were currently playing the Winter Garden and although Ambrose could certainly have afforded his own room at the Clarendon, he preferred rooming with Billy because it gave him someone to talk to and a willing and able masseur. Billy would rub Absorbine linament on Ambrose's back every night so that he would be able to crawl out of bed in the morning. As a result, the room was always pungent with camphor oil and eucalyptus and whatever other ingredients were in the lotion that deadened the pain in the legs of racehorses and in a midget's small, round back.

"I would take that offer if I were you," Ambrose said one Sunday morning. He was seated at a card table that was a permanent fixture in front of the double windows. He wore a red velvet smoking jacket that would have reached an average man's hips but on Ambrose trailed

43

the floor. He had shortened the sleeves himself—being an accomplished tailor—and it was a warm and comfortable garment that he wore constantly. It was his great pleasure on a Sunday morning to sit in front of the windows in a child's high chair, wearing his elegant jacket, sipping coffee from a beer stein with a pewter lid and sifting through an enormous assortment of postage stamps that he would dump from a paper carton onto the center of the card table.

"What offer is that?" Billy asked idly. He lay sprawled on the Murphy bed in his pajamas, leafing through the *New York-American.*

"Why, the offer from California, of course," Ambrose said in his doll's voice.

Billy sighed and scratched his stomach. "It wasn't really an offer. I've been thinking of joining Duckworth and Beane. They're looking for a fat man."

Ambrose plucked a stamp from the pile with a pair of tweezers and held it up to the window light. "I thought you didn't like burlesque."

"I don't, but it's just over on 42nd Street and the money's good. I hate the idea of packing up and moving out."

"I'd miss you, but you have to do what's best for your career."

Billy made a snorting sound and let the newspaper fall apart and drift to the floor.

"Career! Fall guy for a burlycue clown."

"I'm not talking about Minsky's and you know it. Go out to the coast."

"I don't know," Billy sighed. "I don't like pictures. I was in a couple here for Vitagraph. Oh, 1915 . . . '16. They took a bunch of us down to Sheepshead Bay and we ran around on the sand all day and the director yelled at us. Do this. Do that. I never worked so hard in my life and all they paid me was five dollars and I had to buy my own lunch."

"It's not that way any more. You could make big money in California."

"Maybe. I don't know."

He didn't seem to know anything lately. His mind was a fog of hazy, disconnected images. The only clarity was his daydreams about Jimmy and Mae. He would imagine himself taking the subway over to Brooklyn and just walking in on them. They would be happy to see him and Jimmy would pat him on the shoulder and say he was sorry about everything and that bygones were bygones and Mae would go down to the delicatessen and come back with corned beef and pastrami sandwiches, pickles, pretzels and potato salad and Jimmy would take out

44

a couple of bottles of beer and they'd all sit around and eat and talk.

"So how's my fat guy?"

"Just fine, Jimmy."

"You sure look great, kiddo. Don't he look great, Mae?"

"A sight for sore eyes."

"You bet he is. What ya been doin', Billy?"

"Nothing much. I didn't want to join up with anybody."

"Gee, that was white of you, Billy. You don't know what a tonic it is for me to see you sittin' here. I was sick, sure, but I'm right back on top of the world now. I'm the old Jimmy Pepper and we're going to knock Broadway flat on its can."

"I don't want you to think I've just been sitting around crying in my beer, Jimmy. I've been working on a skit for the three of us. Would you like to hear it?"

"Would I! Boy, I was saying to Mae just this morning. I hope we can get Billy to team up with us again."

"See, Mae's a French maid . . . short skirt . . . long black stockings, and I'm a butler in a cutaway coat. A real snob . . ."

"I sure like it so far, Billy boy. I can just see you mincing around playing the English butler bit."

"Sure, and trying to flirt with Mae who's very *frou frou* and flirty flirty but keeps giving me the old duck out from under routine. Well, she tells me that the sink's stopped up in the "mawster's" bathroom and she's called a plumber, then in you come . . . overalls . . . a tool box and you're a real slob . . . a terrible plumber. And the way I see it we'd have a working bathroom . . . water in the pipes . . . we'd have a waterproof floor built . . . a sort of large box with sides about a foot high . . ."

"Zieggy would go for that in a minute! Billy, you're a prince. Isn't he a prince, Mae? I'll tell the cockeyed world you're a prince, fat guy."

What was the point of it? Why did he keep the pipe dream going? All of that was dead. Jimmy . . . and Mae. He was nobody's prince of a fat guy now.

"I have a sister who lives in Glendale," Ambrose said. "She's not very tall, but she's not a midget. She's married to a guy who's a dead ringer for Buffalo Bill. He sells real estate and he's doing just fine. I bet you could stay with them. I bet they'd be happy to have you."

"I don't know," Billy said dreamily.

"They say it's nice there in Glendale. I've never been west, but Donna writes to me two, three times a year. She says you can smell the orange groves from their front porch and it never snows. They'd put you up if I asked her."

"I'll think about it," Billy said, "but I could stay with Mike if I go."

"Sure, but you know how Mike is—here today, gone tomorrow. He might be in Australia when you get there. I'll give you Donna's address. Donna and Roy. Roy Arnheim. A ringer for Buffalo Bill."

"I don't know," Billy said.

The letter from Mike Dale was in the top right-hand drawer of the dresser under a pile of socks and undershirts. Billy had read it a dozen times, unable to make up his mind about what the letter offered.

Billy:

I hope to heck you get this letter as I am sending it to the Clarendon where you always stayed before and putting please forward on the envelope. I never see your name in *Variety*. What's the matter fat boy, you take a powder or something? Listen to your big buddy. If you're not rolling in gelt, or rolling in the hay with some rich skirt (ha ha ha) come on out here to God's country. I know what you think of pictures after that runaround we both got from Larry Semon and the Vitagraph bunch, but Larry's a big shot out here and everything's different than it was in Brooklyn. Dave's an assistant director at Sterling Studios in Culver City and he keeps me working all the time in two reelers and serials. I'm always the heavy, but what the hell, a guy with my mug can never get the girl (ha ha ha) except after the day's shooting. I got a stable of the cutest little tricks you ever saw and one of them is just right for you. She just loves fat boys even after what poor old Roscoe did. To make this short and sweet, Billy, I've got a new Templar runabout and a swell apartment on Mariposa Street just off Hollywood Boulevard. I'd sure like for you to come out here as with my connections, and Dave's (and you know how Dave likes you) we can get you lots of work. You could bunk with me. There's an honest to God lemon tree right outside and where I am it is easy walking to Fox studios on Western and the Vitagraph setup. And the rent's on me, kiddo, but you better have enough scratch to pay for your own food. I can't afford to feed an elephant (ha ha ha).

You hear anything from Jimmy or Mae?

Your pal
Mike

"A lemon tree."

Ambrose peered at a stamp from Spain. "Go, Billy. Go there."

"Gosh, I don't know," Billy said.

There were four Kelly-Springfield tires on the car and a Mohawk spare, but he blew two of the Springfields, the first one before he was

46

even out of Pennsylvania.

"It shouldn't have blown," he had said to the garageman in Pittsburgh. "It's a brand new tire."

"No it ain't," the man had said. "It's a retread, an' a bad one at that."

And then the man had walked slowly around the big Moline-Knight seven passenger sedan examining the other tires while Billy watched him with a sense of dread.

"They're *all* retreads, mister, painted to look like new. You won't get another hundred miles on any of 'em."

But the garageman had been wrong. Billy had gone one hundred and twenty miles before the second tire blew apart like a balloon, almost sending the car off the road. He had to be towed into Columbus, Ohio, where the purchase of four new tires blew a hole in his wallet and cast a bleak shadow over his plans.

It had been Charlie Duckworth who had made the suggestion, in between mouthfuls of corned beef and cabbage at Patsy Muldoon's restaurant on West 44th Street.

"Listen," the top banana had said, "If you wanna go out to California instead of teamin' up with Eddie an' me that's your business. I ain't goin' to try an' stop ya. I like ya, see. I like your timin' an' your moves, but you ain't the only fat guy in town, not by a long shot you ain't. I wanna fat guy I kin get a fat guy. An' I'll give you a word in the ear, Billy, you look like you're slimmin' down. You ain't *sleek,* know what I mean? You better put the blubber on or you won't get nothin' on the coast but a cold shoulder. Know what I mean? So, if you gotta go you gotta go, but don't get out there with small change in your pockets. So, okay, you say you've got enough money, but it don't cost buttons to get out there, they don't give tickets away on them damn trains. Let you in on something, Billy. Cars. They're mad for cars out on the coast and the damn things cost a helluva lot more than they do here. Why, you can buy a good car here, drive it out to California an' then sell it the day you get there for a damn sight more than you paid for it. See? You not only get out there for nuttin', but you make a tidy bundle on the deal. What the hell could be better than that I'd like to know. Now, it so happens that my brother-in-law is thinkin' of sellin his Moline-Knight seven passenger. It's like brand new . . . a 1918 model and my brother-in-law is a hick from Hicksville. He drives like a little old lady so you just know the car's mint. Tires? You worried about tires, Billy? Why, this car has perfect tires. Four brand new Kelly-Springfields . . ."

Simply chicanery or malicious spite? Billy did not know. Dimly he recalled a conversation he had once had with Eddie Beane, Duckworth's longtime foil, during which Beane had mentioned the fact that Duckworth had been an only child and orphaned at six. No sister. No brother-in-law. The car had probably belonged to the boy friend of one of the burlesque girls. The car of some Broadway flash . . . or a bootlegger's runner. It was a capacious automobile and would have been capable of transporting cases and cases of booze. Billy began to have cold sweats as he drove slowly across Ohio and into Indiana. He knew nothing about cars, but the engine sounded ragged and plumes of smoke that seemed to grow darker and thicker by the mile streamed from the exhaust pipe. He had visions of the car loaded down with heavy crates of booze being driven at full speed down narrow country roads on the bootleg run from Canada to New York. Gas station attendants in such places as Springfield and Dayton and Terre Haute, watching him drive in with that plume of greasy black smoke trailing behind him, had muttered darkly about such mysteries as rings and valves, lifters and carbon, fouled points and burned out plugs. They spoke a language that was as incomprehensible to Billy as Urdu, but he could tell by their expressions, a mixture of pity and contempt, that something was terribly wrong. He drove grimly on, leaving a trail of noxious fumes across Southern Indiana. He was burning oil as fast as he was burning gasoline and everything that could go wrong was going wrong. In Terre Haute it had been a new fuel pump and new spark plugs. In St. Louis they had boiled out the carburetor and installed new brake lining and a new storage battery. He had the horrible feeling that he was buying a new car bit by bit and shuddered at the thought of what he might have to be buying by the time he reached New Mexico or Arizona. In Lebanon, Missouri, it was a new fan belt and more spark plugs.

"But I just bought a set in Terre Haute!"

The garageman said nothing. He simply waited for this distraught young man to make up his mind about it. The garageman had all day. Billy shelled out some more of his dwindling dollars and the new plugs were installed, but not before the mechanic pointed out a serious leak in the water pump, so there were more dollars for that.

The trip through the Ozarks from Lebanon to Joplin was a journey of misery. The engine rattled and smoked and Billy had the horrible sensation that the car was about to explode. He felt relieved when he reached Joplin, coasting into the first garage he came to, the car shrouded in a blue haze of vaporized oil.

A valve job and a ring job, the mechanic said. He quoted a price that stunned Billy like a hammer blow between the eyes.

"She'll be good as new, mister," the mechanic said.

"Okay," Billy muttered. "Go ahead and do it." It would take every penny he had. There was a roaring in his ears that he knew to be panic—and rage. He was not a violent man, but if Charlie Duckworth had suddenly appeared before him he would have trampled him into grease.

"Take a few days," the mechanic said. "I gotta get the parts from the R.V. Knight dealer in Kansas City. Now, if you'd been drivin' a Ford . . ."

The sun slipped across the sky into Kansas and the sycamores around the courthouse square cast ragged shadows on the grass. Billy sat on a bench, numb with defeat, watching shirt-sleeved Missourians lounging on the courthouse steps, their hats tilted against the dying sun, sluggish as lizards. There wasn't one of them, he thought bitterly, who had a damn thing wrong with his car.

He followed the sun in his thoughts, breezing along, pulled by a powerful, faultless engine, the tires humming a song to the road . . . southwest out of Joplin and into Oklahoma . . . clapboard and stucco towns rising on the bleak horizon and then dwindling behind him in haze and dust. Dawn at his back into Texas . . . the panhandle . . . the staked plains . . . New Mexico afternoons . . . Navajo pots and blankets in the adobe gasoline stations.

Fill 'er up for ya?

All she'll take. Am I going right for Gallup?

Why sure. No other way. Just follow your nose. And then on to Arizona and the desert and Southern California. The engine purring like some hot-blooded beast.

Burnin' oil?

Not a drop!

That's some car, mister.

The best. I really bought a honey.

A pipe dream, warm and comforting. The wind turned suddenly chill and leaves skated across the path with a dry, horny sound, like tiny crabs clattering over stones. Billy shuddered as the dream faded and the grim reality of his situation sunk in. He was in Joplin, Missouri, and the repairs to the car would take every penny he had. Even if the car remained troublefree—and there was no guarantee of that—how would he buy gas . . . oil . . . food?

Panic shook him like a fever and he stood up and began to walk

49

aimlessly across the park and through the unfamiliar streets of the town.

Stranded. He had been stranded only once before. Some God-forsaken little town in Alabama in 1911. The circus that he had been with coming to grief when the owner ran off in the middle of the night with all the receipts. Somehow he had made it back to Indiana. Sleeping in barns . . . stealing or begging food . . . chased by dogs . . . shot at by angry men with shotguns . . . sneaking onto empty boxcars . . . terrorized by hobos. The thought of that journey made him break out in an icy sweat. Oh my God, was there anything more terrible than being broke? Maybe he could wire Ambrose or Mike and borrow fifty dollars. He hated to do it, but what other choice did he have?

Lights blinked in his face and he realized that darkness had come while he had been walking, darkness and a growling in his stomach. Dusk and dinner time coming together as surely as the turning of the earth. He thought of lamb chops and boiled potatoes sprinkled with parsley; of fried chicken and hot biscuits soaked with butter and honey; of thick slabs of pink ham, mustard greens swimming in the succulent ham juice; of rib roasts, baked potatoes and crusty apple pies. His stomach nagged at him, but he was reluctant to spend money. Of course he had to eat *something.* A sandwich . . . or a couple of frankfurters. Lights blinked on and off, on and off and he became aware of the theater marquee above his head. The Bijou. People beginning to stand in line in front of the box office window where a stout, blonde girl was putting the final touches to her nails before removing the cardboard sign that blocked the window's opening. Three pictures tonight. Twenty cents bought Tom Mix in *A Ridin' Romeo,* Will Rogers in *Honest Hutch,* and Frank Mayo in *The Blazing Trail.* And then he noticed the theatre across the street, the Hippodrome, its marquee less gaudy than the Bijou's with a single word stretched across it, spelled out in wood letters: VAUDEVILLE.

There were no lines in front of the Hippodrome. The man at the box office window was reading a newspaper. He glanced up as Billy ambled into the foyer to scan the playbill.

GATES AND BALL
Fancy steps and snappy chatter

THE GREAT BARDONI
and his trained doves

50

LOLA MONTENESCU OPERATIC AIRS
The toast of Bohemia

THE LARKIN SISTERS
Songs our mother taught us

No one that Billy had ever heard of. Joplin was tryout country. A good place to break in new acts. It was also the last stop before oblivion. Billy could imagine the long road that Lola Montenescu, the toast of Bohemia, had taken to reach the final toast in Missouri.

"You want a ticket?" the man behind the counter asked. "It's a hell of a show."

Billy tilted his bowler to one side of his head, giving him a rakish air, and walked up to the window.

"As a matter of fact, I was just wondering if I could speak to the manager."

"You're speaking to him," the man said. He folded the newspaper and stuck it under the ticket counter.

"My, my, how fortuitous."

The manager's smile was thin as a razor. "An actor."

Billy bowed slightly from the waist. "At liberty. I just happen to be on my way to California . . . to make pictures for Fox and Vitagraph. My Moline-Knight seven passenger touring automobile ran into some minor problems and I'll be delayed here for a few days until they can send the needed parts from Kansas City." He forced a broad smile even though he could tell that he wasn't impressing the man one bit. The face behind the wicket was stone. "We vaudevillians hate to be idle. I'd like to do a turn if you could find a spot for me—and for a fraction of my regular salary."

An elderly couple approached the window and Billy stepped aside as the man bought two tickets.

"Enjoy the show," the manager said. He waited until the couple had gone into the theater and then he turned his bright, probing eyes on Billy's face. "What do you do, Bud?"

"Juggle . . . dance . . . sing . . . walk a tightrope . . . tell jokes. Anything and everything. I used to be with the Jimmy Pepper troupe. We were in the Ziegfeld Follies in 1915 with W. C. Fields . . . Bert Williams . . . Leon Errol . . ."

A glimmer of interest crossed the manager's face like a shadow.

"Well . . . maybe if I got some ballyhoo out. Passed the word around that a genuine Follies star was playing here for a couple of special performances, we might pack the house for a change. Then again, we might not. I couldn't guarantee you a nickel."

"Look, you know what the gate's been. If I draw, and I'm sure I will, you can give me a percentage of the overage. How does that sound?"

"Fair."

"Then is it a deal? I'll help with the ballyhoo. Maybe I could walk a tightrope over Main Street."

The manager grinned. "If you fell you'd bounce like a ball."

"I won't fall. I can do anything on a high wire. Look, I'll be honest. I need the cash."

"Don't we all. Okay, fat man, you've got the job, but no guarantee on the dough, just a straight cut. Say thirty percent of the overage less the cost of the ballyhoo."

"That's fine with me," Billy said. He felt an enormous sense of relief. He grinned foolishly at the redhaired man inside the ticket booth. "My name's Billy Wells."

The manager squeezed his hand through the wicket. "Donovan's my name . . . Earl Donovan."

"Nice to meet you," Billy said.

"Likewise," Donovan said.

CASSETTE

When did it all start? That is to say, your initial involvement. The beginning. Had you been in vaudeville?

Oh, no. I was a circus man—carnivals, tent shows. They were very big before and during the war . . . the first war . . . and I owned a popular circus which I sold to the Ringling brothers. Times were very hard right after the war. A real depression for a while—nobody knew what to do. I had all this cash, but no idea how to invest it. Well, I'd worked for Colonel Selig when I was a kid. Selig was a carny man . . . a circus man . . . and he'd made a fortune out in California in pictures. I guess he went out to the coast around 1910 and built his own studio and everything like that. An important man. I decided to go out to California and look him up.

And that would have been around 1919?

Oh, some time around then. After the armistice. Yes. Selig was making animal pictures and he had a zoo over in East Los Angeles on Mission Road, and a studio. Louis B. Mayer was making pictures there.

I liked Mayer. He was a big, tough, crude sort of guy. Very foul mouthed. A lot of people didn't like him because of that. They called him the Junk Man behind his back because he had started out in the junk business. But I liked him. We got along swell. There were no saints in the carnival business. We spoke the same language.

Did you join up with Mayer?

No. He didn't want any partners, but he offered me advice about going into pictures. Both of them did that . . . Selig and Mayer. I had fresh ideas. I knew I could produce good pictures if I had the right people . . . the right star. Mayer was making dramas . . . women's pictures . . . Anita Stewart was his star . . . Chaplin's wife . . . girls like that. I told Mayer that he should go into comedies because they were the kind of pictures people wanted to see. They wanted to laugh because times were really bad then—millions out of work. Fatty Arbuckle had been the most popular star at that time . . . bigger than Chaplin. The best, but, you know, he had all that trouble and the papers ruined him . . . the Hearst press and the churches just crucified him and all of his pictures were junked. That left a void and I went East to look for another Arbuckle. Mayer was willing to go in on the financing if I found the right guy.

And is that how you met Billy Wells?

Yes. I caught Billy's act in Baltimore . . . the Orpheum house in Baltimore, Maryland. Vaudeville. He was doing a single. He had, oh, I don't know . . . class, style. I liked him right off.

Did you sign him up?

Well, no, not at that time. Mayer had grown cold for some reason and my plans were up in the air. But I knew in my heart that Billy had a big future in pictures and I was willing to take a chance and bring him out to the Coast. To bankroll him. I talked him into leaving vaudeville and he came with me to California . . . by train. That was luxury travel in those days. Everything first class. Fantastic food in the dining car. They had the best chefs in the world on those trains. That was a long time ago.

Yes, it was.

The posters that boys were nailing to telephone poles all over town were anything but flattering. Billy winced when he spotted the first one. It had been tacked to a pole in front of the Joplin Palace Hotel, a three story wooden building that was popular with drummers and theatrical people because of its cheap rates. The poster that Billy saw when he emerged from the musty lobby and crossed the sagging veranda depicted what appeared to be a pink hippopotamus dressed in a man's suit tiptoeing across a high wire with a yellow umbrella in one bloated hand and a brown bowler in the other. A host of circles with smaller circles for mouths and dots for eyes—an illusion of a vast audience—stared up at this prancing creature in awe. Beneath the garish picture was printed

! FANTASTIC FRED !
! THE FABULOUS FAT MAN !

! DEATH DEFYING DEXTERITY !
WILL HE FALL?

SEE SEE SEE SEE

THE HIPPODROME
! ONLY FRIDAY–SATURDAY ONLY !

"Fantastic Fred?" Billy murmured. *"Fred?"* He half ran down Sixth Street to Elm and the theater. The Hippodrome was shuttered, but there were large posters in the glass cases flanking the box office, a small crowd gathered there studying the bloated creature striding so airily thirty feet above the staring round faces.

"Thar he is!" a raggedy boy cried out as Billy approached. "That's 'im . . . that's the fab-u-lus fat man!"

Billy skipped on past, doffing his bowler, grinning like a fool. The group of men and women clustered about the framed posters turned as one. Their expressions mirrored their curiosity. What they had just read had intrigued them. They were all potential ticket buyers. Billy waved a hand.

"Good morning folks! Good morning!"

And then he was gone, beyond their angle of vision, running lightly down Elm to Main, not sure of where he was going because his three days in the town had been spent mostly in the Joplin Palace Hotel, in the boiled beef and cabbage parlor; in the sweaty closeness of his room; or in the large room of Madame Montenescu, a room that mingled the fragrance of lilac water and gin with equal measure. Madame Montenescu was a large, ugly woman with a voice that could bend timber. She had been many places and seen many things, but the closest she had ever come to the birthplace of her parents in Bohemia had been Providence, Rhode Island.

"Ah, that Donovan!" she had said one afternoon, seated on the edge of her bed, a glass of gin with a slice of lemon floating in it held daintily between thick, beringed fingers. "Ah, that redheaded sonofabitch! If I were twenty years younger! Not that I'm much older than that Mrs. Morgan . . . that peroxide hussy . . . but I'd never want a man to slip into *my* bed out of gratitude. No, sir! Never!"

And the gossip had flowed from her the way the gin flowed ceaselessly from the square, frosted glass bottles that she drew from the dark recesses of her wardrobe trunk. Mrs. Morgan was, Billy finally puzzled out, a widow of middle years who owned, among many other things, the Hippodrome theater. She had befriended Donovan when the man, still suffering shell shock from the war—a Marine captain . . . or major . . . much decorated—had wandered into Joplin half out of his head from the Spanish influenza, or some other catastrophic ailment. Befriended the man, saved his life. And he, out of gratitude, ran her theater and . . .

"punches her ticket, I can tell you! Well, no matter. To each his own, I always say. Have a glass of gin, Billy boy, for the sociability. I have always admired men of amiable rotundity as it were."

And there ahead of him was a black Model T pickup, a barefoot boy hopping on and off the runningboard with posters and hammer, tacks in his mouth, while a shirt-sleeved Earl Donovan steered the car from one side of Main Street to the other, from telephone pole to telephone pole.

Billy put on speed to catch up and hopped nimbly onto the runningboard on the driver's side.

"That isn't my whole act, Donovan," Billy said in between deep, breath catching gasps. "Not my whole act at all . . . and why *Fred?* Why didn't you mention the Follies?"

Earl Donovan smiled tolerantly and let the pickup drift to a stop at the curb.

"Now, Billy, you want some dough, don't you? You want more than fifty people in the audience, don't you? Why, I asked around on the QT and I couldn't find a dozen people who gave a damn about the Ziegfeld Follies. You weren't pulling my leg about being a high wire man, were you?"

"No," Billy said.

"Fine. Then that's the act. That's what people will line up to see . . . a big guy walking on a high wire. Folks who have seen you say you can't do it—that the wire'll break or you'll fall off like Humpty

55

Dumpty. And as for *Fred,* why, you don't want to cast your real name in front of all these yokels, do you? You'll be going on to California after the last show and going into the pictures. Your name will be on the lips of every man, woman and child in . . ."

"Don't give me that blarney, Mister Donovan," Billy said stiffly. There was mockery in just about everything Donovan said. Even the minor courtesies of "good morning" or "good night" seemed to fill him with some secret amusement.

"No blarney. I envy you, kid. Pictures . . . the flickers . . . that's where the big dough is." He brushed an unruly lock of chestnut hair from his forehead and glared balefully through the dusty windshield. "Why, for two pins I'd go out to the Coast with you. See that guy down the block, Billy? The slicker in the tight suit standing in front of the barber shop? That's Horace Gobar. He owns the Bijou. Two bits a seat . . . fifteen cents for kids. Why, he makes more in one day than we do in ten. He had a Doll Fairbaine picture last week and there were folks lined up clear round the block. Vaudeville's dead and the smart boys know it."

"You may be right, but I don't see what that has to do with me. I was planning a comedy routine with maybe a little juggling thrown in. I just thought I could do a high wire walk for the ballyhoo."

"Not necessary," Donovan said impatiently. "Why give the bastards something for nothing? We're going to pack the house both days . . . three shows a day. You'll make a hunk of change."

Billy knew that Donovan was right about what would fill the theater, but his resentment lingered. The man could have at least talked it over with him before printing the posters.

"I'll be leaving first thing Sunday morning," he said coldly. "So don't ask for any hold-over."

"Sure," Donovan muttered. "Sure. Got your car fixed okay?"

"It'll be ready Saturday afternoon."

"Good . . . good." There was a faraway look in Donovan's eyes. "I'm glad to hear it."

Three times a day he swayed perilously above the white blobs that were upturned faces in the hot dimness of the theater. The wire ran from the balcony to the stage so that he performed his astounding feat of daring directly above a gasping audience. On the average, three women fainted dead away at each performance and four boys threw up —more from hurried ingestions of caramel corn than fear. Billy wore a suit, carried a cane instead of an umbrella, and wore a pair of brown canvas sneakers that he bought at Woolworth's Five and Dime on Main Street. The wire was telephone cable, rubber coated, and only an acrobat of gross incompetency could have lost his footing on it. Billy Wells was not such an acrobat. He could, and did, do everything on the wire that was humanly possible to do. His feigned gyrations of lost balance; his tottering pauses brought gasps from the onlookers who fully expected this teetering fat man to come crashing down on their heads like an elephant on a nest of mice. Billy's eventual arrival on the platform well above the stage was greeted with audible sighs of relief followed by tumultuous bursts of applause. The turn was a great success and by the third performance there were long lines outside the theater.

"I could hold you over for a week," Donovan said when Billy arrived at the theater on Saturday, an hour before the matinee. "Mean a lot of extra dough for you."

"No," Billy said. "I told you. I want to leave tomorrow morning."

The lobby was cool and dim, smelling of wet dust and carbolic. An elderly colored man in sun-faded coveralls pushed a mop across the marble floor. Donovan sucked his bottom lip and leaned closer to Billy, lowering his voice to a conspiratorial whisper.

"She's madder than a wet hen, see."

"Who?" Billy asked.

"Vera. Mrs. Morgan, you know . . . she owns this flea circus."

Billy had seen her several times, but she had not spoken to him. She would always be waiting for Donovan to lock up the theater at night, waiting for him in her car parked in the alley by the stage door, a large, blonde woman with frizzy hair and too much rouge. Waiting to get her ticket punched, Madame Montenescu would have said.

"What's she angry about?"

"Oh, this and that. She thinks I made a bum deal with you. That percentage of the overage. She gave me some kind of hell about it. She hates to give money away."

Billy began to sweat, a cold trickle of moisture pinpricking his spine. He had no written contract with anyone. If Mrs. Morgan and Donovan chose to cheat him there was very little, if anything, he could do about it. His panic showed.

"Take it easy, kid," Donovan hissed. He placed a hand on Billy's arm and gave it a squeeze. "You got my word on it, didn't you? Earl Donovan's word. So what the hell are you worried about?"

A SHORT SCENE

DAMN HIM. DAMN HIM. DAMN HIM.

A gentle rain had plastered her marcel-waved hair, revealing dark lines of unbleached root. Her face was swollen with rage and tears and lack of sleep. Her cheeks were lilac with rouge: daubs of streaky color on a pallid ground.

DAMN HIM TO HELL.

"Now, Vera," the Chief of Police said.

"Don't *now Vera* me!" the woman shrieked. "I want the cad brought back in chains! In *chains,* do you hear me?"

"Now, Vera," the police chief said, clearing his throat. He turned slowly from side to side in his swivel chair, one hand on the telephone that stood on his desk, the other on the curved wooden arm of the chair. The rain sighed against the windowpanes. "If I've told you once, I've told you a thousand times. I can't have him brought back, in chains or out of 'em, unless you're willin' to sign a complaint chargin' him with a specific crime. Namely makin' off with two thousand five hundred and fifty-seven dollars in box office receipts. Now that's the law, Vera, an' my bein' your cousin doesn't alter that fact. Are you prepared to sign that complaint? Are you prepared to have him tell his side of his . . . unh . . . business relationship with you in front of twelve men of this town?"

Vera Morgan paced the room, tottering on her high-heeled shoes that were a size too small for her feet.

"If Judson was alive he'd take care of this. He'd go after the bastard and shoot him down like a dog!"

The Chief of Police of Joplin, Missouri, picked up a pencil from the desk top and tapped the telephone with it.

"If Judson was alive, Vera, he'd be more likely to shoot you."

She turned her venom on him, speaking through clenched teeth.

"You were always a prissy little man, Nathan. A milk sop . . . a milquetoast . . ."

"Now, Vera," he said.

The engine hummed. Ring tight. Bearing smooth. The oil flowed. The exhaust was clean. The tires gripped the wet road, driving the car toward the arid west. Tulsa came and went in the dawn. Oklahoma City. Sun setting in a sapphire sky over Amarillo. The car purred . . . hummed . . . ticked like a fine watch.

Billy couldn't help grinning. California lay over the horizon. The

Golden State. He felt just as sunny. He had money in his pocket and he was moving smoothly along . . . or rather, they were moving. He glanced at the man seated beside him, his head lolling gently in sleep. Earl Donovan. The man had brought him luck. And he was grateful to him in another way.

"She's going to pull a fast one on you, Billy."

Saturday night. Backstage. The applause still rumbling as Billy headed for his tiny dressing room, meeting Donovan on the way.

"What?"

"No split. If you get fifty bucks, you'll be doing good."

"But I . . ."

"Listen to me kiddo. I'm sick of this whole setup, see. I've been thinking of hitting the trail and headin' west for a long time. I'll see that you get a couple of hundred if I have to choke the old bat to get it. And I'll pay for the gas and all the expenses. How about it?"

"Why sure . . . that'd be swell."

"And we leave right now, see. Don't even bother to change your shoes."

Flagstaff, Arizona. The California line. The vast desert cool under the moon. They said that the road washed away to nothing in the rain, but it did not rain and dust drifted behind them in the moonlight for as far as the eye could see. Redlands at dawn. Orange groves and palms. Vineyards stretched to the mountains above Cucamonga and the mountains tumbled westward to the sea.

Billy drove with one hand on the wheel, left arm resting comfortably on the edge of the open window, the sun warm on his shirt. He inhaled deeply from time to time, breathing the orange blossom and eucalyptus air that was California in the spring. There was a slight haze over Los Angeles as they crested a hill leaving the San Gabriel valley.

"Almost there," Billy said. He felt quite smug about it. He glanced at his companion. "Listen. I don't know what your plans are, but I'm sure my pal could put you up for a few days."

Donovan shook his head. He had no plans, but he'd work something out. The fat guy was a chump . . . a nice chump, but still a chump. He didn't want to move in his circle.

"I figured I'd check into the Hollywood Hotel and sort of look the town over."

"Whatever you want to do. But let's keep in touch."

"Sure. Why not?" Donovan said with a shrug. "You never know."

Billy let Donovan out at the corner of Highland Avenue and Hollywood Boulevard. The Hollywood Hotel looked pleasant—and expensive, more like a country club than a hotel. Trees and flowering shrubs flanked two sides of the rambling, porticoed building and there was a large garden in the back with Japanese lanterns strung through the trees. An afternoon tea dance was in progress and the beat of a foxtrot tune mingled with the traffic sounds along the boulevard. The curved driveway in front of the hotel was lined with limousines and shiny Stutz' and Marmons.

"Pretty fancy," Billy said.

"Yeah?" Donovan said, not appearing to notice his surroundings as he removed his suitcase from the back of the car. "Well, thanks for the ride, kid."

"Thank *you*," Billy said. "And I meant that about keeping in touch. My pal's name is Mike Dale and he's in the telephone book."

"I'll keep it in mind," Donovan said as he turned away and walked up the steps toward the lobby.

The Ramona Court on Mariposa Street was a collection of yellow stucco bungalows with red tile roofs. The buildings flanked a grassy quadrangle dotted with palms, oleander, poinsettia and citrus trees. A fish pond was in front of the complex, the path from the sidewalk branching around it. The water in the pond was deep green and choked with algae. A small plaster of Paris statue of a gnome with a red painted cap stared foolishly into the weedy pool.

Billy left his bags in the car and walked up the path. Mike Dale's address was 1858½ which would make it the end bungalow. A party was in progress there, with a gramophone blaring and men and women standing outside the open front door with glasses in their hands. A young man in a striped sweater was leaning with his back against a palm tree, strumming a mandolin and singing

> *I got a mon-key bride*
> *she is my pride*
> *down where the bam-boo grows*
> *And ev'ry night*
> *when the moon is bright . . .*

"Stop that racket or I'll call the police!"

A short, thick-bodied woman stood in the doorway of the first bungalow, one hand on the partially open screen door. She glared at Billy as he walked past her.

"If you're another of them moving picture people . . . well . . . I'm

60

warnin' all of you. I'm telephonin' the police!"

The screen banged shut and Billy could hear the rumble of the woman's anger as she moved away from the door.

He couldn't blame her. The din was terrific inside the bungalow. The gramophone was stuck and the solitary wail of a trumpet went on and on, but none of the people milling around in the living room seemed to notice or care. Girls in short, tight-fitting dresses flitted past like gaudy moths while other girls, some draped in beautiful Spanish shawls, stood silent and mysterious in the shadows.

"Hey! A guy without a drink!" A young man in a tuxedo, his dark hair plastered to his skull, thrust a glass of gin into Billy's hands. He was too surprised to refuse it.

"Is Mike Dale here?"

The young man cupped a hand to his ear. "What's that you're saying, my fat friend?"

"Is . . . Mike Dale . . . here!" Billy shouted.

"How the hell would I know!" the man shouted back before flitting away into the crowd to fill more glasses.

Somebody had presence enough to flick the gramophone needle and the tom tom repetition of sound ended with a syncopated rumble of muted brass and a voice crying

> . . . my little Hono-lu-lu Lulu . . .
> my little Poly-nesian pal . . .

"Billy!"

And there was Mike Dale coming toward him, shouldering his way out of the kitchen with a bottle of champagne in one hand. He seemed much bigger than Billy remembered him, a giant, bronzed by the sun, his teeth startlingly white against the darkness of his face.

"Billy! You beautiful fat bastard! Why didn't you phone me from the station?"

"I drove out," Billy said as Mike came up to him. "I bought a car in New York."

"*You* drove?"

"Sure," Billy said modestly. "It was an easy trip."

"Well, I'll be a monkey's uncle." His laughter was explosive. "Come on, let's find a quiet spot and you tell big Mike all about it. Son of a gun. *You* drove!"

Billy felt slightly nonplussed. He couldn't understand why anyone should be so amazed that he had driven a car across the country.

"No trouble?" Mike asked as he steered Billy through the living room and down a narrow hall.

"Not at all," Billy said. "When you buy a good car, it's a piece of cake."

The big man whistled softly through his teeth. "You got moxie, Billy boy. I'll say that for you."

There were wooden cases of liquor stacked up in the hall so that both men had to move sideways, Billy sucking in his gut so as not to get wedged between the plaster wall and a stack of Booth's gin.

"I've got one hell of a bootlegger," Mike explained. "This is the goddamndest town for swilling down the stuff and if you don't keep plenty on hand they call you a cheapskate."

"Is this party for anything special?"

"Oh, hell, no. I just like having the gang over."

There was a door at the end of the hall that Mike opened, revealing a room with twin beds and dark, Spanish style furniture and red velvet drapes. A couple were wrestling passionately on one of the beds, mouths glued together, hands groping at disheveled clothing.

"Break it up!" Mike roared. "This ain't no cat house, folks!"

The couple flew apart. The man—a sinister looking bounder, Billy thought—smoothed his shirt and pulled his jacket down to cover an obvious bulge in his trousers.

"Sorry, old chap," the man said with a fake English accent.

The girl, certainly the prettiest girl Billy had ever seen, giggled and batted her pale green eyes as she tugged her dress down over exposed thighs.

"Out," Mike said with quiet menace.

The couple left, the girl still giggling, the man trying to maintain his dignity as he walked stiffly out of the room. Mike slammed the door after them.

"They screw around like cats. I tell ya, Billy, this is the damndest town." He sat on the edge of the nearly violated bed and placed the bottle of champagne on the floor. "I was in the Yukon when I was just a kid . . . went up there with my old man. Did I ever tell you about those days?"

"Sure," Billy said. He was still holding the glass of gin and he set it down on top of a bureau.

"Just like the Yukon," Mike went on. "Everybody has a kind of fever. This whole business is just going to bust wide open. You could get awful damn rich if you're lucky."

"You seem to be doing okay, Mike."

The big man nodded his head gravely. "Okay . . . sure. I work all the time because I'm big, mean and ugly, but it's going to be tough for you, Billy. I'll give it to you straight. Since Arbuckle got all fouled up, every fat guy in the country thinks he can take his place. The town's bustin' at the seams with roly-polys."

"I've got more going for me than weight," Billy said feebly.

"Sure you do, Billy, sure you do. I know that, but you're goin' to have a tough row to hoe. Dave can get you extra work out at Sterling. The pay ain't the greatest, but maybe if they see what you can do they might take a chance and give you some featured parts. I don't know. Hell, I wish I could be more optimistic. You're probably thinkin' you were a damn fool to leave New York."

"No. I'm glad I'm here. Something will work out."

Mike grinned and stood up. He placed one enormous hand on Billy's shoulder and gave it a gentle pat.

"You hold on to that thought, kiddo. An' you can bunk in with me as long as you want, that is, if you can take the noise."

Billy forced a smile. "I don't mind it." He could barely hear himself think. The laughter and music pulsated through the walls. He thought of the quiet Sunday mornings at the Clarendon with Ambrose seated by the windows sorting through his stamps. "Heck, this is Hollywood."

The door opened and the girl with the pale green eyes stepped into the room.

"Gee whizz," she said. "Has anyone seen my panties?"

He signed the register as Major E. P. Donovan, Fort Worth, Texas.

"Will there by any more luggage arriving for you, sir?" the desk clerk asked.

"No," Donovan said. "I'm just making a quick trip. I'm expecting a telephone call from a Mister Doheny. Could you check and see if he called yet and left a message?"

The desk clerk eyed the tall, red-haired man in the wrinkled, decidedly out of fashion suit with sudden respect.

"Would that be Mr. *Edward* Doheny?"

"That's right. Check on it, will ya?" He leaned forward across the polished oak desk top. "I've had a long, hot trip from Texas. Do you folks take prohibition seriously?"

The clerk's smile was faint. "We don't take it lightly, sir, but if you'd care for a pot of tea in the lounge, I'm sure we can arrange it. Do you prefer water or soda?"

"Water—and not too much of it."

The clerk turned away to check the message slots. Donovan lit a cigarette and waited patiently for him to sift through the slips. Edward Doheny and Harry Ashbaugh had been the only two Southern California millionaires he could think of. He had seen both their names in a copy of the *Kansas City Star*. "Edward L. Doheny and Harry Ashbaugh disclaim rumors of Missouri oil exploration."

"There's no message for you, Major Donovan," the clerk said.

"Good. Is there a pay phone in the lobby?"

"Why yes, sir, just past the cloakroom."

Donovan nodded his thanks and strolled off, fishing for imaginary change in his pants pocket. He knew desk clerks. It wouldn't be long before the word got around.

"That redheaded guy in two sixteen. Major Donovan . . . he's a big oil man from Texas. First thing he did was telephone Doheny."

Major E. P. Donovan sat in the spacious lounge in his slightly out of date suit that had Kansas City or Indianapolis stamped all over it, sipping bourbon and water from a teacup and watching the glittering passage of Hollywood's young social set moving in and out of the garden where a jazz band played. Donovan, who had a keen eye and an innate feel for the rightness of things, knew that he would have to buy some clothes in the sharp, California style. But for the time being the suit that Mrs. Morgan had picked out for him when they had gone up to Kansas City for a few days would do just fine. It made him look prosperous, but small town, and thus approachable even if the oil story didn't go the rounds. The lobby of a hotel where rich people stayed was a happy hunting ground. He had used such lobbies himself when he'd had enough money in his pocket to buy an impressive amount of chips. He sipped his bourbon, watched the tea dancers coming and going, and waited.

Donovan spotted the young man talking to the desk clerk and then made a point of ignoring him until the man had meandered casually into the lounge and sank with a sigh into the seat next to him.

"That music gets on your nerves after a while," the young man said.

Donovan glanced at him. He was blonde, tanned, and wore a dark blue blazer and white linen trousers. He was handsome to the point of prettiness.

"It sure does," Donovan agreed. "A bit hard on the ears."

"Still, it's the rage."

"I suppose so. Even in Fort Worth."

"Oh, is that where you come from?"

As if you didn't know, Donovan thought. "Yes," he said.

"I've never been to Texas. I'm strictly a hometown boy. Part of that rare tribe . . . a California native."

"Yeah? Most folks I run into came from someplace else. Can I buy you a . . . pot of tea?"

The young man laughed. "I just had one, but thanks. Damn silly this prohibition, don't you think?"

"Sure is."

"People who never drank before are drinking now just because it's illegal. Especially women. Half the girls get blotto at these tea dances."

"I bet they do, at that."

The man slipped a silver cigarette case from the inside pocket of his blazer.

"Cigarette?"

"Thanks."

"My name's Hammond." He fished a gold lighter from another pocket. "Percy Hammond. I live here in Hollywood. Sort of a permanent resident."

"Donovan's my name . . . Major Donovan."

"Army?"

"Marines."

Hammond blew a thin stream of smoke from the corner of his cupid's bow lips. "I admire the Marines. A damn fine bunch of fighting men. Were you in France?"

"From start to finish," Donovan said, his face suddenly grave.

The young man was silent for a moment as though showing respect for everything Major Donovan must have been through.

"I was in officer's training at Stanford, but the war ended before my group was called up."

"It was worth missing."

"I suppose it was." He took another puff on his cigarette. "What do you do, Major?"

"Oh," Donovan said vaguely, "oil . . . real estate."

"I'm in pictures. An actor."

Donovan looked suitably impressed. "Is that a fact? I've never met a moving picture actor before."

"You'll meet a lot more if you stay at this hotel long enough," Hammond said with a laugh. "Most of the permanent residents here are in the business." He glanced around the lounge, obviously hoping to spot someone who would illustrate his point. "Of course, not all of us are actors. Directors and production people live here too." His face suddenly lit up and he half rose from his chair. A thin, black-haired young man with a worried expression on his face had just entered the lounge. "Irving!"

The man called Irving took a hesitant step forward and then stopped, his large, dark eyes scanning every corner of the room.

"Hello, Percy," he said. "I'm looking for Jack Conway. Have you seen him?"

"No, can't say that I have."

"If you see him, tell him that . . ." He paused to chew on a fingernail. "No . . . never mind. Forget it."

"Irving," Hammond said, "I'd like you to meet . . ."But the man had turned and was walking briskly across the lobby toward the front doors. "That was Irving Thalberg. He sort of runs things out at Universal."

"Seemed to be in a hurry."

"He's a restless kind of guy."

"Young, too."

"But smart as a whip. He's really Uncle Carl's right hand."

Donovan was getting bored with the preambles. He didn't know who Uncle Carl was, but assumed it was Carl Laemmle. He took a sip of his drink and waited for the pitch.

"Say," Hammond said, glancing at his watch. "I'd better be on my way. It's been nice talking to you."

"Likewise," Donovan said.

Hammond stood up, took a step and then hesitated.

"Say . . . are you doing anything tonight?"

"No. Not that I know of."

"Some good friends of mine are having a poker party. Do you play the game?"

So that was it, Donovan thought. The kid was a poker hustler . . . small percentage of the losses of anyone he brought to the game. Probably paid a damn sight more than acting.

"Ever meet a man from Texas who didn't? But I'm not much for poker *parties*. I hate that penny ante, spit-in-the-ocean stuff. Down in Fort Worth we play *poker.*"

"Oh, it'll be a big game," Hammond said, almost too eagerly. "A lot of Hollywood people are usually there. In fact, I better warn you, the stakes get pretty high."

"The bigger the better," Donovan said.

Hammond excused himself to make a telephone call and Donovan ordered another pot of bourbon and watched the last of the tea dansant habitues leave the afternoon festivities. It was dusk now and the Japanese lanterns were being lit in the garden, their lights reflecting off the windows of the lounge and the polished mahogany sills. The band was playing its final number, with a saxaphone wailing like a lovelorn cat.

Two grand in his pocket, more or less. That made for a good pile of chips in anybody's game. It would probably be a fairly straight game run by a couple of pros. Not too many tricks with the cards because they wouldn't have to cheat much to win, not over the long haul. Moving picture people, oil people, real estate people . . . they were in the big money . . . riding the crest. People like that were arrogant players and reckless bettors. He would do just fine. Maybe take the whole game if he handled it right. Lose a little . . . Win a little . . . just keep floating until somebody got careless. If he couldn't clear five thousand he didn't deserve to live.

CASSETTE

I'm sure you've read Jack Turkell's book about the presound era . . . *Hollywood Gomorrah.*

That was a long time ago. Christ, do they still read that book?

I doubt it. It must have been out of print for thirty years.

At least.

Yes, at least that.

That was a crap book, as I remember.

In some ways, yes. But he treated you fairly, or don't you agree?

Oh, sure. Jack was a friend of mine. All the newspaper men were friends of mine. Jack took all his venom out on actresses because he just couldn't get to first base with any of them. He was a good reporter on one of the big San Francisco papers. But he was a runty little guy with the worst skin you've ever seen . . . pimples all over it. A very ugly man and the girls were always giving him the cold shoulder.

Getting back to you . . . he mentioned that you got your first break in the industry by winning fifty thousand dollars in a poker game.

They tell that story about everybody. Zanuck . . . Dave Selznick . . . the Cohn brothers. That's a stock Hollywood story, like the one about pretty girls with big tits being discovered in soda fountains. If they had beds in soda fountains then they'd be discovered there. No, that's a phony story. Oh, sure, I played poker and I've won that much —and lost that much—time and time again. Who hasn't in this town?

I could tell you some fantastic stories about Hollywood poker games. Those big games started about the time De Mille and Lasky came out here and they haven't stopped yet. Why, they had a big scandal not too long ago at the Friars Club in Beverly Hills—rigged poker games. You wouldn't believe the money that's bet in those games. And more in the old days when there was no income tax to speak of and a dollar was worth a dollar. A man could buy a house and raise a family very comfortably on fifty a week and the men in those games were making five, six, ten thousand dollars every week. But no. . . . No. I had my money from the sale of my circus. I didn't need to win fifty thousand at poker, but I loved to play because I met a lot of men who were of great help to me later. Men like Jack and Harry Cohn and old man Schulberg. Poker was always a social game to me.

And a lucrative one?

Well, nobody likes to lose.

He sat on his bed in Room 216 at the Hollywood Hotel in the thin yellow light of dawn and spread his winnings on the bedspread—seven thousand dollars in cash that he had taken from the two men who ran the game, and three IOU's that totaled twenty-one thousand dollars. The biggest marker was for fifteen thousand and it was signed, in a very shaky hand, Niles Fairbaine.

"That shmuck will never pay it," Louis B. Mayer had said. Louis B. Mayer had won five hundred dollars after having dropped six thousand at one point. He had been in a good mood and had offered Donovan a lift after the game had broken up at five in the morning. They had sat in the back of Mayer's chauffeur driven car and Mayer had said:

"Those guys are a couple of fucking grifters . . . a couple of goddamn sharks. I don't know why I play poker. I like bridge—that's a hell of a game, bridge."

"They can take you at bridge, too," Donovan had said.

And Louis B. Mayer had looked at him through narrowed eyes, the street lamps glinting off his eyeglasses.

"I got a feeling they wouldn't take you. I got a feeling you're as slick as those fucking bastards. That's what I think. I may be wrong."

"Don't take a bet on it."

"Don't worry. I'm glad you screwed those sons of bitches at their own game, but never ask me to play at your table—never."

"I won't."

"Are you really a goddamn Major?"

"Does it matter?"

"Not one fucking thing to me."

"Good, because it doesn't matter a damn to me, either. What makes you so sure Niles Fairbaine won't honor his marker?"

"Because he doesn't have a penny, that's why."

"The bozos who ran that game would have taken it if he'd lost to them."

"Some people know how to apply the screws. You don't. There's a way to get that money, but I'm not going to tell you." He had then turned on the seat and placed a hand on Donovan's arm, squeezing slightly, just enough to reveal the awesome power of his bicep. "I think you cheated in that game. I don't know how you did it . . . the way you shuffled the deck, maybe, but you pulled a fast one. To hell with you."

"Why did you give me a ride, then?"

"I'd give a dog a ride—as far as the streetcar tracks."

Donovan sorted out the greenbacks and formed them into a large, tight roll that he shoved into the bottom of his suitcase. The smart thing to do would be to check out of the hotel before Percy Hammond's friends had a chance to analyze the game. They'd dropped seven thousand of their own money and lost out on the big pot. They wouldn't be happy about that. It wouldn't take them long to figure out that the oil man from Texas in the hick suit had dealt that last game from the bottom of the deck.

Donovan tossed his shirts and socks on top of the money and closed the suitcase. He put the markers into his wallet. The smaller ones were collectable. The two men who had signed them, one a director for Famous-Players and the other a well-known character actor, had assured him that their IOU's would be honored as checks at the Bank of Italy's branch on Vermont Avenue. He had no reason to suspect otherwise. The Niles Fairbaine marker was another matter. Fifteen grand. A lot of dough, but it was just so much scrap paper if Niles Fairbaine wouldn't, or couldn't, honor it.

A good looking man in his thirties, but dissipated. Gone to seed, weak mouth, pale, dead eyes and a stupid and reckless card player. A director at Sterling Pictures, and Doll Fairbaine's brother—which might be the only reason he was a director. Maybe he was Doll Fairbaine's cross. But a lot of people bore crosses without necessarily feeling obligated to pay for them. He slipped the marker out of his wallet and

69

held it up toward the light as though hoping that the very paper would offer some sort of clue to its collectability.

IOU $15,000.00
Niles Fairbaine

He had a chance for a big stake if he only knew the right thing to do, the right way to handle it.

"Damn," he said softly. "God damn."

ROADS OF DESTINY

She was loved as no actress had ever been loved before. Her slim figure, sunburnt, freckled face and tomboy hair were adored from California to Calcutta, from London to Cape Town. The most backward savage in the Congo bush who would not have known the difference between a railway engine and an ice box recognized her and shouted for joy when her image appeared on a wrinkled bedsheet screen. She was "Doll" to the world's people. Doll Fairbaine, "America's girl next door."

The advertising slogan, coined by Vardon Bolling himself after viewing her first picture in 1913, was still appropriate in 1921. Everyone on God's earth had aged in those eight years, but not Doll. An increasingly corrosive moral climate had left her untouched. She was a link with a gentler past, those golden summer days before the war.

Jenny Dare Fairbaine, the impish "Doll," was twenty-six years old but could, and did, pass for fourteen in her pictures. To audiences she *was* fourteen, everybody's kid sister, a female Huck Finn. Doll rarely kissed a boy in her pictures, but she did slip frogs into their pockets or pepper them with slingshot or peashooter. A delightful roughneck, a lovable, if exasperating tomboy—laughing, whistling, happy-go-lucky Doll with a smudge of dirt on the tip of her nose and uncombed hair. That image evoked a gentler age. It blotted out for a little while the awareness that the world had undergone a cataclysmic change. Four years of barbed wire and machine guns had spawned the shingle-bobbed flapper, roadhouse sex, the speakeasy and the Palmer raids. The Ku Klux Klan might brand human flesh in Vincennes, Indiana, but Doll remained a Hoosier sweetheart swinging on the apple boughs by the Wabash far away.

And did she love? And did she marry? Like Elizabeth of England she remained virgin in the hearts and minds of her countrymen. It was unthinkable that Doll Fairbaine would give her body to a man—ever. And yet people were realistic, after all. Had Doll Fairbaine announced that she planned to marry some nice boy, say a Richard Barthelmess or a Reg Denny, the world would not have gone into shock over the news. But she did not fall in love, as far as anyone knew, nor gave any indication of marrying now or in the future.

And it was "Hi, Doll!" never "Good morning, Miss Fairbaine" when she drove onto the lot, a tiny figure in the back seat of her cream colored Duesenberg, looking like some waif being driven to an orphanage. The back seat of the car would be filled more likely than not with things grown, cultivated or bred on her huge ranch in the wilds of the Santa Monica Mountains: Mason jars of honey; baskets of eggs, scallions and lettuce and beets that her Japanese tenant farmers grew to such crisp perfection. She would be laden with runner beans and smoked turkey and hams, crockery jars of plum and quince jams, lilac and roses freshly cut and still damp with the morning dew. It was easy to tell when a Doll Fairbaine picture was being made on the Sterling lot. Along with the flowers that graced the desks of secretaries and the bowls of fruit for the girls in the cutting room and the mammoth farm lunches on the set for cast and crew, there was an indefinable atmosphere, a kind of joy, an awareness that everything was going to be smooth sailing.

Vardon Bolling sighed when he heard the Augustan notes of the Duesenberg's horns. He did not have to glance at his wristwatch to know that it was nine-thirty—the time call for Doll to come in for wardrobe tests. The woman's punctuality was as renowned as her other virtues.

He pushed his chair away from his paper strewn desk. So many items of importance lay there, so many complexities, that he felt an enormous sense of relief knowing that she was on the lot. Doll Fairbaine was not a complexity, which is to say that he was not thinking of Doll Fairbaine the woman so much as Doll Fairbaine the product. Her pictures since 1915 had cost between one hundred and twenty-five and one hundred and fifty thousand dollars apiece to make and none had returned less than seven hundred thousand. The Doll Fairbaine product was the solid rock on which the entire Sterling edifice had been built. From that first picture in 1913, *Hoosier Schooldays,* to her last one, *That O'Halloran Girl,* a steady flow of dollars had streamed from the box offices of the world into the Sterling Film Corporation coffers.

Money in the bank, that girl
Oh, yeah, sure fire B. O.

Critics had tended to make sly, oblique attacks on the Fairbaine product of late—*old-fashioned heart tugger* was becoming a common phrase. That, and *reminiscent of an earlier age . . . pure escapist stuff* was another. Bolling was aware that the sophisticates, the younger audiences, tended to shun her films in favor of the new realistic trend, but the money continued to pour in and her salary of seven thousand dollars a week was more than justified by the returns.

The Duesenberg rolled to a stop in front of the executive building. Vardon Bolling looked out of his window on the second floor and watched Doll Fairbaine emerge from the back of the car with a large bundle of fresh lilacs in her arms. The uniformed chauffeur holding the door open for her seemed incongruous. One expected to see a woman dressed in flowing silk with a wide hat adorned with egret feathers step from the car, not a wisp of a girl in cavalry twill riding breeches, dusty brown boots and a checkered shirt. But there she was, her sunburnt face raised in expectation of seeing the studio chief at his window.

"Hello, Vardon!" she cried out in her strong, husky voice—a voice that did not fit the pubescent image. "How's my favorite fella?"

"Fine, Doll. Come on up."

"Is it anything important?"

"No—it can wait."

"Good. Take a raincheck. I have to get to wardrobe . . . then I want to go home. I got a bitch going through her first heat."

"Anyone I know?"

"Oh, Vardon! You're pulling my leg. It's a *dog!* A bull. *Fanny!*"

"Give her my best."

She grinned and attempted to blow him a kiss, dropping several stalks of lilac in the process. The chauffeur, a grave, elderly Negro in dove grey uniform and black leather puttees, picked them up and held them stiffly in his black gloved hands.

"Well, hi there, Doll! Good to see ya."
"Hi, Jim . . . Danny . . . Mary . . . Bill . . ."
"Hello, Doll . . . hello . . ."

Folk passing the time of day in a small town. She thought of the studio in that way, the home town that she had never known. The studio had its own cops and firemen, its own tiny hospital and post office, its wood and stucco bungalows, gravel streets, grassy park and trees. The trees had been saplings when she had first come onto the lot, Mama driving the Ford, she and Niles and Agnes seated in the back. Nobody dared sit next to Mama when she was driving, not unless they wanted to have bruised ribs. Mama had taken driving seriously, her gaunt body hunched over the steering wheel, elbows jutting out at right angles, her arms in constant motion like the wings of some tall, bony bird. So long ago. The trees marked the passage of the years.

The wardrobe fittings took longer than usual. The scenario of her next picture, *The Girl from Kokomo,* called for her to leave the simple life in a rustic orphanage and move to a big city as the adopted daughter of a millionaire. That meant party dresses of organdy and silk and a Little Lord Fauntleroy suit of wine colored velvet for the scene where she masqueraded as a boy. She enjoyed the fitting, not so much because she liked putting on pretty clothes, but because the wardrobe mistress kept up a steady stream of studio gossip, most of it lurid.

"Of course she had a kid by him. Why do you think she went down to San Diego for three months. She gave the little bastard to her sister. Do you remember Velma? She was on the Keith circuit and she married a Navy man. They had no kids, but they've got one now. Have you heard the latest about . . ."

No gossip about her brother, although she would have told her if asked.

"Is Niles on the lot?"

"Oh, sure. He's two days behind schedule on *Mandarin Mystery.* Vardon's upset about it. Don't bend over like that, Doll, I can't get the hem straight."

After the costumes had been fitted to the wardrobe mistress' satisfaction, Doll wandered off across the lot until she found where Niles was shooting. They were on the New York street, a large crowd of extras standing in the shade of the false front brownstones or sitting on the steps in attitudes of bored indifference. She could see Niles slumped in his canvas chair, the megaphone that was the badge of his profession resting on the ground beside him. His assistant, Dave Dale, was setting up the next take, running back and forth, shouting and swearing under a withering sun. An umbrella was adjusted to throw a pool of shade over the camera and crew. A reflector was turned as the cameraman yelled for light on a troublesome shadow. Bit players dressed in the costumes of old world Chinamen scurried to their positions, their long queues swaying against their backs. Dave Dale, looking more like a shaggy, lumbering bear than a man, roared for the street crowd extras to get off their duffs, threatening them with the loss of their lunch chits if they didn't comply—now!

It was the controlled chaos of making pictures that Doll knew so well. It troubled her to see Niles just sitting there and not taking any interest in what was going on. He left far too much of the work to Dale.

"Hi, Doll," one of the property men called out.

"Hello, Sam," she said.

Niles stirred at the sound of her voice, bent forward and groped for the megaphone.

"*OKAY . . . OKAY. LET'S GET IT RIGHT THIS TIME. MOVE THE CHINKS INTO POSITION, DAVE.*"

"They *are* in position," Dave Dale yelled back.

A few of the extras laughed harshly. Niles Fairbaine ignored the sound just as he tried to ignore the presence of his sister.

"*START THE ACTION.*"

But the extras had spotted Doll. They were turning their heads to stare at her and some were pointing and whispering.

"See . . . over there . . . that's Doll Fairbaine . . . that's *Doll!*"

They watched her with a lean hunger. They were not adoring fans. She knew that and had learned to keep her distance from these people who sometimes slept outside the studio gates at night in the hope of being picked for crowd scenes. One dollar a day and a chit for lunch. Their eyes probed her, searching for the elusive clue, the magic quality that had somehow set her so far above them. What did she have that they did not? What was it that made them worth only ten silver dimes and her worth thousands of greenback dollars for a day's work? She sensed their envy and their hatred. The gap between them was too awesome to be bridged by a smile or a gracious wave of her hand.

"*STOP THE ACTION . . . STOP.*" Niles lowered the megaphone and looked petulantly at his sister. "The damn extras aren't paying attention. They're staring at you, Jenny."

"I'm sorry, Niles."

"Oh, it doesn't matter," he sighed wearily. "It's about time for lunch anyway."

He didn't look well, Doll was thinking. His eyes were sunken and his skin had a yellowish, unhealthy pallor.

"Are you all right, Niles?"

He ignored the question and raised the megaphone to his lips.

"*BREAK FOR LUNCH. EVERYONE BACK ON THE SET IN ONE HOUR.*"

75

Dave Dale kicked a reflector stand in disgust as the crowd of extras streamed off like a defeated rabble.

"You don't look at all well, Niles," Doll said, touching her brother gently on the arm. "Why don't you come up to the ranch for a few days?"

"I'm fine," he said curtly.

"You need a week of complete rest. You're just pushing yourself too hard. Are you worried about the picture?"

He looked up sharply. "Why should I be worried? Did Vardon say anything?"

"No."

He stared down at his hands which were like taut, yellow claws on the narrow end of the megaphone. God! he thought. I feel like hell. He closed his eyes for a second and prayed that the day would end, just slam shut like the closing of a door, so that he could go home. The delicate, exquisite Virginia Ashbaugh would be there after sundown . . . the odor of night blooming jasmine coming through the open windows . . . the gurgle of water in the fish pool . . . the golden carp floating lazily, snapping tiny insects from the surface of the green water. He would light a lamp . . . just one . . . the ruby lamp behind the jade screen and he would burn incense in the brass pot by the porcelain Buddha and the beautiful Virginia would be like carved ivory on the silken cover of the Chinese bed. Oh, God! He looked up at the sky, the sun of noon, and groaned.

Doll placed a hand on his brow. "I don't think you have a fever, Niles, but you really don't look well. Are you eating properly?"

He nodded numbly, praying that she would go away.

"Because I can send Juanita to cook for you. I understand you fired your boy."

"He was stealing me blind," Niles said, almost in a whisper. "He went back to Hong Kong."

With five thousand dollars in gold coins sewn into the lining of his coat. To be blackmailed by a stupid Chinese houseboy! Vomit scorched his throat and he swallowed hard.

"I think I'll lie down for an hour," he said thickly.

"That's a good idea, Niles. It'll make you feel so much better." She bent forward and kissed him on the brow. "And please look after yourself better. For my sake. Jenny loves you, Niles."

"I know." His tone was hollow.

"And you're going to do so well . . . be such a big success. I

76

know you will, Niles. I just *know* it."

She kissed him lightly again, noting with a pang of concern how clammy his skin was.

Oh, Niles, she thought sadly. Oh, poor Niles.

FLASHBACK

The rooms smelled of cooking and unwashed linen. Coal oil vapors in the unlit halls. Paper fluttered in the wind over broken windowpanes on the second floor landing.

Where?

Omaha, Nebraska, in the dead of winter with an icy rain slashing the rooming house on Pawnee Street.

When?

February 12, 1904.

And who was in this house?

The owner, a widow, suffering from an ulcerated thigh, sleeping deeply, a half filled bottle of laudenum on the nightstand within easy reach.

A hardware drummer from Chicago secure and happy in his bed after a good week of selling. Allgood's Waterless Cookers and Lite-Wate Dutch ovens being the prime sellers and the big commission makers.

A preacher and his wife from Moline, talking in the dark hours, warm under the blankets and the goosedown comforter the preacher's wife had brought along with her, but troubled nonetheless, talking through tight lips of an errant daughter, a Babylonian whore of a girl (yet loved by both despite their venonous rampages) who had run off with a soldier—a trooper in the Fifth Cavalry. They had been married in Kansas City. The trooper made fifteen dollars a month and the daughter was already with child. It was a terrible thing to talk about at one o'clock in the morning with the rain seething against the windows and the chill of the Arctic wind seeping through the boards. The nineteen-year-old trooper who had seduced and then married their sixteen-year-old girl would win a battlefield commission in Chiahuahua, Mexico, in 1916 and lead an armored division through Normandy, France, in 1944 with three tarnished silver stars on the collar of his wrinkled khaki shirt; a tall, lean, soft-spoken tobacco chewer loved by everybody. A land mine outside the village of Moulins la Marche would deal him the fate so fervently wished if not prayed for this night, but the preacher and the preacher's wife would be decades dead.

The Connery sisters, appearing three times nightly at the Gala Theatre with a full repertoire of popular songs, asleep in one bed, locked in each other's arms for warmth and comfort, their breath sweet and their dreams pleasant.

A dark, Spanish looking lady in bed, but not asleep, with her husband —who was not her husband at all but a corn merchant with a wife and three children in Scotts Bluff.

John Makepeace Fairbaine and his family, including his wife's mother, in one room. John Makepeace Fairbaine, summer tent chautauqua reciter of Shakespeare's more popular soliloquies, wakes with a cry, his long, gaunt body drenched with a cold sweat. His nine-year-old daughter, Jenny, lies between him and his wife. He falls across her in a desperate attempt to touch his wife's shoulder and the child wakes up, whimpering and shaking, her father's terrified face close to hers, his rotting liver breath in her nostrils. Not a day of her life will pass without her remembering that face and that stench of impending death.

Mother and grandmother Agnes Dare, little Jenny (small for her age, passing for six) and her thirteen-year-old brother Niles dress the suffering man and lead him, stumbling and shaking through the bitter streets to the charity hospital where he dies before dawn.

A loss?

He was liked, if not loved. A moody, introspective man with his family. He shone brightest in the saloons where his patrician manner and soft Virginia accent led people to believe that he was a man of gentle upbringing who had seen better days. A ruined child of the South, perhaps. Such was not the case. He was simply a minor actor who had, over the years, committed to memory certain poems and speeches and his recitation of them while in his cups impressed his fellow drinkers and earned him a meager living in tent shows before prairie audiences hungry for culture. What little money he managed to save was invested foolishly in gaudy schemes. He died without a penny in his pocket. He left bar bills totaling twenty-seven dollars and eighty-five cents which four Omaha saloonkeepers graciously declined to collect from his widow. And the widow?

A rock . . . a mountain. Mary Dare Fairbaine was an untrained actress of raw power and passion. Her rendering of Lady Macbeth's capsulated speeches was enough to chill the blood of simple farmers and their wives who crowded the steamy tent on summer nights. She

78

prowled the rough board stage like a murdering cat and sent her howls of anguish and rage to the harvest moon.

> *Out, damned spot! Out, I say!*

She was iron to her husband's velvet—a bassoon to his flute. His speeches were measured, word for word, wrapped in oratorical bunting and dropped like pearls at the dusty boots of his listeners.

> *Tomorrow, and tomorrow, and tomorrow*
> *creeps in this petty pace . . .*

Her speeches were howled and wailed like the strident naggings of a farm wife to some faint-hearted husband.

> *But screw your courage to the sticking-*
> *place, and we'll not fail.*

To kill a king or save a wheat crop from a storm of rain.
"I can do it! I'll keep us together! I will . . . I will!"
That winter was spent in sewing shirts that Niles and his grandmother peddled to Omaha haberdashers, with the profit carefully hoarded away in a tin box for the coming of spring.
Some new clothes for herself, Mother Agnes, little Jenny and Niles. Tickets on the river boat, the Missouri a brown flood dotted with ice after the northern thaws, the boat taking them to St. Louis and then down the Mississippi to Cairo. And then another boat up the Ohio to Evansville, Indiana, where a Mr. Hogarth Boone was preparing his chautauqua.
And this was?
The spring and summer of 1905.

MME. MARY DARE FAIRBAINE
RECITATIONS FROM THE BARD

Agnes Dare insisted that her daughter include her maiden name. She was proud of the Dare's—not that any of them had amounted to very much, schoolteachers mostly, although her husband's brother had once been coroner of Shelby County, Ohio. But it was at least their name, the name they had carried with them since the first Dare brought his family out of New Hampshire to the Western Reserve. Not like the Fairbaine's, which was not—despite John M's delusions of grandeur— a family name at all. No one, not even his wife, knew John M's real name. He had invented a name for himself when, as a virtually unpaid apprentice in a theatrical group, he had played in Fairfax, Virginia. Makepeace had been invented, too, so he had been John something or other. A no name. Probably a foundling boy with pretensions. But Agnes Dare was not one to speak ill of the dead.

Hogarth Boone's chautauqua tent show was a great success that summer, traveling through Indiana and Ohio. The coming of winter found them near Columbus where the show disbanded until the next year. Mary Dare Fairbaine had been frugal to the point of miserliness with the money she had made. She rented a small house in Columbus, bought a new sewing machine from Sears, Roebuck for thirteen dollars plus freight and began sewing custom-fitted shirts for Columbus businessmen. There was enough money in it to keep her permanently rooted in Ohio, but come spring she felt the longing to be on the road again, under the big tent, striding the plank stage that smelled sweetly of sawdust and resin.

> *The quality of mercy is not strain'd,*
> *it droppeth as the gentle rain from heaven . . .*

1906—1907—1908. The years passed quickly. Little Jenny joined her mother on the boards, as did Niles. Jenny, her hair in ringlets and looking all of eight years old although she was now thirteen, recited poetry, her surprisingly strident voice carrying to the farthest row of seats.

> *When Freedom, from her mountain height,*
> *Unfurled her standard to the air . . .*

Niles had inherited his father's long legs and slender, aristocratic face. He wore his chestnut brown hair long to give him a Byronic air. Ladies' fans fluttered more quickly when he strode center stage in doublet and tights, haughty profile turned to the crowd; the handsome, moody, melancholy Dane.

> *How weary, stale, flat, and unprofitable*
> *seem to me all the uses of this world!*

And there were applecheeked country girls who took him at his mournful word and sought to comfort him under the hissing gas lights of ice cream emporiums . . .

"A cherry phosphate, if you don't mind." . . . and then in the dark, summer fields beyond sleepy hamlets in Ohio, Indiana, Illinois and Kentucky, eager to press a love of life into him with their warm bodies and tear stained lips.

"Say you love me . . . please . . ."

And of course he did, and then he was gone, to strut and fret upon another stage, far, far away.

In August 1908, when the chautauqua was in Springfield, Illinois, Mary Dare Fairbaine fell victim to a mysterious brain fever that left her babbling like a demented child. She was taken to a hospital where the fever rapidly became worse, leaving her temporarily blind and in a coma. She was suffering from cerebral meningitis and would have died had she had less will power and a weaker constitution, but it would be many months before she was capable of even walking the length of her bed in the Sangamon County charity hospital. Her illness struck terror into Jennifer who had no idea of what would become of them all without her.

"You must play the man now, Niles."

His grandmother's words, not that Niles had to be told where his responsibilities lay. He was a strapping, broad-shouldered young man on the verge of eighteen, with a painfully cultivated mustache gracing his upper lip like a sharp line from a black pencil. He would provide for his ill mother and for the well-being of his little sister and his aged grandmother.

"I'm going to Chicago."

To become a star. A juvenile lead. The offer was firm, up to a point. He had met an actress ten years his senior who was set for a major part in the touring company of *The Count of Monte Cristo*. Her infatuation had led to promises. A role in the play—and if not, then certainly in something else. Chicago was second only to Broadway. A chap with his looks and talent could not miss. Fourteen dollars was scraped together to furnish him with a suit in the latest style—three button, single-breasted, the coat flaring slightly at the hips, the trousers wide on the upper part of the legs and tapering snugly at the ankles, the outfit completed with the proper accessories including a pan brim hat. And then he was off, a cardboard suitcase of simulated leather in his hand, swinging jauntily onto a car of the Illinois Central Railroad while grandmother Agnes waved and little Jenny sobbed.

81

"Goodbye, Niles . . . goodbye."

Grandma Agnes had no illusions, but to have stopped Niles' impetuous rush to the bright lights of the Loop would have been impossible. She was a Dare, and like countless generations of Dares she was practical. Not for her the idle dreams of misty success. A dollar was a dollar and hard to come by. There was rent to pay and food to buy and lofty dreams would provide neither. Jenny stood beside her on the platform in her guimpe dress of white butcher linen, one tiny gloved hand raised in farewell as the train pulled slowly out of the station, Niles looking back from the top of the steps, waving his hat and grinning.

"Goodbye . . . goodbye!"

Grandma Agnes took the child by the hand and they walked through the streets of Springfield, the girl chattering away in a kind of hysteria until the old woman told her to hush, to just hush up—*now.*

The old lady needed to think, and to think with a clear mind. Jenny's incessant babblings about how rich and famous Niles would become in Chicago were irritating. She took Jenny to a drug store and treated her to a Coca-Cola and herself to a cup of coffee.

They were in deep trouble. Mary ill nearly to death . . . Niles fleeing north to heaven alone knew what, and she and Jenny with no more than ten dollars separating them from the poor farm. The chautauqua was on its final engagement of the year and she doubted if Hogarth Boone would consider using Jenny anyway. The child's recitation of the poetry of Joseph Rodman Drake and H. F. Chorley had always been greeted with favor, but he had never paid the girl so much as a nickel and was unlikely to do so now.

"It's the experience, Mrs. Fairbaine. Why, the child is getting an education in the great art of dramatic oratory without it costing you one red cent."

But, if not the chautauqua, then what?

There is a crossing of stars—meandering paths that touch. There is fate.

RALLY

COME ALL COME

SANGAMON COUNTY FAIRGROUNDS

SUNDAY

THE GREAT CRUSADE FOR TEMPERANCE

Grandma Agnes sipped her coffee and studied the poster so prominently displayed behind the counter. Spokesman from all the factions would be there, the leaders of the Anti-Saloon League, the Prohibition Party, the Women's Christian Temperance Union and the Illinois Friends of Frances Willard among others.

"And a little child shall lead them," Grandma Agnes whispered. It was a revelation, she would stoutly maintain in later years, that had come directly from the Almighty.

Grandma Agnes had been a firm believer in temperance long before she had seen her son-in-law drink himself into his grave. She had never buried a hatchet in a saloon wall, but she had insisted that Niles take the pledge on his thirteenth birthday, and she had taught a little jingle to both of her grandchildren.

> *The devil anxious*
> *to make man sin*
> *invented whisky,*
> *beer and gin.*

and had taken them to meetings of the W.C.T.U., of which noble organization she was a member, though not in any particular chapter due to the nomadic nature of her life. Many of the W.C.T.U. meetings in such places as Albion, Illinois, and Vanceburg, Kentucky, had been little more than revival meetings with a string of ex-sinners falling to their knees and blessing the ladies for doing God's work against the Devil and demon rum. It was at these soul-stirring affairs that Jennifer Dare Fairbaine had learned several temperance propaganda songs and playlets . . .

> *Oh, father, dear father,*
> *come home with me now . . .*

and could recite them with a passion nurtured by her own bitter remembrances.

And the first recognition of her unique talent?

At the temperance rally in Springfield, Illinois, August 23, 1908, the crowd spilling out of the huge, opensided tent. A sea of women in white lawn waist dresses, faces flushed and damp from the murderous heat, fans fluttering, glasses of tepid lemonade constantly refilled, listened as the speakers came and went on the round wooden platform in the center of the tent.

Toward the end of the rally, with the heat and the speeches creating a torpor in the throng, Grandma Agnes spoke softly to a large, hatchet-faced woman with a blue sash bisecting her bosom and this woman stepped onto the platform and bellowed for quiet. She announced that a young child whose father had died of the curse of drink and whose mother was now ill in the charity ward of the county hospital would like to add her tiny voice to the fight against the evils of rum. Little Jennifer, her golden hair curled into tight ringlets, and wearing her best dress, starched and pleated, mounted the platform's steps. She pressed her hands together as though in prayer and raised her eyes toward heaven.

> *I saw a man at the dawn of day,*
> *down by the grogshop door.*
> *His eyes were sunk, his lips were pale*
> *and I looked him o'er and o'er.*

Her voice was startling. It rang out like a trumpet, full and throaty and rich. It seemed astounding that such a tiny wisp of a girl could speak with such authority and passion. A tingle, like an electric shock, passed up the spine of every spellbound listener.

> *His daughter stood by his side*
> *and weeping, murmuring, said:*
> *Oh, father, mama is sick at home*
> *and your children cry for bread!*
> *The drunkard laughed and staggered in,*
> *as he oft had done before,*
> *and to the barkeep faltering said . . .*
> *OH, GIVE ME ONE GLASS MORE!*

There were many men in that gathering who had dutifully escorted their wives. A few of them were friends of John Barleycorn, and secretly contemptuous of the proceedings. Just such a man was Andrew Parkland, owner of a chain of vaudeville houses in Ohio and Pennsylvania. Parkland was not about to be turned away from his daily libation of good rye whisky either by his wife's entreaties or a child's tears, but he knew a crowd pleaser when he saw one. And he was seeing one then in the image of a golden blonde doll with a voice like Sarah Bernhardt's riveting the attention and emotions of three or four thousand people. He signed Jennifer Dare Fairbaine to a week's appearance at his Variety Theater in Cincinnati right then and there. Grandma Agnes made a surprisingly tough deal, but Parkland, overcome by heat and his wife's insistence that such an inspired creature was worth any price, gave in to the old lady's demand that her granddaughter get fifty dollars plus two roundtrip tickets to Cincinnati.

"Done," Andrew Parkland said. "I just hope the child is worth it."

"She is," Grandma Agnes snapped. "And it's the last time you'll get her for fifty dollars and a train ticket, I can tell you."

And it was.

THE GOLDEN DOLL
A CHILD'S PRAYER FOR TEMPERANCE

It was a novelty attraction, a touch of sentimentality on a bill composed of soft shoe hoofers, acrobats, low Dutch comics and a coon shouter. Jenny Fairbaine "The Golden Doll" became a big attraction in Cincinnati and then in Parkland's theaters in Dayton, Cleveland, Pittsburgh and Philadelphia. Her salary rose and, in time, her act changed. Novelty attractions had a way of wearing thin and Andrew Parkland was enough of a showman to recognize that fact. He hired a writer to come up with a skit—a lighthearted farce involving a foxy grandpa, his perky, tomboyish granddaughter, the rent collector and a policeman. A producer from the Biograph Company, maker of moving pictures, would see that skit in Philadelphia in the spring of 1910 and offer good money to photograph it at the Biograph Studio in New York City. Parkland gave his consent, provided that "The Doll" Fairbaine's name was not mentioned on the credit titles and that a print of the film be provided free for projection on his Philadelphia theater's new moving picture screen—another novelty attraction that Andrew Parkland was sure would wear thin in time.

My dearest darling brother . . .

And so began another of the countless letters that Doll Fairbaine wrote to Niles, c/o Tarkington & Poore, Theatrical Booking Agents, The Bowmar Bldg., State Street, Chicago, Illinois. She told him of the excitement and fun of making motion pictures and of the people she had met.

So unlike the people in vaudeville, Niles. More fun-loving and excited

85

*. . . and yet, so sincere about what they are doing, so bemused by their
cameras and so solemn about such things as the time of day and the
position of the sun. Curious . . . and yet, somehow, I like it very much.
I have made five moving pictures and Mr. Parkland is very angry with
me, but I had a wonderful lunch the other day with one of the directors
here at Biograph, a Mr. Griffith who was a fine actor in some first-rate
companies and he said . . .*

And far away, in Duluth, or Kansas City, or Baton Rouge, Niles
Fairbaine received the letters forwarded by Tarkington & Poore (not
with dispatch, for their minor clients were hardly worthy of such postal
considerations) and, in time, he lay back on his bed in whatever rooming house he happened to be in and opened them, one by one.

*I am now making two hundred dollars every week and Grandma takes
most of the money, all of it in twenty dollar gold pieces, and invests it
in what she says are solid common stocks—The Standard Oil Company,
International Harvester, American Telephone and Telegraph, Sears,
Roebuck . . . and, oh, how we all miss you, dearest Niles and pray for
you every night. Mama is really her old self again and would like to visit
you, as would Grandma and I, if you would only let us know when your
play moves east. I'm sure you must be brilliant in it.*

His infrequent letters to her were filled with lies. Roles he had never
played. Cities he had never visited. Salaries he had never made. He was,
by 1912, a total failure as an actor, his once handsome face blotched
and dissipated. He was considered unreliable by theatrical managers
and had been dismissed from the road company of Alworth Bane's *The
Four Brothers* in Davenport, Iowa, for being drunk during a performance and forgetting his lines.

He came to New York after wiring his mother to send him the fare,
coming home neither with his shield nor on it, the high promise of his
youth as frayed as his shirt cuffs, as soiled as his unpressed suit.

"This is my brother, Mister Griffith."

David Wark Griffith saw nothing in the young man's eyes, no bright
innocence, no shiny ideals . . . only a lackluster, brooding resentment
of life. His was not the kind of face that he wanted in his pictures, but
he cast Niles in a few small parts, mostly as a wastrel son, because it
made Doll happy. And he and all of the men at Biograph wanted little
Doll Fairbaine to be happy. She was no longer appearing on the Parkland vaudeville circuit. She was making one moving picture a week, but
not under any kind of contract. Mama and Grandma wanted her to stay
clear of contracts for the moment. The two women had long talks deep

into the night in the kitchen of the roomy apartment on Manhattan's West Side about their little Doll's future (no one called her Jenny any longer except Niles). There were offers to weigh . . . from Belasco, Ziegfeld, the Schuberts, from Edison and Vitagraph, and from Vardon Bolling who was making motion pictures in Los Angeles, California.

Cal-i-for-nia. Mary Dare Fairbaine let that word roll trippingly off the tongue. *Cal-i-for-nia* . . . she liked the sound of it. Such a long way away. The sun shiny all year in *Cal-i-for-nia* and the money excellent, four hundred dollars a week.

"I may not go," Niles had said. "I've had offers."

Doll wept and clung to him. He was her big, handsome brother. They must never be separated again. But, of course, she had to be a brave girl. She wouldn't stand in the way of his career. If he had offers . . . Offers?

From Willie the Weeper and Cokey Joe.

> *Goin' up Broadway, comin' down Main,*
> *lookin' for a woman dat use cocaine*

It had been bewildering and galling to see Jenny become so successful. She had no talent, no true thespian abilities. She would never be a tall, stately woman. Never have great presence on the stage. A child. And yet . . . she had the money. She acted as though she were his big sister. Bought him fine clothes and linens at the very best haberdashers . . . saw to it that he always had cash in his wallet . . . prevailed on Mr. Griffith to give him parts although it was so obvious that Bobbie Harron was Griffith's ideal young actor.

> *I wake up in de mornin' by de city bell*
> *an' de niggers up town givin' cocaine hell,*
> *ho, ho, honey, take a whiff on me.*

The darky gamblers in Natchez and Kansas City used to sing that song, in the hop joints and the barrel houses. Cocaine hurt his nostrils. Made the entire face throb. Liquor made him ill, after a while, gagging and retching on the oily whisky, the perfume taste of gin. Opium was clean. It dulled and soothed and inspired. They gave opium to horses to make them win. Heroin, they called it. Stick it in a vein. Always wipe the hypodermic needle first with alcohol. There was a place near Pell Street on the East Side run by a tall, blonde woman married to, or living

87

with, a Chinaman. The Chinaman was gracious about everything. He wore dark Occidental suits and a straw skimmer. The only thing that set him apart from a gentleman was the wearing of a diamond ring on each finger of both hands. The Chinaman spent his days drinking ice cold champagne and playing solitaire while his wife moved dreamily through the curtained rooms and the sweet smoke, naked under her gown of Chinese brocade.

"I really don't think I want to go to California."

But panic gripped him when he saw the trunks being packed and heard Mama on the telephone arranging for the train tickets. He would be alone with no one to borrow money from . . . no one to wrangle him parts. He wondered how gracious the Chinaman would be if he told him that he could not pay for his toy of hop.

"And yet—I might do quite well in Los Angeles."

"Oh, yes, Niles, yes. You'll see . . . you'll see!"

And Doll had cried out with happiness and clung to him, pressing her face against his chest, smelling the delicious aroma that was her big brother—tobacco and bay rum and soft English tweed. Some people whispered terrible things about Niles. Even Mama and Grandma Agnes said things, but she closed her ears to it. Niles would always be bright and impetuous and gay, so handsome in his new suit, his eyes shiny, his smile radiant, swinging onto the last car of the Illinois Central Railway train so long ago.

LIFE'S DARN FUNNY

Billy felt uneasy and out of place. He was wearing a blue serge suit with a vest, a white shirt with pale blue stripes, a stiff collar and a dark blue bow tie. He was sweltering in his clothes, the perspiration streaming down his legs and into his socks: pounds of healthy fat oozing out of his pores and departing his body forever. He felt thin, wasted and half dead from lack of sleep. Parties did not end at Mike's, they paused briefly for a few hours and then began again. The police knocked on the door constantly . . . the landlord threatened eviction. It was an atmosphere of chaos. He had to move out, but he must get work before he could afford it. He could sell the car, but he hesitated to do so. Distances were so vast in Los Angeles. The studios were spread out. Universal on the far side of the hills in the dusty wilds of the San Fernando Valley . . . Inceville by the sea . . . Sterling in Culver City. He needed the car, but he also needed his rest. A quiet atmosphere, regular hours and good food. Mike kept nothing in the kitchen but ice and seltzer water. Billy had gone shopping once and had cooked a dinner, but the platter of fried chicken had just barely reached the table when "the gang" arrived and the chicken was gone as though devoured by a swarm of locusts. That meant eating out all the time and he couldn't afford to spend a whole dollar for just one meal.

He needed a job and that was why he now stood in the sun waiting for Dave Dale. He stepped out of the way of the extras as they streamed off to get their lunches, a few swore at him for blocking the sidewalk while others sneered openly at his thick, eastern cloths and sweating bulk. Their blatant hostility did not surprise him. He had found most people in California to be unpleasant, especially anyone working in the picture business.

He watched Dave coming toward him. Mike's older brother, as big as Mike, but lacking Mike's grace. Dave always seemed embarrassed by his hugeness and tried to modify it by walking with a slight stoop. It only made him look more menacing, like a gorilla.

"That stupid shit," Dave said. "We could've got that shot in easy. Now we gotta set up all over again."

"You seemed to be doing all the work," Billy said.

"That's right," Dave replied, a tinge of bitterness in his tone. "I do the work and he gets the dough. They pay that asshole ten thousand dollars a picture and he couldn't direct a dog fight." He glanced at his wristwatch. "We're a little early, but we might as well go on over. I'll introduce you and give him a pitch and then you're on your own."

"I certainly appreciate this, Dave."

"Forget it." He smiled ruefully. "I don't know if I'm doing you a favor or not. This guy's the biggest bastard who ever lived. He eats actors for breakfast."

Billy fell into step beside the big man as he hurried off the set and down a narrow alley between two wooden buildings.

"I understand that he's a fine director."

"Yeah, he's good all right, maybe the best comedy mind in the business, but he's still a number one prick. Don't cross him or he'll hound you right out of the industry."

"I get along with most people," Billy said. It was like a prayer. He had heard a lot of wild stories about Chester Pratt, what a sadistic ogre he was, how he brutalized bit players, but he had also heard that when he found good people he hung onto them, used them like a stock company in the many comedy series that he produced or directed for Sterling. That meant status as a guarantee player—seventy-five steady dollars every week, minimum. It could go as high as a hundred and there was always the possibility of his giving an actor a shot in a starring role to gauge public reaction. Cross-eyed Andy Farrel had started that way and now Farrel was starring in one reelers and making a thousand dollars a week.

"In here," Dave said, holding a screen door open. They entered the ground floor of a two story, yellow stucco building and walked down a narrow, gloomy hall that smelled of linoleum and nitrate film. A few of the doors that lined both sides of the passage were open and Billy could see shirt-sleeved men holding long black strands of film up to the light, running the seemingly endless lengths through their hands as they transferred the shiny coils from one cloth lined wicker basket to another.

90

Dave Dale paused in front of a wood door with a pebbled glass panel. Inscribed across the glass in black paint were the words

PRODUCTION DEPT.
BLUE RIBBON COMEDIES

"Okay," Dale said. "Take three deep breaths and pray like hell."

Billy made meaningless dabs at his suit. It was cool in the building and he felt clammy as the sweat began to congeal.

"Wish me luck."

"You'll need it," Dale said. "You're the tenth fat guy he's interviewed in the past two days."

Billy couldn't help thinking of a fox. That was what Chester Pratt reminded him of—a sleek, cunning fox, deadly to all the slower-witted breeds. He sat on the edge of a desk that was piled high with film cans, one shiny brown shoe thumping restlessly against a leg of the desk. He was a tiny man in his middle thirties with a thin, sharp face and a small mouth crowded with oversized yellowish teeth. His hair was ginger, almost orange, and parted in the center of his scalp. His face had the same gingery orange hue and his eyebrows were like clusters of copper wires above dark, beady, volpine eyes.

"So you were in the Follies," he said in a raspy voice after Dave Dale had left the room.

"Yes, sir," Billy said.

The eyes probed, cold, pitiless. The tiny foot bump bump bumped against the desk leg.

"And you're a comedian, you say?"

"Yes, sir."

"Make me laugh."

Billy felt a trickle of icy sweat travel down his spine and into the cleft of his buttocks. He tried to think of a joke, but his mind was suddenly blank.

"Well?" Pratt said coldly. "I'm waiting."

"There were these two farmers," Billy stammered, "and they went down to New York for the first time and . . ."

The director's expression hardened. "You may not have noticed, Mr. Wells, but pictures don't talk. Do something to make me roll off this desk or stop wasting my time."

The door opened and a young man entered the office carrying several reels of film.

"Here's the rough cut on *Pals and Gals,* Mister Pratt."

"Thanks, Tony. Stick around a minute, the fat guy's going to make us howl."

Don't panic, Billy urged himself. He hadn't anticipated this type of cold interview at all. He had expected to do something, but had reasoned that they would tell him what they wanted to see—a pratfall perhaps, or a doubletake. His mind raced through the Jimmy Pepper routines . . .

I hope I can get a good meal here
I hope so, too.

"This is a pantomime of a man *and* a fly sharing a bowl of soup. *I'm* the man."

Not a shadow of amusement crossed the face of Pratt. The young man with the film reels looked vaguely confused.

Billy pulled a chair into the center of the room and then began to set an imaginary table with cutlery and a bowl of soup, carrying the phantom bowl with painful slowness so as not to spill a drop. He then sat on the chair, adjusted an invisible napkin around his neck, picked up a nonexistent spoon and prepared to eat. Ah, but the fly had its designs on the bowl as well. Billy followed its erratic flight with his eyes, the spoon poised near his half open mouth. The fly drew closer . . . closer . . . and came to rest on the tip of Billy's nose. He tried to scoop it up with his hands and only succeeded in spilling a spoonful of hot soup into his lap. He jumped and dabbed at his lap with the napkin. The fly reappeared, buzzing around him and Billy slashed at it with the napkin in a furious duel that brought him heavily against the table. He made a wild dive to save the soup from falling onto the floor, gripping the hot bowl with both hands. The fly landed on top of his head. Slowly . . . slowly . . . he raised his hands, and the bowl, and with a quick movement trapped the fly by dunking the bowl onto his head like a hat. He finished the skit by disgustedly wiping soup from his face and flicking the liquid from his fingers.

The kid with the film chuckled. "Say, that was pretty good!"

Billy only had eyes and ears for Chester Pratt who remained wooden-faced and motionless.

After a long pause the director said: "You look wrong in a bow tie —like you had no neck. Wear a long tie. You have graceful hands for a fat man. Learn to use them more. Flutter them . . . toy with your lapels . . . twit your nose or tug your ear. You can use a long tie as a prop. Twist it . . . wave it at people. Gestures. That's what people laugh at. The way Tom Pipp walks. The way Andy Farrel rolls those cross eyes. Mannerisms. You have to develop mannerisms. The camera catches the little things, Mister Wells."

"Yes, sir," Billy said. He tried to read the man's decision in his eyes, but there was nothing there. No light. Nothing at all.

"You may have been terrific in the Follies, I wouldn't know, but to me, you don't have any character, not yet anyway. You're just fat. Some people think that being fat is being funny, but I don't. I people my comedies with characters people remember and that's why the Blue Ribbons . . . the Pipp two reelers, the Farrel one reelers . . . the Mick and Myer's, the Boarding House Boys are the most successful comedies in the country today—next to Chaplin's, of course."

Billy's voice was barely audible. "Yes, sir."

"And don't 'sir' me. I don't like being 'sirred.' The people who work for me call me either *Mister* Pratt or Chester. You call me *Mister* Pratt."

"You mean I'm hired?"

"Be here tomorrow at six-thirty in the morning. Your salary is ninety a week. And if you've heard any stories about what a bastard I am to work for just forget them, because I'm not as bad as they say . . . I'm a damn sight worse."

CASSETTE

I suppose that the early films of Billy Wells are long gone . . . and the Tom Pipp two reelers.

That's right. I tried to get hold of some years ago for my collection, but I couldn't find one print. Not one, although an exhibitor in Tokyo sent me a reel, but it was just bits and pieces. In the Orient in those days the exhibitors would take comedies and splice together all the gags and stunts. That's all that their audiences liked to see. There might be Langdon, Bevan, Conklin, Pipp . . . maybe a half dozen comedians all jumbled together on one reel. Chaos, but the Japs loved it. No. All those early pictures are gone. They were on nitrate stock and they destroyed all those negatives when safety film came into use. Nobody thought they were worth saving.

That's a pity.

Oh, yes, a shame. All the Chester Pratt films were brilliant.

Did you know Pratt?

Yes, I knew him very well. He died in a car accident in . . . oh, 1924 or thereabouts. A terrible tragedy. He would have dominated the sound era had he lived. There just wasn't anyone like him. A brilliant man.

How did Wells get into his troupe at Sterling?

Well, you know, I thought a lot of Billy . . . brought the guy out . . . talked him into leaving vaudeville . . . bankrolled him . . . and we were close. I was fond of the kid and I did what I could to get him into pictures until I could get my own company rolling. It was a very difficult time for the independents in those days. They were being shut out of the theaters by the big boys, by the Bollings and the Zukors. Zukor and Vardon Bolling were in a dog fight to control the major theaters in the country—sewing up the best circuits to show their product. Famous-Players and Sterling were the giants. I wanted to weigh things very carefully. I didn't want to lay out fifty or a hundred thousand dollars on some pictures and then find that I couldn't get first class play dates. So, I was being cautious, but I didn't want Billy to suffer. I didn't want him to think that I had conned him into leaving vaudeville and then abandoned him out on the coast. I told Doll Fairbaine about him and she talked to Chester and that's how Billy came to be part of the Pratt stock company of comedians.

How did you first meet Doll Fairbaine?

Well, I don't remember exactly . . . at a party somewhere. I was a very social guy and a good dancer. They used to have what they called tea dances in those days . . . afternoon affairs at the Hollywood Hotel, or downtown at the Alexandria. All the picture people attended. I met Doll at one of those dances and we hit it off right from the start.

What a great star she was.

Oh, sure, the biggest . . . the best. Most of her pictures were pretty corny, but the fans loved her and everything she touched came up roses.

It's a pity that she's never written her memoirs.

I guess you could say that.

Miraflores Canyon Road was a dirt road, oiled and hardpacked. It meandered westward out of Mandeville Canyon through hills thickly covered with greasewood, yucca and stunted pine. It was pleasant country and Earl Donovan enjoyed the ride. He had rolled the top down on the secondhand Paige he had bought with some of his winnings and the sun and the hot, dry wind felt good against his face. As the road curved around a hill he could see the ocean off to his left and the ragged line of Catalina Island.

He reached a wide spot in the road, a circle wide enough for a car to turn. A sign was posted there that read

WARNING
PRIVATE ROAD FROM
THIS POINT ON

He pulled the car to one side and smoked a cigarette, running over in his mind what he planned to do. It would work, although he wasn't happy at the idea, but there was no other way. No other way at all.

A SHORT SCENE

"Jesus," Percy Hammond said through tight lips. "You've got some nerve."

"Don't I just," Donovan said as he sat down next to the young actor in the lounge of the Hollywood Hotel. An orchestra was playing under the Japanese lanterns in the sunset glow. Someone was singing

> *I lost my heart at Ava-lon bay . . .*
> *'neath a silvery moon where*
> *palm trees sway . . .*

"I don't think you're an officer *or* a gentleman!"

"I won't argue about that, Percy."

"You made some enemies. They figured out what you did."

"You work for a couple of wise monkeys, but that's neither here nor there. I had a long talk about those two bozos with Louie . . . Louie Mayer."

"Oh?" Hammond said.

"I told him that I didn't think a good looking kid like you was mixed up in that racket. Louie said he hoped not because a guy with your looks should do well in pictures . . . as long as he kept his nose clean."

"I don't really *work* for them," Hammond said weakly.

"Hell, don't I know it? Now, look here, Percy. Let me wash your back and you wash mine. Niles Fairbaine gave me his marker as you know, but that's about as far as it goes. I can't get hold of the guy. I think he's trying to welsh on me. Okay. I've run into welshers before and I know how to put the screws on a bo, but I don't want to do that with him. You get the picture?"

"Yes," Hammond murmured.

"Now, if I collect there'll be something in it for you. There's a way of getting that dough and I think you'd know. You look to me like the kind of a guy who'd know just about everything that's going on in this burg. Am I right?"

"I know one or two things," Hammond whispered. "Look, can I have the money now?"

"I'll give you five hundred. That should buy bread for a while and keep you away from bad company. Okay?"

"Okay. His IOU's money in the bank because his sister'll make it good. They say that some gamblers down in Redondo were going to drop him off a pier in a trunk, but Doll came up with the money. Ever since then she's been afraid something bad might happen to him. She always coughs up."

"Were they really going to do that? Drop him off a pier?"

"I wouldn't know. I don't run around with those kind of people."

A small, grey bird broke from cover and whirled across the road. Other than the rapid flapping of the bird's wings there was no sound on the hillside except for wind and the soft ticking of the car's motor. Donovan finished his cigarette, snuffed it out in an ashtray and put the car into gear.

The road wound steadily upward, past a wooden water tower and a ragged stand of bluegum eucalyptus, their long, silvery green leaves littering the road. Just past the crest of the hill tall iron gates supported by stone pillars barred the road. A leathery faced old man in sunfaded khaki pants and shirt sat on a rocking chair in front of the gates, a holstered revolver strapped to his waist. The man stood up, pushing his straw hat back from his forehead where it had been resting to shield his eyes from the sun.

"Hello, there!" Donovan called out as he braked the car. "This is the Fairbaine ranch, isn't it?"

The man walked slowly up to the car, eyeing Donovan with wary suspicion.

"Might be," he said. "Who wants to know?"

Donovan smiled cheerfully and extended his right hand over the edge of the door.

"Thaxton's my name . . . Amory P. Thaxton . . . Los Angeles County Department of Water and Power. Boy, I tell you, I've been all over these hills. They told me downtown to take Silvercreek Canyon Road and then make a right on Glen View. I sure got lost."

"They don't know horseshit downtown," the old man said. He rested one foot on the runningboard after spitting in the dust.

96

"You can say that again," Donovan said.

"Not horseshit. What can I do for you?"

"Well, let's see . . ." He picked up a map from the seat beside him, a big real estate survey map that he had bought in a downtown stationary and drafting supply store. The map was folded to show this section of the Santa Monica mountains, the Fairbaine estate marked neatly with a red pencil. "Now . . . here we are, and up here . . . yes, up here, we have Benedict Crest reservoir."

The old man was peering over Donovan's shoulder at the map.

"That's right, mister, but that reservoir never was built. Should say proposed on the map. Jesus, they don't know horseshit downtown."

"You can sure say that again," Donovan replied cheerfully, sharing a joke. "But they want me to look it over before bringing in the survey crews. Might just have a working reservoir up there after all. A quarter of the site is on the Fairbaine ranch so that'll sure give you folks plenty of water." He glanced at his watch and scowled. "Sure hope Miss Fairbaine is still here. I've been all over hell and gone for the past two hours."

"She's at the studio," the old man said. "But Pedro's up at the house."

"Pedro?"

"Pedro Sanchez. Him and his wife sort of run the place. He'll take you up to Coyote Canyon . . . that's where they was plannin' to build that water catcher."

"Fine," Donovan said as he put the map away. "That's just fine an' dandy. Yes, siree."

A black, boxy Dodge touring sedan rumbled up the road and came to a smooth stop. It was loaded with people; men, women and kids jammed into front and back. A portly man in a white suit and straw skimmer eased out from behind the wheel.

"Hello there," the man called out in a booming, salesman's voice. "Is this the Doll Fairbaine estate?"

"Holy horseshit," the old man muttered. "They got more nerve than a brass snake. You'd think they couldn't read. A goddamn sign big as a mule's ass an' they can't read it." He looked sternly at the white-suited man. "This here's a private road, friend. Got a sign down there says so."

The man in the white suit tugged a pamphlet from his coat pocket and waved it like a summons.

"I paid a dollar for this at the hotel. It's got Doll Fairbaine's house

97

marked on it and it says in this book that . . ."

"I know what it says," the gatekeeper cut in, not unkindly, "but the book's wrong. The house is a long way from here and no visitors allowed."

"Then why don't they say so? God amighty, we're fond of that little girl."

The gatekeeper stared at the man in silence until he got back into his car, muttering querulously, and backed off down the road.

"A map!" the old man said, spitting in the dust again. "Don't that just take it, though? They sell *maps* just to pester folks. We get fifty, sixty people a week comin' up this road with them damn dollar maps in their hands. It's enough to make a mule chuck his feed."

Donovan glanced at his watch again. "Mind if I go in? I got a heap of work before sundown."

"You wouldn't happen to be from Oklahoma, would ya?"

"Why, sure," Donovan said.

"I knew it. Soon as I saw you I said to myself, why, I bet that fella's a Sooner. Where you from?"

"Where are *you* from?" Donovan asked, smiling.

"Oklahoma City."

"Tulsa," Donovan said.

"I never been to Tulsa."

Donovan put the car in gear. "You ain't missed a damn thing."

The gates divided her life into two distinctly separate poles. On one side of the gate she was America's girl next door, the property of Vardon Bolling and millions of adoring fans. Her receptivity was total. Every scrap of fan mail was answered, few requests for personal appearaaces were denied if Bolling felt her presence was important for the success of the film. She was visible . . . touchable. . . real. But once through the gates she was in her private world, a world bound by a rolling skyline of green hills. The Fairbaine ranch, its boundaries measured in miles, a serpentine, gerrymandered shape with only a fraction of it cultivated and used. Myron Levin and his brother Arnold, lawyers and business managers, viewed the property with dismay. There was no return on a dollar invested. It just lay there, doing nothing, a refuge for coyote, deer, rattlesnake and every conceivable species of bird. The Japanese tenants paid only a token tithe in rent and were becoming rich on the produce they trucked down three times a week to the markets in Santa Monica and the tiny village of Westwood. The two Levins resented the allocation of money for the ranch's upkeep and were in constant battle with their youthful client as to how her money should be spent.

"Land? You want land? We've bought you land . . . The corner of Wilshire and Vermont. Fifteen lots above the Beverly Hills Hotel . . . five hundred acres of farm land in Van Nuys. Three orange groves in Pomona. We lay out a dollar and get five in return . . . dollars that work . . . dollars that produce . . ."

The brothers Levin, cigarette chain smokers, Harvard Law and Harvard Business, believers in God, real estate and good common stocks viewed the ranch with open hostility, scorning its mesquite and rattler infested rocks. They had viewed it once, from the back of their chauffeur driven Rolls Royce, the big car rolling and rocking on the narrow fire roads and the mud-packed cattle trails. The equally vast Malibu ranch of the Rindge family seen beyond a barbed wire fence patrolled by cowboys with guns at their hips and Winchesters in their saddle boots, the lean, bronzed men grinning at the dust streaked car.

"Good God, Myron, those men are armed!"

"And they shoot, too—so I hear." The Rindge cowhands shooting at anything that tried to move north across the Rindge land, but not at Doll. Doll was folks. Doll was neighbor.

The house did not match the grandeur of its setting. It was imposing but hardly magnificent, a long, low building of Spanish mission design, whitewashed brick with a red tile roof, covered verandas and iron grilles across the deep set windows. A cool, pleasant house with tile floors and black oak furniture. A house one could walk into with muddy boots trailed by panting dogs with muddy paws. There were stables beyond the house and kennels—though none of Doll's myriad dogs had ever been confined there. There was a servant's wing and a bunkhouse for hired hands if she cared to hire any to raise the cattle that she did not care to raise. But the Rindges had urged her to build a bunkhouse and so a bunkhouse had been built. Not a soul slept in it and only three people slept in the servants' wing that had been designed for ten. Her mother and Niles detested the place even more than the brothers Levin, which hurt Doll. Niles preferred his house in the less rugged hills above Hollywood and Mary Dare Fairbaine preferred her apartment in Paris with its civilized view of the Luxembourg Gardens and its easy accessibility to the swarm of needy young painters, writers, and poets who jammed the city of light and who were so grateful for her guidance, wisdom and cash.

But Doll loved it. She felt the tension leave her body as soon as the car that the Duesenberg brothers of Indianapolis had designed and built especially for her rolled through the gates that Tom Adams, one time stunt rider for Bronco Billy, swung open.

Howdy there, Doll!

Howdy yourself, Tom!

Home!

She frowned when she saw the Paige. The car was not familiar to her and she puzzled over it.

"Is the man from the city," Juanita said in her poor English. "The redhead man from the water."

Juanita stood on the front verandah, a short, thick set woman with a flat, copper-colored face and long black hair. Dogs yapped and whined for attention, leaping, almost dancing, in the space between the stolid Mexican woman and their slim mistress. Doll patted heads.

"Is Fanny okay?"

Juanita smiled. Gold teeth gleamed. "Sure! Sure! In *la casa* . . . away from the boys."

She wasn't sure if she wanted Fanny to have pups, but certainly not by any of the mongrel males who roamed the ranch. Charles Ray owned a pedigreed bull and he had offered its services if she would kick in with a dowry—a Mexican dinner with plenty of the wafer thin enchiladas that Juanita cooked to such perfection.

Doll was more than willing to give Charles a dinner, but she seemed incapable of making up her mind about the deflowering of her favorite pet. Fanny was high strung for a bull terrier, a breed not known for its sensitivity, and she was afraid that the experience might shock her into some kind of canine lunacy.

Juanita drew a cool bath, Doll watched her to make certain that no bath crystals were added to the water. The Mexican woman was addicted to scents, as were most women. Perfumes, aromatic crystals and oils *pour le bain* were kept only for guests and the infrequent visits of Mary Dare. Doll liked nothing on her skin but the clean, medicinal aroma of Lifebuoy soap.

She did not linger in the tub, but scrubbed her hard little body with quick thoroughness and dried herself with a large, white towel, paying particular attention to the moisture between her toes. She then got dressed in a pair of old, sun-faded Levi pants and a cotton shirt, which she had bought in the boy's department of Bullock's department store, and pulled on well-worn, scuffy cowboy boots. There was time for a ride before dinner, the dogs coursing ahead of her nine-year-old mare, chasing rabbits and flushing quail. She felt badly about leaving Fanny behind, but she kissed the sad-eyed, stocky white dog on the nose before closing the door and striding out to the veranda.

The man stood beyond the shadow of the house, the late afternoon sun adding fire to his hair. He was in his shirt, the sleeves rolled up over powerful forearms, jacket slung across one broad shoulder. He was talking to Pedro who kept nodding his head gravely and murmuring *Si . . . Si.*

The "man from the water," Juanita had said—whatever that meant. She had not bothered to ask.

"Ah, the Senora," Pedro said. He walked up to her carrying his hat in his hand. "That is Mister Thaxton . . . from the water and power company. I took him to Coyote Canyon and he would like to talk to you."

"About what?" Doll asked. She was staring at the man who was smiling at her. He had a good face . . . not handsome, but pug-nosed masculine. A real mick's face. His smile puzzled her. He seemed to be grinning at some secret joke.

"About the reservoir," Pedro said.

"Oh." She recalled dimly that surveyors from the County and the Army Engineers had camped up in the canyon a year or two ago. Only a fraction of the long proposed reservoir was on her land so it was of little importance to her.

"I'd appreciate about ten minutes of your time, Miss Fairbaine," Donovan said. He couldn't stop smiling. He had seen a couple of her pictures and, of course, her image was familiar enough, posters of her plastered to every available fence and pole from Maine to Mexico, and here she stood in the flesh, looking more like somebody's pint sized *brother* than a genuine flicker star. He almost forgot why he was there.

"Well," she said reluctantly. "If it's important."

"Oh, it is, it is," Donovan said. He became conscious of his shirt sleeves and rolled them down, fastened the cuff buttons and put on his jacket. "You might say it's vital." He removed the folded map from his pocket and tapped it with his fingers. "A few changes in the property line that work out to your advantage. Yes, indeed."

She escorted him into the house, down a sun flooded hall, her high-heeled Texas boots tap tapping on the tile floor and into a small, high ceilinged room with dark oak beams. There was an antique Spanish desk, a few hard-backed chairs and a wooden filing cabinet. Nothing

101

else except for some photographs of dogs on the whitewashed walls.

Doll Fairbaine cleared a space on the desk. "Do you want to show me the map, Mister . . . Mister . . . ?"

"Thaxton . . . or Donovan. Major Donovan."

She glanced at him curiously. "Which is it? Thaxton or Donovan?"

"Major Donovan doesn't ring a bell? E. P. Donovan?"

"No. Should it?"

He shrugged. "I thought it might. I thought he might have told you about me."

She leaned back against the desk and studied his face. One hand toyed with the top button of her shirt.

"What are you talking about, please?"

"Your brother," Donovan said. "I've been trying to get hold of him for a week. He hangs up when I call. He avoids me." He pursed his lips and looked displeased. "You should tell your brother never to play cards. He isn't a very good loser."

He wasn't quite sure what it was that he saw in her eyes . . . pain, disappointment . . . defeat.

"How much?"

He pulled out his wallet and opened it slowly, never taking his eyes from her face.

"It isn't the money. It's just that when men play poker they should . . ."

"I know all about men playing poker," she said sharply. "How much did you cheat him out of?"

Donovan removed the IOU and unfolded it. He put his wallet back in his pocket and held the slip of paper between his two fingers.

"Fifteen thousand dollars. Your brother is a very reckless player."

"I'll take care of it, Major Donovan," she said curtly. "Now, if you don't mind, you can get the hell out of my house."

She made a grab for the IOU but he pulled it out of her reach.

"Let's get something straight first, Miss Fairbaine. I don't cheat. I may cut a few corners from time to time, but then I came up a hard road. Sometimes you gotta get a fella before he gets you. I've been a carny man, a circus man, a huckster and a hustler. I'm no more a *major* than you are, but I didn't cheat your brother. I just don't like anybody playing me for a sap. I'd tell him what I think of him only, like I say, I can't get within a hoot and a holler of the bo. *You* tell him. Tell him Earl Donovan thinks he's a horse's patoot."

He tore the IOU into tiny strips and let the confetti flutter to the floor. Fifteen thousand dollars worth of scrap paper. He didn't know whether to laugh or cry.

"I'll tell him." Her voice was toneless. She was rigid against the desk. The man's sudden action had been so unexpected that she was completely off guard. What did she do now? What could she say?

Donovan grinned hugely. "I messed up your floor."

"That's all right."

His eyes were a light reddish brown with tiny sparkles of green. His teeth were broad and very white. The thin, ragged line of an old scar traversed his left cheek. The nose looked as if it had been broken a long time ago. Her fingers touched the smooth skin of her throat.

"It must be a hard life . . . carnivals."

He nodded. "It can be rough, all right."

"I was in tent shows for years . . . always moving . . . one place to another."

"Yeah. It's tough. All those hick towns."

"I used to recite poetry . . . and hawk candy. Ten cents a box. It was awful stuff. Stale . . . rejects. It was packed nicely, though."

"Sure. Fancy boxes. I used to *make* candy for the carny butchers. Beeswax and sorghum. Maybe a little chocolate but not much."

"Folks buy anything at a show."

"Oh, sure, that's part of the fun."

His body loomed above her. He was so close that she could have touched his chest by simply allowing her right arm to move naturally to her side. She kept it bent, her hand at the collar of her shirt.

"It must be interesting working in a circus." Her voice sounded alien. A stranger's voice overheard on a street, speaking of things that had no meaning.

"I was never with a real circus. More of a medicine show. A few acts to draw the crowds and then pitch the product."

"Medicine?"

"Snakeroot, licorice, camphor oil and grain alcohol. Couldn't cure much, but it gave a warm glow."

She felt breathless. His maleness was atmospheric.

"Are you a drinking man, Mister Donovan?"

"I like a glass of good whisky once in a while, I won't lie about that."

"Most men enjoy a snort. There's no real harm. Not in moderation."

He followed her down the corridor and into a large room sparsely furnished with Spanish chairs, a high backed sofa and dark wood cabinets. A Navajo rug covered the center section of the red tiled floor and smaller rugs were hung against one wall. West-facing windows revealed tumbled hills and the sharp line of the ocean with the full ball of the sun dipping into it. Doll poured whisky into a cut crystal glass from a bottle that she took from a carved oak sideboard.

"Here's how," he said.

She said nothing, watching him drink.

"This is quite a house," he said.

"Did you cheat him?"

He took another sip, savoring the liquor. Bourbon. Very old and very smooth.

"I did and I didn't. It isn't that simple in poker unless you bring your own cards to the game. I admit to a trick or two just to shorten the odds."

"What tricks?"

He shrugged. "Tricks with the deal. Keeping my discarded hand in sequence when I shuffled the pack. Things like that. But it was his own foolishness that did him in. I could have won it straight."

"Why didn't you?"

"Habit. I've always played in games where the other guys were crookeder than me."

"Well, at least you're honest about your sins."

Juanita came into the room pushing a rolling tray bearing a bowl of guacamole; a platter of fried tacos stuffed with minced chicken and pork; and a plate of warm tortillas covered with a white linen napkin.

"How did you break your nose?" she asked after the Mexican woman had left the room.

"Sort of a war wound. A Limey sailor hit me with a bottle in Philadelphia. 1916. He threw it. I never saw it coming."

"And the scar on your cheek?"

"Belt buckle. My old man hit me with it when I was twelve or thirteen. I closed the flap with flour and vinegar and left home that night."

"Where was home?"

"Boston . . . Chelsea."

"Ever go back?"

"What the hell for?"

She walked him out to his car. The sky was indigo. A coyote wailed in the dark hills and the dogs yapped frantic replies. She touched his

104

arm lightly as he opened the car door and the feel of the muscled flesh sent a tiny jolt up her spine, like a minor electric shock. Perhaps it was electricity, she thought, because her hand could not leave the arm. Her fingers clenched it.

"Will I see you again?"

"Do you want to?"

"Yes."

"And I'd like to see you."

"When?"

He rubbed the side of his nose and thought about it, looking down into her anxious face. Son of a gun, he thought, the great Doll Fairbaine in the flesh, looking at him the way God knows how many other women had looked at him. He bent impulsively and kissed her forehead, catching the medicinal fragrance of Lifebuoy soap.

"Soon."

"I start a new picture tomorrow. You could come out to the studio."

"I'd like that. Yeah, that would be just fine." And then he was in the car, smiling at her as he started the motor. "Funny how things work out."

"That's life," she said gravely.

She stood in the drive until she could no longer see the red taillights of his car going off down the canyon road. She felt lightheaded and breathless. The man had excited her in a way that no man had ever done. And it was not because he was different from any man she had ever met; on the contrary, she knew his type well—brash, arrogant, the type of hard drinking, swearing, brawling roustabout who used to put up the tent for the chautauqua and take the plank seats off the trucks or wagons and do all the other hard and dirty work of the show. He was the type of man that Mama and Agnes had always warned her about.

If any of those hooligans try to take liberties . . .

They never had. They had liked her and she had liked them. They smoked pipes that they carved from dried corncobs, or chewed plug, slicing the slim mahogany bricks with barlow knives and bragging about how far they could spit.

See that fly over thar, Jenny?

Hard muscled men with sweat stained shirts. Boozers. Profaners. Polacks and Bohunks. Irish and Welsh. Men laid off from the mines or the railroads.

Take liberties? With a little girl? It had been Doctor Jason T. somebody-or-another who had done that. She couldn't remember his name, but the man had joined the show in Elkhart, Indiana, in 1908. Doctor Jason T. whatever-his-name-was had been a disciple of Elbert Hubbard and lectured on that author's works. He was, in Agnes' words, a saintly man who radiated health and goodness. He delighted in buying ice cream for children, especially young girls.

I find the sight inspiring, Mrs. Fairbaine . . . Mrs. Dare. Indeed I do. Girls in their starched white dresses and pigtailed hair. They lick their ice cream so delicately, like fluffy white kittens with pink tongues.

Mama and Agnes had been impressed with such imagery and when the doctor had been so kind as to invite little Jenny out for the day, to visit a museum in Indianapolis, they had not thought twice about it. Of course the child could go! All starched and white, pigtailed and pink tongued. They had not been ten minutes on the road to Indianapolis in the doctor's Ford before he had tried to put his hand up her skirt and pull down her bloomers, all the while talking about the Greeks and the purity of the human body, tugging at her underclothing and pinching her thighs with slender, bone dry fingers.

The human body is a holy thing, Jennifer. I will kiss your holiness and you shall kiss mine.

And he had unbuttoned himself, letting the car drift off the road and into the shade of a hundred-year-old elm, pulling from the gap in his trousers what looked to Jenny like a long mushroom, so pale and speckled and damp it was.

Kiss the godhead, Jenny. Place your dear little virgin tongue . . .

And she had leaned toward the godhead of Doctor Jason T. whoever and struck it with her balled fist, slamming down hard the way a person might strike a rearing snake with a hammer, and the man who loved little girls in starched white dresses had screamed horribly, his body jerking forward, his head slamming against the heavy wood rim of the steering wheel and cutting his parchment flesh to the bone.

So long ago, the detailing blurred by time, and yet so well remembered.

She thought about Donovan . . . Major E. P. Donovan . . . *Earl* . . . until late in the night, the covers pulled up to her chin, specks of moonlight on the Spanish beamed ceiling of her bedroom. Fanny lay at the foot of the bed, curled up in a ball, nose to tail. White virgin dog asleep.

And Doll Fairbaine thought—Gosh, it's got to happen sooner or later, doesn't it? So why not with him? A fine looking man, tall and strong and nothing slicked down about him, no pomade or eau de cologne and no fancy manners. A solid kind of a guy. A bit rough maybe, but not uncouth in any way. Still, not the kind of a man Mama would have picked out, not like that Russian count she had brought all the way from Paris, France, to have her meet. The count had worn shiny patent leather shoes and parted his hair in the middle and had a Van Dyke beard. Very elegant with his jade cigarette holder and all his fancy talk about poets and writers and Nijinsky this and Nijinsky that and would the *mesdames* care for a glass of chilled champagne? And Mama loving it and nudging her every few minutes, bruising her ribs with bony elbows and carrying on about how the count had measured his estates in the Ukraine in versts and versts, whatever they were. But, of course, he had no money now. The dirty Bolsheviks had taken all of his money to buy tractors or something, but they'd be thrown out soon and then the count would be one of the richest men in the world. And she had told Mama that she didn't care how rich he was, or had been, or would be. She didn't like him. He looked . . . greased. And his teeth were stained, like piano keys.

The dog stirred, whimpering softly in its sleep, back legs trembling and kicking at the sheets. She drew an arm from under the covers, reached down and patted the animal on the head.

"Your mama's got a beau, Fanny," she whispered. "A fella. Isn't that something? Isn't that grand?"

REEL SEVEN

BUMPS AND CHUMPS

Chester Pratt formed a frame between thumb and forefinger and squinted at the scene. His fingers approximated the vision of the camera and he liked what he saw, a good pictorial composition once he moved the gawkers out of the way. The sight of the cameras, the silver painted reflector boards, the actors and technicians proved an irresistible lure to the summer crowd on the amusement pier. They looked on such a congregation as just another form of amusement, like the roller coaster or the shoot the chutes.

WOULD YOU GOOD FOLK KINDLY MOVE BACK A FEW FEET, Pratt called out through his megaphone.

The crowd did not shift an inch.

PLEASE.

A few people drifted back, but the bulk remained immovable and unflinching, eyes fixed on the strange paraphernalia of the motion picture company, their tongues gliding lazily over ice cream cones or cotton candy. A carousel thumped its timpani to the warm breeze and the sun danced on the blue water.

"Fuck 'em," Pratt muttered. He glanced at the tall, ruddy faced man standing beside him—Leroy Granville, his head cameraman, cool and composed in white shirt sleeves and straw skimmer, a cold briar pipe jutting from the side of his jaw. "Can we miss those bastards, Granny?"

"No," Granville said. "But we can De Mille 'em whenever you're ready to shoot."

Pratt squinted at the sun. "We're going to have a shadow problem in the long shot."

"Not for half an hour or so."

108

"That's cutting it thin, but I'll take your word for it. Tell Benny to move the crowd out."

Granville nodded and strolled off to where a plump, roundfaced young man with black bushy hair was standing talking to Tom Pipp.

"De Mille the rubes, Benny," Granville said.

Benny Shapiro hesitated, eyeing Pipp with apprehension.

"It'll work, Mr. Pipp."

"No, it won't." Pipp said. "I've been thinking it over and I don't like the idea of the black chap at all. I don't think it's funny for me to be chased by a black chap. I think there's something menacing about it. I think it would be funnier if I'm chased by the fat chap."

"Billy Wells?" Benny Shapiro asked.

"If that's the name of the fat chap, yes."

Christ, Granville thought as he noticed the stubborn set of the little comedian's mouth, half an hour before the shadows crept in along the side of the pier and Pipp was in one of his moods. Pratt would split a gut.

"What's the trouble, Tom?"

"I don't like the scene," Pipp said. "I don't think it'll be at all funny."

"I think it will be, Tom. People will scream when they see Big John chasing you and the car."

"I think different."

Pipp folded his arms and looked down at his feet, a posture that Granville knew only too well. It meant that Pipp had made up his mind and that nothing would change it. He didn't bother to argue, but walked back to where Pratt was still studying the scene, contemplating the correctness of the camera placements.

"Tom doesn't like it, Chester."

"What?" Pratt said. "What did you say?"

"Tom doesn't like the idea. He thinks having John chase him won't be funny. He wants the fat guy to chase him."

"Billy?"

"That's the guy. He says that big John will look menacing."

Pratt's face turned the color of raw beef. He kept the anger bottled in for a second and then let it out through his lips like steam from a kettle.

"The miserable little . . ."

"Take it easy, Chester," Granville said. He removed the pipe from his mouth and tapped the empty bowl against the palm of his hand. "He might just have a point."

Pipp usually did when he balked at doing a scene. He had an intuitive feel for what was funny. Pratt knew that and admired the comedian's taste, but why did he always wait until the last minute before expressing himself? Big John Newberry, the best club fighter in Los Angeles and a fine athlete and stunt man, was already in costume and had practiced the stunts that the scene called for. Pipp had not uttered a word of objection until now, but he had obviously been brooding about it. Now his mind was made up and no amount of cajoling, argument or persuasion would change it back again.

"Damn!" Pratt whispered harshly. He scanned the crew. Billy Wells was seated in front of the makeup table putting half moons of dark greasepaint under his eyes. The fat man was in the scene, as a spectator who Pipp would run into during the chase. Billy would do one of his wonderful brodies, landing on his ample buttocks and bouncing four feet into the air off a concealed trampoline. Having Big John Newberry do the stunt would not have quite the same impact. "Damn it to hell."

"Can't be helped," Granville said. "You know Tom."

Yes, he knew Tom Pipp, only too well. This picture, *Toffs and Copps,* would be in the can in one more day of shooting and then there would be a two week layoff before the next batch of six were ready to go. Two weeks of nothing to do for Pipp except sit around in his apartment and stare at the walls, only he wouldn't be that sensible, he'd stuff his pockets with money, hire a taxi and take off on one of his "trips." Head for San Berdoo or Fresno and hole up in a cat house for a week of solid drinking. Christ, the guy was a mental case and didn't know it. He jammed his megaphone under his left arm and walked briskly to where Pipp and Benny Shapiro were standing in uneasy silence.

"What's the matter, Tom? Unhappy with the setup?"

"Yes," Pipp said, staring moodily at his feet. "I don't much like it at all, Chester."

Pratt forced a smile. "Gee, kid, you liked it this morning when I sketched it out."

"That was this mornin'. I've been givin' it a bit o' thought an' ah've changed me mind."

Pipp could speak like an Oxford don or an Aussie cowpoke, it all depended on his mood. Pratt had learned to recognize the man's attitude by the statue of his diction and he knew for a certainty that there was no point in further discussion.

"Okay by me, Tom, but we can't fit Billy Wells with a chauffeur's uniform."

"The chauffeur was wrong, anyhow. That car's a flivver. It wouldn't 'ave a chauffeur, but it would 'ave a fat chap."

"Okay by me, Tom. I'll work it out."

"I felt sure you would."

Big John Newberry stood waiting. Pratt had to admit that the man did look menacing in his tight black uniform and black boots. The black gloves he was wearing gave an added power to his awesome hands.

"You're out of the scene, John," the director said.

The towering black man scowled angrily. "The hell you say." He had a stunt to do, running in and out of a slowly moving car. That meant extra money.

"Don't worry about the dough," Pratt said quickly. "It's not your fault and I'm not taking anything out of your pocket."

"That's white of ya, Mister Pratt."

"Get out of that uniform and put on some overalls. You can push the fruit cart." He glanced uneasily up at the sun. "And snap it up."

Billy Wells listened to Pratt's rapid fire instructions and tried desperately to let it all sink in. The director was not a man to repeat himself.

"Have you got it, Billy?"

"Sure," Billy said. He had the gist of it at least. The finer points would have to come as he did it. A wooden planked roadway ran along the south side of the pier, a service road used by the many eateries that backed against it, their rear entrances piled high with garbage cans and crates of provisions. Fishing boats could tie up at the end of the pier where a crane on the service road could lift out their catches of lobster, bass, halibut and abalone for the fish restaurants. That roadway was now cleared and three cameras had been cleverly hidden along its route to catch the action. The scene called, originally, for John Newberry to drive onto the road in an open touring car with Mabel Thompson seated in the back acting the grande dame. Newberry would get out of the car, leaving the motor running, in order to buy some fruit from a pushcart vendor, a part that Billy would have played. Pipp would then enter the scene chased by two cops, collide with the vendor, leap into the car and put it in gear. The car would roll slowly down the road toward the end of the pier with Newberry in hot pursuit and Mabel Thompson standing up in the back beating at Pipp with her umbrella. Mabel, an ex-circus acrobat, would tumble out of the car while Pipp and Newberry struggled for possession of it, both men leaping in and out of the front seat. The scene would end with the car going off the end of the pier through a breakaway railing, Pipp grabbing the cable on the crane and Big John

111

leaping into a large basket filled with fish just in time to avoid going over with it. Not the most difficult stunt in the world, Billy had done a dozen that were far more difficult and dangerous, but it did take timing and at least one rehearsal.

"Do you want me to run through it first, Mister Pratt?"

"What the hell for?" Pratt grunted. "Just put your coat on and stick a flower in the buttonhole. You'll be the old man taking the old lady for a Sunday drive. Got it?"

"Got it, Mister Pratt," Billy said without conviction.

"De Mille 'em, Benny," the director called out. He raised the megaphone to his lips, *GET SET FOR A TAKE, EVERYBODY.*

Benny Shapiro wandered to the edge of the crowd of sightseers. His smile was warm and boyish.

"We're going to shoot a little comedy chase scene, folks. You won't see too much from here, just Tom Pipp running past chased by some cops. He'll run into that big, colored man pushing a fruit stand and then jump into a car. Very funny."

The crowd stared at him with hostility. "We'd sure like you folks to stick around and watch us, but I think you'd like to know that Cecil B. De Mille is shooting a picture on the other side of the pier, up the beach a ways. It's a Famous-Players production called *Flaming Sinners.* They're doing the orgy scene so I wouldn't advise anyone who's easily shocked to go on down there and watch it. No, sir! Some of those actresses are practically *naked!*"

The crowd wavered and then broke into scurrying individuals. Women moved as quickly as men and the kids bolted like unleashed hounds. In a moment the area was deserted and only a few dropped ice cream cones and pink blobs of cotton candy revealed that any people had been there at all.

LET'S GO . . . PLACES, EVERYBODY. GET READY TO ROLL, GRANNY.

"All set, Chester," Granville shouted back as he began to run up the roadway toward the cameras at the end of the pier, a hand pressed to the top of his hat to keep it from flying away. "We're ready when you are!"

Chester Pratt was not the kind of director content to sit in chair while the action unfolded in front of him. He was a master of long, complicated takes and he wielded his megaphone the way a symphony conductor used his baton. As his head cameraman ran toward the end of the pier to personally supervise the vital final shots, of which no retakes were possible, Pratt scurried to orchestrate the start of the action, Pipp's entry and the arrival of the old black touring car on the narrow roadway.

START THE CAR, BILLY. DRIVE SLOWLY . . . SLOWLY . . . OKAY, TOM. START RUNNING IN. WAVE YOUR CLUBS, COPS . . . WAVE 'EM ABOVE YOUR HEADS. MOVE THE PUSH-CART, BIG JOHN . . . RIGHT INTO TOM'S PATH.

This was the culmination of the chase scene filmed that morning. Pipp was in his "grandma's boy" costume, short pants and a Little Lord Fauntleroy jacket with an inkstained collar. The cops were after him for having created havoc in their station house—a scene that would be filmed the next day at the studio—after picking him up on the pier, mistaking him for a lost child.

Pipp danced past the first camera, an elfin prance, a pixie chased by flatfooted coppers. Big John Newberry moved on cue, pushing his cart filled with fruit into the scene . . .

A LITTLE COON SHUFFLE THERE, JOHN.

Big John dragged his feet and rolled his eyes, darky dancing into Pipp's path . . .

*HIT HIM AND GRAB THE CART, TOM. . . .*the men collided . . .

TAKE A BROOIE, JOHN.

The black man left his feet and fell backward toward the concealed trampoline as Pipp grabbed the handles of the cart and spun it around . . .

FULL TILT, COPS. . . . into the onrushing cops who plowed into the cart, splintering it, sending its contents flying. Big John bounced upward and the cops went sprawling and sliding on spilled fruit while Pipp danced merrily away, the camera panning him toward the car that had just driven up in the background.

CUT!

Chester Pratt lowered his megaphone and smiled happily. The first part of the scene had gone off perfectly.

"Move the camera, boys . . . hurry it up."

There was a scramble to set up on the roadway, with the heavy camera on its large wooden tripod borne along on the shoulders of several men.

Billy stayed in the car with the motor idling while the camera was set up again and trained on him, the work of less than a minute, everyone moving under the ceaseless goading of the director who had

113

one eye on them and the other on the sun. Shadows were starting to form along the roadway.

"Ready, Dan?"

The camera operator fussed with his lens, opening the diaphragm a half stop.

"Okay to roll, boss."

ACTION. GET OUT OF THE CAR, BILLY.

Billy squeezed out from behind the steering wheel. The motor wheezed, barely turning over, throttled back so that when it was thrown into first gear it would chug slowly up the pier, the steering mechanism fixed so that it would run arrow straight.

SAY SOMETHING TO MABEL.

Billy felt a stab of resentment. He had been in the troupe for nearly two months, working six days a week on every picture that Pratt directed and the man had yet to accord him the slightest degree of respect as an actor. Of course he would say something to the woman in the back seat, he didn't need to be told to do the obvious.

"I'll get you some fruit, my love," Billy said, flicking his tie coyly at her.

Mabel Thompson, a frizzed haired blonde, had her back to the camera so she could say anything without fear of lip readers gasping with shock in some darkened picture palace.

"A bunch of bananas, Billy, and shove 'em up Chester's ass—one at a time!"

I HEARD THAT YOU SKINNY BITCH, NOW MOVE OUT, BILLY . . . AROUND THE FRONT OF THE CAR. OKAY, TOM . . . RUN INTO THE SHOT . . .

They met, the fat man blocking access to the car, Pipp milking the encounter for a laugh by bouncing off Billy's stomach, then darting forward with a hop, skip and jump that took him onto the runningboard and into the front seat.

REACTION, MABEL . . . CAR INTO GEAR . . . FLIP-EROO . . .

Mabel Thompson rose to her feet, bringing her umbrella down on Pipp's head. The car made a gear-lurching jerk forward and Mabel did a perfect back flip out of the car, skirt and petticoat flying over her head.

RUN AFTER THE CAR, BILLY . . .

Billy waved his arms like a madman and dashed for the car, ignoring Mabel who was rolling end over end out of the scene. He leaped onto the runningboard and climbed into the front seat.

114

*PLAY GRABS FOR THE WHEEL, YOU GUYS . . . IN AND
OUT . . .*

Billy and Pipp, standing in the front, grabbing for the steering wheel
as the boxy open touring car rolled slowly up the pier, entering the
angle of view of the second camera now, the operator turning the crank
slower than normal to give the action an illusion of speed.

IN AND OUT, BOYS . . . IN AND OUT . . .

They played musical chairs with the steering wheel. Billy pushing
Pipp out the open side door and Pipp jumping back into the car again
to shove Billy out the opposite door. In and out. Grab for the wheel.
Push and shove.

"Get ready to jump, fat chap," Pipp said breathlessly as he hopped
onto the runningboard and clambered into the front seat. The end of
the pier was twenty yards ahead, the basket of fish on one side of the
roadway, the dangling crane rope on the other. "On my count of three
. . . One . . . two . . ."

Billy made his own quick estimate, gauging the speed of the car in
relation to the railing up ahead. The sea sparkled beyond it and out of
the corner of his eye he could see the third camera and its crew on a
platform slung beneath the pier and extending out over the water.
Granville was working that camera, turning the crank as the car
loomed into view . . .

". . . three!"

Pipp sprang off the front seat, his quick, sure hands grabbing the
heavy, knotted rope of the crane and swinging out in a wide arc. Billy
waited a beat and then jumped as the broad wicker basket of fish came
abreast of the front wheel on the left-hand side. There was a rush of
air in his face as he cleared the door and then he was slammed back
against it with a suddenness and a force that drove the wind out of his
body. His feet were being dragged along the roadway, one shoe torn
loose. He tried to reach back to discover what was holding him to the
car, but his arms felt paralyzed. He sensed that his coat had slipped over
the steering wheel as he jumped because he could feel the painful tug
of the coat under his armpits. Sweet Jesus let the coat split, he prayed
wildly and then heard the crash of the railing giving way and somebody's scream. There was nothing below him but the heaving blue sea.
Sweet Jesus Christ!

KEEP ROLLING . . . GET THAT SHOT, GRANNY . . . GET IT!

"Got it!" Granville shouted back, swinging the camera down toward
the seething waterburst that enclosed the sinking car, his hand steady

and sure on the crank, overcranking to give a slow motion effect. "Beautiful! Beautiful!" A heave of white water and roiling bubbles as the car dipped head first below the surface, Billy's frantic face turned skyward.

"Help!"

The cold sea closed around him, a silent, sun-speckled, salty greenness. His bouyancy pulled him upward as the car sunk like a stone and he broke the surface gasping and coughing, the water hissing around him.

"Help!"

WAVE YOUR ARMS, GODDAMIT.

Chester Pratt screamed through his megaphone as he reached the end of the pier, sliding to a halt a scant inch from the broken railing.

WAVE. SHAKE A FIST. PUT SOME SPIRIT IN IT.

Billy felt the tug of the sea against his body, the swelling surge drawing him toward the slimy, mussel encrusted timbers of the pier, the heavy poles receding into the gloom like a dead forest, the sea dark and oily under the pier as it rolled toward a shadowed beach. Panic gripped him with an iron claw.

"Help! Help!"

DON'T ACT LIKE YOU'RE DROWNING, DAMMIT, THAT ISN'T FUNNY.

Billy raised a hand, clenched his fist and shook it feebly. The water closed over his head and he thrashed his way back to the sweet air.

"Can't swim. . . . Help!"

CUT!

Pratt lowered the megaphone in disgust. "Somebody pull the guy out. Hell, why wasn't Mack Swain doing that bit! Damn it to hell."

CASSETTE

Did you bring Pipp and Wells together?

Well, yes and no. They were in many two reelers for Sterling. Pipp was the star, of course, he was making big money. I don't think they paid Billy very much. A hundred dollars or so a week—which was pretty good money in those days, let me tell you. Billy had no complaints. He was working steady and he was learning a lot from Chester and some of the other fine directors at Sterling. Pratt didn't direct all of the Blue Ribbon comedies, there were other men. Langston Barnes, Gill Brandon, and, as you know, some men who are still around today, or at least well known to this day. Academy Award men . . . top people.

Oh yes, absolutely.

. . . men who made it very big when sound came in.

Yes, indeed.

And Billy learned from them, you know, timing . . . movement. He was developing his character. It took time. So many comedians were trying to imitate Chaplin in those days, even Pipp was trying to be Chaplin. He wasn't the Pipp we all know in *those* days, let me tell you, but he was funny. I have to say that, he was a funny little man, but imitative. It's a pity that those pictures are gone. All on nitrate stock, as you know. All gone. Every one of them.

One or two stills.

Yes. A few stills. You're right there, not more than two that I know of, but they were in at least ten pictures together in 1921 and well into 1922, Billy playing the heavy—cops, crooks, fat bankers—a slipper on Pipp's banana peels . . . always getting the dirty end of the *schtick!*

Ha, ha, yes, very funny . . . and true.

Oh, yeah, sure, a foil. A fat clown. But he was loving every minute of it. Making pictures in those days was a whole lot of fun. Not like today where everything is so deadly serious. It was a joy in the old days. A real joy.

LET'S SEE IF WE CAN GET IT THIS TIME, DAMN IT ALL TO HELL.

Chester Pratt's voice echoed through the railway tunnel, a caustic scourge, sarcastic and venomous.

I KNOW A THOUSAND FAT, UNEMPLOYED ACTORS. SO DO IT RIGHT OR I'LL KNOW ONE THOUSAND AND ONE.

Billy swallowed his rage. He wanted to scream toward the round circle of brilliant light only twenty yards ahead of him and tell Chester Pratt what he thought of him. A bully! A sadist! The ruining of the first take had not been his fault. It had been the fault of the engine driver who had missed his cue and started his train moving too late. Billy couldn't be expected to look over his shoulder as he was running full tilt out of the tunnel, he had to watch the ties which were unevenly laid, to keep from tripping over one of them. It was the engineer's job to keep his train ten to fifteen feet behind Billy's leg pumping, body huffing form. The first take had been a flop because Billy had burst out of the tunnel and raced past the camera set up on the embankment a good thirty yards ahead of the train. The train should have been right on his

117

heels. To Billy, it had certainly *sounded* as though it was and all he had been thinking was what would happen to him if he tripped on a tie and the train ran over him. The train might not be going very fast, but it was no less deadly because of that.

START THE TRAIN MOVING.

A man stood on the tracks in the blazing sun and waved a red flag. Far behind Billy, in the gloom of the tunnel, came the sounds of the engine starting up—an explosive discharge of steam, the grinding rumble of the wheels against the steel rails. The ties began to writhe beneath his feet as the train gathered momentum. It would take the train nearly the length of the fifty yard tunnel to reach an effective speed. Billy glanced apprehensively over his shoulder and made a final adjustment to his conductor's cap, pulling it firmly down on his head so that it wouldn't fly off as he ran. A red lantern gleamed in the cab of the engine so that Billy could effectively gauge his distance from the oncoming locomotive, the bulk of the engine and the boxcars behind it blocking off the light from the opposite end of the tunnel; a great, dark, rattling, steaming mass coming toward him, the sound of pistons and wheels vibrating off the dank tunnel walls, the ties jumping and the rails singing. The red light drew closer: forty yards . . . thirty . . . a vibrating red eye as the train picked up speed. The camera would be turning now and it was time to go. He swallowed hard, looked away from the train and began to run, sensing rather than seeing the worn wooden ties beneath his feet, praying that he wouldn't miss one and stumble on the gravel. He picked up speed as he reached the tunnel's mouth, the train hot and heavy on his heels.

GOOD GOOD GOOD. RUN, BILLY, RUN. . . . bursting out into the blinding sun . . . a comic run . . . legs high, his knees almost slapping his belly, his arms beating the air like a turkey trying to fly.

DIVE. NOW . . . NOW.

Billy dove head first from the tracks into the embankment of sand, the train thundering past him as he tumbled down the reverse slope, coming to rest on his back in a clump of brittle greasewood. He lay there for a moment and sucked the hot desert air into his lungs. Black dots danced in front of his eyes and his lungs were on fire.

CUT CUT. BEAUTIFUL . . . PERFECT . . .

No one raced over to help Billy up, the crew had too much to do and too little time to do it in. The train was stopping and would back up to the tunnel so that Pipp could climb into the cab for closeups. Billy rose shakily to his feet and dusted himself off. His hands were skinned and one pant leg of his conductor's costume was ripped. He found his hat lying in the mesquite a yard from where he had come to rest and he picked it up and trudged wearily back up the embankment and along the side of the tracks to where Pratt stood talking to Leroy Granville. The cameraman's face was grave and he was pointing toward the camera and making circular motions with his right hand.

Pratt kicked the dirt with his booted foot and hurled his megaphone to the ground. "Goddamnit to hell, Granny!"

"Just one of those things, Chester," Granville said.

Pratt glared at Billy as he came toward him. "Gotta do that stunt over, Billy."

"What?" Billy asked, stunned.

"Can't be helped. Granny thinks the crank slipped its gears while he was turning it. May have that shot and may not. Can't take the chance. We'll get another camera loaded and run the scene again." He eyed Billy up and down. "You look a mess, goddamnit! Clean yourself off and get those pants sewn up! Jesus, do I have to watch every goddamn thing around here?"

He was learning something that could be learned in no other way— the painful business of making people laugh—learned in the middle of a city street dodging cars, learned on the desert railroad above Los Angeles, learned on the piers and beaches of Venice and Redondo-by-the-Sea. It was an education of pratfalls, brodies, double takes and hurled pies. He did not have a character. He was simply Billy Wells, working for Sterling Pictures, his salary blossoming slowly but steadily, his worth recognized if not praised, playing any part that Chester Pratt or the other directors cared to hand him. He worked with Pipp, cross-eyed Andy Farrel, Mick and Myer and a bunch of zanies known as the Boarding House Boys. He was part of the stock company, one of several ex-vaudevillians, circus clowns and acrobats who gave the Sterling comedy product its distinctive flair and excellence.

DUDES AND DUDS

LUMPS AND THUMPS

TARS AND CARS

PIPP THE PIEMAN

PIPP AND SQUEAKS

119

The films became a blur to Billy. He was shifted from one to the other, sometimes appearing in three in one day, racing from the costume bungalow on the lot to Stage 3 dressed as a policeman, then back to costume to be turned into a thickly mustachioed heavy for duty in an Andy Farrel picture being shot on Stage 7, then a swift metamorphosis to a country yokel in a checked suit to cap the day doing a pratfall in a Pipp picture being shot on the streets of Culver City. He was making money but had little time to enjoy his new wealth. He spent his Sundays loafing in his new apartment in Hollywood, soaking the bruises out of his body in the bathtub or lounging on his bed reading the weekly *Variety.*

SHAPELY SISTERS SUNK IN JERSEY

The Shapely Sisters, singing duo composed of Anne Marie Shapely, one time partner of popular Irish hoofer, Spanky O'Brian, and Mae Pepper, distaff side of the defunct Pepper Komedy Klub, made their debut and folded quietly at the Bernstein Circuit's Tivoli Theater here last Tuesday night. Though lovely to look at, the girls failed to generate audience excitement with their sweet, but difficult to hear past the third row voices. Act has been replaced by Logan's Bears, Izzy Epstein, Tivoli manager said.

"Oh, Jesus," Billy said. There was no mention of Jimmy anywhere in the thick trade paper although he checked and double checked. So Mae had gone out on her own. Was Jimmy still in the asylum? Had she left him for good? What would she do now? Where could she go?

He groaned audibly and heaved his bulk off the bed and paced the spacious sunny rooms of his apartment. He felt guilty without really knowing why. He had some money in the bank, new clothes in his wardrobe and a spanking new Chandler Six car. Maybe that was why. Or maybe it was his view from his sixth floor apartment in the new brick apartment house he had just moved into, the north windows revealing the leafy hills of Griffith Park, the west windows offering a panorama of the palm lined streets of Hollywood, with the Pacific Ocean a slender blue line on the horizon. It was the middle of February and the air balmy, the morning suffused with a golden light, the soft wind bearing the sweetness of orange, sage, jasmine and oleander into the rooms. It would be bitter cold in the East. Ice on the Hudson and grey sludge on the city streets. Colder still in Jersey City as Mae left the Tivoli Theater, an icy wind in the alleyway by the stage door, the coldness of the wind made doubly bitter by the chill of failure. How much would Izzy

120

Epstein pay for a cancelled act? Not much, Billy thought ruefully as he peeled a banana. He had a vision of Mae's beautiful, stricken face reflected in the dingy, rime-coated window of a streetcar taking her . . . where?

"Damn," he said softly, swallowing a mouthful of banana, downing it the way other men might down a slug of whisky to ease the pain. "Mae . . . Mae."

> *I told my mother . . . I told my father*
> *I told my sister and my brother, too*
> *That it's awful nice,*
> *That it's paradise . . .*
> *Loving a girl like you.*

"Can I speak to you for a minute, Chester?"

"What do you want, Billy? Christ! I'm up to my neck in this crap. You know that new cameraman? The one they said was such a hotshot in Germany?"

"Otto?"

"Yea, the goddamn Kraut bastard! He overcranked all that stuff with Farrel . . . the mad dog and the iceman bit. I'll have to have every third frame cut out of this stuff to make it look right! God damn, what a pain in the butt!"

Chester Pratt stood beside a cloth-lined wicker basket. White cotton undertaker gloves were on his hands and he held a length of shiny black film up to the light, squinting at the images and making obscene sucking noises through his lips.

"I'll come back when you're not so busy."

The director snorted in disgust and let the film coil back into the basket.

"Oh, what the hell. Is it important?"

"It is to me," Billy said gravely.

Pratt looked at him, his dark, beady eyes sharply suspicious.

"You got an offer from Sennett, right?"

"No," Billy said. "Nothing like that."

"Money?"

"No."

"Then what?"

Billy shifted uncomfortably from one foot to the other. He was in a tramp costume and the oversized shoes squeaked as they moved.

"There's this girl . . ." he began and then stopped in embarrassment as he noticed the faint, knowing smirk on Pratt's face. "It . . . it's not what you think."

"Isn't it, kid?" He put a hand on Billy's arm and gave it a gentle squeeze. "Listen, it happens all the time, see. They all want to get in pictures and they'll do anything for the chance. Believe me, I know how these things happen. You make a little promise in the kip and they hold you to it."

"No, no, not that way at all," Billy stammered. His face was beginning to burn.

"Hell, it happens to all of us one time or another," Pratt continued gleefully. "It's one of the risks of the game, but you mustn't let those flappers get a hook into you. Now you take Pipp. Poor old Pipp made a woman a promise two years ago . . . big dame . . . concert singer or something. I don't know, maybe she was in vaudeville, doesn't really matter. Anyway, Pipp told her he'd get her into pictures and brought her out here and the first thing she said was that she wouldn't consider working for less than five hundred a week. Five hundred a week! I kicked her ass down the hall and Pipp came running after me begging me to give her a chance and now he can't get rid of her, see. She's all over him like a leech . . . living in his place . . . telling him what to do . . . handling his money . . . bringing in her relatives. Jesus! What a mess. No wonder the poor little bastard sops up the booze now and then. You don't want to end up a chump, do you? Of course you don't! Tell the skirt to shove off and go find another. They're like streetcars, see. They come around every ten minutes."

"Chester," Billy said, finally getting a word in. "You've got it all wrong. I'm talking about a girl I worked with, Jimmy Pepper's wife. She was in the Follies, on the big circuits . . . part of the act. A terrific comedienne . . . great moves and timing . . . gives you a deadpan look that always brought a howl. I know she'd be great in pictures. I just know it."

"You sleeping with her, fat guy?"

"No! Christ . . ."

"Just a friend, huh?"

"That's right, Chester. You see, I feel sorry for her. She's a fine woman with a lot of talent and . . . well, Jimmy hit the skids and she went out on her own—a sister act. Only I read in the trades that the act . . . well, it didn't go over too good back in Jersey . . . and I'd like to bring her out to the coast. And I thought if I could get her a job out here that . . . well, that she'd . . ."

"Yeah," Pratt said sardonically. "I know the story. Sure, kid, I'll give her a shot in something. Who knows, she might work out. It's happened before."

"Thanks," Billy said, letting his breath out. He felt drained.

"But just *one*, Billy. Do you understand? If she can't cut it. . . ."

"Sure, sure, I understand, and thanks, Chester . . . thanks a million."

"Forget it," Pratt said, turning away. "I just hope you know what you're doing."

He had never felt more sure of anything in his life as he hurried out of the building and ran down the streets toward Stage 4, his tramp shoes slapping against the asphalt, a raggedy tattoo, a bum's shuffle. He'd send a wire to Ambrose telling him to contact Izzy Epstein at the Tivoli and get Mae's address. Then he'd write Mae and send her a train ticket. He'd find her an apartment in his building and bring her out to the lot. Chester would be crazy about her—he was certain of that. The minute he took a look at her . . . that olive and ivory skin, black hair . . . dark, flashing eyes . . .

"Billy? Billy Wells?"

The voice brought him to a complete stop. A husky voice, vaguely mocking. He knew who the caller was even before he looked over at the canary yellow Stutz roadster parked by one of the stages. The man leaning indolently behind the wheel was wearing a dark blue blazer with brass buttons, a blue checked cap pulled jauntily over one eye, the cap not obscuring his chestnut hair.

"Hello, Earl." He walked over to the car, terribly conscious of Donovan's eyes upon him, scanning him from head to toe.

"Panhandling?"

"Sort of," Billy said. He could see his ragged reflection in the car's jeweled surface. "But in front of a camera. I've been working here for months."

"Is that a fact?"

"I work all the time. I'm doing just great."

Donovan took a lazy drag on his cigarette and flipped the smoking butt into the street.

"I knew you'd make good."

The car's Tiffany gleam hurt the eyes. "You look like you're doing okay yourself, Earl."

"Not bad," Donovan said, tapping the steering wheel with a faultlessly manicured hand. "Not too bad at all. I might be doing some producing here if one or two things work out right."

"Gee . . . that'd be swell."

"Yeah, just a few loose ends to tie up. You know how it is."

"Sure."

Donovan flicked an imaginary speck of dust from the dashboard.

"If I make a picture, I'll see that you get a good part. That's a promise, kid."

"It'd be a pleasure to work for you, Earl."

"Likewise."

Billy wondered how Donovan had managed to do so well in such a short space of time, but he didn't see any point in asking him. He could hear one of the assistant directors hollering outside of Stage 4 "Where's Billy? Where the hell's the fat guy?"

"Well, gotta get to work, Earl. Look after yourself."

Donovan pulled out a platinum cigarette case and flipped it open to reveal a neat row of cork-tipped smokes.

"You can bet on that."

HEARTS ARE TRUMPS

He had become important to her, a part of her life. She found herself straining forward on the seat to catch a glimpse of his red hair as the Duesenberg turned on the winding road that led to the house. Before he had come so abruptly into her life she had watched for the dogs, or the mare, but now he was the only creature on earth that she longed to see.

"Earl," she whispered, smiling. She had spotted him by the corral, standing with Pedro. He was stripped to the waist and his torso was brick red from the sun. He never tanned, only grew redder. Her Indian. Big chief Donovan.

"Hi, Injun!" she called out as the big car rolled sedately to a stop. She got out, still dressed in her costume because she had been too eager to get home after a long, frustrating day on location to take it off. She looked twelve years old in her pinafore, white stockings and flat, patent leather shoes.

"Hello, Doll," Donovan said. He retrieved his shirt from a peg on the corral fence and walked toward her, swinging the shirt over one shoulder like a towel. "How's my girl?"

She embraced him and the feel of his muscled, sun warmed flesh brought a catch to her throat.

"Swell," she whispered. "Just swell—now."

"Tough day?"

"Everything went wrong."

"Want to tell me about it?"

She kissed him lightly on the chest, tasting the saltiness of his skin. Good, honest sweat.

125

"Sure. Want to scrub my back?"

He nodded gravely.

It had become a daily routine and one that she looked forward to with almost trembling anticipation. She would eye the sun in the afternoons trying to calculate how much longer they would have to shoot, never asking for the time, not trusting her voice. Watched the sun, the lengthening shadows, and thought about Earl's hands on her back, the heavy fingers caressing her spine. And the day's shooting would eventually end, the director yelling through his megaphone to wrap it up as the shadows became too numerous. And then home, the sun orange on the hills above the ranch, the flowering yucca like thin brass spears among the gorse. Home, and Juanita would draw the bath, sprinkling the water with crystals and unwrapping a fresh bar of French soap because Earl was not partial to the smell of Lifebuoy. She had changed her mind about scents because Earl loved women to smell of rose or lavender, gardenia or hyacinth. And she would tell him about her day as she undressed and slipped into the tub and he would sit on the edge of it and smoke a cigarette, dropping ash into the bath sometimes, the particles drifting down through the water like flakes of grey silt.

"So things went wrong, huh?"

"Yes," she said idly, rubbing soap on her arm as he swished water against her back. "I couldn't get in the proper mood. I couldn't feel sad. Eddie had them play violins. He told me to think about Agnes lying dead in her coffin. Eddie had been there. Did I tell you about Grandma Agnes' funeral?"

"Yes," he said.

"I tried to think about how she looked, so pale and waxen . . . so very dead, dear grandma, but I was still smiling. Oh, not *grinning* or anything like that, but smiling. Mr. Griffith was shooting in Westlake Park and he walked across to say hello. Do you know what he said to me? He said, 'Doll, you're too filled with joy to show heartbreak. You look like someone who has just discovered God!' Wasn't that a nice thing to say, Earl?"

"Yes," he said, running his hand up and down her back in a silky, water-smooth caress.

After her bath she toweled herself pink, dusted her body with powder and walked naked into the bedroom. Donovan sat on the edge of the bed, a red-hued shadow in the final glow of the sun.

"I didn't ask you about your day," she said.

"I kept busy."

126

She smiled and sat next to him, letting her head droop against the warm hollow of his shoulder. She stroked his chest lightly with her left hand, feeling the suppleness of muscles beneath the flesh, taut nipple buds, the smooth hollow of his belly below the rib cage. He turned toward her, his bulk forcing her gently backward across the counterpane.

"Doll," he murmured against her cheek, "little Doll."

And each time was like the first, the same fluttering beat of her heart, the breath catching in her throat and then the jolting waves of pleasure as he entered her, sensations that radiated outward from that one spot until her entire body felt consumed by an inner heat that left her, finally, flushed and damp.

"Earl," she said hoarsely, clenching his wide, cool back. "Earl."

He lowered his head and kissed the swollen tips of her tiny breasts. A boy's chest.

"Do you love me, Earl?"

Of her own love she had no doubts. The love that she had showered for years on dogs and horses was now focused on him. Her commitment was total and unquestioned from the first moment when she had lain naked in his arms, not knowing what to expect, her body rigid and her mouth dry as brass. If her virginity had surprised him he had not shown it, nor mentioned it afterward, but his gentleness had surprised her. She had steeled herself that night for an ordeal, the pain of initiation, but there had been no pain, only a sensation of heat as though her body was being immersed in warm oil and then spasms of such intense pleasure that she had been unable to stop herself from crying out. Her mind had been a whirl of frenzied images and her body had moved without any conscious will, moving against his body as though trying to fuse into his flesh. When her passion had subsided, leaving her drained and exhausted, she had felt an overwhelming tenderness for this her first man, a man who could so easily have torn her apart with his bare hands.

Yes, she loved him and there was nothing that he asked of her that she would not do, but he asked for little. He seemed content to stay in the background of her public life, avoiding the news hawks and the gossipmongers. He spent most of his time at the ranch far from prying eyes and they rarely went out to parties or to dinner. He fully understood her vulnerability as a major star and she appreciated his self-effacement. She delighted in lavishing gifts on him—a Stutz car, clothes, jewelry—and expected nothing in return except his physical presence. And yet he was always doing something that would please and surprise her. He was clever at many things. He could build a fence, chop down a tree, juggle six oranges and make a chili that had brought moans of appreciation from Juanita, the recipe for which, he had stated dispassionately, had been taught to him in the Dallas County Jail. He had a special talent with animals, teaching her mare to bow and curtsy like a lady whenever he made a certain gesture with his hand, and teaching Fanny to walk across a room on her hind legs and to roll over and play dead. All of these varied accomplishments delighted Doll. He was in her thoughts constantly during the interminable hours on the set and sometimes he would suprise her and drive to the studio in his car to pick her up after the day's shooting was over, the chauffeur trailing them back to the ranch in the Duesenberg.

Loved him, and never more so than when she lay beneath him, her flesh still tingling, luxuriating wantonly in the feel of his body against hers.

"Sure I love you," he said.

"You make me so happy, Earl," she murmured. "You're my big red teddy bear. You're my fella."

The days dragged. Sometimes he would saddle one of the horses and ride up along the crest of the hills that bordered the wire-fenced land of the Rindges, with Pedro's old Winchester in the saddle boot. He would swap lies with the Rindge fence riders, or go down into the narrow canyons and blaze away at rocks or the spear tipped yuccas, not shooting worth a damn but relishing the kick of the gun against his shoulder and the smell of the burnt powder as it hung in a blue haze in the summer heat.

Killing time.

Or he would take the Stutz out for a day and drive down the dirt road that was Sunset Boulevard and then along the coast past the clapboard and stucco beach towns with their boardwalks and piers.

Venice.

Canals cut in the brackish ground beyond the dunes, the ditches spanned with wooden bridges, the murky, stagnant water dotted with wooden poles for the gondolas. Pink plaster palazzos. Gasoline stations. Coney Island red hots.

Redondo-by-the-Sea.

There was a speakeasy in a building beyond a Moorish arch flanked by salt withered date palms.

"Right off the boat, mister."

"Pumped from the bilge?"

128

"Say! You're some kidder! Have one on the house. That your Stutz? Say, ain't that one honey of a car, though? Costs a bundle, I bet. You in the oil game? Say, do you go for the pasteboards? Some birds I know think they're real hotshots at stud. I bet you could show 'em a thing or three."

Gambler country those little towns on the bay. Cards and booze, the gamblers coming west from Chicago and the booze coming north from the border. Mexican Scotch. The bartenders pushing the booze and hustling the back room games, sizing up the customers by the cut of their clothes and the make of their cars. Butter and egg men. Men in the oil game . . . the real estate game. Money being made now after the hard times. The smell of a boom in the air. Subdivisions being staked out in the bean fields. A forest of oil derricks rising on the nude brown hills.

Donovan sipped his Scotch, smoked a Camel and felt out of things. Doll's big red teddy bear with a few bucks in his pocket, just enough for gas and a couple of drinks.

"Keep the change, Mack."

"Listen mister, about that game . . ."

Not enough dough for a game. And only a sucker played poker in the back room of a stucco Moorish temple in Redondo-by-the-Sea anyway. The bartender snarled. The Stutz howled as Donovan shifted through the gears and hit the road for Long Beach. The rocker arms of the oil wells bobbed up and down on Signal Hill.

"How was your day, Earl?"

"Okay. I drove to Long Beach."

"Why?"

"To join the navy, Doll. Got a hankering to see the world."

"Oh, Earl!"

"I was only half kidding," he said, blowing a smoke ring toward the beamed ceiling in the bedroom. "The fleet was pulling out. Heading for the Orient, some guy said. Those ships sure looked swell, Doll. You could see the brass shining in the sun and all the flags flying. A knock-out. Going to Hawaii . . . China. I got restless feet, I guess."

She turned to him quickly, her hands roving anxiously over his body.

"Don't talk like that, Earl. Not even in fun."

"Would you miss me?"

Her lips were hot against his throat. "I'd die, Earl. Just curl up and die."

"Yeah? Well, I said to myself: Earl, you gotta fever to move, that's your big trouble. No roots. Just a bo movin' in the wind. I went into a place near the docks and had a cup of coffee. I could see the ships headin' out toward the horizon. Smoke pouring from the stacks . . . cuttin' that blue water. Honolulu . . . Manila . . . Shanghai. It set me to thinking. So many places in this old world that Earl P. Donovan hasn't seen."

"Please don't talk that way."

"I dunno, Doll. I guess I'm just a rover. What I need is a good woman to tie me down."

"Earl!" She gripped him, pulling him toward her. "Oh, Earl! Just ask me . . . just say it!"

"No," he said quietly. "It wouldn't work, Doll. Not for me. These past few months have been swell, but I gotta do more than just scrub your back. I'll never make the kind of dough you make, but I gotta make *something*."

"You will, Injun, you will."

"I'm not the kinda bo who can just sit around on his duff and let his little woman bring home all the bacon. That would cut the guts right out of me. You understand that, don't you?"

"Sure I do . . . sure. And I love you for it, Earl."

"I've got a head on my shoulders. There's lots of things I could do."

"Sure there are . . . sure." She was under him now, her arms locked tightly around his waist. "Just love me, Earl. Love me . . . and . . . and I'll talk to Vardon. We'll work things out. You'll see. Everything's going to be swell."

The realization that Doll was having a love affair had come as something of a shock to Vardon Bolling. The news of it had been given to him by Frank Gilboy, who had heard rumors on the lot and then had confirmed them by giving Doll's chauffeur a bottle of gin. As far as Gilboy was concerned there was nothing to worry about. After all, the woman was entitled to a roll in the hay and she was certainly being discreet about it. Still, it was his job to pass on information about the private lives of Sterling's stars to Bolling and so he had reported Doll's affair with Earl Donovan.

"He's living up there," Gilboy had said, "but he seems to be a regular sort of guy. He works like a mule around the ranch and he and Doll go to bed early. Kind of a cross between a hired hand and a gigolo."

"What do we know about him?" Bolling had asked, a worried expression on his face.

"Nothing. He just drifted in and I guess he'll drift out—in time."

"Check up on him. Find out if he's on the square."

"That might be tough to do. Like I said, he stays up on the ranch and I can't just walk in there for no good reason. And even if I talked to him, I don't know what the hell I could find out that we don't know already. Doll bought him a few things, but he hasn't hit her for any big dough."

"How do you know?"

"I dropped by the Levins' and put it on the line to Arnold. I said, 'Arnie, how much is this palooka that Doll's running around with costing her?' And Arnie said nothing, not a red cent . . . just a few presents. She bought him a Stutz and some glad rags, but the car's in her name, so if he walked out tomorrow he might be into her for a couple of grand. That's all."

"What does Arnold know about him?"

"Not too much. The guy was in the marines during the war. A major, or something like that, Arnie said. Doll told him he'd been blown out of a trench and suffered a little shell shock. That's why he stays up there. He's happy to be alone. The guy doesn't worry Arnold or Myron one bit . . . and he doesn't worry me. Pipp worries me—and a couple of other people I could mention—but this looks like a clean setup."

"Not so clean if the gossip vultures got hold of it," Bolling had said, gazing through the window at the ordered rows of studio buildings. "It wouldn't look good in print. Doll Fairbaine *living* with a guy. Living in sin. No. That isn't the kind of publicity that would do anyone any good, especially now. Nose around, Frank. Find out all you can about this man . . . but be very discreet."

"Ain't I always?"

Scandal after scandal had swept the motion picture industry like so many evil winds. First there had been sweet Olive Thomas dying of poison in a Paris hotel room. Suicide? Murder? There had been ugly rumors of dope dealers and Apache toughs clustering around Olive in the Left Bank bistros. And then Bobby Harron had blown out his brains in New York City because Griffith had found a fresher faced youth to replace him in pictures. Legions of fans had no sooner recovered from those shocks when Roscoe Arbuckle raced to San Francisco in his Pierce Arrow to seal his fate in a bedroom at the St. Francis Hotel. A drunken orgy. A dead girl. How had Fatty killed Virginia Rappe? Did he do it with his elephantine knee, pressing it against Virginia's naked body until her bladder had burst? Or had he, as the more lurid statements in the press had hinted, done the foul deed with a bottle, jamming it into the wretched girl's vagina as a glassy substitute for his own flesh? It hardly mattered. Fatty was in and out of court. So were Virginia's female organs floating in glass jars. A sordid spectacle that seemed without end. And then as if the motion industry in general and Paramount Pictures in particular hadn't had enough trouble, someone had to go and shoot Bill Taylor in his apartment. William Desmond Taylor, Famous-Players director, would-be ex-British Army officer, man about town and dashing Lothario, dead on his Oriental rug with a bullet in his back. And in his bedroom were pink nighties and love letters. Mary Miles Minter and Mabel Normand had been his frequent guests. So had Mary's mother. A tangled, ugly web.

The furor of outrage following the Arbuckle orgy had swept the country. There had hardly been a preacher in America who hadn't damned the movies from his pulpit every Sunday, urging his flock to boycott the local picture palace until "the makers of trash and the purveyors of pollution" had cleansed themselves of sex and sin. Those bony blue fingers had not been pointed in Bolling's direction. On the contrary, Sterling, with its steady output of Doll Fairbaine pictures and wholesome comedies, had been the one shining example of what was right about Hollywood. But Bolling had known that the good could suffer with the bad and he had led a group of concerned producers to seek Draconian remedies for the industry's ills. A thorough housecleaning. Immediate blackballing of any star whose off-screen behavior might offend the public sense of morality. Respectability had been needed and Bolling had suggested that a man with impeccable credentials be found to become the titular head of the entire motion picture industry. Bolling had been chairman of the Republican committee in California and had led the delegation to Chicago in June 1920, where he had sweated through nine interminable ballots before helping to nominate Warren Gamaliel Harding on the tenth. One of the men who had been instrumental in plucking the bland faced Mr. Harding out of the smoke filled rooms was a jug-eared Indiana politician by the name of Will H. Hays. After Mr. Harding's overwhelming victory in November, Mr. Hays had been induced to give up his twelve-thousand-dollar-a-year appointment as Postmaster General and head the motion picture industry at one hundred thousand dollars a year. The appointment had stilled the critics, but now, only a few weeks after Mr. Hays had taken office, the storm of the Taylor case had broken and there were more headlines in the press, more blue fingers wagging in scorn and condemnation. Mabel Normand and little Mary Miles Minter might be as pure as snow, but their names were linked. Their names were in the headlines. Their careers were over.

The studio lay stretched out before him, *his* studio, a film factory where raw stock came in one end and a finished, saleable product emerged from the other. That concept was now standard for the industry, but there had been nothing to compare it with when he had first come West. He and Lasky. De Mille, Ince, Anderson. They had made their films in the open air in those days with maybe a barn or two to house props, costumes and cameras. But he, Vardon Bolling, had been taught efficiency in the workrooms of his father's glove factory. No sweatshop that . . .

"You get what you pay for, Vardon," his father used to say.

Yes, no doubt about that. The highest paid workers in the world were on the streets and in the buildings of Sterling Studios. Bolling's heart had swelled with pride. *His* people, from the lowliest day laborer to the richly recompensed cameramen and film editors. The sun glinted off the glass panels in the stages. A man swept up leaves that had fallen from the pepper trees lining the streets. The camera car that Chester Pratt had designed and that had cost ten thousand dollars to build—the only one of its kind in the business—rolled toward the front gates. Everywhere he looked he saw neatness, order, industry. The sky above his studio was a faultless, imperial blue. A panoply of heavenly favor day after day . . .

"Miss Fairbaine to see you, Mister Bolling."

Rose Hanover in the doorway, pencils in the gray bun of her hair. She was smiling. Everyone smiled in Doll's presence.

"I hope I'm not disturbing you, Vardon," Doll said as she hurried into the office. It was 9:15 in the morning and Doll was in makeup and costume. She was dressed as a schoolboy—knickers, a white shirt, a short jacket, her lovely legs encased in knee-high woolen stockings, her tiny feet encumbered by ugly black shoes.

"Of course not, Doll." The sentiment was heartfelt. She was like sunlight entering the room. He could remember the day she had first come into his office (not this grandly decorated one on the second floor of a modern stucco building, but a cubbyhole in a wooden bungalow) holding onto her mother's hand, a child–woman of seventeen in a white dress, a Leghorn hat pinned to her curls. She had sat on his lap when the contracts were being signed—an act that had momentarily embarrassed him until Mary Dare Fairbaine had explained that Doll always sat on Mr. Griffith's lap before the start of every picture. A gesture of good luck. Doll had called him "Uncle" on that day. She still did, on occasion.

"Oh, Uncle Vardon, I'm so happy!"

Even the dour Miss Hanover smiled as she left the office, closing the door silently behind her.

"Doll, you look radiant!" Bolling came out from behind his desk, arms outstretched in welcome. "I take it that Myron or Arnie called you."

She frowned. "The Levins? Why?"

He gave her a hearty, avuncular hug. "Good. I'm happy to break the news. Your share on *Halloran Girl* and *Wabash Moon* come to a cool quarter of a million. Two hundred and fifty thousand dollars. And that's not counting English and French rentals. Both pictures are cleaning up in London and Paris. Which reminds me. I think the time's ripe for a European personal appearance tour. You'd be mobbed!"

"That'd be swell, Vardon . . . and I'm glad the pictures are doing so good, but I have something else to be happy about." She pulled away from his embrace and clutched his hands. "Vardon . . . dear Uncle Vardon . . . I'm going to get married."

He stared at her with a frozen smile. Had she just confessed to cannibalism he could not have been more stunned.

"Married?"

"Oh, yes, Vardon. Yes! He asked me last night and I said yes . . . yes . . . yes!"

"Who . . . who asked you, Doll?" He knew who and his legs felt unsteady. He had to sit down in one of the leather club chairs. Doll sat on the arm of the chair and placed her hand on his shoulder.

"I know that you've *seen* Earl and I'm sure you must have *heard* all kinds of wild stories."

"Stories?" he croaked. "What kind of . . . wild stories?"

"About him living up at the ranch. Well, it's true. He's been living there, but it's been . . . oh, sort of innocent."

"*Sort* of?"

"Nothing terrible. You know what I mean, Vardon. I'm not like some women I could mention—women we both know. My relationship with Earl has been . . . normal."

"I'm sure it has," Bolling said weakly. It was foolish of him to be so shocked by the news. After all, she wasn't a child any longer, nor was

134

she the simple rustic she portrayed in her pictures. She was a twenty-six-year-old woman having an affair with a man. A discreet affair at that. What was the harm? But as for marriage. . . . "Doll, I'm happy that you're happy, but who is this man? You know, marriage is a very important step, a lifetime commitment. It would be wrong to *rush* into it because of . . . let's say . . . a physical attraction."

"He's the only man for me. I know it. I waited, Vardon. I kept myself pure for that one special man to come into my life and come into it he did. It's as though God Himself led him to my door."

"Yes, well . . . that may be so, but who is he? Where did he come from? What does he do for a living? You know, if you were just Jenny Fairbaine of Columbus, or Wabash City, it wouldn't make much difference, but you're not. God knows you're not, Doll. Your getting married will make headlines in every newspaper in the country and half the newspapers in the world. Millions of people are going to want to know everything there is to know about this Earl . . . this Earl . . ."

"Donovan," Doll said, smiling. "Earl Patrick Donovan from Boston, Massachusetts."

"Boston, eh?" He felt better, not knowing why.

She got up from the arm of the chair and walked slowly toward the windows.

"He's led an odd life . . . ran away from a terrible father . . . joined a circus when he was just a boy. He's had to fight and kick all of his life, but he's a man of noble courage and I admire him for it. Tough metal must go through the fire, as grandma used to say."

"What kind of fire?"

"Oh . . . fire . . . the vicissitudes of fate. It isn't an easy world for some people, Vardon. In order to survive, there have been times when he . . . when he stepped on the wrong side of the line. He's been very honest with me. Told me everything about himself, but the good far outweighs the bad."

"How bad is bad?" His momentary relief was rapidly dissipating.

"Jail a couple of times—for very *minor* offenses. A man doesn't have to be a hardened criminal to be put on a chain gang in Alabama for thirty days of brutal labor."

AMERICA'S GIRL NEXT DOOR MARRIES CHAIN GANG FELON

Bolling felt a stab of pain in his chest. He took a deep breath and swallowed hard. A vein in his left temple began to throb, like

135

a thick, blue worm under the skin.

"I see. That might create certain publicity problems."

She turned from the window to face him. Her eyes had an evangelical radiance.

"All of that could be overcome, Uncle Vardon. No one need know about it. Small town sheriffs placed him in those hell holes. Hundreds of men are jailed every day. They'll jail a man or put him on a road gang for the most trivial things. Why, my own father nearly went to jail in Lincoln, Nebraska, for failure to pay a saloon bill that he felt had been grossly padded. Earl has nothing to be ashamed of and neither do I for loving him. I'll stand by him no matter what storm breaks!"

DOLL DEFENDS JAIL BIRD HUSBAND. "I LOVE HIM," SHE CRIES

"Don't rush into anything. I'm sure we can work things out if we put our minds to it."

"Oh, Uncle Vardon, we weren't going to rush anything. I have this picture to finish and I'd like Earl to get established here in some capacity. He has such a quick mind . . . such wonderful, fresh ideas for motion pictures. I'm sure you could find a spot for him. Sort of a roving job so that he could learn all phases of production. If he was a producer that would solve the publicity problems, wouldn't it? He wouldn't be just some unknown man that I married, he'd be Earl Patrick Donovan, producer at Sterling Pictures."

"That might be a good angle," Bolling said. His voice was hollow. "Let me talk it over with Frank. He'll know the right way to go about it. No one in the publicity department has a better touch than Frank Gilboy."

CASSETTE

According to my research, your marriage to Doll Fairbaine was hardly the social event of 1922. In fact, I couldn't find anything about it in any of the Los Angeles papers until the close of the year.

That's right. We had a quiet wedding. Just a few of our closest friends: Vardon Bolling, Griffith, Sam Goldwyn, Louie Mayer, Dick Barthelmess and the Gish sisters . . . people like that. The marriage was kept secret strictly for business reasons. Bolling was afraid that the public would be turned off at the thought of Doll getting married. You know, she was thought of as being no more than sixteen years old in her pictures . . . a child. It wasn't unusual in those days. Audiences were more caught up in the make-believe than they are today. Francis Bushman was married, you know. He was a big star—a great romantic actor. Millions of women would have been horrified and angered if they had known this screen idol of theirs was a married man with children. It would have ruined his career. The same reasoning was applied to Doll.

Yes, I can understand that.

We intended to let the news slip out in time . . . after I began producing. I had plans to change Doll's screen image . . . bring her more up to date.

Into the mainstream.

Yes. Audiences were becoming more sophisticated, although Doll still had a huge and loyal following.

Did Bolling encourage you in this idea?

Bolling encouraged me in everything I did. We may have had our differences from time to time, but not where Doll was concerned.

You saw eye to eye, right?

I guess you can put it that way.

Frank Gilboy slipped his hand under the tail of his jacket and felt the lump in the back pocket of his pants where a leather covered sap rested like a coiled snake.

"You guys wait in the car," he said.

There was a big, beefy man behind the wheel of the black Chalmers and another beefy, red-faced man seated in the back. They wore identical black suits and Panama hats. Both men were off-duty detectives on the Los Angeles force.

Gilboy dropped the sodden butt of a cigarette on the neatly raked gravel drive and walked across the red-tiled verandah to the front door. The Mexican woman opened it after he rang three times.

"Good morning."

"*Buenos dias,* Senor Gilboy," Juanita said.

"Is Mister Donovan here?"

"Oh, yes . . . *si, si.* " Gold teeth gleamed. She opened the door wider and Gilboy stepped into the foyer. He could smell the aroma of bacon and eggs.

"Is he having his breakfast?"

"Oh, yes . . . *si.* "

He knew the house and didn't wait to be escorted. Donovan was taking his breakfast on the patio and Gilboy paused for a moment in

137

the shadow of an adobe arch to size up the man. Big. Maybe one-ninety. Heavy hands and thick forearms. The sonofabitch could pack a wallop. Not that Gilboy gave a damn.

"Mister Donovan?"

Donovan had just cut into an egg covered with green salsa. He popped the dripping morsel into his mouth and chewed thoughtfully, watching Gilboy come toward him in a heavy-footed slouch. A cop's walk.

"What can I do for you?" Donovan said.

"Gilboy's my name . . . assistant publicity director at the studio. I'm afraid I have some bad news. Miss Fairbaine broke her leg doing a stunt on the set."

"Oh?" Donovan said. He wiped a speck of green sauce from his lips with a linen napkin. "You should have telephoned."

Gilboy's smile was like mush. "I guess she knows you pretty well. She said don't phone Mister Donovan. If he knows I'm on my way to the hospital he'll jump into his car and come down that canyon road ninety miles an hour. A broken leg will mend, but not a busted neck."

Donovan burped slightly. "She said that?"

"Her very words. Fighting back the tears. That little girl is as spunky as they come."

"She sure is."

"She's at Hollywood Hospital by now. She'd like you to be there when they set her leg."

"Oh hell, yes," Donovan said.

He had to laugh when he saw the two red-faced, hardeyed men in the car. He was still laughing when Gilboy gave him a shove into the back seat and climbed in after him. Donovan was wedged in between Gilboy and the detective and their combined weight made the Chalmers grown.

"What are you laughing at?" Gilboy asked.

"Doll's broken leg."

Gilboy thought about that for a moment as the detective in front put the car into gear.

"A wise monkey, aren't you?"

"Well, I've been around," Donovan said. He nudged the beefy detective seated beside him. "Your pal here has a pistola under his arm as big as a tree."

"He shoots people from time to time," Gilboy said.

"With our without a badge?"

"What do you care?"

"I like to know who I'm dealing with."

"You're not *dealing* with anybody, buddy. I call the tune and you dance, but if it makes you happy, Charlie has a badge. So does Sam. Sam's driving the car and he has a big gun, too."

"Where are you taking me?"

"You have a choice—the docks or the Santa Fe station. It depends where you want to go."

"What if I don't want to go anywhere? What if I like it here?"

Gilboy sighed and leaned forward. He drew the sap from his back pocket and let it lie in his hand like a dead mouse.

"I don't want to convince you about shuffling along. You're to make up your own mind about that. No pressure . . . no coercion. That's an order from the horse's mouth. You understand?"

"Sure."

"And Charlie and Sam will testify to that, won't you, boys?"

The two detectives grunted.

"We want to handle this in as pleasant a way as possible," Gilboy went on. "Clean and fair."

"That's jake with me," Donovan said. He settled comfortably back in the seat and crossed his legs. He thought of slugging Gilboy, but the big detective on his right had his coat unbuttoned and a meaty paw buried under his armpit. Also, he wasn't that sure that he could take Gilboy with one punch. The guy had a jaw like a pile of rocks. He might just stun him and make him angry. He had seen what an angry man could do to a human face with a lead sap.

"Helluva great day," Donovan said, "you can see Catalina."

They drove in silence until they got downtown, then Gilboy tapped the driver on the shoulder and said: "Pull up at Sixth and Spring."

The two detectives stayed in the car, looking malevolent, and Gilboy and Donovan walked into a coffee shop across the street from the City Bank Building. Gilboy took a table in an area that was marked CLOSED —PLEASE SIT AT COUNTER.

"That area's closed," a boy in a white jacket called out. "We don't serve there until lunch."

Gilboy shoved his hat to the back of his head. "Two coffees."

"You'll have to come to the counter," the boy said.

Gilboy stared him down. "Two coffees and a piece of peach pie."

Donovan sipped his coffee and watched Gilboy eat the pie in about four bites. When he had finished he shoved the plate away from him

139

and took a fountain pen and a folded piece of blank paper from his pocket. Then he took out his wallet and extracted a check. He placed all of these articles in front of Donovan.

"The check's signed. The amount is open—and I do mean open."

"I can see that," Donovan said.

"Those guys in the car think you're a blackmailer. You and I know different. So does the guy who signed that check." He took out a pack of cigarettes and lit one. He didn't offer the pack to Donovan. "We get a lot of blackmailers in this town—or did. You don't take blackmailers to court. You bust every bone in their hands and put 'em on a train East. The word gets around. We haven't had to deal with a blackmailer for a year now."

Donovan said nothing. He tapped the edge of the table with his fingers and studied the check. It was drawn on the bank across the street and it was signed by Vardon Bolling.

"You're a special case. We haven't had to deal with your kind before, but that doesn't mean we don't know how."

"You're doing just fine," Donovan said.

"You may be one hell of a good Joe," Gilboy said, smoke dribbling from the corner of his lips, "but that doesn't mean you're good enough for Doll Fairbaine. There's more at stake there than true love. You following me?"

"All the way."

"The idea is that you write a farewell note . . . a kind of it's-been-nice-but letter. Maybe you could say that you've already got a wife."

"That sounds good."

"It'll break her up, but she'll get over it. It happens to dames all the time."

"I suppose it does at that."

"You write the note and sign it. Then we fill in the check."

"How much do we fill it in for?"

"How does twenty grand sound?"

"Thirty sounds better."

Gilboy stared at the ceiling where a black fan turned lazily. There was dust on the blades and dead flies. The cigarette burned down to his fingers.

"Okay. I can go that high. We'll step across to the bank and you can take it in cash or get a letter of credit. That's up to you." He dropped the smoldering cigarette butt in the dregs of his coffee and took a watch from his vest pocket. "There's a boat leaving San Pedro for Shanghai at four o'clock. I can get you on it. Thirty thousand American dollars will go a long way in Shanghai, China."

"I could go into the bible business in Canton."

Gilboy scowled. "What?"

"Forget it. What if I don't want to go to China?"

"Then you can hop the train in an hour and a half. I can get you a drawing room as far as Chicago."

"I've never been to Chicago."

"You've missed something. That's all I can say. A guy can get rich in Chicago these days if he's got a big enough stake. You'll forget all about California—if you're smart."

Donovan wrote a note. It was short and to the point, mixing a little regret with cold lies.

. . . and I know you'll hate me, but I know that you'll find a good man one day, a man who is free to return your love . . .

"That's fine," Gilboy said after reading it. He folded it carefully and slipped it into his pocket. He then took the pen and filled in the check.

"No hard feelings?" Gilboy asked as he handed the check to Donovan.

"None at all," Donovan said.

They saw him off, the two detectives standing behind Gilboy on the platform. The cops looked disappointed that Donovan was getting on the train without his hands entombed in plaster casts.

Donovan sat in his drawing room and smoked a cigarette while the train pulled out of Los Angeles and headed east. He had a bank draft for thirty thousand dollars in his pocket, which was safer to carry around than cash. As the train began to slow on the long grade up to San Gabriel, Donovan left his drawing room and strolled down to the observation car. A few people were standing on the open platform looking at the orange groves that lined both sides of the tracks. A man wearing plus fours and plaid socks waved his cigar at the trees.

"I'm going to miss that in Cleveland," he said.

Donovan climbed the rail next to him and jumped nimbly off the train.

Doll found the note when she returned to her dressing room at the studio after a long, hot day on location. She had to read it five times before its contents sunk in and then she went into hysterics. Bolling and

141

the studio doctor were conveniently outside the dressing room when she began screaming and they rushed in to console her.

"No! No! No!" Doll shrieked over and over like a mad woman.

"There . . . there . . . there . . ." Bolling kept saying, holding her in his arms.

The doctor gave her a strong sedative that calmed her down but turned her legs to jelly. Her chauffeur had to carry her to the car.

Her dreams were vivid but disjointed. D. W. Griffith and God were in the dreams, walking in and out. She sat on Griffith's lap in a starched white dress and he tried to pick up her skirt. His fingers were like frail dry sticks. God had a red beard. A fat woman wearing nothing but a chemise sat drinking wine in a room that looked like the front parlor of a rooming house in Moline. Where was Donovan? She was looking for him, but all she found was D. W. Griffith, God, the fat lady and a dead white dog.

She woke up screaming and drenched with sweat. Moonlight fell across her bed through an open window. A shadow stirred.

"Hey now, what's all the shouting about?"

"Earl!" She sobbed, reaching into the darkness. "Earl!"

He sat on the edge of the bed and she buried her damp face against his chest.

"Oh, God, Earl . . . Earl . . ."

"It's okay, Doll. It's okay."

"I don't care about that woman in Toledo," she whispered harshly. "I just don't give a damn. You can divorce her. I don't care how much it costs."

"I don't have a wife in Toledo. The note was a fake."

She raised her head, her distraught tear swollen face close to him. "Why? Why did you do it? You put me through hell."

"I thought it was the best thing to do. The best way to get out of your life. I could ruin your career."

"I would have killed myself." She clung to him, her nails digging into his shoulders. "If you hadn't been there when I woke up I would have put my head in the oven. I swear before Almighty God. I can't live without you. I don't want to live without you."

"I got halfway to San Berdoo on the train and then couldn't go any farther. I want to marry you, Doll, you know that."

"Then do it. I don't care about my career. I'll tell the whole world. Yes! yes! yes! I married him. Maybe he isn't a saint, but he's the man I love."

142

She began to kiss his neck and face with little whimpers of pleasure, her mouth slack and wet. She was still groggy from the sedative.

"Get dressed. We're going to Yuma."

"Tonight?"

"Yes, right now."

He helped her into her clothes and then half carried her to the garage and lifted her into the Stutz. It was a chilly night with fog drifting in from the ocean. He found a plaid rug in the back seat and wrapped it around her.

"Oh, Earl, am I dreaming?"

"No, baby."

"Drive like the wind," she murmured.

OUT TAKES

She would never forget the dawn tingeing the mountains a pale rose or how the dust boiled away behind them, obscuring the road. (The great desert and the car hurtling across it at eighty miles an hour.) And she would never forget Yuma, Arizona, early in the morning and leaving the car, her ears ringing from the sound of the engine, and walking beside him to the white clapboard house that looked so tiny under the cottonwood trees or how a dog barked and a cock crowed.

She would never forget the old man and his wife standing together in the parlor. (The soft whirring of a clock in a rosewood case. The smell of furniture polish.) The old man had forgotten his teeth and his wife excused herself with a painful smile and brought them down from the bedroom and the old man turned his back to insert them.

"So you wish to be married?"

She gave her name as Jennifer Dare Fairbaine.

"Fairbaine? Like that moving picture actress?"

"Lots of Fairbaines back East . . . Ohio . . . Indiana . . ."

"Oh, yes," the old man said gravely. "Oh, my yes. We do surely hear a lot of names here. Now, kindly join hands and repeat after me . . ."

And she would always remember the heat of the border town and the soldiers in their sunbleached khaki uniforms lounging in a wooden shack beside the road and waving the car on into Mexico. And the town was squalid with its low adobe buildings and dirt streets and there were vultures perched on the flat roofs with folded wings.

And she would remember the hotel on the far side of the town (that a Mexican general had spent one million dollars to build) and the coolness of the courtyard with its fountain and trees and flowers. The whitewashed halls and red tile floors. The dark Spanish furniture and crisp linen sheets. So much like home. And Donovan called down for champagne and it came in a silver bucket filled with shaved ice. Moët y Chandon, 1913. The first alcoholic beverage she had ever tasted.

"I talked to Vardon about us," she said.

"I know," he said.

"Did I tell you that?"

"No, I just guessed."

"You're so smart, Injun."

"Ain't I just."

"He will . . . I think."

"Will he?"

"Yes."

"Not just a job, Doll."

"No, of course not. Not just *any* job."

"Like I've told you, I want to produce . . . one or two pictures just to show what I can do. There's no big trick in it. Just dough."

"Yes."

"And if he'll meet me halfway . . ."

"I'll help you, Injun."

"No. Not a penny, Doll. It's my deal and I'll put up the pot— fifty–fifty with him. I didn't tell you, but something I was working on paid off . . . not cards, don't give me that look. Poker's a sucker game and I haven't touched a pack since God knows when. No, this was a legit deal I had in the works and it paid off. I got a bank draft for thirty thousand and I'll put it right on the table if he'll match it."

"He will, Earl . . . he will. Oh, my big red teddy bear!"

And she remembered making love through the long day and falling asleep and waking up and making love again. She remembered the sunset and the guitars beneath the balcony in the courtyard where the fountain tumbled green water and the swirl and dip of the swallows that nested under the tiled eaves.

WHAT FOOLS MEN ARE

Pipp tried to remember where he had met the woman, but it seemed that the harder he thought about it the less he could recall. Her name was Thelma and she said she had been a nurse at one time. Had he met her in a sanitarium? He couldn't be sure and Thelma refused to tell him.

If you don't know, why should I tell you?

It upset her when he asked her, and her brooding silence would last all day.

He had met her. That much was certain. She had come into his life during a low period and he could remember her moving through the chaos of his apartment with the calm sureness of a battleship on a troubled sea.

You live in a hole! A man of your wealth and stature!

He rather liked his small apartment on South Alvarado. It was within easy walking distance of restaurants and streetcar lines. He had never learned how to drive a car and one of the studio drivers lived a few blocks away and would take him to the studio every morning and bring him home at night. He used the apartment only for sleeping. His dirty laundry was taken care of once a week by a colored lady who lived over on Hope Street. The colored lady never dusted the apartment and neither did Pipp.

No wonder you're sick all the time.

Thelma simply moved in and took over. It was a period between pictures and he only dimly remembered her staying with him. She dried him out and tried to pump a little life into his small body with her large, capable hands. She cooked beef broth for him and made him eat mashed carrots. But she did more than cook for him and sleep next to him

145

(cradling his head in the warm billows of her breasts), she began to reorganize his affairs, paying bills that had accumulated, depositing checks that he had shoved away in bureau drawers among mismatched socks and wadded underwear. He was making twelve hundred dollars a week at Sterling and after Thelma had made the deposits and paid the bills she showed him a balance sheet that was extremely impressive.

I'll manage your money for you, Thomas, because it is quite obvious that you are totally lacking in fiscal responsibility.

He couldn't argue about that. Thelma made arrangements for his pay to be deposited directly to his account in the Bank of Italy. She then marched down to the bank branch near Westlake Park and presented a power of attorney that Pipp had signed one night without reading the document. She had legal authority to handle his money jointly and she made him promise not to draw large sums of money out in cash, because, as she put it, he handled money like a drunk marine.

Thelma Robeck was of German ancestry and came from Milwaukee where her father had been a brewery worker. She was a big woman, close to six feet tall and built to proportion. She was fifteen years older than Pipp and had once had some minor success in a road company opera troupe. Her voice had been sound enough, but her acting ability had been abysmal and her personality so overbearing that theatrical managers had soon grown tired of her. She had still clung to a shred of illusion about becoming a star when she nagged Pipp into taking her out to the studio. Her humiliation by Chester Pratt turned her into a demented virago for a week. From that moment her hold on Pipp became absolute.

She convinced him to place a substantial down-payment on a large Victorian-style house on Irving Boulevard, a street lined with imposing homes, and moved Pipp into it. He missed the coziness of his tiny apartment and he especially missed the bootleggers. For a brewer's daughter, Thelma held puritanical ideas about drinking and getting hold of a bottle became a major problem. He never drank while working, but he had become used to downing half a quart of Scotch at night and being forced to give up the habit made him edgy. Thelma told him that it was just a question of will power—which he could have told her —and she attempted to supplant his craving by teaching him how to play cribbage and encouraging him to drink cocoa. He was hopeless at cribbage, a game that required at least a rudimentary understanding of addition, and cocoa made him feel sick to his stomach.

He was not happy with Thelma Robeck.

146

If it wasn't for me, you'd be dead drunk in a whorehouse!

That was true. How did Thelma know about his alcoholic peregrinations? Is that where he met her? Some cathouse in Stockton, Salinas, San Bernardino? He remembered dimly being in a place in Red Mountain. Small, neat rooms. Antimacassars on the chairs in the parlor. A clean, old-fashioned place. Gold miners trade. An honest shot of whisky. Sentimental tunes on the player piano. A large woman in a red dress singing *When the Angelus was Ringing . . . Shine on Harvest Moon . . .*

Had he met her there?

If you can't remember, I won't tell you.

It made no difference. She had entered his life somehow, somewhere, and presumably she was in it to stay. He was not happy with her because he felt intimidated. She overpowered him and he was afraid to cross her. Of course, he had to admit that she had done wonders for his health. His eyes had lost their bloodshot hue and his skin was no longer clammy all the time, but a week taking the cure would have accomplished as much.

No, he was not happy with Thelma Robeck, but he could see no way of getting her out of his life and every day that passed only increased her hold on him. A week after they had moved into the big house on Irving Boulevard, an assortment of people began arriving, all of them tall, dark-haired and morose. They had simply moved in, bag and baggage, with hardly a word of explanation from Thelma as to who they were.

Friends . . . relatives . . . what does it matter?

The first to arrive had been a large, untidy looking man of middle age. Thelma said that his name was Rolfe and that he was a cousin of hers from Milwaukee. Rolfe was some sort of an engineer, Thelma said, and he had a good job waiting for him at an oil refinery in Long Beach, but Rolfe showed no sign of going down there. He stayed in an upstairs bedroom all day, only coming down for meals, occupying his time by clipping items from newspapers and magazines and pasting them into a scrapbook. Then Gretchen arrived, a lank-haired, blank-faced girl of eighteen, well along in pregnancy. Her arrival was followed a few days later by Hank who looked enough like Gretchen to be her brother— the two of them enough like Thelma to be her children. Hank was nineteen, sharp-faced and vaseline slick, a gum chewer who smoked cigarettes and cracked wise. He carried gin in a hip flask and his clothes in a rotting cardboard suitcase.

147

Henry is a stockbroker. He'll need a car to get around in and establish himself.

And so a car was bought for Hank so that he could drive off at dusk and drive back at dawn, drunk and boisterous, lipstick and rouge stains on his shirt and collar.

How long are these people going to stay, Thelma?

Stony silence.

The atmosphere became increasingly more unnerving for Pipp. Sometimes he would wake in the middle of the night and hear the muted sounds of argument coming from downstairs. Once he peered around his bedroom door to see Gretchen stumbling along the hall toward her room weeping hysterically, Thelma almost dragging her, grim-lipped and silent. And once he had seen Rolfe dressed in a shoddy grey bathrobe, hands clenched to his head, pace the landing muttering, "Why? Oh, dear God, why did I do it? Why did I ever do it?"

Why did he do what, Thelma?

I don't think that's any of your business, Thomas.

Why wasn't it his business? It was his house, wasn't it? Or was it? There seemed to be some question of that. Thelma held a paper that would transfer title to the house to her once the balance of the modest mortgage was paid. He couldn't recall having signed such a document, but there it was. Thelma plucked it from the cavernous hollow between her breasts like a dagger and showed it to him. It was his signature all right—Thomas Fanning Pipperal with no dots over the i's.

I don't remember signing that.

There are many things you don't remember, Thomas. Drinking destroys the brain . . . drop by drop . . . cell by cell.

Pipp threw himself into his work with a passionate dedication that had Chester Pratt clapping for joy. Every one of the two reelers of the third series were coming in on schedule and well under budget. And Pipp's timing had never been sharper or his sense of comedy more acute.

"This'll be the best series of 'em all, Vardon," Pratt told Bolling one day.

"Fine," Bolling muttered. "That's just fine." Bolling was secretly concerned. The last picture was being shot and Pipp had come to him with a request that he could not very well refuse. The little man wanted his salary for that week paid to him in cash.

There would be a ten day hiatus between the last picture of the third series and the first picture of the fourth. Pratt's stable of gag writers would hole up in their offices and hammer out plot lines and situations, creating loose structures that would be given substance later when the pictures were being shot. Pipp required only a vague idea. His peculiar genius could not be written down. It came out of impromptu bits of business that he and Chester Pratt would work out on the set. And so Pipp was not needed for the story conferences because he could not articulate what he thought would be funny. He had ten days of free time ahead of him. Ten days of staying home with his menage on Irving Boulevard. Cribbage and cocoa for ten days. The gorge rose. Pipp took his pay in cash on a Friday afternoon, rented a car and driver from a Culver City livery service and headed south for San Diego after a stop at Al's Barber Emporium on Alvarado Street to load a suitcase with bottles of Scotch. He left one out and got pleasantly stewed during the long drive down the coast. By the time he reached San Diego he had forgotten all about Thelma, and Rolfe's midnight wanderings, and Gretchen's interminable pregnancy, and Hank's gutter manners. The Pacific fleet was on a stopover before leaving for Manila and sun gleamed off the white hulls as they lay moored side by side off Coronado Island. The Hotel Coronado was booked solid with naval officers and their wives and so he checked into a large hotel in downtown San Diego, requesting a suite with a view of the bay. He signed the register Albert Sydney. A plump bellhop lugged the deadweight of his suitcase to the elevator.

"Say," the bellhop said as they rode slowly upward. "If I hadn't seen ya sign the register as Mr. Sydney I'd swear you was Pipp of the movies." He winked broadly.

"Lots of people make that mistake," Pipp said, staring at the elevator doors.

"Say, listen, don't get me wrong. I ain't about to tell on ya. No, siree. I know how you film folk like your privacy. Why, we had Mabel Normand stayin' here a coupla weeks ago, Checked in under another name, but I spotted her, see. I know all the stars. I said, Miss Normand, I sure loved you in *Mickey,* saw it twelve times. Boy, were you great. Your secret is safe with Shiloh Waterbury."

"Who's Shiloh Waterbury?"

"That's me, see. Only that's my stage name. I have strong ambitions to be a thespian."

"I wish you luck"

"Thanks. Of course, acting lessons are expensive, see, and I don't get as many as I should."

Pipp peeled off a five dollar bill from the roll in his pocket and gave it to the bellhop.

"Thanks. You're a sport. If there's anything I can do for ya, just ask."

Pipp thought it over as the bellhop went through the rooms, opening windows and pointing out the view.

"I hate to be alone at night," Pipp said, his voice barely audible. He always felt embarrassed around bellhops for some reason.

The boy's face became as grave as a banker's. "I know a fine bit. An actress."

"Can she read Shakespeare?"

"She'll do anything you ask her to do, but I gotta give her a little advance, if you get my drift."

Pipp took the roll out of his pocket. "Will twenty be enough?"

"A double sawbuck'll be just swell. She's trying to work her way through elocution school and every little bit helps."

Lights were dancing behind his tightly closed eyes and there was a roaring in his ears as though a thousand Niagaras tumbled through his head. He struggled to open his eyes a crack but all he could see was a gleaming whiteness that shot bolts of pain through his eyelids. His head was in a sink and the water was running. He had sensed that much. He opened his mouth to say something, but all that emerged was half a pint of rancid Scotch. He wanted very much to die.

"Just take it easy."

Was that Gilboy's voice? He hoped so. He wanted to see Gilboy more than he wanted anything in the world. The thought of Gilboy and hot coffee drove the longing for death away. A large hand was sloshing cold water in his face. Gilboy's hand?

"Gil . . . boy? Gil . . . boy?"

"Take it easy, buddy. Just take it easy."

Later, after kneeling in front of the toilet bowl for half an hour, during which time everything that could conceivably come up from his stomach had come up and been flushed into Mission Bay, he staggered out of the bathroom and collapsed in a drained heap on the bed. He lay on his back and watched the ceiling move. It was like a sheet of white mist blowing in the wind. Then a face intruded into his line of vision.

"Gil . . . boy?"

"Nobody here named Gilboy, buddy. How about puttin' some clothes on?"

Not Gilboy? Pipp puzzled over it for a moment, struggling to get his wits together. The ceiling continued to roll on and on and the face moved with it. Not Gilboy? He stared hard at the face until, finally, it stopped drifting with the mist and came into sharp focus. It was the face of a total stranger.

"You . . . you're not . . . Gilboy."

"That's right, buddy. Johnson's my name. Detective Sergeant Johnson. San Diego Police Department."

Pipp sat up. He realized with a shock that he was stark naked and a man that he had never seen before was standing by the side of the bed.

"Not Gilboy."

"Put your clothes on, buddy. I gotta take you downtown."

"Downtown?" His brain flickered from darkness to light. "It seems . . . to me . . . that I am . . . downtown."

"The DA's office. We gotta ask you some questions."

"Questions?"

"About the rape and sodomy of a fifteen-year-old girl."

Pipp's eyes rolled back in his head as he slumped forward into the detective's pitiless hands.

The house detective at the El Mirador Hotel felt there was something fishy going on when he spotted Casper Eidelberg sneaking in the back way with a camera case under his arm. The house detective didn't like Casper Eidelberg because the big fruit was always putting on airs about being an actor. Sometimes he called himself Shiloh Waterbury, a phony monicker if ever there was one. So, the detective trailed the bellhop up the service stairs to the fourth floor and saw him knock three times on the door of Room 415. A naked girl opened the door just enough for the bellhop to squeeze in. The house detective waited fifteen minutes and then let himself into the suite with a pass key. He tiptoed through the empty living room and into the bedroom. A naked man, glassy-eyed with passion, sat on the bed with his back against the headboard while the naked girl knelt beside him with his penis in her mouth. Casper Eidelberg stood at the foot of the bed with his face glued to the stiff leather hood of a Graflex camera.

"Got ya!" the house detective cried.

The naked girl screamed and the bellhop injured his left eye on the hard leather rim of the camera's hood. The man on the bed slumped to one side in an obvious faint. It was a clear case of *something* and the house detective telephoned the police department.

Detective Sergeant Biff Johnson of the Flying Squad answered the call. He formed certain conclusions two minutes after entering the room. The guy on the bed was dead drunk and there was enough unopened hootch in a suitcase to give joy to a Legion convention. The girl, now partially dressed, was an obvious tart and the whole setup smelled of the old badger game. Then the girl began to wail that she'd been wronged, that the man on the bed had promised her a starring role in a moving picture if she would perform a certain act and if he could have a photograph of her doing that certain act so that the could study it at his leisure. Oh, she cried, I never knew there were such wicked men in the world! She had large, very round breasts with nipples of a startling shade of pink. Those breasts kept peeping in and out of the gap in her hastily buttoned dress and Detective Sergeant Biff Johnson couldn't keep his eyes off them. He asked her how old she was and she broke down into paroxysms of weeping, her breasts bouncing in and out of the gap like balls into a net. She said that she was fifteen years old —and could prove it.

Sergeant Johnson then set about determining the identity of the man on the bed who was either a victim or a child molester. The house detective said that the man's name was Albert Sydney and Casper Eidelberg kept his mouth shut because he still clung to a vague hope that he could salvage something out of the debacle. Sergeant Johnson went through the drunken man's clothes, which were heaped in an untidy pile on the floor, and found a wallet with close to a thousand dollars in it (money that the bellhop had counted while dreaming about the vast sums that Pipp, or Sterling Pictures, or both would be paying him every week to keep a set of pornographic photographs off the French postcard market) and a printed card which read . . .

> I SOMETIMES PASS OUT DUE TO INCIPIENT
> DIABETES. IF FOUND IN A COMA, PLEASE
> TELEPHONE MR. FRANK GILBOY DAY OR NIGHT
> AT CULVER CITY 7216. THERE WILL BE A
> REWARD FOR YOUR KINDNESS.

The detective then found a note mixed in among the bills

Pipp—Call Chester re wardrobe
fitting Lovers & Loafers.

"That's Pipp of the movies," he said. "I thought he looked familiar. Well, I'll be damned."

Sergeant Johnson did what he felt was the right thing, he telephoned his chief at headquarters and passed on all the information that was available to him, as well as his opinion.

"It's the badger game, Chief. Pipp's drunk as ten lords and this fifteen-year-old tart was giving him a little Frencheroo while her boyfriend was taking pictures with a Graflex. I'll bet it ain't the first time this guy's taken pictures of guests in compromising poses and then . . ."

"How old did you say the girl was?" the chief asked.

"Fifteen. Looks older, but she says she can prove it."

"Stay right there and don't let anybody in or out of that room."

The chief of the Flying Squad then called the D.A. The D.A. was up for re-election and although he wasn't in any deep trouble he wasn't exactly a shoe-in either. There had been a few protests that the D.A. was soft on vice, that he looked the other way regarding some boarding houses near the U.S. Navy's destroyer base, boarding houses that for some peculiar reason held nothing but female roomers between the ages of eighteen and twenty-five. The D.A.'s reason for looking the other way was civic—he and his older brother, the mayor, were trying to lure the entire First Fleet permanently away from Long Beach. Making San Diego the best liberty port outside of Honolulu was one way of going about it. The chief of the Flying Squad's interest in the boarding houses was more basic. Their operation was putting enough money in his pocket to insure him an early retirement. He was a firm believer that one hand washes the other. His call to District Attorney Owen D. Jessop went something like this.

"Owen, this is Chief Harkshore. What would you say to having a Fatty Arbuckle case to take into court? Yes, Owen, it's all there: drunken picture star, sex orgy in a hotel room—only the girl's no Hollywood sweet potato, she's a fifteen-year-old-local. Are you listening, Owen? *Fifteen* years old! a mere child forced into an unnatural, perverted act. These Hollywood degenerates think they can get away with anything if they drive down here. If folks want to know how you, and this city, stand on the subject of morality, you can sure as hell show 'em."

Owen D. Jessop was excited yet cautious. He didn't want to leap into anything that he might be sorry for later. He wanted to weigh all the angles, and so while Detective Sergeant Johnson remained on guard in Room 415, a squad of detectives brought Casper Eidelberg and his girlfriend down to City Hall where they were interrogated and the plates developed. It was soon apparent to Jessop that the girl was something of a juvenile whore and that the bellhop was a would-be blackmailer or shakedown artist, but the photographs were plain enough. Pipp the comedian, a man whose pictures were suddenly very popular with the kids in San Diego, Jessop's own son and daughter included, was caught in Kodak clarity doing obscene things with a girl of fifteen. That would be sufficient to bring Pipp to trial on a charge of statutory rape and contributing to the delinquency of a minor. But the moral character of the girl and her bellhop pimp was bound to come under harsh scrutiny by Pipp's lawyer, no doubt one of those high-priced Los Angeles shyster showboaters who could slip jurors on their fingers like so many gaudy rings. Pipp could come out looking more sinned against than sinning. His brother the mayor felt the same way about it. They both knew that they had something on their side of the table but they weren't quite sure what it was.

"A Fatty Arbuckle kind of thing would sure generate a lot of publicity," the mayor said. Willard Jessop had been, and for that matter still was, a real estate man. He was a San Diego booster of the first water and the thought of Los Angeles made his blood pressure rise. San Diego had so much more to offer than that burgeoning metropolis to the north. The thought of Hollywood particularly irritated him. By all rights San Diego should have been the moving picture capital of the world. The early film makers had fled west seeking limitless sun and to escape the hard eye and long arm of Tom Edison. Edison held patents on the basic structure of the moving picture camera and felt that only those men who were willing to pay him fat royalties should be in the moving picture business. Willard Jessop didn't understand all of the ramifications of the rebellion against the Motion Pictures Patents Company amalgam; all that he knew for certain was that film makers who were not members of the Patents group had come west to avoid prosecution under the patents law. Sun was a consideration, but so was the nearness of the Mexican border in case the Patents Company goons closed in on them. Laemmle, Fox, Ince, Zukor, Lasky and De Mille, all of the men who had fought against the Trust had gone to Los Angeles, although San Diego had more sun and was closer to the border. Lasky had rented a barn in Hollywood and now *Hollywood* was known throughout the civilized world and San Diego was just a name on a map.

Would a juicy sex trial boost real estate values? He somehow doubted it. He glanced at the photographs that his brother had spread out on the desk.

"She sure doesn't *look* fifteen, does she."

"No, Willard, she does not. She is an unusually well-endowed girl."

"And she seems to be enjoying herself. I mean to say, Owen, *she's* smiling and Pipp ain't."

The two brothers who only had the future of San Diego at heart stared glumly at the photographs.

"Still," Willard said, "we've got *something* here."

"Oh, yeah, we sure as hell got something."

Owen Jessop placed a call to Culver City and asked to talk to Frank Gilboy. He spoke in his best D.A. manner and informed Gilboy that a warrant was being issued for Pipp's arrest and that he was prepared to press a statutory rape charge in court unless Sterling Pictures could convince him that such drastic action was unwarranted.

They were leaving a door open and Gilboy wondered why. "There might be more here than meets the eye," he said as he and Vardon Bolling and Sterling's chief attorney, Maurice Caiden, drove from the studio toward the airport in Santa Monica where a four passenger Junkers F-13 was waiting to whisk them to San Diego. Bolling, hollow-eyed with dread, said nothing. Thirteen Pipp films were ready to go out to the exchanges and thirteen were already in release.

PIPP GUILTY IN RAPE CHARGE

Sterling comedy star called "monster"
by judge. Sentenced to ten years at
hard labor.

The monetary loss would not wreck the studio, but the storm of bad publicity would stain the Sterling image forever.

"If Pipp pleaded guilty in a closed session . . ." Maurice Caiden said gloomily.

"Nuts to that," Gilboy cut in. "They're after something down there. They're not *that* sure. Rape, my butt! Hell, the little guy can't get it up. Everybody knows that. They're prepared to deal, but I can't figure their angle."

"A guilty plea would eliminate a trial. It would eliminate publicity . . . to a certain extent," the lawyer said. He looked even more haunted than Bolling.

There was no conversation during the flight down the coast. The engine sent shock waves of sound through the thin metal partition that separated the pilot from his passengers. Bolling, who was afraid of height, was too petrified to say anything even if he could have heard the sound of his own voice. It was a brilliant afternoon, clear and sunny, but the magnificence of the view was wasted on the brooding, silent passengers.

A police car and driver were waiting at the San Diego airport and the three men were driven to City Hall and taken immediately to the mayor's office. Only the brothers Jessop were there and Owen Jessop, who looked more like a small-time insurance salesman than a hardhitting D.A., presented the facts in a droning monotone. They had, he said, got Pipp dead to rights, caught in the act by the house detective at the El Mirador Hotel, an ex-San-Diego police officer and a man of unimpeachable honesty.

"Sure," Gilboy grunted.

The pictures on the table were proof positive of an extended orgy that Pipp had conducted with a fifteen-year-old child. But, in all fairness, there could be mitigating circumstances—to a certain extent. A warrant had been issued for Pipp's arrest, but no one knew of that warrant yet except himself, the mayor, and a few detectives of the Flying Squad. In other words, Jessop had intoned, they had done everything possible to keep the news of the scandal from leaking out to the press.

"That's good of you," Bolling said.

"Yes, it is," Maurice Caiden said.

"Why?" Gilboy said. "Why kid-glove the guy? If you've got a case, you've got a case. What the hell does Pipp mean to you? Then again, may be you ain't got a case at all, maybe you'd get laughed out of court."

"Now, Frank," Bolling said uncomfortably.

"Now, Frank," Caiden echoed.

"Now, Frank, *hell,*" Gilboy said. He was mad, madder than he had ever been in his life. He had spent a couple of years wetnursing Pipp through his periodic drunks and he had come to like the little guy. A rabbit, a harmless little rabbit who had never hurt a living soul. Rape. The charge was fantasy. "You say you got proof positive. Let me see those pictures." He lunged toward the desk where the photographs had been stacked, image side down, and spread them out across the surface like a deck of cards before the brothers Jessop could stop him.

Bolling and Caiden peered over Gilboy's shoulder. What Bolling saw shocked him to the core. He had never seen a dirty picture in his life and the sight of the naked bodies on the bed disgusted him.

PIPP EXPOSED IN PORNOGRAPHIC PICTURES POSES

"Good God!" he said.

"And that girl is . . ." Caiden began after clearing his throat.

"Fifteen," the brothers Jessop said in unison.

"Good God," Bolling repeated.

"You certainly have proof positive," Caiden said, pursing his lips. "That is, if you're sure of the girl's age."

"We have her birth certificate," Owen Jessop said. "She was born right here in San Diego on April twelfth, 1907. She is a mere child."

"A wise child," Gilboy growled. "She sure as hell knows what to do. She's giving him the French mouth like an expert, but she's damn near pulling his prick off to get it up. Why, it looks like she's trying to pluck a daisy from the ground. You call that a picture of a man enjoying an orgy? Hell, I call it a passed out drunk having his prod pulled. What the hell kind of a burg is this where a man can't drink in peace in the safety of his own hotel room without badger sharks breaking in on him, and taking pictures and trying to pull his prod off? You oughta toss those tinhorn blackmailers in the hoosegow and chuck away the key."

"She may be involved in a blackmail plot," the D.A. said doggedly, "but she's still only fifteen years old and Pipp *is* with her. We could go to court on this evidence."

"Sure," Gilboy said. "You might even ruin Pipp's career, but you wouldn't do yourself any good, I can tell you. Pipp looks like a starved cat next to that Amazon. A jury's going to wonder who the hell's raping who."

"We're not being vindictive," Mayor Jessop said. "We don't want to ruin the man's career. Perhaps we could work out some kind of compromise solution."

"I'm sure we could," Bolling said.

"The dropping of charges for . . . well, we could work something out."

"Of course," Bolling said. "You just name it."

Los Angeles: Vardon Bolling, president of Sterling Pictures, announced at a press conference today that he will shortly undertake one of his most ambitious projects. A scenario is now being written for a moving picture to be filmed entirely in San Diego. The production will cost a quarter of a million dollars. Tentative title is *Here Comes the Fleet* and it will deal with the lives and loves of the crew of a battleship on ship and shore. Full cooperation of the United States Navy and the city of San Diego has been assured. Should be a thriller.

Bolling spurned the waiting airplane and traveled back to Los Angeles by train. He was in a black, bitter mood. The stark photographs of Pipp were seared into his brain. He was certain that he could never look at the man again without feeling a sense of revulsion. Pipp was on the train too, three cars back in a drawing room with Frank Gilboy. Gilboy was welcome to him.

"I want you to take a close look at Pipp's contract," he said to Caiden. "I want out of it. Sooner or later that man is going to cause a major scandal. Let some other producer suffer. Maybe Sennett would take over the contract."

"I doubt it," Caiden said.

"Or Bill Fox."

"I doubt that, too."

"Well, I'll find someone. If I can't then we just cancel and pay the penalties. But I swear to God, Maury, that immoral little bastard will never make another picture under my banner. Some people are such damn fools when it comes to . . . to . . ." Words failed him.

"Sex?" Caiden suggested.

Bolling glared through the window. A deserted beach flashed by.

"Yes. And all that fooling around. Well, Pipp has gone too far. I built my studio on decency. On a high moral tone. Pipp has caused nothing but grief, and people who cause grief will damn well pay a price for it, so help me God!"

At that moment Doll Fairbaine and Earl Patrick Donovan were crossing the border into Mexico and driving toward the Hotel Casa del Sol in Santa Rosario. And in New York City a midget wearing a wool overcoat with an Astrakhan collar was alighting from a taxi in front of a brownstone in Greenwich Village. And thus fate moves, as imperceptibly as the shadowed darkening of the sea.

Ambrose Pike checked the address before paying the taxi driver. The building was badly in need of repair and several windows on the first floor were boarded up. A couple of tough-looking men lounged on the front steps despite the bitter wind.

"I better wait for you, Ambrose," the driver said. His beat was the theater district and he knew Ambrose well.

"No need of that," the midget said in his tiny, high-pitched voice. "I don't know how long I'll be."

"I'll wait anyway," the driver said, scowling at the bruisers on the steps. The driver had once gone seven rounds with the great Honey Mollody and he knew a couple of pugs when he saw them. "I got nothin' to do."

"Suit yourself."

The plug uglies barely glanced at Ambrose as he mounted the steps, as though the sight of a midget in an Astrakhan collared coat and derby hat with spats over his shiny black shoes was the most common sight in the world on Sullivan Street.

The entranceway was dark, but enough light filtered in from the street lamp outside for Ambrose to read the names above the mail slots. Most of the names were barely legible scrawls, but there was a neatly printed card above the slot marked 3B which read ANNA MARIE SHAPELY & MAE PEPPER. The bottom two-thirds of the card had been ripped away and Ambrose assumed that it had contained the words SHAPELY SISTERS—SONG AND DANCE with perhaps a number where they could be reached.

"Klopstein and Maguire used to handle 'em," the manager of the Tivoli Theater had said, "but they dropped 'em like a hot rock. Only hot they ain't, see. They sure look swell but they can't sing worth a damn. I told 'em to try burlesque."

Ambrose labored up the dark stairwell to the third floor. It was a noisy building and a cacophony of sound assailed him. He was sensitive to noise and placed his tiny gloved hands over his ears as he mounted the steps. A sailor and a girl emerged laughing from a room on the second floor, a blaring gramophone spilling the raucous beat of jazz onto the landing. A large woman with hennaed hair stood framed in the doorway for a moment.

"Don't do nuthin' I wouldn't do!" she yelled before closing the door with a bang.

The sailor and the girl locked arms and came down the stairs whooping and hollering and Ambrose pressed his body against the wall to keep from being borne along with them like a twig in a surging tide. When he reached the comparative quiet of the third floor he felt shaky in the legs and out of breath. He waited outside the door to 3B until his heart stopped pounding and he felt capable of talking coherently. He was out of shape, having left the adagio act to take a legitimate part in a Belasco play. Out of shape and getting fat, he thought ruefully as he reached up on tiptoe to pull the handle on the doorbell.

A tall, blonde woman opened the door a crack and peered out into the dark hall, well above his head. The woman had a round, pretty face, but there were mauve circles like bruises under her eyes and a thin, bitter set to her mouth.

"What the hell . . ."

"Excuse me," Ambrose said. "I'm looking for Mae Pepper. I'm a friend of a friend of hers."

The woman stared down at him in horror.

"Christ! What sort of friend would send *you?*"

"I beg your pardon," Ambrose said, removing his hat.

"Skip it," the woman sighed. "Beggars can't be choosers." She opened the door fully and stepped inside. She was wearing nothing but a silk wrapper and Ambrose could see the outline of her full hipped body through the gauze. He lowered his eyes.

"I hope I'm not disturbing anything."

"Not a damn thing," the woman said as she closed the door and bolted it. "Want a drink?"

"No, thank you."

"Afraid liquor'll stunt your growth?"

Ambrose ignored the crack. He was immune to disparaging comments about either his size or his pristine habits.

"What I have to tell Mrs. Pepper will only take a minute. I have a message for her from Billy Wells in California."

The woman plucked a cigarette from a pack on a table and lit it with a kitchen match that she ignited against a mottled plaster wall.

"Do what you want, it's no skin off my ass." She inhaled deeply and blew a stream of smoke through pursed lips. "She's in bed."

"I'm in no hurry."

"Take your coat off and sit down."

"No, thank you, I prefer to stand."

He would rather have died than sit on the only available space—a broken-down couch littered with articles of female apparel, mostly slips, silk stockings, camisoles and panties, spread out as though on

160

rocks to dry in the sun. He realized then that the room was virtually airless, and certainly sunless; the single window in the small living room faced a brick wall. An unvented gas heater belched raw heat into the room and the couch with its damp adornments had been turned to face it. The rest of the room was virtually barren. A table . . . a crooked lamp. That was all. Nothing on the walls but the scabrous yellow blotches of dry rot. Nothing in the air but the smell of burning gas, stale and acrid cigarette smoke, the lingering odor of fried food. He closed his eyes for a second and thought of his room at the Clarendon with its wide vistas of the Hudson and the Jersey Palisades, the cream colored walls covered with the pictures that he had bought in Paris September last on his final tour with *The Sky Highs*. The two oils by Georges Braque that had cost him a hundred dollars apiece, and the half dozen watercolors of Nice and Morocco by Raoul Dufy that had cost him no more than a few dinners and hours of enjoyable conversation about postage stamp designs in a cafe on the Rue Blondel.

The woman, who he assumed must be Anna Marie Shapely, smiled crookedly at him as she bent forward to flick ash from her cigarette in a cracked plate. Her body was a pasty white and he could see the deep folds of her abdomen and a thatch of dark hair between her thighs. He blushed and stared at his feet. Anna Maria Shapely tickled him under the chin.

"You're sorta cute, you know that? I bet you're a killer with the girls."

And then, gratefully, she was gone and he looked up only after he heard a door open and close. There was a sound of muted laughter from behind the bedroom door and then, in about five minutes, the most beautiful woman he had ever seen in his life opened the door and came into the room. Blue black hair was coiled tightly on top of her head revealing a swan-like neck. The woman's mouth was wide and sensual and the oval eyes had a smoldering luminosity that made Ambrose think that she might have a fever.

"Mae Pepper?"

"Yes," she said, drawing the folds of a heavy woolen robe tighter around her body. "So you're a friend of Billy."

"That's right. We used to room together."

"I haven't seen him in a long time. Is he doing okay on the Coast?"

"I believe he is, yes. He wants you to come out there."

"Oh?"

She leaned back against the door as though guarding it. Her eyes

161

burned more intensely than ever.

"Did he say that?"

"He wrote to me. He saw a blurb in the trades about you playing at the Tivoli. I think that he wrote you there, but you had moved on."

Her smile was a shadow. "Yes . . . moved on."

"I got your address from Joe King at Klopstein and Maguire."

"That was nice of Joe," she said with faint bitterness.

"Well, as I said, Billy wrote me and asked my help in finding you. He'd like you to come out to California. He said in his letter that he could get you a job at Sterling. He'll pay your way out, of course."

She was staring at him with an intensity that made him feel uncomfortable. He reached inside his coat and withdrew his wallet.

"I'm to advance whatever you need. Will two hundred dollars be enough?"

She glanced fearfully over her shoulder and then came to him quickly, kneeling in front of him.

"Yes" she whispered fiercely. "But I don't want the money now. Please put your wallet away and get out of here. Where can I meet you tomorrow?"

"I live at the Clarendon . . ."

She rose to her feet and pushed him toward the door. "I'll be there first thing in the morning. Goodbye."

"Goodbye," he said, stepping into the hall. "It's been nice meeting—"

The door closed in his face.

Ambrose walked slowly down the hall to the black pit of the stairwell. Gramophone jazz echoed through the walls of the old brownstone. Cheap music and loud laughter. It made him think of Oscar Wilde's *Harlot's House.* He had never slept with a woman, never having found one of his own size that he could fall in love with, and his sense of personal pride and innate fastidiousness had kept him from buying the favors of a woman of normal stature, as many affluent midgets were prone to do. But he was a wise young man who certainly knew the ways of the world even if he himself had been cut off from them by a cruel trick of genetic fate. He was not sure in his heart that Mae Pepper was whoring to keep alive, but the atmosphere in the room had depressed him. The other woman's flagrant nudity and her vaguely suggestive remarks nagged at him. Would the white-fleshed blonde, or even the exquisite Mae Pepper, have taken him to bed for a few dollars? It wasn't something he wanted to think about. He had done his favor to Billy and this was the end of his involvement. He had no desire to see Mae Pepper in the morning and made up his mind to place the money in an envelope and leave it with the desk clerk. He wrote Billy a letter that night.

. . . I located Mrs. Pepper with no trouble. She was living in the Village and we had a nice talk about you, show business, etc. She is certainly a beautiful woman and should do very well in pictures. I gave her two hundred dollars which she felt would be enough. There is no urgency in my being reimbursed. Keep well, Billy, and write from time to time. I am sending this letter by air mail and would appreciate your sending me back the envelope for my collection.

Your good friend
Ambrose.

He sat in bed late into the night and sorted aimlessly through a small mountain of loose stamps that he had dumped at the foot of the bed. His heart wasn't in it. He kept seeing the soft curves of flesh as the blonde bent over him . . . the bright luster in Mae Pepper's eyes . . . the way she held the edges of the robe tight against her body as though she, too, had been naked beneath it. He tried to think of her and Billy in a physical, carnal sense (for surely there had to be more than friendship in Billy's desire to find her and pay her way out to California). Try as he might he couldn't picture them together. It wasn't Billy's fatness in contrast to the woman's slenderness that clouded his vision of them, but rather Billy's innocence and air of naive wonderment. He doubted whether Billy knew as much about the complexities of love and sex as he did himself. Of Mae Pepper's knowledge he had no doubts whatever.

He sighed and let the stamps drift through his fingers. Some of them fluttered to the floor, tiny patches of color on the pale beige rug.

Billy waited nervously on the platform as the long train ground slowly to a stop in a haze of escaping steam. He studied his reflection in a small mirror above a vending machine, giving his bow tie a final tug and setting his straw skimmer at a slight angle. He was wearing new clothes, dark pants and a white jacket, well tailored to his girth, and he looked prosperous. His constant glances into mirrors and the glass windows of the station served to bolster that image in his mind. He remembered how Mae used to kid him about his appearance during the lean times when he had been forced to buy suits off the rack, suits that

163

had always been too tight or too baggy. Mae had an eye for men's clothing and had often said that she had fallen in love with Jimmy because he wore clothes so well. Billy cast a sideways glance at himself in the station window as he walked across the platform. What he saw was a well-tailored fat man, a bigger reflection by far than anyone around him. He had put on sleek pounds since coming to California and he wondered if Mae would make a crack about it.

He saw her before she saw him. She stood for a moment in the doorway of the train, then took the porter's hand and came down the steps.

"Gosh, she looks swell," Billy murmured before waving his hand and shouting her name. She was wearing a traveling suit of pale beige wool, a dark brown cloche covering her hair. Several men standing on the platform glanced at her. "Mae! Mae!"

"Billy!" She came toward him, walking stiffly in her hobbled skirt. He pushed his way through the crowd to reach her and embraced her with clumsy affection.

"Mae. Gee, it's good to see you. You're really a sight for sore eyes."

She kissed him lightly on the cheek and then stepped back to eye him up and down.

"You look wonderful, Billy. On top of the world."

He patted his belly and grinned foolishly. "Adding to the spare tire, I'm afraid. But the studio likes me fat . . . the fatter the better."

"Sure. Like Jimmy used to say—fat's fun."

He continued to grin at her, amazed that she was standing in front on him.

"Say, I want to show you the town. Let's get your bags and get out of here."

"I've only got one. I didn't have much to bring."

"As long as you brought yourself. That's all that counts."

The suitcase was found in the baggage room and a redcap carried it out to the car for them and placed it in the trunk. The Chandler had just been polished and it gleamed in the sun.

"This yours, Billy?"

"Bought and paid for," Billy said proudly. "I tell you, Mae, the money can sure flow out here once you get started. I've got you into pictures for sure and I just know you'll do swell."

"I hope so. I've never faced a camera before."

"You've got nothing to worry about. Not with *your* face."

"It takes more than that."

"Don't worry about it. You had the best timing of anybody I ever saw on the circuit. Remember the hotel skit? When Jimmy played the bellhop and you and I were honeymooners?"

She smiled faintly. "That was a long time ago."

"Yeah, the Follies. You used to get a laugh with your eyebrows. Boy, that was a great skit."

He wanted to ask about Jimmy but was reluctant to bring up the subject. He knew that she'd get around to telling him sooner or later and he knew in his heart that the news would be bad. How could it be otherwise? He gave her a reassuring smile and started the engine.

"You must be hungry."

"A little," she said.

"Have you ever tasted Mexican food?"

"No."

"Good. That's the first treat I've got in store for you, a stop at the old plaza for lunch. Then I'll give you the ten dollar tour from the mountains to the sea. Gee, Mae, you're going to love it here."

There was a cafe near the plaza where the tables were set up in the shade of pepper trees and a mariachi band strolled among the diners. Billy pointed out half a dozen celebrities to Mae. Selig's zoo and the Louis B. Mayer studio were only a short distance away on Mission Road. The Sennett crowd often drove over the hill from Edendale and Tony Moreno, who had an interest in the place, was usually there at his private table with some of the Vitagraph people. Billy pointed out Chester Conklin and Kalla Pasha.

"They're with Sennett," Billy said.

The names meant nothing to Mae. She picked at an enchilada covered with melted cheese.

"Don't you like it?" Billy asked.

"Very tasty," she said. "But I'm terribly tired, Billy."

"Gosh, yes, you must be worn to the bone." He bolted down the enchilada on his plate and beckoned to the waiter. "I'll get you settled in and we can see the sights tomorrow."

"I think I could sleep for a week."

"You can't sleep later than Thursday afternoon," he said with a broad smile. "That's when you meet Chester Pratt at the studio." He couldn't stop smiling. "Honest to God, Mae. I just can't get over your being here . . . in *California!*"

'I can hardly believe it myself."

"Gee, I wish. . . ." He stopped himself in a hurry before the name slipped out.

She reached across the table and placed a hand over his.

"Look, Billy, let's not act like he's dead and buried. Jimmy's alive and living with a butcher's widow in the Bronx. She's staking him to a comeback. He's working the subway circuit. You wouldn't believe all the clubs that are popping up. They're nothing but speaks, but they've all got a jazz band, a couple of chorus line tarts and a comic. Jimmy's doing pretty good, but he's drinking like a fish and he can't stay away from the hop. Our relationship is over . . . it's been over for a long time. I feel bad about it, but I ran out of tears in Cleveland."

His eyes brimmed with sympathy. "Gosh, I'm sorry, Mae. You know, you and Jimmy were . . ."

"Sure, Mister and Mrs. Santa Claus. Face reality, Billy. We had a stormy marriage, even during the good years. You must have known that."

"Yes," he said somberly. "Sure I knew it. I guess I just closed my eyes."

"Now you can open them." She gave his hand an affectionate squeeze. "We're in California and the sun is shining. You're going up in the world and so am I. To hell with yesterday."

He had rented an apartment for her on the fourth floor of his building, a single, one large room with a Murphy bed hidden in the wall, a good-sized bathroom and a small kitchen. Like all of the other apartments at the Cabrillo Arms it was furnished in Spanish style.

"I hope you like it," Billy said. "It was the only vacancy they had and I took it for a month."

"It's lovely." She walked to one of the windows and gazed out. A garden was below her. Palm trees, bougainvillea, clumps of star jasmine. The hills of Griffith Park were in the distance, lush and green after the winter rains. "But you didn't have to do it, Billy. I could have stayed with you."

"Heck, Mae, I'm in the chips," he said blithely. "This isn't Cedar Rapids. Remember? All of us in one room . . . two blankets . . . ten below zero outside."

"That isn't what I meant."

Her voice was so quiet he could barely hear her. He knew what she meant. It was all he had thought about lately, to ask her or not to ask her. His ears began to burn and his collar felt like a noose.

"You don't owe me anything. A train ticket."

"More than that, Billy."

"So I helped you out."

166

"You saved my life."

"Christ, we've known each other forever."

"A lot of people have known me forever. You're the only one who held a hand out." She turned away from the window. The sunlight was behind and her face was shadowed. "That counts with me, Billy. Every guy I've known lately has kicked me in the teeth."

She was no more than ten feet away from him, but she might as well have been in China. She was waiting for him, but he couldn't make his feet move. God, he thought miserably, if it was any woman but Mae Pepper.

"I . . . I don't want you to feel . . . obligated. No. Not in any way." He was beginning to sweat, globs of moisture rolling down his back. He had never felt so fat, so gross. "Christ, you've been like a sister to me."

You roger her yet, fat guy? Or can't you get it past your gut?

"I'm not your sister, Billy."

"I know it. It's just that . . . that . . ." It was impossible to explain. His brain whirled with a thousand reasons. She had said to hell with yesterday, but yesterday hung over both of them like a cloud. She was there, but so was Jimmy, tall and bony, lips curled in a sardonic smile.

She came close to him and the scent of her perfume blinded him like a bright light. She touched his cheek with a cool, soft hand.

"Oh, Billy, you're such a dear, sweet sappy guy."

COMING ATTRACTIONS

It amused Harry Ashbaugh to invite Vardon Bolling to play a round of golf at Rancho Vista Country Club. It was amusing because Bolling had applied five times for membership, listing his occupation as "industrialist." Five times he had been blackballed by the membership committee and his application and check for twenty thousand dollars returned to him. The amusing thing about it was the fact that the last application had only been blackballed by one member of the committee and that member had been Harry Ashbaugh.

"Well, Vardon," Harry Ashbaugh said. "How do you like your lie?"

Bolling, a handsome figure in his impeccably tailored plus fours and tweed jacket, squinted against the sun and asked his caddy for a spoon.

"Spoon, eh?" Ashbaugh said, rolling a cold cigar from one side of his mouth to the other. "I'd use an iron myself and drop the ball this side of the sand."

"No doubt you would," Bolling muttered as he addressed his ball.

167

He felt angry. He resented being patronized, as he sensed he had been since arriving at the country club. He was an outsider, there only by the good grace of a member, and the men who made up the foursome had pointed that out in subtle ways. They had talked over his head about club matters, a contemplated grand fete for the fourth of July. The debutante ball. The current standing in the tennis tournament. Pompous, arrogant men, secure in the knowledge that *their* money had been built on good, solid, *respectable* foundations. (One of the men manufactured the sewer pipes that ran beneath the streets of Los Angeles, and the other owned a Pasadena bank.)

Anger gave strength to his arms and surety to his grip. The wooden clubhead descended with force and power. The ball sailed off, skimming the clipped grass and then rising in a graceful trajectory that carried it over the distant bunkers and onto the green beyond. It was a shot that would have made Walter Hagen proud.

"Not bad," Ashbaugh said as he trudged into the rough after his own ball. "Not bad at all."

The whisky in the clubhouse bar was not bootleg. It came from the vast cellars beneath the ornate Victorian building. The members of the club had voted to a man for prohibition, but they had taken the precaution to stock those cool catacombs to the bursting point with wines, cordials, brandies and hard spirits before the law went into effect. They had never thought of it as a law that applied to them anyway. Prohibition had been designed to keep the poor from squandering their money on booze. Gentlemen could hold their liquor and drink with grace. Why, even the president kept a bottle handy. Harry Ashbaugh had had more than one drink with Harding, Secretary of the Interior Albert B. Fall or Attorney General Daugherty right there in the White House.

"Well, Vardon," Harry Ashbaugh said, "here's mud in your eye."

Harry Ashbaugh drank his whisky straight. He was a tall, craggy-faced man of fifty-two with short, curly gray hair and bushy gray eyebrows. His eyes were gray, too, and as cold as slate. Harry Ashbaugh had the eyes of a gambler, which he was. He had parlayed a minor strike in the oil fields of Pennsylvania into a million dollars worth of oil leases at Spindletop, and that million into untold millions in Oklahoma, West Texas and California. He had started life as a two-fisted roughneck and now he was a man who drank with presidents and had lunch with kings, but the gloss was less than skin deep. His nails, Bolling noted, badly needed cutting.

"And to you, Harry."

"Hell, Vardon, we only seem to have a snort or two at conventions or party fund raisers. This makes a nice change, damned if it don't."

"Yes, it does."

Bolling sipped a gin and grenadine cocktail, his gaze wandering. They were seated at a table in the room reserved for male golfers only. The walls were paneled in mahogany and there were silver cups on shelves and framed photographs of tournament winners and famous guests on the walls. Willie Anderson's picture was among them, as was John McDermott's and Walter Hagen's. Beyond bay windows of leaded glass stretched the eighteenth green, shadowed now in the late afternoon by sycamore and elm. This country club, California's most exclusive, was also its most beautiful and the view of the trees swaying against the sky, the greensward rolling like an emerald sea toward the foothills of the San Gabriel's brought a lump to Bolling's throat. He was there, but he was outside of it because of a stupid prejudice against his profession. It was so damned unfair he felt his hand shake with suppressed rage as he lifted his glass to his lips.

"You know something, Vardon," Harry Ashbaugh said. "I'm getting bored with the oil game. Yes, sir, all the fun's gone out of it. Running out of land, that's the trouble. A man looks for a likely spot to sink a hole and then finds the land staked out by the real estate developers. Why, I know of some property down Long Beach way that just cries out for test drilling, but you know what's on that land? Bungalows! Five solid acres of bungalows! And each bungalow has an orange tree in the backyard and a flivver in the driveway."

"And those flivvers use gasoline and oil," Bolling said with a faint smile.

The oilman nodded. "That's a fact, Vardon, but that's a job for all the pencil pushers I hire. Consolidation, that's the word now in the oil game. Consolidation and marketing. We use what we've got and most of us have just about the same amount of chips. Gasoline stations, that's the way we all go now. You'll be seeing my Indian Head sign all over the state, and as I build one station on a corner the other boys'll be building one right across the street. Four to every major intersection, one of mine and three of theirs." He signalled for the liveried waiter and the man glided over bearing a double shot of bourbon on a silver tray. "Not much of a challenge there, Vardon. To tell you the truth, we're all hand in glove on this. Not like the old days when we toted shotguns along with the drilling rig and used 'em, too. Times are changing. This Townsend highway bill for instance. A billion dollars or more to be spent on roads. Over a quarter of million men working now, building highways to hell and gone. Gasoline stations, Vardon, that's what all the drilling has come down to and we're all in the game. No fun in that."

Bolling sipped his drink. He was not a drinker. One was his limit and he always managed to make it last throughout an entire social event.

"Why are you telling me all this, Harry? Are you thinking of retiring?"

Harry Ashbaugh snorted and downed his whisky in one gulp.

"No. I still have a surprise or two to pull before I cash in my chips. I've been looking in your neck of the woods, if you want to know the truth."

Bolling choked on his drink. "Motion . . . pictures?" he gasped.

"I was wrong about it. Just closed my eyes to it. Should have known better when I saw all those Jews getting out of the cloak and suit business. They saw something in those nickels that I didn't. I give you credit, Vardon. You saw what they saw . . . and only you and Zukor see what's ahead . . . as do I."

Bolling dabbed at his mouth with a linen handkerchief. "I don't think I follow you, Harry."

"You follow me all right. Theaters. They're just like gasoline stations, only you boys have the gloves off. Bare knuckles—knock 'em down and drag 'em out. The man who controls the picture palaces controls the business lock, stock and barrel. Now, that's the kind of fight I'd like to get into."

"There's a lull in that fight, Harry. The FTC filed a suit against Zukor for restraint of trade. I expect to be served myself. The independent theater owners are crying foul, claiming that Famous-Players and Sterling are trying to lock them out of the marketplace. They have a point, but, personally, I have a clean conscience about it. Why shouldn't Zukor and I own our own theaters to show our own product? What's wrong in that?"

"Why, nothing as far as I can see. That's just good old American business sense." He leaned forward across the table and lowered his voice to a whisper. Not that it was at all necessary—there was no one seated near them. "I am very close to certain people who are *very* close to the President. You know the gentlemen. We all shared a drink and a cigar or two at the convention. I have the assurance of these gentlemen that Mister Harding thinks the same way as you and Zukor about this theater business. Mr. Harding has no bleeding heart attitude when

170

it comes to a beneficial monopoly. He isn't about to stop Henry Ford from making a cheap car and he isn't about to prevent men from acquiring chains of picture palaces. No, sir, he is not about to lend a hand in preventing that at all."

"That's nice to know," Bolling said guardedly. He tried to read the truth of that statement in Harry Ashbaugh's eyes, but there was nothing to be read there. The eyes were stone.

"Nice to know? Vardon, you tickle the hell out of me. You should be whooping with joy. I was in Washington a week ago and had a very interesting talk with Daugherty on some other matters of concern to me, and then all of that FTC business came up. I asked him straight out. I said, Harry, how is this monopoly suit by the Trade Commission against Famous-Players-Lasky going to affect Indian Head gasoline stations? And he said, Harry, as far as the Justice Department is concerned, not in any goddamned way. It is not the *American* way to limit the expansion of free enterprise. Well now, that got me to thinking. I enjoy going to motion pictures, just like every other man, woman and child in this country. It's not a nickel through the turnstile operation any longer."

"No, it isn't."

"It's a major industry. Zukor was right in saying that the baby is growing into a giant. I *like* giants, Vardon."

"As do we all."

"And I want to get my feet wet. You and Zukor are going to need a lot of fresh cash. Let Zukor go to Kuhn, Loeb. You don't have to put yourself in the hands of those Wall Street sharks . . . you can come to me."

"That is certainly something to think about," Bolling said, struggling to keep his voice steady, to maintain the proper objective tone. The question of Wall Street financing in order to increase his theater holdings had been much on his mind lately. Kuhn, Loeb and Company had floated ten million dollars worth of securities for Zukor, a sum that the private coffers of Sterling Pictures could not possibly match. Sam Goldwyn had a group of individuals behind him, including the du Ponts. The message was clear: finance or perish. And now Harry Ashbaugh of Ashbaugh Oil was asking to buy a stack of chips.

"I'll talk things over with my attorneys, Harry. Just in a general way —sound them out about it."

Harry Ashbaugh removed a leather cigar case trimmed with gold from his pocket and offered a cigar to Bolling.

171

"You do that, Vardon. Tell them that I am thinking in terms of a partnership and a reorganization of the Sterling structure. The infusion of say . . . fifteen million dollars into the theater division should make some people sweat. It's my understanding that Kuhn, Loeb believe that fifty first rate theaters in the proper places would skim all the cream from the milk."

"Absolutely."

"Then I think we should seriously talk about how to go about skimming it. Might take a little time to iron out all the wrinkles, but it could be time pleasantly spent." He lit Bolling's cigar and then his own. "Why don't you join the club, Vardon? That way we could combine business with some first rate golf playing. And seeing as how I control the membership committee I don't see any problem in getting you selected. How about it, Vardon? Or do you have to talk that over with your lawyers, too?"

"No, Harry," he said, barely trusting his voice. "I can make that decision on my own."

CASSETTE

I'm sure you remember this still.

Let's see. Well, I'll be damned. Of course I remember it, but I don't think I've seen that picture in fifty years. I'm in there somewhere.

You're standing directly behind Doll Fairbaine.

That's right, so I am.

There's no caption and the librarian at the Academy wasn't certain of its place in the archives. It was in the Sterling Pictures general collection. What was the occasion? A groundbreaking ceremony of some kind?

No. As far as I can recall it was a visit by Harry Ashbaugh and his group. A short time after this picture was taken, the name of the studio was changed to SBA, Sterling–Bolling–Ashbaugh. Ashbaugh bought into Sterling and used Ashbaugh Oil stock as collateral for loans from the Bank of Italy. That's A. P. Giannini standing between Ashbaugh and Bolling.

Do you recognize all of the people in the picture?

Some of the men were from the bank, or from the oil company, but I recognize all of the Sterling crowd.

That's Chester Pratt, isn't it?

Yes, with cross-eyed Andy Farrel and Tom Pipp. All of Sterling's top

172

players are in the front row: Pipp, Farrel, Homer Roth, Hobart Boswell, Marie Rhodes, Virginia Ervine . . . Doll. The stock players are in the back. There's Billy Wells and Kewpie Dolan. They were the two fat men on the lot, but Billy was the better actor. Kewpie died in a car crash with Pratt. A nice guy.

Is that Dave Dale?

Yes.

I didn't recognize him without his glasses.

His eyes were fine in the early days. They started going bad much later. He was nearly blind at the end and had to have a special magnifying glass fitted into his Moviola. Didn't bother him any more than it bothered Beethoven not to be able to hear all the notes. He worked by feel—sense—won all those Oscars half blind or not.

Who's that man? An actor?

No, Doll's brother, Niles. The tall blonde next to him was Ashbaugh's daughter.

And the dark-haired woman on the far right?

I don't remember her name.

A beauty.

Yes, she was.

It's a terrific picture. Very historic. Everyone looks so *enthusiastic.* All of you seem to be aware that you're part of the golden age.

Well, I don't know about that, but we're all smiling.

Bolling was stuck and he was smart enough to know it. Still, Doll was happy and that's what really counted. She was working like a plow horse and her latest picture had been her best. Her face glowed on the screen with an inner joy. Everyone who had seen the rough cut swore that it was the greatest Fairbaine picture ever. It would make a million. So what was a few thousand dollars? Hell, he thought, it wasn't the money, it was the idea that the red headed sonofabitch had pulled a fast one on him. Earl P. Donovan was now a bona fide producer on the lot with his own office and a full time secretary. Christ! The bastard didn't know the first thing about motion pictures. The only thing he knew how to do was please Doll. That was something, he supposed. A woman loved is a woman beautiful, as Mrs. Bolling was apt to say from time to time. There was probably some truth in that, although he didn't quite understand why. But there was no point in brooding about Donovan. He tried not to think about the bastard at all, except that his presence during this visit by Harry Ashbaugh and the bankers was so pervasive.

Always walking beside Doll . . . seated across the table from him at lunch. No matter where he looked he had seen that shock of red hair. He struggled to shift his thoughts to other things, to what was important. The complicated deal had been signed. Stock transfers had been made. Sterling Pictures, studio facilities and theater holdings, were now linked to Ashbaugh Oil, if not body to body at least hand to hand. Giannini had eagerly accepted Ashbaugh stock as collateral for big loans. They needed ready cash to beat Zukor to the punch in buying out the smaller theater circuits in the South, Midwest and New England and to buy up strategically located independent theaters. To meld those fragments into one vast network of picture palaces. All first run houses. Plush seats. Ornate lobbies and facades. Dress the ushers in smart military uniforms. Hire pretty young girls, too—usherettes. A "Sterling Palace" or "Sterling Hippodrome" in every decent sized town in the country and every one of them showing nothing but Sterling pictures. And what pictures they would be! Scenarios by world famous authors. The best directors and cameramen. The most popular screen personalities. Lesser companies making lesser pictures would be forced to show their shabby products in shabby houses. Converted nickelodeons. Hard seats and creaky projection machines. Flicker hole-in-the-walls on back streets. It would take fifteen million or more. A whirlwind campaign of buying. A tough crew of salesmen to acquire the independently owned theaters in the best locations, men tougher than those working for Zukor—"the wrecking crew," as Stephen Lynch and his boys were known. Harry Ashbaugh knew how to do that. His real estate men had been buying corner lots at strategic crossroads for the past two years. They had the technique down to a science, knew how to play on an owner's fear and greed. *"The carrot and the stick,"* Harry had said one afternoon after blasting his ball from a bunker with a wedge. *"Carrot and stick—and the stick a damn sight bigger than the carrot."*

"How about a big smile, Mr. Bolling? Fine! Hold it everybody. Thank you very much."

174

NINE SECONDS FROM HEAVEN

It was funny. In all of his thirty-three years of living he had never seen his name in print, but there it was, big as life on the front page of *The Moving Picture Weekly,* in the middle of a column entitled Minerva's Hollywood.

E. P. Donovan is a new producer on the Sterling lot and rumor hath it that he is number one in lovable Doll Fairbaine's heart. The popular screen star has been too busy with her fantastic career to pay much attention to this town's list of eligible bachelors, and as your correspondent reported last month in this column, her sparking with the popular Charles Ray was nothing to be taken seriously. Mr. Donovan is from a fine old Massachusetts family and the personal protege of Vardon Bolling. Young Mr. Thalberg at Universal had best look to his laurels!

Donovan scanned the column carefully, but there was no further mention of him. *E. P. Donovan.* The initials gave a certain dignity to his name, a connotation of success, like B. P. Schulberg or J. P. Morgan. That might fool the readers of the magazine, but it didn't give Donovan any bloated ideas about himself. Vardon Bolling's protege! He wondered who had thought that one up.

He folded the magazine and flipped it into a wastebasket where it landed with a dull thud. The basket had been empty. Not much scrap paper accumulated in the office of E. P. Donovan Productions. The office was in the production building, a few doors down the hall from Chester Pratt's suite of offices where typewriters clacked from early morning to late night and where gag men and writers spilled out into

175

the hall in frenzies of argument. Wastebaskets overflowed in those offices like so many stopped-up storm drains.

Donovan sat on the edge of his pristine desk and lit a Camel. The door to the outer office was partially open and he could see his secretary behind her desk. She was filing her nails and taking her time about it. It was ten o'clock in the morning and another long day stretched ahead for both of them.

"Miss Blackwood," he called out, "you can go home if you want. I'll be out of the office all day."

She left her desk and stood in the doorway. "Shouldn't I be here in case the telephone rings?"

It was a gesture. The telephone never rang unless Doll called, and she was up at Big Bear on location.

"That's okay, Miss Blackwood. Don't worry about it."

She needed no further urging and was off like a shot.

Ten-fifteen. Donovan lit another cigarette and then picked up his telephone and asked the PBX girl to connect him with Bolling's office. That, too, was a gesture because he never got any further than Bolling's secretary, the efficient and protective Rose Hanover.

"Mr. Bolling is in conference, Mr. Donovan," Rose Hanover said.

"Do you know when he'll be free?"

"I'm sorry, Mr. Donovan, but he'll be busy all day. I'll leave word that you called."

Calling Bolling was a pointless ritual. Donovan understood the strategy well enough. The publicity department was busy sending out statements to the press—of which the item in *The Moving Picture Weekly* was one—planting the idea that E. P. Donovan was an important producer. They might even put his name on the credit titles of Doll's newest picture. Bolling knew that keeping the marriage secret was impossible for any length of time. It would be announced when E. P. Donovan was established as a man worthy of such a prize.

In theory there were sixty thousand dollars on the books to finance a picture that E. P. Donovan would make, the profits from said picture to be split equally between Donovan and Sterling. That deal had been put down in black and white with Doll as a witness after their return from Mexico. After breaking the glad news to Bolling and showing him the marriage paper. Bolling's face had turned from purple to paste, but he had kept his composure. He had remained calm.

"It may be some time before we can fit Mr. Donovan's project into the schedule, Doll," he had said.

That news hadn't bothered her, if indeed she had even heard him. Her happiness was complete. Her Earl would have an office on the lot . . . a secretary . . . his name on a door . . . a place to go every day.

"We can come to the studio together, Earl!" Walking hand in hand to school.

"I *will* make a picture," Donovan had said, looking Bolling straight in the eye.

"Of course you will," Bolling had replied with a tight smile. "When you have a scenario—actors, a director—you just come to me and I'll give the okay."

When hell freezes.

Gales of laughter came down the hall from one of Pratt's offices. Gag men at work. The sound mocked the silence of the room. Donovan dropped his cigarette on the floor and crushed it with his foot. Ten-thirty.

He left the office and walked across the lot, not going anywhere in particular, just trying to walk off his frustrations. A couple of secretaries passed him and gave him arch, knowing smiles before hurrying on their way, heads close together, tittering—or so it seemed to Donovan. Rumors about his relationship with Doll were pandemic, with each section of the studio having its own pet theory. He wondered how many people on the lot had read the latest issue of *Motion Picture Weekly. "the personal protege of Vardon Bolling."* Perhaps the comedy writers had been laughing at that and not at their own jokes.

He only felt comfortable around the workers, the carpenters, electricians, painters and property men, almost all of whom had worked in the carny and circus world before drifting into motion pictures. He had spotted them instantly by the way they walked and the slang they used. And they had spotted him, and had given him the high sign. Had he shouted *Hey, Rube* at the top of his lungs they would have come running.

Ten-forty-five. There was activity outside Stage 2, a large crowd of extras in costumes of the French Revolution milling around while a squad of assistant directors bearing megaphones struggled to herd them into some kind of order. *A Tale of Two Cities* was being made, utilizing the most expensive sets that the studio had ever constructed. Further swarms of extras, dressed as colonial Americans, were being shepherded toward Stage 5 where Niles Fairbaine was directing *Father of His Country.* Donovan spotted the burly figure of Dave Dale as he darted in and out of the crowd, trying to keep his Green Mountain boys

177

and Minutemen from becoming hopelessly mixed up with Jacobin soldiery and the Paris mob. The activity was frenzied and the atmosphere only increased Donovan's feeling of depression and impotence. He was being cut off from this carnival of greasepaint and costumes, lights and cameras. Bolling had pigeonholed him and there wasn't a damn thing he could do about it.

"Niles is anxious to help you when you find the right story," Doll had said one night when Niles was at the ranch for dinner.

Niles had only smiled across the table as though saying, *"My sister is such a child. You and I know better, don't we?"*

Not that he wanted Niles' help. He had watched the man on the set enough times to know how incompetent he was. He was a director because it pleased Doll to see her brother working, just as it pleased her to see her husband's name on an office door. The only thing that concerned Doll at the moment was the secrecy of her marriage. She longed to tell the world, but Bolling had convinced her to wait until her last picture, *Polly Ann,* was in release. In the meantime, the publicity department would continue to slip the name of E. P. Donovan into their press releases. A phantom personage was being slowly created. A dynamic young producer, Thalberg's cross-town rival. It was enough to make Donovan puke.

Eleven-o'clock. He felt in the way. A bystander. An outsider. Sweating assistant directors corraled the last of their charges and drove them inside the stages with megaphoned curses and threats. A studio musician, violin tucked under his arm, ran toward Stage 5 to provide mood music for General Washington's passionate farewell to his Martha before going to the wars.

Eleven-ten. There was no point in walking around looking conspicuous and so he ambled back to the office. Miss Blackwood's typewriter was covered. The phone sat like a black ornament on her desk. Nothing moved in the tomb but a spiral of dust in a shaft of sunlight—and a thin coil of tobacco smoke drifting from the mausoleum of his own office. He stepped into the doorway between the two rooms to see Frank Gilboy seated in a chair, smoking a cigarette and reading the rumpled copy of *Motion Picture Weekly* that he had retrieved from the wastebasket.

"What the hell do you want?" Donovan said.

Gilboy looked up from the paper. His eyes were heavylidded and weary.

"You busy?"

"Do I look it?"

"Just wondered." He refolded the paper and chucked it back into the basket. "You get a laugh out of it?"

"What do you think?" Donovan snapped.

"At least they spelled your name right. What the hell difference does it make?"

"It makes a difference to me," Donovan said as he walked to his desk. "Bolling's protege! What kind of crap is that?"

"They're building you up, Bub. They don't want Doll getting hitched to just any old Tom, Dick or Harry."

"Tell 'em to lay off. That's your department, isn't it?"

Gilboy squashed his cigarette between his fingers and tossed the still smoking residue into the wastebasket. "It was—and it wasn't. I had a lot of duties around here."

"Had?"

"I turned in the badge, so to speak. These Ashbaugh guys are going to be a pain in the ass."

"Why tell me about it?"

The big man shrugged his shoulders. "We've got no beef, Donovan. So you pulled a slicker on the boss. That's no skin off my nose. It was bound to happen sooner or later. What the hell, she could've done worse."

"Thanks." He leaned against the corner of the desk. He felt taut, explosive. It wouldn't have taken much to trigger him. Gilboy sensed it and smiled wryly.

"I'm just a bull to you, ain't I? Once a bull always a bull. Okay, and so what? This is a funny kind of business. It doesn't mean buttons what you were before you got into it. Zukor made fur coats. Bolling and Goldwyn sold gloves. Lou Mayer peddled scrap iron. This Valentino bird that everybody's going nuts about was a waiter. Me, I was a cop. I don't know what the hell you were, but I could make a good guess."

"You really ask for it."

"Any time you want to try, go ahead. I'll give you one free swing."

They stared at each other without malice. Donovan jammed his hand into his pockets. Gilboy dug wax out of his ear.

"The old man's got you in a box. He won't help you because he hates your guts. He'll put your name on a lot of pictures that you had nothing to do with because that suits his purpose and makes Doll happy. Doll doesn't care if you make pictures or you don't make pictures as long as you're home for dinner. I've known the girl for years. She's pretty

179

as a sunrise but she's got a twelve-year-old mind."

A typewriter began to chatter in another part of the building, the sound dulled by the walls.

"You go right for the throat, don't you?" Donovan said.

"I don't beat around the bush, if that's what you mean. A spade's a spade in my book. I'll put my cards on the table. I'm leaving the studio and taking Tom Pipp with me. Bolling gave me the kid's contract with his blessing."

"Why? I thought he was a moneymaker around here?"

"Sure. The kid's pictures clean up. *Photoplay* says he'll be right up there with Keaton.

"And the old man's dropping him?"

"Off the lot as of today."

"Just like that?"

"Well, he's been thinking about it for a couple of months. Paying the kid, but not working him . . . for some reason."

Donovan turned away from the desk and opened a window. "Your cards are on the table, Gilboy, but they're face down."

"I'm giving you first shot at the little guy. Of course, it'll mean you'll have to leave here, but, what the hell, you're not exactly burning the joint up, are you? You just go to the old man and tell him you're going independent. That you're planning to rent space at the Simberg studio, or from the Cohen brothers, and turn out a feature starring Pipp. He can't stop you from going and he'll have to give you that thirty grand. You've got him by the short hairs on that, con."

"You're trying to kid a kidder, Gilboy. You're talking like a bo selling a gold brick to a rube."

Gilboy pulled a wrinkled cigarette from his vest pocket and smoothed it between his fingers.

"Okay, Donovan, the cards are up. Pipp's out because he scares the pants off the old man. The kid's a boozer. He never lushes on the job, but when the shooting's over he takes off for a periodical. You could sink a lot of dough in a picture and if Pipp did something stupid you couldn't sell it for scrap. Mr. Will H. Hays would see to that. Taking him is a risk, but you don't strike me as a guy who'd be afraid of risks. You can't sell a picture today without a star and I'm offering you one. Take it or leave it."

"Don't rush me." He began to pace the office. He knew it by heart . . . seven paces to the filing cabinet . . . seven paces back to the desk. He'd been prowling the office for weeks like a caged animal.

"It's a clean deal, Donovan. You can start right off with a guy who can bring shekels into the box office."

"A rummy, huh?"

"I can handle the kid."

"I hate drunks."

"You can't make much of a picture these days with thirty grand, but you'll find all kinds of people willin' to lend dough on Pipp. For instance—"

"I said . . . *I hate drunks.*"

Gilboy lit his cigarette and blew a perfect smoke ring toward the window.

"He never hits the bottle on the set. Not like some Paramount stars I could mention."

"I'm not interested." He qualified that. "In Paramount stars."

Donovan traversed the office a couple of times and then sat in his chair behind the desk, tilting it back to stare at the ceiling, as though the answer to everything lay hidden in the round glass bowl covering the light fixture. Maggie Klopf, the great Madama Tauras, used to read the future in glass bowls. She always swore that it wasn't a trick, that she sensed the future by staring hard into the eyes of the people seated across the table from her in the gypsy tent. The eyes are the mirror of the soul, she used to say. Donovan switched his gaze and looked at Gilboy. He saw the eyes of an honest man.

"Why the hell did you come to me, Gilboy?"

Another smoke ring, more perfect than the first, drifted lazily toward the window.

"Because I think you're a gambler. Sennett, Bill Fox, Roach, boys like that . . . they don't have to take risks. They've probably heard one or two stories about Pipp and they're cold on the kid. Bolling found that out when he tried to dump the contract."

Donovan's laugh was short, explosive and laced with scorn.

"And if I sign the guy, I'd have to pay his salary out of my own pocket until I could raise dough. Then I go around and find that everyone and his uncle has heard the same damn stories."

"Wrong. The only thing the banks or distributors know about Pipp is what they read on the box office receipts. His pictures make money. Pipp has *fans.* Keep that in mind . . . *Pipp has fans.*"

"Okay. I'll take your word on it. But Fox and Sennett aren't the only guys in this town making pictures. There must be a lot of people who'd take a chance on Pipp."

"Sure there are." He dribbled cigarette ash at his feet. "Christie'd take a shot . . . so would Joe Simberg. But I'll be dead straight with you on this. They won't go for anything but a one picture deal—salary and not a damn thing more. I want percentages . . . a piece of the pie for him *and* me. And I'm not talking about two reelers with . . ."

"What makes you think I'd part with a share?"

"Why not? What have you got to lose? What's fifteen or twenty percent of nothing? Hell, I tell you money can be raised on Pipp—and I'm not talking about two reelers. The swing is to features and that's the way to go. Five . . . six reels. A real story with a beginning, middle and end, not just a lot of slapstick and chases. I figure you'd need seventy-five grand for a feature and it should gross five . . . six hundred thousand if it grossed a penny."

"I could probably get seventy-five grand without using Pipp to raise it."

Gilboy's smile was faint. "Yeah? You think you can get that kind of money out of Doll? I got news for you, kid, she can't buy Fanny a dog collar without the Levin brothers okaying the check. She made that kind of a deal with them years ago and it was the smartest thing she ever did. Niles tried to tap her for a hundred grand once to make a picture and the Levins turned it down cold. She pouted for a month, but they stuck to their guns. They think pictures are lousy investments."

Doll had never discussed her financial arrangements, but Donovan had sensed that Myron and Arnold Levin controlled the purse strings. Now he knew. It was just as well—he hadn't wanted to go to her anyway.

"Fifteen percent is a big share."

"Fifteen *or* twenty," Gilboy said evenly. "It all depends on how tough it is to put a package together. I'll have to shop around. FBO . . . maybe First National. I don't know. Money's out there, but we don't want to give an arm and a leg to get it."

"We? What are we, partners all of a sudden?"

The big man sighed like a weary elephant and squashed the fire from his smoke between two fingers.

"Maybe I'm wasting my time here. I've been watching you go round in circles and I thought you might appreciate a hand. You know something, Red, you've got a lot going for you. You're Doll's husband and the whole world'll know about that in a week or two. And you've got the nerve of a brass ape, but you can't tie strings into a rope. You're

182

a small towner and there are men out there who'll cut you up like a piece of beef steak. Okay, you look at me and all you see is a big gumshoe blowing smoke in your office, but I've been around this business since before the war and I know my way through the woods. I could dig up more bones than a dog in a tan yard and everybody knows it. There are some men in this town who just pee in their pants when they see me coming, but I was a good cop, I never blabbed then and I don't blab now. That counts for something. Respect. I can walk into any office and they'll listen to what I got to say. Partners? Hell, you can be the producer . . . the boss . . . the guy with his name in lights, I don't give buttons for that. I want Pipp to get his twelve hundred a week plus five percent of the deal. I only get commission. Ten percent—which I will work my butt off for, let me tell you. I'll put your little show on the road because I know where to go and what to do when I get there. You want me to keep on talking?"

Donovan settled back in his chair. "Mister Gilboy, I got all the time in the world."

CASSETTE

There was a series of articles in *Cahiers du Cinema* a few years ago written by Gerard Dubec, in which he traced the role of Hollywood agents. He began, in that typical *New Yorker* style you know, with the present, the MCA's, CMA's, Abe Lastfogel's, and then he went back to the beginnings, to the powerhouse agents of the thirties, the Orsatti brothers, Jaffe, Gilboy Associates. The reason I bring this up is because Dubec mentioned that you had a lot to do with Frank Gilboy's start as an agent. That you were, in a sense, the godfather of the agency structure as we know it today. Did you ever read those articles?

No.

Would you say that that was a fitting observation on his part?

I'd say it was a lot of crap. Now you take those Frenchmen with their *cinema* this and their *cinema* that, they talk so much junk most of the time. They really get carried away. That's a ridiculous thing to say about me, I don't know what the hell he means by it. Back in the silent days there were very few agents. The big agents, the Broadway theatrical managers, they wouldn't touch motion picture people. They just never did get a toe hold on the Coast until the thirties. People made their own deals in the early days, or had a relative make their deals the way Syd Chaplin made deals for Charlie. Why, there were very few

183

stars who even had business managers. That's why so many of them died in the poorhouse. Valentino . . . all the money that man made . . . just staggering to think about. He spent it as fast as he made it. Lucky to die while he still had a few bucks to pay for his funeral. Keaton, a millionaire, spent every penny. Langdon . . . they gave Harry a fortune to make his own pictures. Didn't know a dollar from a doorknob, that man. Died broke. A sad thing. Doll, Harold Lloyd, Swanson, and oh, many others of course, got good advice and became richer and richer, but so many stars were just children when it came to money. They made so much of it so fast. No taxes to speak of—the stock market going up to the sky. Hell, life was an ice cream cone. Frank Gilboy understood them. When he took a client he handled everything: their careers, their money. It made them rich . . . made him rich.

There's a wall of mystery around him that I find very difficult to penetrate. Even men who worked at the Gilboy agency during the thirties and early forties seem reluctant to talk about the man in any depth.

That's because they didn't know him. They can't tell you anything because they don't know anything. Frank was a loner . . . a recluse. He built that beautiful building in Beverly Hills . . . had all those agents working for him. They were all young, all wearing the same dark grey suits. Gestapo headquarters, that's what they called the place in '39, '40. Gestapo headquarters. Frank had been a cop back around 1910 or so. He was tough, cynical, and as he got old he withdrew from people. He had a private section in that building and only a very few people could get in to see him. All those young men in grey suits and black loafers never did see him. Not once. A couple of those guys are now studio heads. Top TV packagers and they brag about how they once worked for Gilboy and what a holy terror he was and how he had RKO in his right pocket and Warners in his left pocket and all that kind of bull. They talk that way in the hope that some of the Old Hollywood glamor will rub off on them, but they never were anything but flunkies. Frank tossed a ball and they ran after it. Like dogs.

I see. Well, getting back to your relationship with him . . .

I had no relationship with him. We had a deal at one time. He handled Tom Pipp, who was an established comedy star, and I wanted Pipp to make a picture for me—*The Bubblehead* . . .

Of course!

. . . which was really the start . . .

Oh, sure.

. . . and all those Frenchmen give me a pain right where I should have pleasure.

It began to rain during the first week in November, a soft drizzle that never seemed to end. Day after day the rain drifted from an ash colored sky and all outdoor shooting was suspended until the weather should clear. Most of the comedy units relied on the great outdoors to film the chases and stunts, but it was impossible to work on the slick streets even if the light from the sky had been strong enough, which it was not. The clouds hung low and a murky pall lay over the city for three solid weeks.

No shoot—no pay. The paymaster at Sterling had stuck that little handwritten admonishment in the window of his office. It didn't apply to those extras and bit players who were working on productions that were being shot inside the stages, but it spelt hardship for Chester Pratt's stock company of comedians. The stock company actors had status as guarantee players, which meant only that if pictures were being made a guarantee player would be in them. A guarantee player could drive right onto the lot in the mornings and did not have to stand in the sun with a hundred other actors in the hope that an assistant director would pick him out of the herd and give him a day's work. But, no shoot, no pay. The sky was a dark haze. The rain came down.

Chester Pratt stared morosely through the window in his office. Rain whispered against the glass. Behind him on his desk were piles of film cans, pictures that had been cut and were now ready for his final viewing and okay. The shiny metal towers nearly obscured Billy Wells from his view. He had phoned Billy that morning and asked him to drop in. The fat man was waiting patiently, straddling a wooden chair, but now that he was in his office Pratt didn't quite know what to say to him.

"Hell, I don't think it'll ever stop."

"If it would just open up and . . ." Billy left the sentence unfinished. It was a cliché. Open up and pour . . . get it over with. It was what everyone was saying.

"Yeah," Pratt muttered, "but it won't." He shifted a stack of film cans and sat on the edge of his desk. "Well, Billy, hope you're not hurting."

"Oh, no, I have a bit of dough put aside."

"Not like that dope, Kewpie. He's in to me for fifty bucks already."

185

Billy grinned. "Me, too."

"And half a dozen other people, I bet."

"Could be."

"The nerve of the guy. He came in last week and said, 'Chester, if you don't lend me fifty bucks for eats I'll quit the company and go over to Sennett's.' Well, I looked him dead in the eye and said, 'Kewpie, you mean to tell me it ain't raining on Mack Sennett?' That shut him up in a hurry. But, what the hell, I lent him the fifty anyway."

"He's a nice guy."

"Oh, sure, he's aces."

Pratt shifted his buttocks on the hard wood desk and tapped the side of it with his heels. Billy was waiting for him to speak, to tell him why he wanted to see him. He cleared his throat uncomfortably.

"You keeping busy, kid?"

"Well, you know . . ."

"Sure."

"I was hoping that maybe you were going to shoot some interiors for the next batch."

"Interiors? No, the fact is, nothing's scheduled."

Another moment of heavy silence. Billy stared at him, puzzling over the remark.

"I mean . . . *nothing*," Pratt added quietly.

"I don't understand, Chester."

Pratt gave the side of the desk an extra vicious kick and then pushed away from the desk and began to pace the office, hands clenched behind his back. His agitated prowling made him look more foxlike than usual.

"I like you, Billy. I think you've got a barrel of talent. And damned if you don't have the best comedy mind on the lot. Always coming up with some idea we can use on the spot . . . not like those damn, drunken writers. I told Bolling more than once that we oughta pay you extra for those gag ideas, but he's a—"

"Heck, that's okay, I . . ."

"damn cheap sonofabitch. So, okay, that's how it goes. Nothing you can do about it. Actors act, writers write. That's what he told me. Anyway, that's neither here nor there, but when Pipp left—"

"Gee, Chester, that was a shock."

The director dismissed the outcry with a shake of his head.

"No shock at all to me, but it left a void, a blank space in the Blue Ribbon schedule. So, I went to the old man and I said, Vardon, I'd like to take a chance with Billy Wells . . . the fat guy. The fat guy who can *act,* the one who was in *the Follies.* Christ! You gotta spell everything out with him. If it isn't Charles *Ray* or John *Barrymore* or Tom *Mix,* he doesn't know who the hell you're talking about. Well, he just stared at the ceiling for about an hour and a half and then he looked at me kinda funny and said, 'You know, Chester, I'm not sure that all these comedies are worth the trouble.' 'What does that mean,' I asked, but then he got a phone call from New York and he never did tell me. That was two weeks ago and now I know."

There was a distant rumble that could have been thunder, or only a truck entering the lot. Billy glanced toward the window, looking away from Chester Pratt's eyes that had been suddenly fixed on him. Something had happened, something bad, and Billy felt his stomach contract as though in expectation of a sharp and painful blow.

"There are going to be some big changes around here, Billy," Pratt said, "and I wanted you to be the first to know."

"What sort of changes?" His voice was as soft as the rain.

"Harry Ashbaugh thinks big. One reelers . . . two reelers . . . that's small potatoes to him. Niles Fairbaine agrees with him, so does Bolling."

"Niles Fairbaine?"

"Closer to Ashbaugh than two bears in a barrel. About to be his son-in-law, I understand. Anyway, Bolling called me in the other day and told me the new plans. Just wants big features to go into those big, new theaters they're building. The Blue Ribbons will be phased out. He sold Farrel's contract to Sennett. Mick and Myer and the Boardinghouse Boys are being cancelled. Kaput. Just like that."

Billy licked his bottom lip which felt, and tasted, like a piece of old cardboard.

"Are you out, too, Chester?"

"No." He sounded guilty. "They're giving me a war picture to do— a flying picture. Sort of my meat, in a way. I joined the Royal Flying Corps in Canada in nineteen fourteen . . . two days after the war started. I taught aerial photography for four years. Anyway, do you know Gilbert Rostand, Bolling's chauffeur? Well, he was a French ace and he wrote a yarn about the Lafayette Escadrille and sold it to the old man. Holmes Grant and Violet Dane are doing the scenario. The budget's going to be close to a million. It's a terrific break for me. Something different, for God's sake, but I feel rotten about letting the old stock company split apart."

"That's how it goes."

187

"Sure. But I wanted you to hear about it from me and not read it in the papers tomorrow. Maybe I can get you on the picture, but we won't be shooting for months."

"I understand." He couldn't see himself in it anyway. Audiences would laugh at the sight of a fat soldier and war pictures were always serious.

"If you're smart you'll hot foot it over to Edendale and see what's cooking at Sennett's. Or you could try Vitagraph. Larry Semon's a friend of mine. I'd be happy to give him a ring."

"I know Semon." He'd be lucky to get a single day's work out of the man. His face showed it.

"Cheer up, Billy. It's not the end of the world. You've got a talent as big as your body and you'll do just fine."

He tried to eke some comfort from those words as he ran through the rain to where he had parked his car. It had been a truck after all and not thunder that he had heard. A dozen trucks, their loads of lumber covered with tarps, rumbled down the main studio street toward the back lot. A small, damp group of studio carpenters stood under the eaves of the wardrobe bungalow watching them pass. They were all smiling.

"Hi there, Billy," one of the men called out.

Billy ducked among them as a passing truck sent a spray of water into the air from its back wheels.

"What's all the wood for, Tom?" Billy asked.

"Sets," the carpenter said, grinning. "A year's work. Honest to God, Billy, you wouldn't believe it. Three sets for *Robin Hood* . . . sets for something called *When Knights Were Bold* . . . a French village set for some war picture. A year's work, honest to God."

One man's misery is another man's joy.

He would be just another fat man looking for a job in pictures. He was more expert in his craft than most and could do a 108, or any other kind of pratfall, without breaking his neck, but so could a lot of other fat men. Getting a day's work here and there would be no problem, but it would be tough finding anything even remotely like the security he had enjoyed at Sterling. His income was about to take a plunge from very good to very rotten. He had enough savings to cushion him for a couple of months, but after that . . . He tried to dismiss the unthinkable from his mind as he parked the car in front of his apartment building. The place looked somber in the rain, the bricks stained almost black by the incessant drizzle, the palms untidy with their sodden skirts of dead fronds. He walked through the chill lobby and took the elevator up to Mae's floor and knocked on her door.

She was getting dressed to go out and was wearing a blue silk kimono over her slip.

"You look like something the cat dragged in," she said. "What's the matter?"

"I just got a kick in the butt." He slumped onto her couch with an explosive sigh of misery and told her all about it while she heated up a pot of coffee.

"So what?" she said. "They're not the only picture company in the world."

He glared at her. "That's easy for you to say. You can get all the bit work you want. I'm not that easy to cast."

She sat next to him on the couch and lit a Murad. "Honest to Christ, Billy, you're a real pain sometimes. If you want security, why don't you join the post office or something?"

"It's not security," he mumbled.

"Yes it is. I know you like a book. You're only happy if you're in a comfortable little slot. It was the same when you were with Jimmy. He treated you like a doormat and paid you like a coolie." She blew smoke in his face. "And stop squirming like that, you know it's the truth."

"I'm not *squirming.*"

"Honestly, you're such a child. So you're out at Sterling, maybe it's for the best. Look at it that way. You were in a rut. You're too good of an actor to get pies thrown in your face all the time. You could be another John Bunny if you got the right parts." She patted the back of his neck and kissed him on the cheek. "Come on, snap out of it. Go put on your blue suit. Tommy Armbruster's taking me to Baron Long's for dinner."

"Gee, Mae, I don't think Tommy'd want me tagging along."

She blew lightly on his ear lobe. "Tommy does what mama Mae says. Now run on up and change like a good boy."

He was at ease with her, a tensionless camaraderie, a bond that none of her lovers had ever enjoyed. Friendship, she had once told him, is more important than sex. It certainly was to her. There were times when Billy wasn't so sure, times when he ached for her body, but those feelings were never more than fleeting pangs of desire that came over him when he saw her in some particular way, a light falling across her

189

face from a lamp perhaps, or walking across a room in her kimono, the soft fabric whispering against her long, silk-covered legs. Or on the mornings when she had driven to the studio with him, dawn flushing the sky, the windows up in the car and her subtle perfume making his head spin. But those momentary erotic tortures were a small price to pay for the affection she showered on him in so many ways—the socks she darned, the gourmet meals she cooked, her sincere and never-flagging concern for his welfare. She had even found him a girl, a roguish, plumpish blonde with bobbed hair who worked as a cashier at Musso and Frank's Grill on Hollywood Boulevard, a girl who knew all the latest jokes and the newest dance steps. Billy was a fine dancer himself, light and quick on his feet, and the sight of him doing the tango with the amply endowed Lois Boyce at the Montmartre or Baron Long's club in Vernon always drew a crowd—and often a silver plated cup when dance contests became an overnight rage. Lois lived with her mother, who ran a boarding house near Gardner junction where Rudolph Valentino had lived while he was struggling along as an extra. Lois had been around actors all of her life and had a low opinion of them, but she had seen some special quality in Billy and had gone to bed with him on their first date, more out of fun than uncontrollable passion. That suited Billy. He wasn't in love with the girl, but he enjoyed her company, on the dance floor or under a blanket.

Tommy Armbruster was a young bond salesman who lived in the building. He had ridden up in the elevator with Mae one evening and had been hanging around her ever since like a lovesick hound. He had no objection to Billy tagging along with them. He could have accepted a platoon of marines as long as Mae sat next to him in his three-passenger Haynes couplet where he could touch her leg from time to time as he shifted gears. She would let him do that without objections, but Billy knew she kept him dangling because he had told him so.

"Christ!" Tommy Armbruster had moaned after dropping in on Billy one night, bringing a bottle of good gin with him. "I just don't understand the woman, Billy. I mean to say, old chap, what's the matter with me? I'm good looking, a college man, making money . . . got a swell car and dress like a fashion plate. I can go all the way to third base with her but I can't get home. I don't understand it."

Billy had failed to explain Mae's capricious attitude toward men, because he didn't understand it himself. He knew of at least six men she had slept with while she was married to Jimmy and there had been no common denominator between any of them. Short and fat, tall and thin, young, middle-aged, poor and uneducated, rich and cultured . . . they had touched some chord in her that Tommy Armbruster, for all his college man charm, had not. Whatever her need had been for these men it had always passed quickly. Her affairs had rarely lasted longer than a week or two, sometimes no longer than a single night.

"Mae, you look terrific. Like Nita Naldi!" Tommy Armbruster flung his tuxedo-clad arms wide as though in anticipation of her rushing into them with a happy cry of surrender. "You really are the bee's knees."

Mae ignored both the arms and the compliments as she stepped out of the elevator in a swirl of black chiffon and a wash of perfume, Billy walking stiffly behind her, self-conscious, muttering apologies.

"Stop it, Billy. Tommy doesn't mind, do you, Tommy?"

The man who sold bonds on commission saw only Mae Pepper adjusting her stocking seams and giving a final inspection to her makeup in the gilt framed lobby mirror. The legs in their sheer silk hose were perfection, the face angelic, the dress a knockout, the perfume intoxicating. He could forget Billy coming along for the ride in a suit that was a shade too blue.

The band was playing "Dardanella" when they entered and then segued into "Argentine Tango."

> *Argen-tina*
> *where gauchos ride and play*
> *Argen-tina*
> *they dance the night away . . .*

Closely linked bodies swayed and dipped to the pulsing beat. A mirrored ball hanging from the ceiling above the dance floor turned slowly, shooting myriad specks of light from its prisms. The maitre d' led them to a table, the only empty one in the room, removed the RESERVED sign and then looked about for an empty chair. The table was barely large enough for two slender people.

"Listen," Billy said, "don't bother about a chair. I'll stand at the bar."

"Oh, no," Mae protested.

"I want to," Billy said.

Tommy Armbruster offered no argument, for or against.

"Slim Summerville's there and I want to talk to him. You know, Mae . . . about maybe getting in at Sennett's."

"Well, okay," she said reluctantly, "but I want one dance with you. Let's knock 'em cold with a comedy Charleston."

If prohibition was the law of the land, that law stopped at Baron Long's. It wasn't the only speakeasy in Los Angeles, but it certainly drew the best crowd. Federal agents stayed clear of the club on Santa Fe Avenue. It was a melting pot where motion picture people rubbed elbows with established Los Angeles society. A raid there might net a few stars of the silver screen, but it might also net the governor of the State.

Slim Summerville stood at the far end of the long mahogany bar, a tall, angular man hunched over his drink in brooding melancholy. Billy had worked with him in vaudeville and knew that he always looked a good deal sadder than he actually was.

"What are you putting down, Slim?"

"Gin, Billy. It tastes less like creosote than the whisky . . . but not much less."

Billy smiled and tapped for the bartender's attention.

"At eighteen bucks a bottle it should taste like gin."

"It should," Summerville agreed moodily.

Billy waited until his glass of gin and ginger ale had been placed before him and then began the delicate job of sounding out Summerville on the employment possibilities at Sennett's, where the gaunt comedian was a fixture.

". . . of course, I *like* Sterling, but I feel I could do with a change of scene. Sennett makes the kind of pictures that I could—"

"Save your breath, Billy." Summerville tilted his glass and crunched an ice cube. "I know all about the shakeup at Sterling. Everybody does, including Mack Sennett. Andy Farrel may be cross-eyed, but he's not blind. He tipped Mack off that Bolling was dropping his comedy stable. The old man could've picked any of you guys up before the ax fell, but he's got more clowns now than he can use—or pay."

Billy took a big slug of his drink. The gin helped.

"I gotta find a spot somewhere, Slim . . . and I'll work cheap."

"Not cheap enough, Billy. Mack's taking a bath right now. He has half a million of his own coin tied up in *Molly O* and he can't release it until this Taylor business is cleared up. Hell, I don't think anyone really thinks Mabel Normand shot the poor sonofabitch, but there isn't a theater in the country that'll run one of her pictures just now. The old man's tearing his hair, but there's nothing he can do but sweat it out. Heck, I'm leaving. Got sort of a deal with Joe Simberg to make

192

some one reelers. I guess Joe could use you in 'em, but it'd just be bit work—ten, twenty bucks a day, maybe.

"Thanks, Slim." He downed the balance of his drink in one gulp. "I'll think about it."

"What the hell, it's eats."

"Sure. That's something."

Eats! Self-pity shook him like a fever. Pratt had been going to star him in his own series: *Fat Billy Wells . . . A Ton of Fun . . . A Barrel-Bellyful of Laffs.* That was how Andy Farrel had started. Pratt going to Vardon Bolling with a suggestion. Just a question of timing, he thought bitterly, signaling for another gin and ginger. A month or two earlier and Bolling might have said, *Fine! Make half a dozen with the fat guy and we'll see how they go over. We might have another Arbuckle, Chester, you never know.*

The gin had a medicinal flavor, like liniment. Billy choked it down. Ten or twenty a day doing pratfalls for Joe Simberg or Hal Roach. The twenty bucks if he did something spectacular like a 108 and then a backflip down a flight of stairs. And if Bolling had said *Sure, Chester, go right ahead—we need someone to take the place of Pipp* he might be getting five hundred a week right now, and a thousand a week if the first batch of pictures had pleased the exhibitors, and of course they would have been pleased. He was Billy Wells, wasn't he? Fat Billy Wells . . . one hell of a funny fellow.

"Hey, you're hitting that giggle water pretty fast," Summerville said as Billy ordered, and downed, his third gin.

"I damn near made it, Slim. Came *that* close." He attempted to snap his fingers for emphasis, but they were wet from the glass. Thumb and index finger met in a soundless caress. *"That* close."

There was a fanfare of trumpets and then the bandleader raised a small megaphone to his lips and called out: "All right, folks. Boys and girls. Sheiks and shebas. It's time for the contest . . . the dance that's going to sweep the country . . . *Charle-ston!"*

The band swung into the beat, the music nearly drowned by claps, cheers and squeals of delight. Sheiks and shebas, from sixteen to sixty, headed for the dance floor.

"Come on, Billy, come *on.* "

Hands were tugging at him and he turned slowly as though coming out of a trance, and there was Mae standing in front of him, her body already moving to the syncopated music.

"Come *on!"*

193

He felt lightheaded and strangely reckless as he followed her to the dance floor.

Charleston . . . Charleston . . .

Other dancers gave way before him, like birds fluttering from a prancing hippo. His high kicks and exaggerated hip jerks brought howls of laughter from the crowd.

"Shake it, big fella!" someone shouted.

Mae moved beside him giving her own interpretation of the dance, mingling the shimmy with the Charleston so that her firm breasts swayed despite the binding designed to keep them flatly in style.

"Oh, I wish I could shimmy like my sister Kate," the bandleader bellowed through his megaphone.

Mae became brazenly seductive, bumping her well-rounded hip against Billy's thigh, shaking her torso at him. He ignored her blandishments, which was part of the fun . . . the happy rube image—Fat Freddy from Corn City. Every part of his body either bounced, rolled or quivered as he pranced around the floor.

"Look at the fat guy! Isn't he a scream!"

People were leaving their tables and moving closer to the dance floor. They came to Baron Long's for fun and sights like this kept them coming. Even the high stakes bridge players were being lured from the back rooms by the din of applause and laughter.

"Roll it, big boy!"

Billy grinned at the crowd. Lights flickered across their laughing faces. Christ, he was thinking, how he loved that sound. It was what he missed making pictures . . . the laughter, the feel of the audience. He never should have left vaudeville, *never.* The gin was out of his stomach now and coursing hotly through his blood. He felt possessed by magic. There was nothing that he could not do. Nothing at all.

"Show stopper, folks!" he cried out before taking a few quick running steps on the slick floor and flipping his body backward. He knew in one terrible moment that his feet had slipped and that he would never complete the back somersault. The glittering orb of light dangled above him for a split second and then exploded behind his eyes into a million fragments of yellow and red.

SOMETHING ALWAYS HAPPENS

She both feared and despised Frank Gilboy, but it was her fear that conditioned her attitude toward him when he came to the house. She was polite to the point of servility while he was there, but the moment he was gone, and she heard the sound of his car backing down the driveway, her anger flashed out like a naked blade that slashed to the bone anyone unfortunate enough to be within earshot. That anyone was usually Pipp.

"I don't understand how you can permit that man to step into this house! He looks dirty! And will you just look at the rug in the den! Well, you just look at it! Doesn't he know what an ashtray is for? Was he raised in a saloon?"

"He's my representative, Thelma," was all Pipp could manage to mutter through the storm.

"Your representative! Is that what you call him? I call him a flatfoot with the manners of a pig! That's what I call him!"

But she feared his cold, probing eyes. He had seen Rolfe one afternoon as Rolfe came slowly down the stairs wearing his shabby bathrobe. The two men had stared at one another and then Rolfe had gone hurriedly back to his room.

"Who was that?" Gilboy had asked.

"A relative of Thelma's from back East," Pipp had explained.

"Yes," Thelma had echoed, her words seemingly trapped in her throat. "A . . . relative."

Gilboy had frowned. "Oh?"

That "Oh?" had sent a nameless fear into her bones like a chill, and she had felt the same fear when Gilboy had spotted Hank one day, coming into the house with a girl he had met at a tea dance, a flapper with rouge on her knees, but not a bad girl despite her uncorseted body posturings. Gilboy had looked at the two of them the way he might have regarded two cockroaches walking on a ham sandwich. She knew that he had been a policeman because Pipp had told her. She could have guessed it. He had a cop's stare.

"Your representative! And look what he's done for you! Signed you up with a nobody!"

"I'll be getting a percentage, Thelma."

"A percentage!" She spat the word out as though it were phlegm. "A percentage!"

"He's Doll Fairbaine's husband and—"

"I don't give a damn about that!" Her voice rose to a scream. "Do you hear me? I don't give a damn!"

But it was *"Would you care for a cup of coffee, Mister Gilboy?"* when the big man came by, and come by he did, every day, to stay for hours, or to take Pipp to the Simberg studios on Santa Monica Boulevard and La Brea where Donovan had rented space. *"How about a nice piece of fresh apple pie to go with that coffee, Mister Gilboy?"*

But at night she paced the hall and the upper landing, muttering to herself, or bursting into Rolfe's room to shriek unintelligible things at him—the muted words echoing through the walls—or into Gretchen's, causing the girl to go into hysteria and her baby into convulsions. She went into Hank's room only occasionally, principally because Hank was rarely in at night, but also because he could give as well as he got. He would stand toe-to-toe with her and howl vulgarities until she left, slamming the door behind her with such force that the entire house rocked. Pipp was sick of all of them, except Gretchen and her baby, a girl named Frieda. He felt deeply sorry for both of them. Gretchen had managed to talk to him a few times when Thelma was elsewhere and she had told him a good deal about her life—such as it had been—but she refused to say anything about Rolfe or Thelma. She spoke of growing up with stern Lutheran grandparents in Milwaukee, and of a man, much older than herself, married, a lawyer, who had convinced her to run away to Chicago with him one mad summer night. He had mumbled something about divorce . . . a new start . . . fantastic opportunities in Florida . . . and had taken her to a shabby hotel where he had spent the night weeping over her body, as she put it, with his own body drenched with sweat. In the morning he had telephoned his wife and wept for forgiveness. A man of many tears, Gretchen had said with

196

some bitterness. But he had shed none over her eventual plight. She was a girl with good features and would have been pretty if she would comb her hair and use a little rouge on her sallow, misery-pinched cheeks. Her eyes were a deep shade of blue, but they lay dead as marbles in mauve shadowed sockets. She rarely slept, she said. Always thinking . . . thinking . . .

Pipp would also lie awake at night, his thoughts skipping from one image of gloom to another. He felt disoriented. Leaving Sterling had been a shock to him. He had felt secure there, an important cog in a highly efficient machine. Chester Pratt, the small army of writers, the technical skill of Granny Granville—all of those elements had combined to bolster his feeling of security. He had known that the pictures would turn out well. Now he wasn't so sure. He had no way of knowing if Earl Donovan could even produce a picture. There was no scenario yet and he had little faith that the writer Donovan had hired would come up with one. The man had written some "Lonesome Luke" stories for Roach and Harold Lloyd as well as some gags for Sennett, but he didn't seem to be capable of coming up with an idea that could be sustained for five or six reels. And if a continuity were written, who would direct it? Who would be the cameraman?

He would groan and toss and worry.

He found the Simberg studio depressing. It was so small after Sterling, so cramped and cluttered. Four of the six stages were the old fashioned open kind, which made the place look like an abandoned lumber yard. Short, muscular, jovial Joe Simberg had clapped him heartily on the back and told him not to worry about the look of the place, that a lot of good pictures had been made there over the years and that E. P. Donovan was going to put the old place right back on the map. Charlie Chaplin's studio was just a few blocks up the road and they'd show the Limey a thing or two.

And he fretted and turned in a troubled half sleep.

Thinking . . . thinking . . . He had no money worries. He was being paid and the percentage of the gross would make him some big dough, Gilboy had assured him. He had no reason to doubt that, but what if Donovan didn't make a picture? What would he do then? Who would take him? Roach? Sennett? Or had Bolling told everyone in the industry about what had happened in San Diego?

What *had* happened?

Try as he might, he couldn't bring that episode into focus. He could remember a pretty woman with warm, comfortable breasts sitting on

197

his lap and reading the part of Rosalind to him from *As You Like It.*
Everything after that was a blank—except for the policeman and a
dingy, barren room in the San Diego City Hall. Rape and sodomy, the
cop had said. He couldn't conceive of himself doing anything like that.
Did he turn into some kind of Priapic monster when he drank? Impossible. He knew the limitations of his body only too well.

Sigh and sweat in uneasy slumber.

It was not all quarrels and discord with Thelma. There were times
when she comforted him. She could sense the degree of his tensions and
would permit him a glass or two of Scotch at bedtime and then sit next
to him in the big bed that they only occasionally shared. She would read
to him and then fill his mouth with a heavy, blue veined breast while
stroking his groin until he fell asleep. He felt a sense of obligation to
her for that intimacy, and for other things, yet prayed that he would
wake up one morning to find her gone, and that Rolfe and Hank had
left with her. She'd never leave. He knew that in his heart, just as he
knew that he would never kick her out. He had been sucked into a
quasi-marriage. A relationship . . . a family.

Till death do us part?

The thought made him tremble and distorted his sleep with feverish
dreams.

"Donovan's gettin' a little worried about the way you look," Gilboy
said one morning. "Those circles under your eyes are terrible."

Pipp looked away and stared out the side window of the car.

"I haven't been sleeping very well. It's all this worry about the
picture."

That was true. That was part of it. The writer Donovan had hired
just wasn't coming up with anything. And so much depended on the
director, and one hadn't been picked yet. He had told Donovan after
every story conference: You must get a director so that we can all work
together on this.

Pipp thought about Donovan as they drove toward the studio. He
liked the man and had faith in him. His energy and enthusiasm were
contagious and Pipp's spirits always perked up after being around him.
And so far he had done everything he had said he would do. He had
raised the money for one picture with an option for three more from
First National, probably the most aggressive distribution company in
the business. *"You'll make a damn sight more dough with me than you
ever made at Sterling,"* he had said. Pipp felt certain that he would, but

the nagging doubt persisted that they would never get the first picture off the ground. A month had gone by and there wasn't one page of story written.

He felt overwhelmed with bleakness when Gilboy pulled up at the studio gate. A bored guard let them in and then closed the gate behind them. There was the usual crowd of people standing outside, men and woman, anxious, even desperate to work in motion pictures. A few people a day were let in to work as extras and that slim hope sustained the dreams of all. There was a boom in brothels, Gilboy had told him —all those young girls coming out to the coast to make it big in pictures, going into a cathouse when their shoe leather wore out. Where the men ended up only God knew. Selling door to door, or taxi dancing in the tango parlors. The sight of those desperate people only added to Pipp's depression. They reminded him of doomed animals in a pound.

Donovan had taken over a large bungalow and carpenters had partioned the interior to form three offices and a story conference room. The only other available space on the lot had been in the two story stucco building that ran for half a block along Santa Monica Boulevard. Joe Simberg had his office there as well as cutting rooms, a projection theater and offices for the gagmen, scenario writers and directors who ground out the hundreds of cheap one and two reel comedies, cowboy dramas and action serials that Simberg produced every year. The building was musty, dark and noisy as a factory. Donovan's bungalow had once housed the wardrobe department and still smelled faintly of camphor even after two coats of paint had been applied to the walls. But at least the place was quiet. A green and gold sign hung over the front door.

THE DONOVAN FILM CO.
RELEASING THROUGH FIRST NATIONAL

"Good morning," Donovan said, standing in the open doorway, a mug of coffee in one hand, a cigarette in the other. He was wearing jodhpur pants and riding boots, a white shirt, open at the throat, sleeves rolled up. His skin was reddish bronze and he looked overpoweringly healthy. Pipp winced.

"Morning," Gilboy grunted. "That pencil chewer come up with anything yet?"

"I canned him," Donovan said. "Kicked the bastard out on his ear. Well, actually, I called him at home last night and dispensed with his services. He called me a rotten son of a bitch."

199

"Good riddance." Gilboy spat beyond the solitary wood step toward the poorly tarred roadway. "Hire another?"

"No . . . but I signed a director. He's in my office now putting his John Henry on a contract. One of the Sterling crowd—Dave Dale."

Pipp chewed his lips and looked bleaker than ever. "He's not a comedy chap."

"No, but he's big, ugly, tough and mean. He keeps a crew in line and the extras jumping. What the hell, every time I went on a Niles Fairbaine set it was Dale who was doing the directing."

"That's true," Pipp agreed.

"And a director's a director, if you ask me. He walked out of Sterling yesterday and came by here looking for work. I got him on the cheap, but he's happy as hell about it."

Dave Dale could barely stop grinning. Niles had pushed him a step too far and he'd blown up, the straw to break the camel's back, he said to Pipp, gone into a rage and taken a roundhouse swing at Niles, missing him. "Thank God, or I'd have taken his head clear off his shoulders. Jesus, what a punch, but the horse's ass ran screaming to Bolling. I knew my number was up so I took a powder. They owe me for a week's work, but I can go whistle for it. And I fall into this! Damndest thing, Pipp . . . came by to see if Simberg could use another assistant director, spotted Donovan's sign and stopped to say hello. He signed me on the spot. Two hundred a week. I still can't believe it." His grin turned foolish and made him look like a drunk bear.

"I'm happy for you, Dave," Pipp said solemnly. "I hope we can work well together."

They were alone in the conference room, at opposite ends of a rough, unpainted table. The room smelled of pine resin and turpentine and the sun beat in through curtainless, awningless windows. The hulking director wiped his face with a handkerchief.

"I know damn well we can. I was Chester's assistant before you came on the lot. He taught me plenty, but I've always had a good feel for timing and pace. I've seen all your pictures. Hell, I've studied everything Chester's ever done—and I've got some ideas about you."

"Such as?"

"Oh, the little Lord Fauntleroy suits . . . the man in kid's clothing routine. Funny, but not for a feature. I think you need a new look, in step with the times."

Pipp nodded gravely. "Bolling's idea. He thought that playing me as a child man would be funny. I guess it was. Those two reelers were successful, but I never began that way. In Sydney . . . London . . . in the music halls . . . I was the little chap, the clerk, the weak chap and the other blokes were bruisers, huge fellows, but I always get the best of them. Turned the tables on them. I was a damn fine acrobat in those days. I can still tumble, but I'd like to stay away from that type of comedy. I'd like to see the chases held down, not build the picture around them."

"More character comedy."

"Yes. And a greater utilization of props. There was a skit that we did in the halls during the war. I played an officer . . . monocle . . . smashing uniform . . . terribly swank. That in itself always drew a laugh. An absurd costume for my size and build. I used a swagger stick as a prop and I would slap this stick under my arm with great elan and cause havoc with whatever, or whoever, was behind me. Knock over a table and lamp, partially disrobe a woman. Oh, we were racy in the halls and the audiences loved every minute of it."

"You can have a lot of fun with a stick."

"Certainly. A ladder . . . length of stove pipe . . . anything that can poke holes or knock things down, provided that the one creating the havoc remains imperturbable, oblivious to the chaos around him. There was a character in a skit . . . can't quite recall the idea . . . something about a plumber."

"Was that in the music halls?"

"Perhaps."

"Vaudeville?"

"I don't know." The plumber skit had gone right out of his head, a fleeting shadow of memory.

"How are you guys coming along?" Donovan stepped into the room and straddled a chair by the table. "Making any headway?"

Dale nodded. "We're knocking ideas around. At least we agree on what we don't want."

Donovan lit a cigarette and watched the smoke coil and billow in the hard sunlight streaming through the windows.

"Christ, what a country. Five days before Christmas and you could bake bread in this room." He tapped cigarette ash to the floor. "First National wants this picture in release by March fifteenth. Five to six reels. Frank's talking to them now, calming 'em down about you, Dave. They said they'd never heard of a Dave Dale and I told 'em that was their tough luck—that you're a diamond in the rough and the best damn director in the business. Frank's telling 'em the same thing."

Dale stared down at his hands, heavy slabs of meat resting on the unpainted table.

"Thanks for the confidence. I won't let you down."

"Hell, you don't have to thank me. I know what you can do."

"I appreciate your trust."

"Don't fall all over yourself. Just come up with a story. When you need someone to write the gags—"

"I don't like gagmen," Pipp interjected. "I can come up with my own gags once the basic format has been crystallized."

"Yeah?" Donovan sucked on his cigarette. Pipp bothered him. The little man was so damn serious, like a college professor, and he had a habit of tossing five dollar words around. All the comedians he had ever known had been illiterate buffoons with a rapid patter of filthy jokes laced into their conversations. He didn't doubt Pipp's ability to be funny on the screen, but he half wished that he had signed a Hank Mann or a Ben Turpin instead. "Well, I'll leave you guys alone. Work it out in your own way, but we gotta have something ready within the next couple of weeks."

It was an ultimatum and Dave Dale knew it. He glowered at his hands after Donovan had left the room. He had reached blindly into the darkness and grasped a brass ring and he wasn't about to let go of it.

"I see you as an ordinary guy doing ordinary things and letting the comedy grow out of normal, everyday situations. The type of stuff Lloyd is doing. If he'd stuck with 'Lonesome Luke' he'd be washed up by now."

"I could never be the stalwart American chap."

"No, of course not. We can't move completely away from Pipp the pixie, just modify him. Get rid of the funny costumes and the obvious gags . . . work within a frame of reality."

"It was a mechanic wallah . . . a chap with tools," Pipp murmured. "Can't quite grasp the idea of it, but somehow . . ." He shook his head in despair. "It's no use. I can't bring anything into focus. Brain's a ruddy blank lately."

The euphoria that Dave Dale had felt that morning when Donovan had so impulsively hired him was giving way to apprehension. Pipp looked grey-faced and prematurely old. All the stories he had heard about his erratic behavior and crippling depressions flooded in on him. This was his first real break after years of trying and he couldn't allow the chance to slip away from him. If Pipp folded . . . if Donovan scrapped the project—what then? He could never get his job back at Sterling, and he knew the extent of Niles Fairbaine's vindictiveness. The man would pass the word around the Directors' Association that Dave Dale was a hard case, a wild-eyed Wobbly, or some other kind of radical, and directors would shy away from hiring him as an assistant. His palms felt sweaty and he withdrew his hands from the table and folded them tightly in his lap.

"We'll come up with something terrific," he said with heartiness. "Something that'll knock 'em cold."

Pipp's eyes had a moist appeal, like those of a puppy begging for a kind hand.

"I hope so." He leaned forward across the table, his voice lowering to a conspiratorial whisper. "I don't mind telling you this, Dave, but I haven't felt at all funny lately. I haven't felt that I could make anyone laugh no matter what I did."

"That's crazy," Dale said hollowly. "Crazy as hell. You're a very funny man."

Pipp's bottom lip was quivering and there was a noticeable tick under his right eye.

"I lie awake nights trying to visualize myself on the screen as a new character. I can't see anything, Dave. Nothing up there but a flicker of shadow as though I had been and gone and no one was aware of it. No one laughs. No one cares."

"I care." He unfolded his hands and placed them back on the table, fingers gripping the rough, unsanded planks. "I care very much. This picture is important to me, Pipp. And, goddamn it, it's important to you. I won't let you talk that way. It's defeating. We've got to put our heads together and think this project out. We'll come up with something really good. You'll see."

His mouth felt dry as brass. He stared Pipp in the eye until the little man slumped back in his chair.

"I'm sorry," Pipp murmured. "I shouldn't talk like that. Of course we'll come with something. Why shouldn't we? We're both intelligent men. We both understand the business. It's just a question of coming up with the proper image. The gags will follow."

"Of course they will." He tried to smile, to show confidence, but his face muscles seemed frozen. He hoped that his expression was not one of terror.

Pipp leaned far back in his chair so that he was looking up at the ceiling.

"This plumber chap that I mentioned. He was a fraud but the funny part about him . . . the amusing part, you see, is that he isn't aware of his pitiful shortcomings. He thinks he's the best plumber in the world —the prince of plumbers. He does the most absurd and outrageous things with tremendous elan. I don't suppose that he has to be limited to plumbing. Or that his trade is that important. I suppose he could be anything at all. I meant to ask him about that aspect of it because I'm not all that keen about plumbing jokes . . . about water closet jokes, you see."

Dale tried to lick his lips, but his tongue was stuck to his palate. "Ask who?"

Pipp waved a hand airily. "Oh, *him*—you know—the fat chap."

"What fat chap?"

"Whatever his name is . . . we were on location out in the desert by the railroad tracks. Forget exactly where that would have been, out in the Mojave someplace. You know how Chester is . . . always picking the most ridiculously uncomfortable places to make a flick. Well, we were there . . . terribly hot afternoon, you see . . . sitting in the shade . . . and he told me about the plumber wallah and I said to him yes, yes, that's not a bad idea at all. I could see myself playing that type of bloke because I love machines and tools and all that sort of thing but I'm so hopelessly inept with them." He allowed his chair to propel him forward with a bang. His eyes were wide, a misty innocence. "Did you know that I can't drive a motorcar? I tried, you see. Oh, yes, I tried, but I can't coordinate my hands and feet. All that shifting about. Clutch and gears . . . spark . . . throttle . . . I just can't make my hands and feet cooperate. Some blokes are so terribly good with mechanical objects. I can't drive a nail with a hammer. Bloody hopeless twit."

"Was it Billy Wells who told you about the skit?"

Pipp yawned and rolled his eyes upward. "Suppose it must have been. Only fat chap I worked with steadily. Wasn't Kewpie. Must've been Billy."

"Was it a routine he had done with Jimmy Pepper in vaudeville?"

"Don't know," he said, yawning wider. "God, but I get so tired during the day. Never sleep at night any more."

"We'll be shooting during the day," Dale said pointedly.

"Know that," Pipp mumbled. "Everything . . . be okay . . . then."

"Let's hope so."

Pipp suddenly climbed up on the table, cradled his head in his arms and curled up in a ball.

"Must sleep. Be okay . . . little while."

He was asleep instantly, mouth open, a thread of spittle dangling from his lower lip. Dale drummed his fingers lightly on the table and then left the room. Donovan was in his office across the hall talking to Frank Gilboy. Both men looked up expectantly as he appeared in the doorway.

"He fell asleep on me . . . on the table."

"He does that from time to time," Gilboy said.

Donovan appeared exasperated. "Doesn't he have a bed at home?"

Gilboy scowled. "Something's wrong there. Don't know for sure what it is. Domestic problems—an atmosphere you could cut with a knife."

"What kind of atmosphere?" Donovan said.

"Disturbing to Pipp. He won't talk about it, but he supports an odd group of people. He's not happy, that's for sure."

"Neither am I," Donovan said. "What the hell, I'm paying the kid his twelve hundred a week. He's got no gripe with me. I expect him to pull his oar. I didn't build that story conference room so he could sleep on the table."

"Don't worry about it," Gilboy said. He stood up and walked ponderously across the office to the door. Dale stepped aside to let him pass.

"Close the door and sit down," Donovan said after Gilboy had left the room.

Dale sat on the edge of a chair, stiff and expectant. The whole setup was falling apart. He sensed it. There was a ringing in his ears and his body felt clammy. Christ, he thought, what a goddamn day. A roller-coaster ride . . . up and down.

Donovan tilted back in his chair and chewed the end of a pencil.

"I got problems with the kid. You can see that."

"Yes, I can, Mister Donovan."

"The name's Earl. Jesus, I don't know what to say. I've got to have a picture in the can by March fifteenth and we don't have a scenario yet. I thought the kid would be overflowing with ideas and all he does every day is go to sleep on the goddamn table."

"He seems . . . depressed."

"That makes two of us."

"I'm sure we can come up with an idea."

"You can't rely on him to help you. He likes something one minute and then he changes his mind. Well, there's nothing in his contract that gives him story approval. I'm relying on you to come up with some-

205

thing, Dave. Now, I know I'm not paying you what you're worth, but—"

"I'm satisfied," Dale said quickly. "I appreciate the break."

"Forget it. I just want you to know that there'll be bonus money for you if we get this goddamn thing off the ground and make it within the budget. First National is putting up the bulk of the money and they're going to be on my neck if we're not shooting by the first week in January."

"We will be." It was a statement without meaning. He was painfully aware of Donovan's raised eyebrow and he hurried to back up his remark with something at least halfway concrete. "Pipp was talking about a comedy sketch that holds some promise. An idea for a character that he could play. It's just a germ of an idea and he didn't explain it very well, but I think there might be something to it. It's an idea that one of the fat guys at Sterling came up with."

"Fat guys?"

"Yes, one of the fat men in Chester's unit—Billy Wells."

Donovan spun his chair gently from side to side. "Oh, yeah, Billy Wells."

"Do you know him?"

"Seen him around the lot a couple of times. Half promised him a part if I ever made a picture."

"He's a damn fine comedian. I'd like to use him in this picture, but I guess that's out. The poor bastard busted his neck. He's flat on his back with a plaster collar on him that'd cripple a mule."

"In the hospital?"

"Not now. He's home. The Cabrillo Arms on Commonwealth."

"I'll drop in and say hello. Sound him out. Maybe he could put something on paper."

"Want me to come along?"

"No. Let me see what he's got first. If I like it, I'll put him on the payroll."

"That'd be great. It's tough on the guy being laid up and out of work."

"Yeah," Donovan said. "It sure as hell must be."

CASSETTE

Since we talked last time I was able to look up some data on *The Bubblehead* at the Academy library. They were very sketchy on credits

206

in those days, weren't they?

Oh, sure. There was no struggle for credits like there is today. People were just happy to be working in pictures and they didn't give a damn if they got screen credit or not. Audiences didn't care who did the costumes or the lighting. Hell, they still don't. What does it mean? There are credits on some pictures that are as long as the goddamn film. No point to it. Of course, we didn't have the unions and the guilds that there are today. Everyone pitched in. Actors helped move the cameras and the lights. They brought their own props and did their own makeup if they wanted to. There were no union representatives saying that you can't do this or you can't do that. The directors had an association. So did the cameramen. They didn't regulate salary or anything like that, they were true guilds dedicated to keeping up a high standard of excellence among their members. A man didn't have to join those organizations in order to work. Everything was a lot simpler back in the twenties.

A good time for producers.

A good time for everybody, if you ask me.

I had always assumed that *The Bubblehead* had been a Sterling release. I don't know why. I've never seen it, of course . . .

No. There are no copies of it. I've always regretted that I didn't stick a print away in a vault, but, what the hell, it was just the first of so many pictures. It didn't seem important at the time.

Was there a reason why you didn't make the picture for Sterling?

Oh, sure. I didn't want people saying that the only reason I was a producer was because I was Doll's husband. She was such a major power at Sterling—as was Niles, her brother. Bolling had put him in charge of production. There were politics involved in that move. Niles Fairbaine was very close to Harry Ashbaugh, and it was Ashbaugh who controlled the destiny of Sterling through his money. Bolling was still the boss, of course. He called the shots, but Niles had a title and some say about what was to be made. Niles begged me to make my pictures there, but I wanted to sink or swim on my own.

Turned out to be a good decision, didn't it?

Yes, it did.

Getting back to the credits on *The Bubblehead.* Who wrote it?

It was my idea. I wanted to change Pipp's character on the screen and the picture grew out of my vision, but everyone had a hand in it.

Community effort!

That was how we did things. Everyone putting ideas into the pot.

207

That must have been enjoyable. One thinks of the picture industry today . . . TV . . . the jealous guarding of specific areas of creation. But, moving away from that aspect for the moment, this was a crucial turning point in your life, wasn't it?

Yes, it was.

Out on your own . . . first picture . . . career on the line. How did your wife view your new venture?

She was very happy about it.

Her marriage to you was known by then, but in looking through *Photoplay* and other fan magazines from the fall of 1922 through the winter and spring of 1923, I could find only one short article about the two of you. A piece showing you together on the ranch. There were many articles about her: what she was wearing, how she did her hair, what her favorite recipes were—stuff like that. Any reason for that neglect?

It wasn't neglect. Doll wanted it that way. She was cool to the press regarding our personal life, but generous where she was concerned. She'd give them all the copy they wanted if they'd leave *us* alone. That was jake with me. I hated publicity.

But there was some of it after the marriage was announced. I was struck by the way they glamorized you. World War hero, the incident with Pancho Villa in 1914, very much a swashbuckling tone. Was all that true?

Yes, but exaggerated. Publicity people have never changed. They take a grain of truth and make an epic out of it.

The story about you and Villa fascinated me because I think you told me that you didn't become involved in the making of motion pictures until after the war . . . 1919 or thereabouts . . . and the article I read stated that you were with Villa on the border in 1914 and that he agreed to recreate the taking of Juarez for your camera.

I was with Villa, but I didn't have a camera. They were wrong about that part of it. I was a carnival man in 1914 and Pancho Villa was a popular figure at that time, sympathetic to the American public. Carnival men . . . wild west men . . . the Ringling brothers . . . people like that . . . There was talk of inducing Villa to appear under the big top for a great deal of money. He needed cash to buy guns to keep his revolution going. I went down to see if I could get him to join my carnival. That was a long time ago and I forget all the details.

Time is corrosive to memory, isn't it?

Well, it does blur it a bit.

He recognized the woman who opened the door, but he couldn't recall where he had seen her—not that she would have been easy to forget.

"Earl Donovan's my name," he said, staring hard at her.

"I know," Mae said. "I've seen you at Sterling."

He smiled and pushed his hat to the back of his head.

"Sure. Knew I'd seen you around some place. You're an actress."

"A bit player," she corrected. "Your wife's an actress."

She sounded faintly mocking, but he didn't care, barely heard her in fact. His senses were too involved in her physical presence. She was wearing a pale green silk dress, open wide at the neck. It was hot in the apartment with the afternoon sun beating on it and a film of perspiration clung to the soft swell of her unbound breasts. The deep cleft between them would be hot and moist. He felt a tightness in his throat.

"I'd like to see Billy . . . if it's okay."

"Sure. It'll do him good. He's been awful low the past few days." She brushed a damp strand of hair from her forehead. "This damn heat doesn't help."

"It's got everybody down. The papers say it's a Santa Ana, a wind off the desert."

"It can go back where it came from." She stepped aside, holding the edge of the door. The dress clung to her hips, but the bottom of the skirt rippled like green water. "Come into the hot box."

He glanced at the room as she closed the door. Curtains stirred in the wind, keeping out the sun but not the heat. A wrinkled white sheet was spread on a couch, a blue nightgown draped over one arm.

"I didn't get your name."

"Mae Pepper."

"Are you looking after the big guy."

"As best I can." Her face was drawn, the skin taut across high cheekbones, dark half moons under her eyes. "It isn't easy. He's a rotten patient."

She crossed the room toward an archway that led into a narrow hall and Donovan trailed after her, watching her uncorseted hips sway. He imagined her body under the dress, supple and vibrant, firmly fleshed. There was a bedroom at the end of the hall, the door open, the shades drawn. A double bed dominated the room, Billy Wells lying on it, his neck and torso encased in plaster. He lay flat on his back, the pajama clad legs moving restlessly, reminding Donovan of an overturned beetle waving its legs feebly in the air. The room smelled sourly of sweat.

209

"You've got a visitor, Billy," Mae said. "Mister Donovan from the studio."

Donovan leaned against the bedpost while Mae went to open a window.

"How's the kid?"

"Swell," Billy muttered. He struggled to sit up, but it was too much of an effort. Neck and upper body had been fused into a solid carapace. His eyes were sunken and flesh hung from his jowls in yellowish strands, like melted wax.

"You look rotten," Donovan said. "What the hell are you doing out of the hospital?"

"Waiting to die."

Mae let a window blind go up with a snap. Sunlight poured into the room.

"Stop talking like that," she said angrily. "If I thought you meant it I'd buy you a gun."

Billy blinked at the light and looked sheepish. "Heck, Mae, I was just griping."

"Do your griping when I'm not around, then. I'm sick and tired of it."

"I'm sorry," he mumbled.

She stood with her back to the sunlight— a silhouette of fury.

"You should thank God you're not paralyzed. Honestly, I've never known anyone so full of self-pity. You just make me sick."

Billy squirmed and avoided looking in her direction. "I said I was sorry. Just calm down. Is there anything cold to drink?"

Her anger faded almost as quickly as it had come. "I'll make some lemonade. Want some, Mister Donovan?"

"Sure."

Donovan waited until she had left the room and then he sat on the edge of the bed and lit a cigarette.

"Well, Billy, you sure got yourself into a fine mess. What the hell happened? A stunt go wrong?"

Billy held out his hands. "Give me a pull up. Jesus, I feel like a beached whale." He struggled up with Donovan's help and leaned back against the headboard with a grunt of pain. "I did something stupid on a dance floor and busted a bone in my neck."

"Yeah?" He smiled wryly. "Fantastic Fred—the death defying wire walker."

Billy managed a wan smile. "Good thing I didn't fall in Joplin."

210

"Yeah. We might still be there." He blew a thin stream of smoke through his lips. "You read all that crap they wrote about me in the papers?"

"Sure. What of it?"

"Lot of bull. Publicity stuff."

"I figured that. What the hell, that's how it goes in Hollywood."

"Sure, the build-up routine. I liked that stuff about my being from an old Boston family. The Chelsea cops musta got a laugh out of that!" He looked around for an ashtray. Not seeing one, he flicked ash on the carpet and ground it into the nap with his foot. "You ever tell anyone about Joplin?"

"I might have told Mae, but she's family."

"Family, huh?"

"Well, sort of."

"A good looking woman." He puffed in silence for a moment, eyes narrowed against the smoke. "You must've lost fifty pounds, kid."

Tears of self-pity welled in Billy's eyes. "Easy. I've taken a beating, Earl. Lost my savings . . . my car . . ." His voice choked up. "Really hit the skids."

"You hear about my deal with Tom Pipp?"

"Yes," he croaked, fighting back the tears.

"Got a feature to turn in by the fifteenth of March. I just hired a director, Dave Dale."

"Good man."

"He thinks you're aces, too. I got a star, a director, a First National release, a swell office at the Simberg studio. I got just about everything, in fact, except a scenario. I hired a writer away from Sennett and he couldn't come up with a damn thing that Pipp would go for. Couldn't blame him. Just a bunch of tired old gags." The cigarette had burned down to his fingers and he stood up, walked over to the open window and flipped the butt through it. "I'm in a spot and maybe you can help me out."

"Jesus, I don't see how. I'm all busted up."

"You didn't bust your brains, did you? Do you remember talking to Pipp about a story?"

Billy scowled. So much had happened to him lately of such a catastrophic nature that he had difficulty in remembering happier times. He tried to recall his days at Sterling but drew a total blank.

"Story? I'm afraid I don't . . ."

"Dale said it was an idea. A character of some kind."

211

"And I told him about it?"

"Dale? No. He said you had talked it over with Pipp and he had liked the idea."

"Pipp?" He struggled to work his thoughts backward, out of the chaos of his ruin . . . the bills . . . the dwindling balance in the bank . . . the awful day when Mae said he'd have to sell his car. She'd given up her own apartment so as to pool the expenses, but things had been slow in the business and she had had only a few days work in the past three weeks. The spectre of poverty and eviction squatted on his chest and clouded his thoughts with images of gloom.

"Pipp and I used to talk a lot out on location." He rubbed both hands over his face as though washing it. "Seems to me we used to talk over gags, bits of business that Chester overlooked . . . and I told him about Billy Bubblehead once. Was that it? Billy Bubblehead?"

"Beats me."

"That must have been it," Billy said excitedly. "Sure. I had an idea once for a skit . . . for Jimmy Pepper. He did a great blackface."

Donovan shook his head dubiously. "Blackface? I don't see Pipp doing—"

"No, no," Billy said hurriedly. "Not for Pipp to do. That would have been ridiculous . . . no . . . but I told him the idea. A plumber, a guy who acts like he really knows what he's doing but gets it all wrong— hooks everything up cockeyed, water leaking from all the pipes, shower running when the sink faucets are turned—stuff like that. I would have played the straightman, the guy who hires him. Pipp didn't like the idea of the guy being a plumber. He said he didn't like jokes in a can, so I told him that the guy could be anything . . . a carpenter or an automobile mechanic. Say he was a carpenter measuring a piece of wood to fit an opening. He measures it with great pains . . . cuts the wood . . . it's an inch too short. That sort of stuff. Or . . ."

"I get the gist." Donovan lit another cigarette and paced the room slowly, from the window to the bed and back again. "Could be funny. But would that hold up for five or six reels? This has to be a feature."

Billy squirmed on the bed. He sensed an opportunity and the thought made him itch. "Sure . . . if a story is worked around the routines. Plot, subplots . . . maybe a mistaken identity kind of thing."

"Such as?"

Billy waved his hands as though trying to pluck an idea from the air.

"Oh, say . . . well . . . Pipp's a rich young man . . . an eccentric."

He swallowed hard, closed his eyes and plunged ahead, praying that a

212

story would materialize out of a few routines he had envisioned Pipp doing. "We open up in the garden of a mansion—one of those huge places in Pasadena. Pipp is holding a watering can . . . watering something. We then go inside the mansion where a group of people are standing in front of a window. One of them is a doctor: Van Dyke beard, pince-nez glasses. We'll get over the fact that these people want Pipp put away in a loony bin so that they can take control of his money. They're his relatives, see. They look at the doctor and point toward the window and we have a title that reads something like . . . 'Would you call our ward's behavior normal? All that money and not a penny's worth of sense.' We then go back to Pipp with his watering can. Camera pulls back and we see that he's dribbling water on a tree—a huge, towering tree—a redwood or something like that. He skips to another tree and waters that and then on down a row of huge trees, watering each one carefully with his little can. Then men . . . men in white coats run onto the scene carrying nets. Pipp sprinkles water on them before they catch him. His relatives—the heavies—shake hands as they watch the doctor and the men in white coats carry Pipp away." He paused to gauge Donovan's reaction, but there was nothing to indicate his feelings one way or the other as he paced the room puffing on his cigarette, hands thrust in the pockets of his jodphurs. Billy rubbed at his cast to try and appease an itch beneath it, licked his lips and continued. "The next scene is at the mental hospital. The place is being painted . . . or repaired . . . anyway, there's a truck loaded with equipment parked in front of the building. There are ladders on the truck, cans of paint, lumber, tools, all kinds of stuff . . . a real handyman's truck. There'd be some business as the booby hatch truck pulls up and the doctor and the men in white jackets haul Pipp out of the back and try to get him inside the building. Pipp wants to try on one of the white jackets. The doctor tells an attendant to humor him. Anyway, somehow, Pipp gets on a white jacket that makes him look like the man painting the building . . . or doing carpentry . . . you know, whatever works best. Somehow the two men get mixed up and the guards haul the workman into the loony bin and leave Pipp outside— just for a minute, just long enough for him to get into the work truck and roar away. The moment he drives off, every guard in the building explodes through the door followed by the irate workman. They leap into the padded paddy wagon and give chase."

"That could be funny," Donovan said quietly.

Billy's heart gave a leap. "Yes . . . sure . . . pandemonium. A car chase

213

now—all over the place—across fields, through little towns. Pipp driving like a maniac."

"Is he really supposed to be crazy?"

"Oh, no. No, not at all. Just an eccentric millionaire who's been kept apart from the world because the trustees of his estate want to grab his inheritance. Anyway, the chase ends when Pipp eludes the paddy wagon and drives into a swank resort hotel . . . like the Biltmore up in Santa Barbara. A millionaire's playground. The manager of the hotel is a big, officious fellow . . . a part I could play if I ever get this cement off me. The manager is expecting a handyman to make some repairs to one of the bungalows and to paint the dining room. Naturally, he assumes that Pipp's the man. He tells him where to go and what to do and then—"

"Okay, that's enough." Donovan flipped his cigarette butt through the open window. "Put the story down on paper. Can you work a girl into it?"

"Sure . . . of course . . . a maid at the hotel. An orphan who the manager is on the make for." He felt dizzy with confidence. There was no end to the rabbits he could pull out of his hat. "In fact, someone else is on the make for the girl as well. Some stuffed shirt staying at the hotel and trying to cheat on his wife. And I can see a scene in which . . ."

Donovan glanced at his wristwatch. "Look, kid, I better run. You get some paper and a pen and put all that stuff down. As of right now you're on the payroll. Is a hundred a week okay?"

"Fine," he blurted. "Swell."

"How long do you have to wear that cast?"

"Gee, I don't know. I gotta go back to this doctor, but—"

"You go to our doctor . . . Doll's doctor. Name's Gilpin, got an office in the Guaranty Building. He's the top man in this town. Tell him to send the bill to me."

"He should be in a hospital." Mae stood in the doorway holding a tray with three tall glasses of lemonade on it. "He needs proper care."

"I'm okay here," Billy said.

She shook her head emphatically. "No, you're not. Look at yourself. You're wasting away to nothing. I don't feed you properly . . . can't bathe you." Her hands were trembling and the glasses clinked against each other. "You need two weeks in a hospital."

"She's right," Donovan said. "They'd get you back on your feet in no time."

"I can't afford it," Billy said. "It's as simple as that."

"I'll write it off as a production expense. You got a telephone here?"

"In the living room," Mae said. "It goes through the switchboard downstairs."

Donovan took a glass of lemonade from the tray as he left the room.

"Did you hear what he offered me?" Billy said as he sunk back on the pillow in exhausted relief. "It's like a miracle, Mae."

"I heard enough. It sounds to me that he needs you as much as you need him."

"So what?" Billy sighed.

Mae set the tray on the bedside table and removed one of the glasses for herself. She took a couple of short, almost angry sips and then walked out of the room.

Donovan was seated on the couch talking on the phone. The blue nightgown was on the arm next to him and he stroked the light fabric idly as he talked.

"Doctor Gilpin? Earl Donovan. Sure . . . we're both fine. No problems. I'm calling about a friend of mine. Name's Billy Wells, a comedian in pictures . . . busted his neck. When?" He glanced at Mae who was standing in the archway.

"Five weeks ago," she said.

"Five weeks," he repeated over the phone. "Guy should be back in a hospital and I'd like you to arrange it. Now. This afternoon. His doctor?"

"Dr. Becker," Mae said. "Harold A. Becker in Vernon."

"A Doctor Becker," Donovan said. "But I'd like you to take over completely. He looks in rotten shape to me. Hollywood Hospital? No, I couldn't get him there. You'd need four strong men to lift him out of here. He's a big man with a heavy cast on him. Cabrillo Arms Apartments, Commonwealth Avenue up near Griffith Park. Wells, that's right, Billy Wells. Sixth floor. I appreciate this, Doctor, the guy's important to me and I want nothing but the best. Private room . . . the works." When he hung up he was grinning with self-satisfaction. "That's how I do things. They'll be right over with an ambulance."

"That's good of you," she said coldly.

"Heck, he's a pal of mine."

"Do you always shortchange your pals?"

He continued to smile at her, one hand toying with her nightgown. "I don't know what you're talking about, lady."

"I'm talking about a hundred dollars a week for a scenario. That's pretty damn cheap, even with a hospital bed thrown in. Billy has a fertile comedy mind. What happens if he gives you a shooting continuity in two or three weeks? Is that it?"

"I didn't put him on for life, but, no, that wouldn't be it. I'd slip him a bonus."

"How much of a bonus?"

His smile broadened. "Say, what are you, his manager?"

"I look out for him. And stop pawing my nightgown."

He let go of the garment and folded his hands in his lap. "I'll do right by the kid, don't worry your head about it. He'll clear a couple of grand out of this if he clears a penny. That is, if he delivers. I'm counting on him."

"He'll deliver." She studied him, trying to make up her mind if his smile was genuine. He looked cool and comfortable in his white shirt and jodphur pants. Short brown boots gleamed with polish. He made her feel shabby just to look at him.

"Are you from Louisiana?" he asked pleasantly.

She shook her head. "Montreal."

"Sure. It's the French blood. Same as the Cajuns. You remind me of a woman I knew in Shreveport . . . only I'd say you're about a hundred percent prettier." He retrieved his lemonade and took a sip, looking at her over the rim of the glass. "Not bad, but it could use a spark of something."

"There's some gin in the kitchen."

"Gin's just the ticket."

She made no move to go after it. "Are you going to wait for the ambulance?"

"If you want me to."

"I can manage. I'm sure you have more important things to do."

"Nothing's more important than Billy at the moment." He held out his drink. "About three fingers. And fix the kid a slug. Best thing in the world for a busted neck."

"Gin got him into this."

"Okay. Make yourself one. We'll toast the future."

"Yours or Billy's?"

He stood up, still smiling, and walked over to her. "You sure carry a chip, don't you? Look, I'll give the kid a written guarantee. Five hundred bucks now and all hospital expenses and then a cool fifteen hundred if we go with his story. I'll put it down on paper. Signed, sealed and delivered. Will that make you happy?"

She took the drink from his hand and turned toward the kitchen.

216

"I'll take your word for it."

He followed her out of the room, watching her buttocks move under the thin fabric of the dress. He thought of the Cajun woman in Shreveport who had always slipped out of her kimono halfway up the stairs and who wore pink garters and not a damn thing else.

"How long have you known Billy?"

"Years. We were in vaudeville together."

"Right. I remember him telling me about it. The Jimmy Pepper troupe . . . the Follies." He leaned against the kitchen door and admired her legs as she reached to a top cupboard for the bottle of gin. "Is Jimmy Pepper your old man?"

She laced gin into his lemonade and handed it to him. "He was my husband. He died last month."

"Hell, I'm sorry."

"That's all right. We busted up a long time ago. There was a notice about his death in *Variety*. Near the back page."

There was no bitterness in her tone, just a quiet resignation as though she had always known that Jimmy's life would come down to that, three terse lines in the back of a trade paper.

Donovan swallowed half his drink and held out the glass for her to take.

"I better run. Tell Billy I'll drop by the hospital tomorrow. It's been swell meeting you."

And then he was gone, letting himself out. She could hear his footsteps receding down the hall toward the elevator, but she still sensed his presence in the apartment; a faint aroma of bay rum, brilliantine and cigarette smoke.

"Sure of himself, isn't he?" she said to Billy. He lay on the bed grinning like an imbecile, giddy with the rapid turn in his fortunes.

"Gee, he's a swell guy."

She crossed her arms over her breasts. "He looks right through you."

"The salt of the earth. Did he go?"

"Yes."

"I wanted to thank him again."

"He said he'd drop by the hospital. You can thank him then."

"That guy! I don't know, things just seem to happen when he comes around."

"I bet they do," she said.

217

INTERLUDE

She had watched the castle growing day by day until now it towered over the small bungalows that lined the far end of the field and she wondered what the people who lived in those houses thought of it. They would see only the back of the gigantic structure from their windows, a maze of scaffolding, a skeleton jumble of boards and catwalks, the inner shell of rough plaster. The gargantuan framework became a medieval castle only when seen from her vantage point on the Sterling studio lot. The central keep, the walls and guard towers were faced with plaster, but plaster artfully molded and painted to resemble granite. The set was by far the largest ever built at the studio and in a month or two it would be swarming with thousands of extras, with knights in armor riding prancing steeds, with men-at-arms, bowmen and serfs. A moat was being dug by an army of laborers wielding picks and shovels. A drawbridge would then be constructed to bridge that moat and afford access to the courtyard of the Earl of Arundel's mighty bastion. Her own Earl could have commanded the glittering host that would flow across the bridge. Vardon had assured her of that, as had Niles. Executive producer in charge of production. That was the title she had sought for him. His actual duties would have been vague, perhaps even nonexistent, but that didn't matter to Doll. She wanted Earl back on the lot. She wanted to drive to the studio with him in the morning and come home with him in the evening. She hated where he was now, so far away in Hollywood, miles from Culver City. She insisted on having lunch with him every day and would walk off the set promptly at noon and not return until well after three o'clock to the despair of her director and the anguish of Bolling, who watched the cost of her current picture mount steadily because of the delays.

She thought of Sterling in the symbolism of the Norman castle, a place of glittering towers and bright banners, a Camelot, a jewel of Christendom, peopled by the beautiful. There was order and stability at Sterling, the confidence of money and success. The Simberg studio on the other hand was a place of chaos, a sun-bleached stucco ghetto, a tenement of dark, evil smelling corridors with rotting sets piled behind the main building like debris in a slum. Earl seemed happy there and she failed to understand way. His bungalow was always crowded with Simberg people, the lowly clowns, buffoons and cowboy actors who peopled Simberg's quickie two reelers. They hung around the Donovan bungalow not just because of the booze that could always be found there, free for the asking, but because they sensed in Donovan an awakening, as though his very presence on the lot foretold better times to come. He was a man on the move and they hoped to move along with him.

"You shouldn't let those people sponge off you, Earl."

"Oh, hell, they're okay, Doll. What's a slug or two among friends?"

She tried, in subtle ways, to talk him into abandoning his project and returning to Sterling, but he would only set his jaw firmly and shake his head. He had to see it through. Success would come. Billy's scenario was first rate and if the picture proved to be a hit—why, there was no end to his plans. Four or five more features with Pipp, perhaps a partnership with Joe Simberg.

"Joe's close to bankruptcy, Earl. Everyone in the business knows that."

"I know all about it. He got stuck with a bunch of lousy pictures. We talked over some ideas and really hit it off swell. I tell you, Doll, there's no better partnership than a Jew and a Mick. And this could be one nice studio if it was fixed up. Hell, I don't want to go back to Sterling and just sit on my can all day while other people run things. That's not my way, Doll."

They would lunch at Musso and Frank's grill, she pecking at a salad, he digging into chops or a steak, hash brown potatoes, a wedge of pie for dessert, endless cups of coffee. Energy radiated from him like heat from an engine.

"I miss you, Earl."

"Now, honey, I come home every night, don't I? That's all that counts."

She lived for nights at the ranch when all of his power and vibrancy, that electric energy, belonged to her. Her lovemaking was wantonly feverish and she would daydream about ways to please him. (Vardon Bolling seeing the rushes one day was moved to tears by the sight of Doll's face as she gazed at a doll that, as a poor orphan child, she could not afford to own. There was an expression of such wistful longing in her eyes that it seemed to encompass the pathetic dreams of every impoverished child in the world. "She'll tear their hearts out," he had cried. She had been thinking of Earl's body.)

But she could sense his restlessness. His moving picture lay between them. His motley friends and associates at Simberg's became a cloud that she could not disperse. Even as she licked his flesh like a cat he would murmur "Must have Billy tighten that lobby scene . . ." or

219

"Hope to hell Dale lines up a cameraman tomorrow."

"Is that all you can think of?"

"Why, no, Doll." Genuinely surprised.

"You make me feel like a whore."

"Now, baby, what a thing to say." Pulling her onto him, hands tight on her buttocks, moving her, guiding her. "I've just got things on my mind, that's all. Like talking in my sleep. I'll keep my mouth shut. I won't say one damn word about the picture for the rest of the night. I promise."

Her annoyance would fade with her groans, her little whimpers of pain and pleasure as she impaled herself on him. Later, wet and exhausted in his arms, she would bite his earlobe and chide him.

"My brother runs an entire studio with less fuss than you're making about one tiny comedy."

"That's because Niles is a genius."

"He is, yes. And he could teach you so much if you were his assistant, Earl."

"Sure. The guy's a wonder."

She was deaf to irony or sarcasm where Niles was concerned. "Helping to supervise all those big pictures. Wouldn't you like that better than being at Simberg's? That's a dreadful place, teddy bear. Like the carnival, in a way."

"I liked the carnival—in a way."

Yes. She had sensed that. Those were his feelings about the motion picture business—a carnival, the biggest sideshow midway in the world. The people around him: little Pipp, fat Billy Wells, lumbering Frank Gilboy, the Simberg cowboys, buffoons and clowns. Of course he was happy there. He was at the center. The ringmaster. The boss.

"Niles would like to bring the movies out of all that slapstick. Give it grace and stature. The eminence of theater. That's what Niles says."

"Let me tell you something, Doll." Stroking her back, fingers gentle on the ridges of her spine. "Just between you and me. Niles is a real pain in the ass."

"Good morning, Mister Fairbaine."

Secretaries stood up respectfully when Niles Fairbaine entered his office. Such minor symbols of homage pleased him.

"Good morning, girls."

It was ten minutes before noon.

"Mister Bolling would like to see you, Mister Fairbaine."

That could wait until his morning ritual had been completed. There was coffee served to him in a Sevres cup and the trade papers to read. He settled comfortably behind his desk as the coffee and the papers were brought in on a silver tray.

He scanned the papers, looking for his own name. It was mentioned enough because he made certain that the studio publicity department saw that it was.

Niles Fairbaine, production manager of SBA Pictures, announced today . . .

"When Knights Were Bold" will be under the personal supervision of Niles Fairbaine. No director has been set for this lavish photoplay, but Mr. Fairbaine, a top director in his own right until he took over the helm at SBA, scotched reports that D. W. Griffith would meg the opus. "I'm seeking a man with fresh, up to the minute ideas," Mr. Fairbaine said, giving some credence to the rumor that there is a degree of antipathy toward the Great Man by this rising production chief.

"May the son of a bitch rot," he muttered, lips touching the slim porcelain rim of his cup. He detested David Wark Griffith and he didn't care who knew it.

Vardon Bolling, general manager and vice-chairman of Sterling-Bolling-Ashbaugh, has handed the production reins of Doll Fairbaine's next picture to Niles Fairbaine . . .

That was probably it, he thought. Bolling was touchy on that subject. The publicity department had gone just a little too far.

An item caught his eye and he set the cup down as though the coffee had turned bitter.

PIPP FEATURE TO ROLL
Earl P. Donovan announced Monday that shooting will begin on "The Bubblehead," Tom Pipp comedy feature, on February 12 with a Santa Barbara location. This five reeler will mark Mr. Donovan's initial . . .

He tossed the paper aside with a grimace of disgust. Donovan! The very thought of the redheaded bastard made his blood boil. He hoped that the son of a bitch would fall flat on his keester. It would serve Doll right for marrying the yahoo.

The daily ritual was now completed. The coffee was cold and the papers read. There was very little else for him to do, but that didn't bother him in the least. He was gratified by the trappings of his job. To Virginia Ashbaugh and her father he, Niles Fairbaine, was production

221

chief. It was hardly necessary for them to know the details of his job, to know that the mainstream of decisions swirled past him, leaving him high and dry. Had he picked up the telephone and told Chester Pratt, or any other director on the lot, what to do or how to do it he would have received nothing but a hoot of laughter for his trouble. He knew that and so he did not pick up the telephone except to call his bookmaker, bootlegger, tailor or various restaurants for reservations. He glanced at the antique clock on the wall, a present from Virginia. He had a date to meet her at three. A tea dansant at the Alexandria Hotel.

Bolling was understandably angry when Niles strolled into his office and settled languidly into a chair. He could always tell when Bolling was furious because the man's skin turned a peculiar shade of mauve. Furious, but, as always, holding it inside.

"Now look here, Niles—"

Niles raised a limp hand. "I'm sorry, Vardon. I know what you're going to say, but I had nothing to do with the printing of that story. Some foul-up in the publicity department, I expect. There are one or two chaps down there who I suspect are pansies and they put out some of the goddamndest nonsense from time to time."

"I wouldn't know about that," Bolling said icily. "All I know is what I read in the papers. Everyone in this studio, yes, even pansies in the publicity department I dare say, know that your sister is under exclusive contract *to me*. The merger with Harry did not change that fact. That was a covenant in our deal. Doll's pictures are *my* pictures and I'm not about to *hand over the reins* to anybody."

"Now, Vardon, you know me better than that. It certainly wasn't my doing. The very thought is ridiculous."

"Yes, Niles, it is," he said with great emphasis.

And that was that. A slight slap on the wrist. He had a grudging admiration for the man for doing that much. Fifteen million dollars rolling into the company coffers because of Harry Ashbaugh. Only a man of Bolling's stature would dare to find fault with the oil man's future son-in-law.

He concealed his contempt for Harry Ashbaugh because it was politic to do so. The man was a ruffian in gentleman's clothing, an illiterate ignoramus who could talk about nothing with any coherence except the making of money. He admired Niles because he considered him to be "cultured," a gentleman born.

"Yes, Harry, the Fairbaines were Tidewater Virginians since before the Revolution. My father, dear soul, was a ruined child of the South.

Educated at home on the classics . . . Greek . . . philosophy. No doubt he would have gone to the University that Thomas Jefferson built, as his father had before him, but he was still a mere boy when the fury and lightning of the Great Rebellion swept the family fortunes into dust. There was little sustenance in that ruined soil, saturated by the blood of the men in gray and the men in blue. The cannon's roar set him wandering as swallows wheel and fly to the doleful ringing of great iron bells."

Harry Ashbaugh was bewitched by such rhetoric.

"I was a poor boy, too, Niles. I could tell you a story or two about ruined soil. God knows my pa grubbed in it long enough. But I said to myself, Harry, Harry, I said once . . . it ain't what's on top of the ground that counts, it's what's under it. I saw 'em pumpin' that oil outa the ground and ladelin' it into barrels. Dirt cheap it was then when I was a boy . . . no real market for it. But then I saw them cars bein' made and I knew they'd amount to somethin' someday. I learned the oil drilling business, Niles. Learned it from the ground up and the ground down to bedrock. Learned a simple truth, too. It ain't just the drillin', it's the leases. The mineral rights. A lawyer taught me that before I was old enough to shave more than once or twice a week. I didn't drill a hole when Spindletop came in, but I had more goddamn leases than a hound has tics."

Harry Ashbaugh lived in a house that was so ostentatious, so filled with the vulgarity of poor taste, that Niles could not enter it without a sneer. The butler and the liveried footmen, the gold dining service, the hideous plates with their encrustations of gold and seed pearls, the ormolu clocks on the mantel, gilt chairs and golden salvers. So much gold, Niles would often say to his friends, that it reminded him of a rich nigger's mouth.

Once he had gone on a trip with Harry Ashbaugh to see some of the source of that wealth, traveling north from Los Angeles in Harry's private Pullman car, sipping bourbon and water in an oak-paneled interior, on horsehair and mahogany chairs with red velvet drapes masking the utilitarian windows of the train. North, into a harsh brown landscape of flint dry hills. The stench of crude oil on the hot wind. Men meeting them at a clapboard depot above Bakersfield. Men in dusty black suits without collars or ties. Wiry, lean-jawed men. His kind of people, Harry Ashbaugh said, stripping off his own celluloid collar. Taking off his coat. Rolling his sleeves up over brawny, hairy arms. They had ridden east into the hills in the back of a jolting, springless tin lizzie to where black wooden drilling derricks covered canyon floors and hill slopes like a forest killed by blight. A signboard here and there on corrugated iron shacks. ASHBAUGH #3 . . . TULE HILLS—ASH-BAUGH . . . U.S. NAVY RESERVE #5 . . .

"Is this where the navy gets its oil?" Niles had asked.

Harry Ashbaugh had only winked, then glared with narrowed eyes at roughnecks on a rig.

"Tighten up that bull rope, goddamn it!" And then he had turned to the lean-jawed men who had met them at the depot and to whom he referred as "high powers," and spoke angrily of sucker rods and beam hangers, bridles and jars, while the men nodded their heads and muttered that everything would be done right. It had been a depressing trip for Niles—except for the hours spent in the Pullman there and back. It seemed incomprehensible to him that such bleakness could buy so much, that those oil-soaked timbers and sweating, swearing men wrestling iron pipes into lunar ground could provide Harry Ashbaugh with the trappings of kings.

How different the pale Virginia was! A rose among thorns. He had met her in 1919 at a meeting of the Los Angeles Shakespeare society, a dinner to raise money for the starving children of Europe. He had recited Hotspur's speech, Act the first, Scene the third, "But I remember, when the fight was done, when I was dry with rage . . ."

He had noticed her watching him from a table in the first row, watching him the way so many women had watched him during the struttings of his youth. Her eyes had burned with a sapphire chatoyance and her little pink cat's tongue had flicked now and then across her unpainted child's lips. Yes, a child—fifteen, sixteen—but with a woman's desires. He had thrilled her with his speech and they had met briefly afterward, her gloved hand clenching his arm, her praises coming in a breathless rush. Oh, she did so want to meet him alone. To speak of the Bard of Avon—and did he know the poetry of Dante Gabriel Rossetti? And what did he think of Dr. Sigmund Freud? A behemoth of an aunt swaddled in a sealskin coat hovered in the background, but she had whispered her name. Virginia Leslie Ashbaugh . . . at the Marlborough School for Girls on West Third Street and could they please meet?

They had met for an afternoon, she seated beside him in his car in her school uniform, giggling, telling him how clever she had been, how she had told her aunt one thing and the school another and that she wouldn't get into even a speck of trouble if she were home at her aunt's house no later than six-thirty. He had taken her to his place because he had felt it more discreet than taking her out in public, to a restaurant or an ice cream parlor, and she had nearly swooned at his Chinese screens and ivory Buddhas and joss sticks. They had sat on cushions to drink jasmine tea prepared by his boy Ching who had come from Hankow and spoke mission English in a delightful sing-song that set her laughing. After the tea and the conversation, after his recitation of Hamlet's discourse to the jester's skull, and her fervid rendition of "The Ballad of Dead Ladies of Francois Villon" (. . . And where, I pray you, is the Queen who willed that Buridan should steer . . . sewed in a sack's mouth down the Seine?), she had let her head fall against his shoulder like a drooping lily and had whispered in his ear, "I dreamed about you last night." And he had said, "What did you dream?" And she had whispered with jasmine-scented breath, "That you made love to me in Xanadu and I was the damsel with a dulcimer singing of Mount Abora." And he had pinched her gently on the thigh, where gray cotton school stockings ended in rose silk flesh.

He had expected her to weep, as girls were apt to do after their virginity had fled, but she had simply glanced at the tiny Austrian clock that rested on the carved teak table beside the divan and then she had explored his body with her long, curiously waxen fingers. And he had asked her what she was thinking and she had frowned and said, "Do all men wear French letters? Doesn't it tickle when you put it on?"

My oh my
When you roll those eyes . . .
my little Georgia peach . . .

"You're late," she said.

"I'm sorry. I had a long meeting with Vardon."

"I've been sitting here feeling foolish and some greasy lounge lizard tried to pick me up." She lit a cigarette. Her hands were trembling. "I hate this place."

"It was your idea."

"I think dancing is boring."

"What do you want to do?"

"You know what I want to do."

"I gave Lin Po the day off."

She stabbed her cigarette in an ashtray. "That's just an excuse, Niles.

225

He never goes anywhere. He just sits in his room."

"I'm beginning not to trust him. I know these Chink boys. God knows I've had enough of them."

"He's fine. He enjoys it."

"Does he? I wonder."

"Why shouldn't he?" She plucked another Fatima from the box in her purse. Niles lit it for her and she blew a thin stream of smoke in his face. "They know things about sex that would never enter a white man's mind. Do you know how they punish a woman in China, Niles? They strip her naked and fold her into a basket so that her . . ."

"That's just an erotic story."

"Well, I like erotic stories." She took a quick puff on her cigarette. "I had a terrible fight with Father this morning. He wants us to have the wedding in Washington with the reception at the White House. He even went so far as to phone Harding. I had to stand there and listen. Warren, he said, Warren, my little girl is getting hitched . . . *Hitched!*"

"Be tolerant, Virginia."

"He's such a fool. He really makes me sick. Then he got sentimental about my mother and took out the album and I had to sit there while he pawed over her photographs and told me what a dear, sweet, saintly woman she was. She had lunatic eyes, my mother. Have you ever seen her picture?"

"No."

"Terribly thin little creature with the maddest eyes you've ever seen. My aunt Jessica would never talk about her. She was twenty years younger than my father, did you know that?"

"Yes. You told me."

"And died in childbirth. Do you think my father hates me because I killed her?"

"Don't be ridiculous."

"Subconsciously, I mean. I bet Doctor Freud would have a field day psychoanalyzing *him.*" She crushed out her cigarette and squirmed on the seat. "Niles, I'm getting itchy. I have little bumps all over my body. If we don't leave this place I'm going to cause a scene."

And he knew she would, because she had created scenes in the past. He held her firmly by the arm as they walked through the lobby. She was beginning to tremble while they waited for the man to bring his car around, and her teeth were chattering by the time they drove away.

"Did you run out of the stuff I gave you?"

"God, yes," she said through clenched teeth. "I finished it this morning. Nearly fell asleep in the tub, but it felt so good." She stared intently ahead. "Drive faster, damn it."

Opium calmed her down and she went to sleep on his bed. While she was sleeping he readied the living room, drawing the heavy wine colored drapes, igniting pellets of incense in brass bowls and lighting candles that he placed behind small, ivory screens. He then took off his clothes and put on a silk Chinese robe after first rubbing his body with sandalwood oil.

The China boy was in his stuffy room off the kitchen, smoking a pipe of opium as he lay on his narrow cot. His bare body was oily with sweat, the flat, hard muscles of his belly reminding Niles of carving on a well-smoked meershaum pipe.

"No sleepy now, John. Missy here. Me and missy want you front room . . . velly soon. You savee, John?"

The young Chinaman looked at Niles with glazed eyes, then nodded his head slowly and licked a bead of sweat from the corner of his mouth.

He was a stupid boy, but obedient and tractable, placid as a sheep. But lately Niles had noticed that little things were missing. A jade carving, silverware. He was beginning to mistrust the boy. Maybe he wasn't as stupid and slavish as he acted. He would have to watch him more closely. He went into the bedroom and Virginia was awake, staring dreamily at the ceiling.

"I feel so wonderful, Niles."

"Of course you do."

"Come here, precious Niles."

He stood by the side of the bed and she sat up and reached out for him, parting his robe and pressing her mouth against his groin. He drew gently back and placed a hand on her head to keep her from falling off the bed.

"Take off your clothes, Virginia. Let us begin."

They were lying on the divan, on a silk brocade cover when the houseboy came into the room like a sleepwalker and began to prepare the pipes. Virginia watched him over Niles' shoulder. The thought of what they would be doing with the boy in a little while made her squirm with the ecstasy of anticipation.

"Coke, Niles," she whispered feverishly. "Cocaine for the Chink and me. Please, Niles . . . *please.*"

Judge and Mrs. Crenshaw were just sitting down to dinner when they heard the screams. It was a Brunswick stew with baking powder biscuits, lovingly prepared by the Crenshaw's cook, Hattie. The judge tended to ignore distractions at dinnertime, being somewhat of a trencherman if not a gourmet.

"I heard a scream, Henry," Mrs. Crenshaw said. "Did you hear a scream, Hattie?"

"No, ma'm," Hattie said as she ladled the steaming concoction on the judge's plate.

"Ah," he said, "ah, Hattie, you outdid yourself."

"There it is again," Mrs. Crenshaw said as a high-pitched shriek intruded the dining room, muffled by the closed windows and the drawn curtains.

The judge frowned. "That was a scream all right."

"Might be a runned over dog," Hattie said. "Lotsa poor dogs gittin' runned over lately."

The judge scowled. "I don't think it was a dog. Didn't sound like a dog to me."

"They can holler like they was human," Hattie whispered, her head cocked to one side, listening.

They all listened, but heard nothing more.

"I suppose it *could* have been a dog, Henry," Mrs. Crenshaw said dubiously.

"Let me check and see," he said, knowing full well that the tone of his wife's voice had implied that he take some sort of action. He got up from the table with obvious reluctance and went to the front of the house. Nothing seemed amiss on the quiet street. Lights burned in the houses across the way. A car or two moved placidly in the direction of Larchmont Boulevard. He went to the back of the house, stepping into the garden through the kitchen. The night was moon flooded and the bamboo at the end of the garden stood out sharply against the sky. He detested bamboo and had complained to Niles Fairbaine, in a gentlemanly way, when the director had planted them.

Bamboo is just a monstrous grass, you know. It's bound to spread into my wife's gladiolas.

But the man had planted them anyway and the bamboo now formed a living fence between the two properties. The judge walked to the end of the garden until he stood in the shadow of the leafy green stalks. (He would say later that he had heard a suspicious sound, but he would never understand why he had been drawn to the bottom of the garden on that night.) The bungalow beyond the bamboo was a dark, angular mass with not a glint of light showing at the windows. He could hear the gurgle of the carp pool and see tiny prisms of moonlight reflected off the water. It was only then that he heard a sound, as though someone were wading or splashing in the pond. He thought that curious and parted the bamboo with his hands. What he observed through the reeds was Fairbaine's houseboy kneeling beside the water, his arms immersed to the elbows. The Chinaman was stark naked and there were great dark splotches of what appeared to be oil on his body. The man swayed slowly from side to side and then raised his arms out of the pond and let water pour onto his chest from his cupped hands. The black, oily stains dissolved into a hundred rivulets that dripped to the ground and the lily pads and it was then that the judge, who had fought so long ago in the canebreaks below San Juan Hill, knew that the substance was blood.

REEL TWELVE

ON WITH THE DANCE

There were cars parked all up the canyon road, Fords mostly, their black canvas tops glistening ebony in the rain. Cops in yellow slickers saw to it that the sightseers kept their cars parked on the shoulder of the road and many of the cars had sunk hub deep in the soft earth, the owners not caring for the moment, they and their passengers being too caught up in the cavalcade of expensive automobiles winding their way toward the gates of the Fairbaine ranch. All the greats of the motion picture world were coming up the mountain that rainy February morning to pay their respects to one of their own.

Vardon Bolling sat in moody silence beside his wife in the back of their limousine. His wife seemed particularly radiant, almost gay in her ostrich plume hat and he did his best to keep her incessant chatter from interfering with his own serious thoughts.

"Of course, everyone knew he was a pervert," Mrs. Bolling was saying, repeating herself. "Boys and young girls and dope. A man like that was bound to come to a bad end. I can't think of a soul who'll miss the poor creature."

Only Doll, Vardon was thinking. He dreaded seeing her. What would he see in her eyes? What distressed him was what he feared he would *not* see—no life, no laughter. The finish of her picture would have to be postponed. But for how long? So much of his own money tied up in it . . . three hundred thousand so far and the end not in sight. It would gross at least five million, but that was in the future. Everything at the moment seemed to be in the future.

Money. A river of dollars had flowed in and then flowed out of the company during the past several months. Millions poured into the theaters and into preparations for the massive epics that would draw hordes of people into those picture palaces. Harry Ashbaugh had been a titan, clearing the path of all obstructions, ramrodding the complex negotiations with the bank, with real estate brokers, architects and contractors. The man's energy had seemed limitless, an untiring dynamo in perpetual motion between Los Angeles, Washington, D.C., and New York. The theaters had become an obsession with him and they were being built to his taste: thick carpets, crystal chandeliers, plush seats, gilt everywhere.

"Gilt's the color of gold, Vardon, gold's the color of money. Never forget that."

Pleasure domes. Luxury. People would pay just for the joy of spending a few hours inside those opulent walls, but they would also be entertained with a lavishness never before seen on the screen. When the first three Sterling Palaces were completed in September, the ones in New York, Boston and Chicago, the debut picture would be *When Knights Were Bold* followed two weeks later by the war picture that Chester Pratt was directing. Two weeks after that there would be an epic saga about the Oregon trail to be shot on location in Wyoming. One hundred Conastoga wagons, scores of actors, thousands of extras, a regiment of cavalry, tribes of Indians. And then other pictures . . . one following the other. And the Sterling Palaces opening in other cities month after month . . . Cleveland . . . Philadelphia . . . Pittsburgh . . . Richmond . . . Atlanta . . . St. Louis . . .

"Mary Minter once told me a perfectly horrible story about Niles. Something that he asked her to do that is beyond the comprehension of a person with a moral mind."

Rain peppered the windows. The gates to the ranch were open, cars backed up before it as the gatekeeper and a studio policeman scanned the occupants to make certain they were the "right" people.

. . . Kansas City . . . Indianapolis . . . San Francisco. A Sterling Palace in every large city in the nation. That was the goal. And those gilded structures would show nothing but Sterling pictures and if Adolph Zukor or Sam Goldwyn or Bill Fox or Carl Laemmle didn't like it they could go lump it. They could go running to the Justice Department screaming about anti-trust laws and monopolies and Harry M. Daugherty would set them straight.

"Harry will tell 'em to start their own damn monopolies, that's what he'll tell 'em, as if you had to tell a smart Jew a goddamn thing about makin' money. And if they keep on hollerin', why, ol' Daughtery'll tell

231

'em to just go fuck themselves."

"I suppose this will be more on the order of a wake, wouldn't you say, Vardon? Canapes and champagne . . . perhaps something more substantial for you boys. Whisky, cold roast beef."

Not that Zukor would say anything to Daugherty. How could he? He was busy doing the same thing. He might be sore because they were beating him to the punch, but if there was one thing you could say about Adolph it was that he knew the rules of the game. Control of the motion picture business was at stake. It was a business of seats. That was the beauty of it. Nothing more to it than that. Comfortable seats and a first rate projection machine. A first class organ. Pleasant surroundings. Even mediocre pictures could be successful in such an ambience. Only, of course, Sterling would never run a bad picture. He'd see to that. By God, but the future seemed rosy. And yet . . . and yet . . .

"Do you think that Doll's Mexican girl will cook those little thin things with the melted cheese over them? Did I tell you that I had lunch yesterday with Nazimova?"

Doll worried him . . . and Harry. Harry should have been here to offer his courage and to share his sorrow with Doll. But the death of Virginia had hit him hard. It seemed to have shattered him, taken the drive and the thunder right out of him. He was sitting in that big barn of a house in San Marino staring at a wall.

"Oh, dear, I wish it wasn't raining. The damp is wilting my plumes."

"You okay, Doll?"

Donovan stood by the side of the bed. He wore a dark suit and a white shirt that made him look like a pallbearer. Doll was lying on the bed, staring at the ceiling. She wore a long, black dress that had taken Juanita an hour to get her into.

"He's dead, Earl," she said with startling fervor.

"Yes, Doll."

"Only the sweet Lord Jesus could bring him back to me, but that's not His will."

"No, Doll, it isn't."

"Grandma Agnes taught me how to pray, and she taught me all about God's mercy and God's plans. God wanted Niles, Earl."

"Yes, he did, Doll."

"He wanted him in heaven among the saints. Among the golden choir." She raised her arms as though seeking an embrace. "Niles rests above this house, Earl."

"Yes, he does, Doll."

232

They had all come out of respect for Doll, not to mourn Niles Fairbaine. Their silence was awkward and their solemnity forced. The large room that had once been vibrant with the color of Spanish shawls, Navajo rugs and Mexican artifacts was now sterile as a tomb. An oil painting of Niles that had been copied from a photograph and rushed to completion during the eight days since his death hung above the fireplace, the frame draped with black crepe. Beneath the painting, resting in solitary magnificence on the mantel, was a two foot high urn of hand-carved alabaster.

"What awful taste," Nita Naldi murmured to Blanche Sweet.

Bolling eyed Doll keenly as she entered the room with Donovan. He felt reassured by what he saw. Her face was not swollen from weeping and her eyes were shining. She looked composed and almost happy. He remembered her grandmother's funeral. The service in a small, white frame building in a bleak suburb of the city. A Fundamentalist church of some sort. Singing and shouts. The poor old woman's soul bound for glory . . . going across Jordan . . . Hallelujah. Well, there was probably something to that old rock-ribbed religious belief. It robbed death of terror. Goin' home. God and the Host waiting up there with harps and wings. Doll would be all right in a few days. A little sadder, a bit wan —yet accepting what fate had decreed. She would go back to work, the memory of her dead brother adding, if anything, a certain poignancy to her performance.

"I'm so happy that you all came," Doll cried out, her voice clear as a trumpet. "May the good Lord bless you all!" She dropped suddenly to her knees and clasped her hands in front of her. "Please join me in prayer!"

There was a rabid insistence to her voice. She was not asking. It was a demand. Her eyes, Bolling noted with alarm, were not so much shiny as they were burning.

"Sweet Jesus, beloved Savior, bless all those who have sinned . . ."

It seemed incredible to Donovan that he had only been away from the office for ten days. He felt like a man who had just been released from a long term in prison. He touched every item on his desk in the early morning light as though the untidy assortment of papers belonged to some dim, half forgotten past. He felt older by ten years. Certainly he looked older, his face drawn and his eyes sunken after days without sleep. It had been a nightmare, starting with the call from the police. He had gone downtown to identify the corpse, meeting Vardon Bolling there and Harry Ashbaugh. The oil man had been led into one

233

screened-off cubicle in the morgue and Bolling and himself into another. He thanked God that Doll had been spared the ordeal of identifying the butchered remains. Her grief had been frenzied enough without having to see her brother removed bit by bit from a canvas sack.

Eight days of grief that went beyond reason, and now this strange calm, this retreat to Jesus. She kept nightlong vigils before the urn of ashes and he had joined her for the past two nights, not wanting her to be alone, trying, unsuccessfully, to bring her back to reality.

"Life must go on, Doll."

Perhaps if her mother had come, but they had been unable to locate the woman. Gone from Paris . . . a cruise to Egypt with three young poets and a Dadaist painter—whatever the hell *that* was.

"Well, look who finally showed up."

Frank Gilboy stood in the doorway. An ox in a raincoat.

"Hello, Frank," Donovan said.

"I bet you've had a time."

"It hasn't been easy."

"Was it as clean as they said in the papers?"

"No. They were naked as fish."

"I figured as much. I knew his tastes. I feel kinda sorry for the Chink, but I guess he'll burn."

"I guess so." He touched a small stack of scripts. "Any changes?"

"No. Everybody's still happy. Billy wrote a helluva continuity, but Groton at First National is worried that we won't make the release date. And Pipp's worried that we won't shoot at all."

Donovan pressed his hands against his eyes. "I'm under a lot of pressure to drop out of this thing—pay everybody off and just chuck it in."

Gilboy drew a sack of Bull Durham and a packet of cigarette papers from his pocket, a sure sign that he needed time to think. Donovan watched him roll a smoke and said nothing.

"I still got boys around who tell me things. I know what's going on. Doll hasn't been the same sunny Sally since you left the lot. Losing Niles won't make her feel any happier. Did Bolling offer you a deal?"

"A thousand a week and a two secretary office."

"Any responsibilities?"

"Well, you can't have everything."

Gilboy licked the cigarette paper with surprising delicacy.

"You going to take it?"

"It'd make Doll happy."

"Oh, hell yes." He lit his cigarette and blew smoke through his nose.

234

"Is that your job in life, Donovan? To make Doll happy? I ain't knocking it, you understand. Not the worst job in the world looking after a dame who makes a million bucks a year, not counting all that property. Blocks and blocks of it. No, not the worst job a Johnny could get hold of."

"Can the crap, Gilboy."

"What am I supposed to say? So you'll pay everybody off. That's real white of you. That'll sure make Pipp happy. He can use the money to buy a rope and then hang himself with it."

"Don't get carried away."

"You think I'm laying it on too thick? Listen, bub, I'm a one client agent so my own pocketbook is in trouble if you go back to Sterling. I won't kid you about that, but I'll get along. You could kick me off a mountain and I'd land on my feet. Pipp's different. If you pull the rug out from under him he'll curl up and die."

"You could take him anywhere."

Gilboy shook his head like a dying bull. "No, I can't take him just anywhere. There was a lot of talk after Bolling cut him loose. People wondered why a moneymaker like him was being given the gate. All those stories about him lushing it up went the rounds and some people think that Will Hays told Bolling to dump the kid. If you let him go, too . . . Well, I think you get the point. There's a blacklist in this town even if nobody wants to talk about it."

"Don't blow a gasket. I told Bolling I'd think about it. Anyway, what the hell would I do with two secretaries?"

"You'd think of something." He blew a cloud of smoke in relief. "I think we have a shot at making a damn fine little picture. That's what I think."

"We'd better make a honey or I'll never hear the end of it."

CASSETTE

While browsing through the Academy library I came across a review of *The Bubblehead* in the March 22, 1923, issue of *The Moving Picture Weekly*. It was a fine review, but what really gave me a kick were the comments on Billy Wells' scenes with Pipp. The reviewer was quick to note the chemistry between them, that almost indefinable quality that makes for a great team. Pipp and Wells were born.

No, I wouldn't say that. They weren't a team then. Pipp carried that picture. Billy was just a featured player. There was no talk of teaming them up. There were no teams in comedy pictures at that time. Teams were for vaudeville. Teams were thought of in terms of dialogue, snappy patter, Dutch jokes. Vas you dere, Sharlie? Gallagher and Shean . . . burlesque . . . the Follies . . .

Yes, I see what you mean. Still, that review struck me somehow as being the fountainhead. You certainly came in for accolades as well. That gave me a kick, too. Your first picture. The first of God knows how many to follow.

Yes, the first.

Off to a roaring start.

First National was pleased. I had come in on time and within the budget. The death of Doll's brother had thrown me off schedule by two weeks or more. We had to work eighteen-hour days to catch up. Shooting in Santa Barbara . . . in a big resort hotel and at a small studio up there. American Studios, I think it was. Now long gone, of course.

Speaking of that—the death of Niles Fairbaine, I mean—certainly intriguing. There was a curious lack of newspaper coverage. After all, there seemed to be so many elements that would have thrilled the readers of the age: the Chinese houseboy, the dope they found on him, the glamor of the victims . . . a studio chief . . . a millionaire's daughter . . .

Yes, all there, but there was nothing to be gained by delving into it. The newspapers weren't reluctant to print sensationalism, but that was a scandal free crime. Harry Ashbaugh's daughter was planning to marry Niles. She had come to his house for supper and the houseboy had stabbed them to death. A tragedy. The boy was a hophead and the papers attacked the loopholes in the immigration laws that permitted such people to come into the country and work as servants. There was an outcry about the Yellow Peril, but very little written about the murders.

And a flame still burns at the Hollywood cemetery for him, I understand.

Yes. Doll interred her brother's ashes there in oh, '23 or '24. A perpetual flame . . . something of a tourist attraction, although few people today have any idea whose ashes are there. The inscription is cryptic. Jenny loves you, I believe it says.

Getting back on the track, so to speak. You were off and running after *The Bubblehead*—no pun intended!

Yes. I'd learned a lot. I was in on every facet of the making of that picture, from script to final cut. There were producers in town who didn't know a damn thing about the making of moving pictures. They sat in their offices and worked on figures. Accountants. That's all they were. Money manipulators. The very term *producer* was a joke to directors and cameramen. There were directors who'd toss their producers off the set if they showed up there. But directors had a respect for me because I knew what the hell I was doing, and if I didn't know I sure as hell asked.

Nothing but blue skies and no problems.

Well, no problems that I couldn't handle.

Billy sat in the back row of the theater next to Mae. He had seen Pipp arrive with Thelma Robeck and had spotted Donovan and Gilboy conversing in the lobby with executives from First National, but he had no idea where they were seated. The theater in Long Beach was jam packed because of the PREVIEW TONIGHT sign on the marquee. To a soul the audiences had been looking forward to a De Mille picture, or perhaps Valentino in *The Young Rajah,* so there were boos and catcalls when Pipp's name came on the screen.

"Oh, God," Billy whispered, sinking lower in his seat. "I don't think this preview was a very good idea."

"Shush," Mae whispered back, "if it gets too nasty we can sneak out."

The credit titles came to the end: DIRECTED BY DAVID DALE. PRODUCTION UNDER THE PERSONAL SUPERVISION OF EARL P. DONOVAN. There was no writing credit of any kind, a slight that Billy felt keenly. He had written a fine scenario and continuity. His name should have been on the screen as the writer as well as being listed as a feature player.

"That bastard," Mae hissed.

"One credit to a customer," Billy muttered ruefully.

The audience was still hooting its disappointment and several people got up and left, making a big show of their departure.

"That's the damndest gyp I ever heard of," a man shouted as he stamped up the aisle. "Previewing a pie-throwing two reeler. Goddamn gyp!"

But then the theater quieted down as the opening scene irised in. The photography was crisp with strong highlights and shadows. The opening shot was of Pipp's mansion (a millionaire's home in Santa Barbara) and the audience could tell by the slow pace of the establishing shots that this was no ordinary comedy short. The camera lingered on the beauty and opulence of the setting and then dollied to a medium shot of a mullioned window, the relatives standing behind it, peering out with grim, disapproving expressions. A bunch of flint-hearted, avaricious blue noses. The audience recognized the stereotypes and greeted their appearance in the film with appropriate hisses.

"Okay so far," Billy breathed.

The first shot of Pipp sprinkling a stand of towering eucalyptus trees with a tiny watering can brought a howl of delighted laughter. The once reluctant viewers were now into the picture, the plot quickly grasped. The laughter came faster now, a sustained chuckle of delight punctuated every few minutes by rollicking guffaws.

Billy stopped sweating and slumped comfortably in his seat to enjoy the picture. It was the first time he had seen any part of it; Donovan hadn't shown the rushes to anyone but Dale and the cameraman. Like any actor, he was primarily concerned with his own part, the role of an officious hotel manager. To do it had been a challenge.

"It's going to require a good deal of acting," Dave had said. "I don't want to do the Chester Pratt sort of stuff—the physical gags, pratfalls and 108's. It would be out of character and, besides, I'd be afraid to have you do anything like that. Jesus, you've only been out of a neck cast for two weeks. You could kill yourself if you took a bum fall."

"I can act," Billy had said.

"You look right, is the point. Big . . . overbearing. You're supposed to be a man who caters to millionaires. You feel superior to the lesser breeds . . . bellhops, maids . . . Pipp the handyman. You can handle the others. They jump when you tap the little bell on the reception desk. But Pipp is a free soul. He exasperates, then maddens you, especially when he always seems to get the upper hand—usually inadvertently. An obvious type of gag would be for you to upbraid Pipp while he's say, eating a banana. You win the point, impress onlookers by your authoritarian manner, then slip on the banana peel and fall flat on your can. That might have been okay a few months ago, corny but good, but one bad fall and you could end up a basket case. We have to come up with something more subtle."

"I could reach out to ring the bell and hit the inkstand instead. Get ink on my face. Wipe if off slowly with my tie after doing a slow burn."

"Yeah . . . good idea. Or . . . you could do a slow burn and then wipe the ink off with *Pipp's* tie . . . or his shirt tails."

"That would be even better. Then something happens that gives him the upper hand again. Always leave Pipp triumphant. Make me the patsy all the time."

The scene with the inkstand was on the screen now and Billy studied himself critically. His face was not quite fat enough to suit him (Thank God he had filled out since that was shot) but he looked all right, big

238

and imposing. The scene played like a charm and the laughter was explosive. Smug vindication as he wiped his inky face with the tail of Pipp's white shirt. Then, as he stepped back from the little man, he made contact with the pen lying on the edge of the desk and was impaled on the nib. More laughter.

Mae gripped his arm and squeezed it. "Swell, Billy, swell."

That remark seemed to express everyone's reaction to the entire picture. When the lights went on, the applause continued, dying away slowly as people drifted, almost reluctantly it seemed to Billy, up the aisle and into the lobby where personnel from First National were waiting to ask questions.

"Did you enjoy the picture?"

"Have you ever seen Tom Pipp before?"

"Did you prefer this feature length comedy over a two reeler?"

"What did you like best about the picture?"

A few people recognized Billy as he strolled into the lobby.

"Hey! That's the fat man!"

Mae leaned closer to him, an arm locked in his. "Billy, I'm real proud of you."

A smiling Donovan pushed his way through a cordon of people.

"Don't run off, kids. I've booked half the tables at Baron Long's. We've all got some celebrating to do."

"Did you just book them?" Mae asked. "Or were you that sure of yourself?"

"You're damn right I was sure. I knew we had a hit when I saw the rough cut. But this is even better than I thought. Wait until I tell you what the boys from First National just said. Your boyfriend has a big surprise in store, girlie."

And then he was gone, ducking back into the crowd before Mae could set him straight or Billy could question him about the lack of writing credit.

"He really rubs me the wrong way," Mae said, letting go of Billy's arm. "He always has that smile on his face as though he knew something you didn't."

"I know. I always get the feeling that's he's laughing up his sleeve about something."

"He might just laugh out of the other side of his mouth one day."

"Well," Billy sighed, "that's Earl and there's nothing you can do about it. I shouldn't knock him. He's done swell by me, by and large."

Mae only grunted and drew a Spanish shawl tighter around her shoulders as they stepped outside into the bright square of light cast by the marquee's bare bulbs. Pipp was standing on the sidewalk waiting for his car, with Thelma Robeck towering above him, her body swathed in a beaver coat that nearly touched the ground. Pipp looked wan and the woman looked angry.

"Hi, Pipp," Billy said. "Went pretty well, didn't it?"

"Yes," Pipp said morosely. "I suppose it did."

"Pipp, I'd like you to meet Mae Pepper. Mae . . . Tom Pipp."

The little man extended a limp, slightly damp hand. "How do you do. I've certainly heard a lot about you from Billy. A pleasure, I'm sure."

"Same here," Mae murmured. Pipp's eyes fascinated her. They were like the eyes of a lonely child.

"And this is my . . . friend. Thelma . . . Thelma Robeck."

Thelma nodded imperiously, her eyes dark and brooding, flicking from Billy to Mae and then back again.

"Where *is* that car," she said, looking away.

"Listen," Billy said, almost too brightly. "We'll see you at the club in about an hour."

"What club?" Pipp asked.

"Why, you know, *the* club . . . Baron Long's place in Vernon. Didn't Donovan tell you?"

Pipp looked uncomfortable and cast a nervous glance at Thelma. She was looking impatiently up and down the street.

"We . . . I . . . didn't speak to Donovan," Pipp whispered. "Thelma's sore at him about something but she won't tell me what it is."

"Why don't you ask her?"

He shook his head sharply. It was almost like a twitch. "I'll find out soon enough."

"Find out what, Thomas?" Thelma asked, giving him a hard, bitter stare.

"Where Baron Long's is," Billy said blithely. "There's a marvelous supper party planned for the cast and crew. You're invited."

"Naturally I'd be invited, Mister Wells. Why wouldn't I be? Who's throwing this shindig? Donovan?"

"No. The top guys at First National. They didn't announce it in advance in case the picture was a flop."

Thelma drew herself to her full height. "Thomas doesn't make flops. Do you, Thomas?"

"No, Thelma." He was studying the sidewalk as though something terribly important lay at his feet. "I only make hits."

"Exactly!" Thelma said. "You keep that in mind. Every day, in every way, you're getting better and better. You remember that."

"Yes, Thelma."

"Artistically, physically and spiritually. Better and better." She smiled at Billy. A taut mask covering pure hate. "I suppose you and your lady friend will be there?"

"That's right," Billy said.

Thelma looked Mae up, and down, a brief, whittling glare of disdain.

"I suppose you'll help him to crow about how funny he was in the picture."

"Now, Thelma," Pipp blurted in an agony of embarrassment.

Mae's smile was pure honey. "Well, I'm sure you'll do some crowing of your own. But then, you know how us *lady friends* are."

Billy coughed, then placed a hand on Mae's shoulder and gave her a slight push. "Gotta be on our way. Hope you two can make it."

They walked in silence to where Billy had parked his car, a second-hand Moon that he had bought with his script money.

"Jesus," Mae finally said. "What a bitch."

"I'll say she is. She watches that poor guy like a hawk. Dave and I went over to his house a couple of times to work on the continuity and she practically listened at the keyhole all the time we were there and couldn't wait for us to leave."

"What does he see in her?"

"Damned if I know. I feel sorry for the sap. That's why I told her it was a First National party. She's mad at Earl for some reason and probably wouldn't go if she knew it was his party. But heck, I like the guy and we've got something to celebrate."

"Sure you do. You were great together." She pinched his arm as he opened the car door for her. "My jolly round straight man."

Billy winced. "I thought I looked tall and imposing, myself."

"Tall, imposing and talented. You really made Pipp shine." She kissed him lightly on the cheek before getting into the roadster. "And I have a feeling that he's professional enough to know it."

Donovan knew how to throw a party and Baron Long knew a high spending customer when he saw one. There was nothing but the best on the tables that Donovan had reserved. Mumm's champagne and bottles from the dwindling supply of preprohibition Scotch and London gin had been brought up from the cellar. Two-inch thick steaks were spluttering on the kitchen grills. Platters of sliced smoked salmon,

Russian caviar and other hors d'oeuvres abounded. A lot of picture people who had nothing at all to do with *The Bubblehead* drifted over from adjoining tables. Everyone was welcome. The more the merrier as far as Donovan was concerned.

Donovan rapped for attention, slapping a spoon against an empty champagne bottle.

"Well, folks, we did it. Do you know what Mister Groton and Mister Wiesenthal told me? These two fine looking gentlemen seated to my left?" Groton and Wiesenthal, First National executives, looked stupefied with food and drink. They grinned sloppily when they heard their names. "Well, Mister Groton and Mister Wiesenthal told me that they think *The Bubblehead* is going to be the comedy sleeper of the year, and who am I to say nay to that?" There were cheers and Donovan raised his hands for silence. "There were folks in this town who said that I was making a big mistake. That Pipp would run out of steam after two reels. They were wrong." Pipp, seated stiffly beside Thelma Robeck, was slapped vigorously on the back by half a dozen people standing behind him. "And there were folks who said I was crazy letting Dave Dale direct the picture. Who's crazy now?" More cheers. "And there were good folk who urged me to get an established comedian like Chester Conklin to play the role of the hotel manager, but who the hell could have played that part better than our own Billy Wells? Stand up, kid, and take a bow."

Billy stood, his mouth full, a napkin tied around his neck. Everyone was clapping him except Thelma Robeck.

"As a matter of fact," Donovan went on, "Mister Groton and Mister Wiesenthal who are the powers that be at First National, the fastest growing distribution company in the business I might add, were so darn impressed with Billy's scenes with Pipp that they insist he be in the next picture . . . which brings me to the high point of my speech. Pipp—the one and only Tom Pipp. Let's hear it for the little guy."

Pipp, waxen, torn between smiling and not smiling, glanced at Thelma Robeck who stared straight ahead.

"On your feet, Pipp," Donovan shouted over the applause. "Quiet down, everybody . . . quiet down."

Pipp stood up, gripping the edge of the table for support. He had not had a drink—Thelma had seen to that—but he looked half drunk.

"Thank you," he muttered. "It was marvelous working with all of you and . . . and I'm glad the picture turned out so well. Thank you all very much." And then he sat down, his forehead beaded with sweat.

"Thataboy," Donovan said. He held up a glass of champagne. "Let's all drink to the funniest Englishman since Charlie Chaplin. And let's drink to the future, because I have the great pleasure to announce that First National wants six . . . count 'em, folks . . . six more feature length Tom Pipp pictures within the next two years. And they say that the gold rush is over in California! As Al Jolson would say: folks, you ain't seen nothin' yet!"

Billy could only stare dully at his plate, the words not sinking in yet. *Six* pictures. *Two* years work. Somebody slapped him on the back. Somebody else shoved a glass of Scotch in his hand. His brain whirled. It meant big money, real dough for a change. He'd build a house. Somewhere along the coast . . . up in the wilds of Palos Verdes perhaps . . . build a gallery on top and place a telescope there . . . A big, brass telescope to watch the ships coming into San Pedro . . . steaming out . . .

"Oh, Billy, that's wonderful!"

Mae kissing him on the cheek. He downed half the Scotch.

"Mae, I'm going to get pie-eyed."

"Just don't dance," she said.

It was four in the morning before the party started to break up. Groton and Wiesenthal, who looked, respectively, like a butter and egg man and his bookkeeper, stayed until the band caved in from fatigue and the trombone player blew Taps. They had spent the night drinking champagne and dancing with Mae or any other good looking woman they could grab hold of. When they finally passed out, their chauffeur carried them, one by one, to their car.

Mae tried to repair the damage that Groton and Wiesenthal, and two or three other men, had caused to her dress, shoes and silk stockings. The stockings were *Holeproof,* but they had failed to live up to their name.

"Men . . ." she breathed to the powder room mirror. The only man who hadn't pawed her while dancing had been Pipp. She had danced one foxtrot with him before Thelma Robeck had seen what was going on and had intruded, complaining of a sick headache. Pipp had smiled wistfully at her before being dragged away from the party by what Mae felt certain was his jailer. A tall blonde girl stumbled into the room and collapsed on her knees in front of a toilet bowl and Mae exited before the heaves began.

"You got a ride home, baby?" A tanned young man with patent leather hair leered at her. She ignored him. She didn't have a ride home, come to think of it. She'd seen Billy leave about one in the morning, drunk as a lord, happily supported by Dave Dale and Al St. John. But there were always cabs—if she could borrow a dollar or two from someone.

Donovan was signing tabs at a table littered with plates, glasses and bottles, most of them empty. Baron Long sat next to him, smoking a cigar and nursing a mug of coffee.

"There go all the profits," Donovan said as he signed a final tab.

"No one told you to invite the world," the club owner said dryly. "You're sure a patsy for freeloaders."

"What the hell, it's only money." He stood up and brushed a strand of confetti streamer from his jacket. "Every night is New Year's Eve."

"Come by more often." Long shuffled the tabs into one pile like a deck of cards and then pointed to a bottle of Mumm's. "Might as well take that with you, Donovan. You paid for it."

Donovan shoved the bottle under his arm and headed for the door. His head was throbbing and he paused in the club's foyer and held the cold bottle of champagne against his brow. A dark-haired woman was looking at him and it took a moment before he recognized her.

"Headache," he said lamely.

"I know," Mae said. "I've got one of my own."

"Where's Billy?"

"Sleeping it off somewhere by now."

"When I throw a party I throw a party, don't I?"

"If you say so."

"You waiting for someone?"

"No. Just anyone who can lend me cab fare."

"I've got a car. Don't worry about it."

"Think you can see the road?"

"Maybe not, but who the hell cares?"

It was cold with the top down and plumes of mist blew across flat, wet fields. The powerful Stutz plowed through the mist like a dreadnought through the sea.

"I'm freezing to death!" Mae shouted over the roar of the motor. She sat huddled on the seat, her shawl wrapped around her head.

"It's good for you!" Donovan shouted back. "Smell that clean air!"

"Where are we?"

"Damned if I know! We don't seem to be on a road!"

"What?"

"I said . . .!" He slammed his foot on the brake and the car slid sideways to a halt. "I said we don't seem to be on a road. I missed

Western Avenue and made a wrong turn somewhere. It looks like we're driving across a bean field."

"How could you miss Western Avenue?" She sat up and leaned back against the door. "Did you plan this?"

"Yes and no. I wasn't taking you home. I thought you might like a bowl of clam chowder. I know this place in Redondo and I was taking you there." He glanced around at the pearl misted wasteland. "It's a bean field, all right. We could be anywhere."

"What do we do now?"

"Wait till the sun comes up, I guess."

"I'll be dead by then."

"Are you really cold?"

"I'm wearing a silk dress that weighs about an ounce and a half. Yes, I'm cold . . . right down to the bone."

Donovan sighed and got out of the car. He wrestled the canvas top out of the well, struggled with the supports and then locked the top in place with the levers on the rim of the windshield. He then opened the boxy trunk in the rear and took out a thick wool car blanket.

"It is cold at that," he said as he got back into the car and closed the door. He unfolded the blanket and handed it to Mae who took it eagerly and covered herself from the chin down.

"Do you want part of it?"

"No," he said. "Nothing like a little cold to clear the head. That and some champagne."

The bottle was lying on the back seat and he reached over for it and began to twist the wire around the cork.

"Want some?"

"Out of the bottle?"

"Either that or from your shoe." He eased the cork out with his thumb and it made a satisfactory pop. A foam of wine sheeted his hand.

"I know a guy who has a real bar in the back of his car." He took a pull from the bottle and then set it carefully on top of the dashboard. "Think of that . . . a bar. Damn thing is solid walnut and folds down, slides up. Full of glasses, bottles. Damndest thing you've ever seen."

"Sounds ostentatious."

"Sure, but the bo's in the big money and he wants to let people know it. Oranges. Owns half the trees in the state. And Doll owns the other half. That's a hell of a way to make money, let me tell you. Just sit on your keester and watch Mexicans pick fruit off the trees for about two bits a day and a plate of frijoles. They pack the oranges in a box, ship 'em east and the money rolls in like a river. Goddamndest thing you ever saw." He retrieved the bottle and took another drink. "Want some?"

He held it out for her and she took a sip and handed the bottle back to him.

"Nice."

"Sure. Not as good as chowder, but it'll have to do."

"Why don't you go into oranges if there's so much money in it?"

"There's no fun in an orange. I like pictures."

"You just made a good one."

"Yeah . . . and I'm going to make a lot more. Six more Pipps. Hell, that's just the beginning."

"I thought Billy was great."

"So did everybody else."

"It was a well-written story, too," she said, an edge to her voice.

Donovan chuckled softly and took another swig of champagne.

"Let me guess what you're driving at."

"I'll save you the trouble. He should've had a credit for it."

"I did him a favor. They don't like people who wear two hats in this town. He ain't Charlie Chaplin."

"Do you expect him to write these other pictures?"

"No. Just stick in his oar from time to time—for pay, you understand. Hell, he'll be making some real dough acting for a change. So if you're thinking of marrying the guy . . ."

She turned her head and looked through the window. The mist hung over the field in flat, luminescent sheets. There must have been a moon, but it was not visible.

"Have you got a cigarette?"

"Sure," he said, lighting one for her. "He is your boyfriend, isn't he?"

"We're just friends." She let the blanket slip down to her lap. "I don't sleep with him, so you can get that thought out of your head."

He lit a cigarette for himself and looked at her in the orange glow of the match.

"You're a real good looker. You could make it big in pictures with that face."

"Tell me something I haven't heard before. Every hot-eyed assistant director in town has the same line. They make me sick."

"I'm not an assistant director. If you want some parts you've got 'em."

"Fine. I can use the money."

"You don't like me, do you?"

"What makes you think that?"

"Come on, you're like a cat with its hair up most of the time. We can't talk for five minutes before sparks fly."

"Maybe I just don't like men who leer."

He laughed and reached for the champagne. "Baby, you've got me all wrong. I might enjoy looking at a fine piece of stuff, but I sure as hell don't leer." He drank from the bottle and passed it to her. "Anyway, if you don't like being leered at why don't you wear a sack? You go around half naked most of the time."

"I like to be comfortable."

"You make a bo's mickey rise just to look at you."

"Is that what I'm doing now? Making your mickey rise?"

"If you do, I'll let you know."

She sipped at the champagne and then placed the bottle on the seat between them.

"A woman shouldn't drink from a bottle."

"No, she shouldn't. There are hotels in Long Beach that have glasses in every room."

"Is that a proposition?"

"Sure sounds like one to me."

"Why?"

"Does a man need a reason?"

"Maybe not, but I do."

He rolled the window down and flipped his cigarette into the mist. "When I was a kid I was in a street gang. Toughest damn gang in—"

"God," she moaned. "Not the story of your life."

"Pipe down. It's important. Where was I?"

"In a gang somewhere."

"Boston . . . Sons of the Shamrock. I was maybe twelve, thirteen. No older than that because I ran off when I was fourteen and hitched up with a medicine show in Brookline."

"Bully," she said, retrieving the bottle. "I was sixteen when I was laid, married and went into vaudeville . . . all on the same day."

"That's your story, lady. I'm telling mine. A couple of kids would meet on the street. Tough kids, see, tough as nails. Strangers. You get my point?"

"No."

"They had to find out about each other. Test each other out to see if they'd be pals or blood enemies. They'd rassle . . . two falls out of three."

"Is that what you want to do with me? Wrestle?"

"In a manner of speaking. Yes."

247

"Oh, Jesus. I knew you'd be a problem the moment I set eyes on you."

MONTAGES

She lay on her left side, her head on his shoulder, her breasts pressed against his rib cage. Her left arm was beneath her, her right draped down across his body. Beyond him, through lace curtains stirring gently in the morning wind, she could see the vivid blue of the harbor, a battleship resting there as though painted on the sea.

Wind and water.

Coming down Rue de Bleury to St. Antoine with the wind off the river tugging at the hat that Aunt Marie had made for her, the straw with the bright red roses sewn to the crown. Montreal. The summer of 1912.

What had she been thinking of when he had stepped out of the shadows of Notre Dame? Charles Chambrun probably because he had been in her thoughts during those summer months. Very proper Charles Chambrun. So Catholic. So deferential toward her virginity. So willing to wait *pour la marriage.* We will honeymoon in France, he had said. Poor Charles Chambrun. He would go to *la belle France* in three years time with the Princess Pats and die among the wire at Festubert with his legs blown off at the hips. *C'est la vie.*

Bonjour, mam'zelle, are there any more in la maison like you?

A vaudevillian, of course, with his chocolate brown suit and yellow shoes, a brown bowler and a malacca cane. Tall, thin, horsefaced. He followed her to William Street, trying, in his bad French, to pick her up. What was there about him that intrigued her? Something. The underlying gloom of the man perhaps. His mordant jokes. He hated Montreal as much as she did, only he would only be there for a few days, playing the Rivoli, and then on to Toronto, Detroit, Chicago, Cleveland, Pittsburgh. Back in New York by winter, thank God, he said.

She could have kept on walking, pretending that she did not speak any English. And if she had done that her life would have been different. But she had stopped long enough to speak to him and he had taken her to a cafe and bought her pastry and a cherry phosphate. He had ordered a cup of coffee, but hadn't touched it, seated there with his long legs crossed, smoking cigarette after cigarette. And then he had taken her to the theater to see him perform in the matinee and she had fallen in love with him.

Had she really done that? Or had she only fallen in love with the magic of his life, the gypsy closeness of the backstage people, the powder, paint and the make-believe? Another world. She's a natural, the stage manager had said of her. Can you sing, baby? And she had said yes, yes I can sing and she went on that night in the costume of a bedridden soubrette, but not before the great Jimmy Pepper had initiated her into yet another world on a sagging divan in his airless dressing room.

God, she thought, stroking Donovan gently, listening to his deep, regular breathing, hearing the blood thump through his veins, Jimmy was a ghost who would never leave her alone. A ragged, dried out wraith. He had destroyed his manhood and his talent with hop and booze and then had blamed her for it. She felt no guilt, but the phantom was always there, squatting on the bedpost, pointing a bony, accusing finger at her. No guilt, but a kind of dull sadness from time to time, a regret that all Jimmy had really wanted was a woman to fuck whenever he felt the urge, a woman who would always be waiting for him when his anger and frustration went beyond his control. She could have helped him if he had only talked it out with her, but he kept so much of himself hidden, a private well of gall. Some of his rage came out in his humor, monologues that often went far above the heads of his audience and left them feeling uncomfortable and, at times, angry. He had come just a bit too soon. The solid citizens of Terre Haute and Indianapolis did not take kindly to ridicule. Babbitt was yet to be born.

Poor Jimmy, she thought, feeling Donovan stir beneath her hand. When success had come in the Follies it had been too late. He had burned himself hollow by then. That had been the final agony and the lushness of her body had only mocked him. No guilt about that, either. She had told him. Ziegfeld had told him. Sandow had told him. Everyone had told him, but he had kept on the booze and the hop anyway, digging his grave deeper day by day.

She could have joined him on that road to death. He would have been grateful for her company. They could have shut the dressing room door and mocked the world over bottles of rye and the little brown pills that he brought back in his pocket from Chinatown. Drift off together in dopey dreams.

If you love me, Mae . . .

Not that much, but too much to leave him. She had held on to life and he had hated her for it.

Donovan turned with a groan and reached out for her as many men

249

had reached out for her and she was waiting for him, warm and open, real.

Sunlight. Wind off the sea. There was a shadow in the room, but she closed her eyes to it.

You're nothing but a whore, Mae . . .

Whispers. But she did not hear.

A SHORT SCENE

"Damn but I feel great."

"You're driving better, I'll say that."

He took his hands off the wheel and held them up for her to see.

"Look! I can steer this baby with my knees."

"Don't."

"Oh, hell no. Let's get home in one piece."

"What are you going to tell your wife?"

"Doll's in Catalina—at a seance." The grin of the happy rassler faded and he looked glumly at the road ahead. "She has a new friend, see. A woman evangelist. Not a bad broad. A Texas pulpit thumper. She's teaching Doll how to play some screwy game called Mah-Jongg . . . five hundred bucks for a set of Chinese dominoes. She's also teaching her how to speak with the dead."

He pulled up at a roadside stand and bought two glasses of freshly squeezed orange juice.

"About you and me," he said.

"What about us?"

"I enjoyed every minute. You're a crazy lady in the kip."

"You're sorta screwball yourself."

"Doll's been a trial lately, but she's still my wife. I'm not planning on leaving her."

"No one asked you to."

"And I'm not the sort of bo who'd set up a dame in some fancy apartment."

"Swell. I don't like strings."

"Which doesn't mean I don't want to see you . . . from time to time."

"Drink your orange juice, Donovan. You talk too much."

REEL THIRTEEN

SHADOWS AND SUNSHINE

Pipp knew that Thelma was waiting, just biding her time before dropping the ax. She had been tight-lipped for weeks and virtually silent, an uneasy calm before an inevitable storm. That storm finally broke after a messenger boy from the studio delivered a mimeographed copy of Donovan Production No. 2, the completed scenario of *Sons of the Sea*.

"Ah ha!" she cried after leafing through the manuscript. "Just as I thought."

"Just as you thought what, Thelma?" Pipp asked. They were at breakfast, she with a plate of ham, eggs and hash brown potatoes in front of her, he with a glass of prune juice and a piece of dry toast.

"I take it that you're the 'thin sailor' and Mister Wells is the 'fat sailor'?"

Pipp moistened his lips with the prune juice. "We'll be given names in the continuity. I'll be Tom and he'll be Bill."

"You'll be Tom and he'll be Bill," she sneered. "How original. Or will it be *Bill* and *Tom* on the title cards? Answer me that if you can."

"I don't understand you, Thelma."

"No, of course you don't. You don't understand the simplest things. Your thinking processes have rotted away in your skull. Half of your mind is gone."

Pipp squirmed on his seat and avoided looking into her furious eyes. "Don't talk that way, Thelma."

She banged the manuscript on the table with such force that the plates jumped.

"Don't you dare tell me how to talk and how not to talk! Don't you

251

dare! If you didn't have me to look after you—"

"I know that, Thelma," he said quickly.

". . . you'd be nothing by now. *Nothing!* A skid row bum, that's what you'd be!"

"Yes, Thelma."

"Or locked up in a loony bin." She picked up the script and waved it at him. "It's right in front of your eyes and you can't see it. You can't see what they're doing to you. My God, I've never met a man as stupid as you." She pushed her plate away and stood up. "Get your coat on, Thomas. We're going to the studio right this minute and have it out with your precious Mister Donovan once and for all."

Pipp's brain whirled in bewilderment. He felt suddenly sick to his stomach and could barely find the strength to stand.

"Have what out, Thelma? What?"

"Shut up! Don't you talk back to *me*. Don't you dare!"

Hank drove them to the studio, slouched indolently behind the wheel, ignoring his two silent passengers in the back seat. Pipp looked green and he wondered what all the commotion was about, not that he gave a damn. Just so long as the bitch stayed off his back.

"Don't drive so fast," Thelma snapped.

"Go fuck yourself," he muttered, but slowed down.

Donovan tilted back in his chair and folded his hands behind his head. The gesture of nonchalance seemed to goad Thelma into such a paroxysm of rage that she became inarticulate.

"You're not making any sense," Donovan said, finally getting a word in.

Thelma almost hurled herself against the desk. "Well! Well, mister high and mighty, we'll see about that! We'll soon see. There are lawyers in this town . . . yes . . . lawyers . . . we'll see about *that!*" Then, spluttering, her face scarlet, she turned away, grabbed an ashen, quaking Pipp by the hand and pulled him out of the office. Her words seemed to linger in the room for a moment like the echo of distant thunder.

"What the hell was that all about?" Gilboy asked, stepping in from the adjoining room.

"I'm trying to sort it out in my head. Is Dave here?"

"Yeah, he went out for coffee."

"Part of that storm was directed at him . . . the poor bastard."

"What did he do?"

"I dunno. Far as I can make out he's been screwing some dame

252

named Gretchen and Thelma doesn't like it."

Gilboy scratched the side of his nose. "Gretchen, hunh."

"You know her?"

"Yeah, That is, I've seen her around Pipp's house. One of Thelma's relatives. Her daughter, if you ask me."

"Under age, you think?"

"Oh, hell no. Got a kid."

Donovan pulled a pen from the inkstand and toyed with it. "I don't know what she's getting a lawyer for. Damned if I do. She went on and on about the script. About Billy . . . about Pipp being thrust into the background . . . about my ruining his talent."

"The woman's a mental case."

"Maybe so, that only makes her more dangerous. I think we've got a problem on our hands. Did you talk to that navy guy this morning?"

"Yeah, just hung up when that bitch started screaming. We can use the four stacker for a week, then they tow her up to Oakland for wrecking. So, the way I figure it, we'll have to start shooting on April twenty-seventh and be done with the exteriors by May fourth. The twenty-seventh is a week from tomorrow. Doesn't give us much time, but we'll be ready."

"If Pipp doesn't fuck us up."

"Pipp? Why should he? He loves the story."

"Maybe, but she sure as hell doesn't—and what she says goes, if you ask me."

Gilboy pondered over that for a moment. "You got a point. I guess they'll go home. I better hightail it over there and see if I can smooth the waters."

"Forget it. She threatened me with a lawyer. I bet she's dragged Pipp off to some shyster."

"What the hell is she after?"

"Damned if I know for sure, but I guess we'll find out soon enough."

Dale passed in the hall, a script under his arm, a mug of coffee in one hand. Donovan called out to him and he stuck his head around the door.

"Yeah?"

"Come in for a second, Dave. I want to ask you something."

"Sure. What is it?"

"Can you think of any reason why Thelma Robeck would be sore at you?"

The director blushed slightly. "No, why?"

"Because she was in here blowing her cork about a hundred different things. One of those things had to do with you . . . you and a girl named Gretchen."

"What did she say?"

"That every time you go to the house for a story conference you sneak upstairs and screw the girl silly."

Dale clenched the cup so tightly it shook in his hand, coffee slurping over the rim and dripping to the floor.

"That's a goddamn lie!"

"You don't know the girl?"

Dale struggled for composure. "No . . . I mean . . . sure, I *know* her, but we've never done anything except talk. God damn that filthy-minded bitch!"

"Okay, okay," Donovan sighed. "I believe you, but stay away from her until Thelma calms down."

"I'd like to get her out of that house," Dale said, his voice tight with rage. "She lives in hell there . . . absolute hell."

"Maybe, maybe," Donovan said, "but the battle-axe is on a tear, so for Christ's sake use your head and stay away. Don't even write the girl. What is she to Thelma? Frank thinks it's her daughter."

"Could be," Dale said solemnly. "She won't talk about the old bag. I dunno, there's something funny going on there, but I can't quite put my finger on it. All I know is that she's a sweet girl who's never had anything in her life but a whole lot of pain."

"Is she married? Frank says she has a kid."

The director squared his huge shoulders and looked defensive.

"So she has a kid, so what? She got in trouble. It happens."

"No skin off my nose," Donovan said.

"She's a nice girl," Dale almost shouted.

"I'm sure she is. Let's drop the subject. The Navy's giving us a destroyer for a week. Take a run down to Long Beach and look her over."

"Okay." He had a determined look in his eyes. "I'll do that right now."

"Yeah," Donovan grunted. "Stay out of sight. I've got a funny feeling that we haven't seen the last of Thelma today."

She was back at the office at three o'clock, Pipp trailing along in her shadow. A man that Donovan had never seen before was with them, a tall, bald-headed man who introduced himself as Harold Cornwall, attorney-at-law.

"I told you there were lawyers in this town," Thelma crowed triumphantly. "Mr. Cornwall is going to set you out to dry!"

"That'll do, Mrs. Robeck" the lawyer said, a slight edge to his tone. "Let us not resort to acrimony." He rubbed his hands together as though washing them and smiled icily at Donovan. "I feel certain we can work out our problems with both civility and dispatch."

"I've got no problems," Donovan said dryly.

"I differ in that opinion," Cornwall said. "May we sit down?"

Donovan waved airily at some chairs. "Make yourselves comfortable." He smiled at Pipp who was staring at the floor. "If I'd known you were unhappy about anything, Tom, we could have talked it over."

"I do the talking for Thomas," Thelma said as she sat in a chair next to the lawyer. "He knows nothing about business."

"Maybe not," Donovan said, "but I'd like to talk to him alone for a few minutes."

Thelma's face was stone. "Never. You've bullied the poor man long enough. Treated him like dirt!"

The lawyer cleared his throat noisily. "Let's get down to the facts of the argument as I understand them. The contract with Mr. Pipperal is quite specific in that you agree to star Mr. Pipperal, professionally known as Tom Pipp, in a series of feature moving pictures at a sum of twelve hundred and fifty dollars per week plus five percent of the net profits, that twelve hundred and fifty dollar stipend to be increased to fifteen hundred dollars per week after the third picture."

"Right," Donovan said. "Only I told Pipp I was raising it to that for the second picture and then up to two grand for the third. I've done right by the kid. He has no kicks."

"That's *your* opinion," Thelma snorted.

The lawyer pursed his lips and looked up at the ceiling.

"The bone of contention as far as Mr. Pipperal is concerned is not the money, although the sum of fifteen hundred dollars is quite inadequate, but rather your violation of the spirit of the contract, namely that Mr. Pipperal is to *star* in these films and not, in the argot of comedians, share the laughs with another comic."

Donovan leaned back in his chair and swung his legs onto the edge of the desk. He had the picture now, could see the look of brooding resentment on Thelma's face, an expression now tinged with righteous triumph as Mr. Cornwall continued talking.

"The increasing comedic role of a Mr. Billy Wells, as evidenced by the scenario of *Sons of the Sea,* detracts from the star status of my client and violates the basic covenant of the contract."

255

"Horse balls," Donovan said.

The lawyer raised a pencil thin eyebrow. "I beg your pardon?"

"I said horse balls. Pipp, how do you feel about sharing a laugh or two with the fat guy?"

Pipp was incapable of speech. He was standing behind Thelma, hands gripping the back of the chair, his face devoid of expression as though in a trance. Scared out of his wits, Donovan was thinking.

"What exactly are you after?"

The lawyer glanced briefly at Thelma Robeck.

"Spell it out for him," she said.

"First of all," the lawyer said, fixing Donovan with a judicial stare, "Mr. Pipperal demands an immediate increase in salary to one reflecting his status, say, three thousand dollars per week now and four thousand in six months time. Secondly, Mr. Pipperal must have total script approval so as to avoid the watering down of his roles. Thirdly, and most important of all, the inclusion of Billy Wells or any other comedian as a quasi partner to Mr. Pipperal must end forthwith. That will in no way be tolerated. Mr. Pipperal is the star and will remain the star. I might remind you of Paragraph Ten, Subsection D of Mr. Pipperal's contract which provides for full salary to be paid in case of Mr. Pipperal's illness and subsequent inability to work. The realization that he will be forced to share the spotlight with Mr. Wells in this upcoming production is making Mr. Pipperal quite ill. Yes indeed, the nervous strain and anxiety are taking a heavy toll on the man's health. I would not be a bit surprised if he found himself too sick to report for work when *Sons of the Sea* goes before the cameras in a week's time unless there is a radical revision of the script."

Donovan rubbed a thumb across the bridge of his nose. They had him in a bucket and he knew it. He avoided looking at Thelma Robeck because he knew the limits of his temper. Hurling an ashtray at her wouldn't solve one damn thing.

"Let me think it over," he said.

"Take your time," the lawyer said, standing up. "My office is in the Bradbury building. I shall expect to hear from you by noon tomorrow. Time is somewhat of the essence. We don't want to drag this matter out, do we?"

"No," Donovan said quietly. "We don't."

Lights burned in the Donovan Productions bungalow long into the night and shadows crisscrossed the shaded windows as the men inside

256

paced the rooms. Billy was there, Frank Gilboy, Benny Shapiro— production assistant—and two writers, Max Gilder and Harry Knight. Donovan had two options: to ignore the threat or to give into it. An evaluation of the scenario was being made to see how it might play if the role of the fat sailor were eliminated. Billy, who had helped to write the story, was incapable of contributing anything to its surgery. He sat miserably at one end of the conference table while Max and Harry, two excitable New Yorkers, screamed suggestions at one another, chewed pencils and drank coffee. They reached a sudden accord at three o'clock in the morning and went into Donovan's office, Billy walking leaden footed behind them.

"Well?" Donovan asked.

"It won't work," the two writers said in unison. "It just cuts the heart right out of it."

"The fat sailor is more than just a straightman," Max said.

"He's an integral cog in the entire machinery," Harry added.

"The comedy comes out of the interplay," they said together.

Donovan rapped a pencil against the telephone on his desk.

"Go on home. Get some sleep."

"Do you want us to think up a new story?" Max asked.

"No." The pencil rattled against the phone like a drumstick. "We go with this scenario or we go with nothing. Nobody's going to push *me* around." He glared at everyone in the room as though daring an argument.

"Listen, Earl," Billy said wearily. "There's no point in cutting off your own nose. What the hell, I know we can come up with something that'll make Thelma happy."

"I'm not interested in making Thelma happy," Donovan said tightly. He plucked the phone from the cradle and dialed a number. "That goddamn Dave should be here. What the hell did he do in Long Beach? Join the fucking fleet?"

Gilboy yawned. "Maybe he stayed down there for the night. What do we need him for anyhow?"

Donovan hung up in disgust. "He's the director, ain't he? The picture's in trouble. He oughta be here. Jesus, I don't know what to do. Fight it out in court, I guess."

"Is that what your lawyers think?" Billy asked.

"They don't know what to think. Neither do I. Thelma'd slip rat poison in the little guy's booze. They'd haul him into court on a stretcher with ten doctors hovering around him. That pay-if-sick clause

257

is legit and it's her big ace in the hole."

Billy took a deep breath. He was aching with weariness and depressed to the point of weeping, but he felt a sense of obligation, a sense of nobility.

"Look, Earl, let's be sensible about this. The woman's got you by the short hairs. You know it. Hell, we all know it. Scrap the goddamn thing. Write me out of the picture. I appreciate your sticking up for me, but . . ."

Donovan's smile was cryptic. "I'm not sticking up for you, Billy. I'm Earl Patrick Donovan, see, and nobody plays me for a sap."

Donovan spent the butt end of the night in his office, stretched out on a leather couch, smoking cigarettes and glowering into the darkness. Dawn inched into the room and he was happy to see it. He phoned Myron Levin at home and the lawyer advised him to go along with Thelma Robeck's demands, except for the money, they could negotiate on that point . . .

"Hell," Levin said, "it isn't the dough, you know that, Earl. She's just got her nose out of joint because she thinks the tubby fella is stealing laughs from Pipp."

"But he isn't," Donovan said. "Damn it to hell, why can't she see that? Something happens when Billy and Pipp are together. I can't quite explain it, Myron, but something clicks. The audience sensed it on the Bubblehead picture, so did the brass at First National. Billy makes everything Pipp does seem a whole lot funnier than it is. Anyway, that's not the point, see. I don't like anyone getting their hooks into me like this. If I give her a fingernail she'll snatch my whole arm."

"Swallow your pride. Go along with it. What the hell, it's only for six pictures."

Donovan hung up in disgust and there was Dave Dale standing in the doorway. He gave him a savage glance.

"Where the hell have you been?"

"Around," Dale said quietly.

"The tin can okay? Or is it messed up like everything else around here?"

"I didn't see the destroyer. I . . . I didn't go to the navy yard yesterday."

"Terrific. What the hell did you do, then?

Dale shifted his feet and scowled at the floor. "I got married."

"You got married," Donovan said dully. "Congratulations."

"I married Gretchen . . . Gretchen Robeck. Thelma's daughter. We eloped."

"I didn't figure Thelma gave the bride away. What made you do a dumb thing like that?"

The big man looked shaken. He ran a hand through his hair and came into the room to walk slowly back and forth in the space between the desk and the couch.

"God . . . what that poor girl's been through. You wouldn't believe it, Earl. It's like something out of a horror story, I swear to God."

Donovan lit a cigarette and handed it to Dale as the man shambled past.

"Thanks," he said. "I had to get her out of there. That's where I went when I left here. I drove by the house, didn't see the car and so I went in. She was alone . . . and crying. She cries a lot."

"Maybe you'll get used to it."

The director puffed on his cigarette and stared into space.

"Not with me. Never cries with me. I make her happy. She told me that the first time I talked with her. Gosh, she's got the cutest little kid you ever saw. Frieda. That's her name. Frieda."

"She cry, too?"

"Cute as hell. Just a baby, and by God that kid won't have a rotten childhood like her mother. I'll see to that. We'll both see to that." He stood transfixed at the window as though seeing their future in the rosy clouds of morning.

Donovan cleared his throat. "Okay. I'm happy for you, but there's going to be hell and fury from a certain party."

Dale dropped his cigarette on the carpet and crushed it with his heel.

"If I see that woman I'll sock her in the jaw. I swear to God I will!"

"That's all we need right now, you socking Thelma. Sit down, we have a lot to talk about."

If Dale heard him, he paid no attention. His pacing became more agitated.

"She told me everything . . . every detail of her life. A whore, that's all her mother was, a traveling prostitute. The guy who lives there, Rolfe, that's her father, but he's been in and out of jails or institutions for as long as she can remember. A year or so ago he got in big trouble in Milwaukee for trying to abuse a five-year-old girl, but ran off before they got him. She lives in terror that he might try to harm little Frieda and—"

"Hold it a minute," Donovan said as he came around from behind his desk. "Is all this on the level?"

Dale looked blank. "Level?"

Donovan gripped him by the shoulders and shook him. It was like trying to shake a tree.

"Is it true? Can you back it up?"

"Back it up? You mean about Rolfe?"

"What the hell do you think I mean? Sure, Ralph, or whatever the hell his name is."

"I guess so. I don't think Gretchen would lie. Hell, I know she wouldn't lie."

"Where's Gretchen now?"

"At my place."

"Get her out of there. Thelma's bound to put two and two together when she finds the girl gone. She'll be out looking for you and it'll be Nellie-bar-the-door. Take her to Mae's place . . . and you stay with her."

"I don't see why I have to hide," he protested.

Donovan reached for the telephone. "Don't give me an argument." He dialed Gilboy's number and whistled softly between his teeth until the man answered. "Frank, do you know any cops in Milwaukee?"

Her anger surpassed anything that Pipp had ever seen before. She was a demented creature storming about the house, venting her rage on the furnishings, particularly in Gretchen's room. The night was hideous with Thelma's inarticulate shrieks, the splintering of wood and the crashing of glass. Pipp crawled into bed fully clothed and pulled the blankets over his head, but there was no shutting out the storm. She came into his room every few minutes to shout obscenities and threats, blaming him personally for "the rotten underhanded" behavior of his associates.

"But . . . you don't know if she went off with Dave," he muttered into his pillow.

She did not hear him. Anyway, she knew that Gretchen and her baby had gone off with Dave Dale. The maid had seen him come to the house. She hadn't seen Gretchen and little Frieda leave with him, but it was obvious that they had done so.

"Kidnapped!" she howled. "I'll have that bastard put in jail!"

There was no point in trying to reason with her. At dawn she was on the phone to the police and their reluctance to become involved in what appeared to be a family matter drove her fury to a new pitch. He

260

heard her leave the house at seven in the morning, chauffered by a silent Hank who knew when to keep his mouth shut. She was home by noon, the quarry uncaught, murder in her eyes.

It was not a day to get out of bed, Pipp reasoned. He was still hiding under the blankets when he heard the muted sound of a car pulling into the drive. He jumped out of bed and peeped through the window to see Donovan and Frank Gilboy getting out of the Stutz.

Pipp stood on the upper landing and tried to make out what was being said in the living room, but could hear only the low rumble of Gilboy's voice. He crept timorously down the stairs, overcome by curiosity, and yet fearful of being seen by either Thelma or Donovan. How could he ever look Donovan in the face again? He felt flushed with shame for the words that had been put in his mouth by the lawyer. He had wanted to cry out—*Look . . . listen . . . this is wrong. I like working with Billy. I like the laughs we get. Yes, we . . . a laugh is a laugh. It doesn't matter how you get it. I won't be a party to this. Never!* So easy to speak with such conviction in the safety of his thoughts. "You poor twit," he whispered, crossing the hall toward the closed living room door, moving with a mouse's caution.

OH, GOD! DAMN YOU TO HELL!

Thelma's voice. A howl of such despairing rage that it reminded Pipp of the scream of a horse caught in the quagmire of a Queensland river. The sound turned his blood to wax and drove every thought clear out of his head. When the door burst open and Thelma charged out of the room beyond, he was helpless to move from her path.

GODDAMN YOU, TOO.

She swept him aside with one swing of her powerful arm and he staggered against the glass front of a grandfather's clock and cringed there, limp with terror.

GODDAMN EVERY ONE OF YOU.

And then she disappeared from view up the stairs. There was the slamming of a door followed by an awful silence as though the house had swallowed her.

"Well, that's that," Donovan said. He was strolling casually out of the living room, folding a piece of paper. His eyes, sparkling with amusement, met Pipp's blank stare. "You can come out now, Pipp. Frank and I have the situation well in hand."

"What . . . situation?" Pipp asked, his voice cracking in his dry throat.

"Why, your domestic situation, of course. Thelma Robeck has decided to leave Los Angeles with her husband."

"Her husband?"

Donovan shook his head in pity. "You knew Rolfe was her husband, didn't you?"

Pipp nodded dumbly. Of course he knew that. He had figured out the relationships a long time ago. But what did it mean? Why was she leaving? He couldn't trust his voice to ask.

Donovan waved the paper at him before slipping it into the pocket of his coat.

"You are now free and clear. For a price, you understand. You can't sleep with another man's wife for a year or so and not pay a red cent. Wouldn't be the decent thing to do, would it? Still, Frank and I worked out a reasonable settlement. Ten grand in cash and the car. Hell, you can't drive the damn thing anyway, so what's the loss of a Maxwell sedan?"

"Nothing . . . I guess."

"And she'll be giving back her power of attorney and the deed to this house." He glanced over his shoulder at Gilboy who was ambling his way into the hall, thumbs hooked in his vest pockets, a self-satisfied look on his face. "You can tell Pipp how we did it, Frank. And keep a closer eye on the kid from now on. He may not be as lucky next time."

YOU'RE A FREE SOUL, PIPP. REMEMBER THAT. SKIP ALONG THE DECK . . . DON'T WALK . . . THATABOY . . . NOW WAVE TO THE CAPTAIN ON THE BRIDGE. TRY TO STOP HIM, BILLY . . . SMILE UP AT THE CAPTAIN IN APOLOGY AND SALUTE. YOU KEEP WAVING, PIPP . . . THAT'S THE WAY . . . CUT.

The sun shimmered off the water of the harbor. Noon. No shadows. Dave Dale lowered his megaphone and pulled a pouch of chewing tobacco from his back pocket.

"Good," he called out. "That was a good scene. We'll do the dockside business right after lunch."

The thin sailor and the fat sailor smiled at each other. Pipp did a softshoe shuffle and a buck and wing.

"What if I did that in the shot . . . before they take the camera away?"

Billy looked dubious. "Wrong spot for it, Tom. Do you think you could do that on a gun barrel—if we coated it with resin?"

Pipp glanced forward at the old destroyer's three-inch gun.

"Sure. As long as we keep it horizontal."

262

"And then the gun crew swing the cannon outboard."

"Righto . . . jolly good. And the captain yells down to you to get me off of there."

"And I climb up and walk across . . . wobbling, unsure of my footing . . ."

"And then the gun swings up . . ."

"And you slide down and hold onto me . . ."

"And we sway back and forth . . ."

"And then the captain yells at the crew to lower the gun . . ."

"Only they lower it too much and I fall off into the sea."

"No, you hold on and I fall off. I'm the slob who always pays."

Pipp shook his head in concern. "That's a long fall. You could hurt your neck."

"No," Billy said. "The neck's swell. And anyway, I'd go into the water feet first. It's not that much of a drop."

"Well, it's up to you. Be a funny bit. I could hold onto the gun by sticking my arm down the barrel. They could cut to a shot of the crew putting a shell into the gun and then . . ."

Ideas flowed from them like a cool, clear spring. The continuity of *Sons of the Sea* was nothing more than a guideline. Gags and bits of business came to them at the spur of the moment, effortless and effective ad libs. Dale allowed them free rein. The first reel of the picture was in the can and it was all pure gold.

They were not as compatible off the set. They had nothing in common socially, no shared interests—other than the picture—that they could talk about. When the assistant director yelled for the company to break for lunch Billy would go with the gang, to eat and then to join the crap game that the crew invariably started, while Pipp would seek a quiet spot where he could read a book and perhaps nibble an apple and a handful of raisins. No one resented his need for solitude. He was not thought of as being "standoffish" or "too good for the rest of us," he was just being Pipp. That was the way he was and everyone accepted it.

He tried to concentrate on the passage he was reading, but his eyes kept going over and over the same lines. *Perhaps the smile and tender tone . . . came out of her pitying womanhood. Perhaps the smile and tender tone . . .* He set the book aside and gazed out past the railing at the dock. Iron roofed warehouses, a crane immobile against the hard blue sky, the cameraman walking along the dock checking angles, his assistant tossing bread crusts to the gulls, Dave Dale pitching a baseball to one of the grips who had brought a catcher's mitt. *Perhaps the smile*

263

and tender tone . . . came out of her pitying womanhood. He closed his eyes for a moment and recalled the lines that followed . . . *for am I not, am I not, here alone . . . so many a summer since she died . . . my mother, who was so gentle and good?*

"Yes," he said softly. His fingers toyed with the leather binding. Alfred, Lord Tennyson. Tennyson . . . Lord Alfred Tennyson . . . Alfred Tennyson, Lord . . . *Half lost in the liquid azure bloom of a crescent of sea . . . the silent sapphire-spangled marriage ring of the land . . .* "Lovely bit of verse, that. Lovely."

He saw Billy emerge from the shadowed alley between two buildings and cross the dock toward the gangplank. A woman was with him— tall, slender, dark haired. They were both laughing, Billy's laugh like a tug's horn, her's like a golden bell. Up the gangplank and along the deck toward where he was seated below the bridge. Where had he seen the woman before? Of course, Mae Pepper. Eyes weak. Needed glasses. Vanity. Bloody hopeless twit.

"Tom, you remember Mae, don't you?"

"Of course," Pipp said, getting to his feet, blinking in the sun. "Nice to see you again."

"Same here," Mae said, smiling at him.

"Mae's going to play the girl on the dock and I thought we might run over a few things with her before they set up."

"Oh yes? Jolly nice little part, that."

"Yes," Mae said. "Mr. Donovan phoned me last night and told me I'd got it."

How graceful she looked, Pipp was thinking. Long, smooth neck, slender hands and wrists . . . high cheek bones . . . olive skin . . . very large bosoms for such a delicate frame. Exquisite. He wiped a bead of sweat from his upper lip with a pallid hand.

"I'm sure Dave has ideas about the role," he said, "but Billy and I sort of play around with things and see what tickles our fancy. The girl has to play it straight, you know, no mugging about. Not a *girl*, really. A woman. Anxious to be with her boy friend, not knowing that he's a rotten chap, a bully, our nemesis the bosun's mate—Mike Dale—all muscles and swaggering malehood."

Mae laughed. "That's Mike all right!"

"Yes," Pipp said, his voice flat. "Quite a contrast to me . . . to the part I play."

"But you flirt with me, don't you?"

"Well, in a way. You see, Billy thinks of himself as a lady's man and he thinks you're giving him the glad eye, and I think you're giving me the glad eye, but what you're really doing is smiling at Mike who is coming down the gangplank behind us. That sets up the complications and the shoving match with Mike."

"Do I have to get pushed into the water?"

"Does she?" Billy asked. "I was going to ask Dave about that. It seems to me that there might be too many falling into the water gags. I mean, I fall in . . . and the admiral falls in."

Pipp scratched his head. "Bit overdone. I think Dave might like to change that. I don't think she should fall in the water. Mucky bit of sea that . . . oil . . . orange peels and stuff. Point is, this leads up to the final scene in the picture. Shooting it out of continuity, but this leads up to the fade-out scene. I rescue you and we walk off together. Finis. How would it work if she fell off into a boat? Little rowboat and the boat drifts away? Somehow . . . don't quite know how yet . . . but I get into the boat and we fade out drifting off into the sunset . . . using my jumper as a sail. How would that be?"

"Sounds okay to me," Billy said. "I'll talk it over with Dave."

"Good chap that," Pipp said after Billy walked away. "Awfully hard worker."

"Yes." Mae said.

"Vaudeville. The only school. So many people coming into pictures now are terribly lazy. They can get by on their looks and so they don't bother to learn anything."

"That's true."

"You were on the boards, I understand."

"Yes . . . with Billy."

"You're very beautiful. You should try for dramatic roles."

"Oh, no," she laughed. "I'm not a very good actress. I can play straight and help a gag along. That's about it."

"That's a talent, too, you know. I . . . I think we can work well together in the scene."

"I hope so."

"Yes, so do I." He could think of nothing he wanted more. "If you feel at all insecure about anything, please let me know and I'll help you."

"That's very nice of you, Mr. Pipp."

"Just Pipp," he said, blushing slightly. "Or Tom."

"Pipp, then. It sounds better than Tom. *Tom's* are big, hearty guys who sell cars."

That made him laugh. A rare sound, he thought wryly. In the business of making people laugh and never laughed himself. Nothing to laugh about. He felt giddy, as though he had downed a glass of cold champagne on an empty stomach. An odd, but wonderful sensation. He touched Mae lightly on the arm, feeling the resilient flesh beneath the soft fabric of her dress.

"Always call me Pipp, then, but never *mister*. Pipp has a Dickensian ring to it, don't you think? A bit old wordly. Have you ever read *Great Expectations?*"

"No . . . I don't think I . . ."

He gripped her arm. "Lovely book. Not the same spelling. Two p's in my name, one in his. Just Pip . . . one p. Beautiful story. You should read it some time. Mrs. Haversham . . . the beautiful and provocative Estella."

God, he was thinking. I'm speaking like a drunk, words tumbling out in a rush. Bloody twit. He let go of her arm and wiped his forehead with the palm of his hand. "Awfully hot on this deck, isn't it?"

She knew men well enough to sense his infatuation. She also sensed his discomfort. She smiled at him, but he avoided looking at her.

"Maybe we'd better go down to the dock," she said.

"Yes," he mumbled, glaring at his feet. "About time to start."

As they came down the gangplank, two cars bearing the second unit camera crew and some cast members turned onto the dock. Mike Dale was standing on the runningboard of the leading car, a deeply tanned giant in a white sailor suit. When he spotted Mae he let out a shout, jumped nimbly from the slowly moving car and ran up to her.

"Mae! You goddamn beautiful babe!"

He swept her off her feet with one arm and held her against the barrel of his chest.

"Damn! It's good to see ya, babe! How come we keep missing each other?"

"Put me down, you big ape!" She kissed him on the nose. "Come on, muscles, you're breaking my ribs!"

He grinned wickedly as he reached up with his free hand and pinched her lightly on one breast.

"You've got too much padding there to break anything." He set her back on her feet and then held her at arm's length. "Damn, but you're a sight for sore eyes. Let's go off some place and pitch woo for an hour."

"Same old Mike," she laughed. "Can't you find enough women out here without bothering me?"

"Hell! They don't make 'em like you, babe. You're my type."

"Anything in a skirt is your type."

He let go of her and stood arms akimbo. "Yeah, I guess you're right, Mae baby. I want to make every dame in the world happy."

Dave Dale slouched past, glowering at his brother. "Get your mind off your pecker for a minute and let's run through the scene. Places, everybody."

Mae smoothed her hair and straightened her dress.

"Where do I go, Dave?" she asked.

He pointed vaguely down the dock. "Oh, just stand over there some place. I'll have you walk into the shot."

Mae wandered off to one side, past the camera and the light reflectors to where Billy and Pipp were seated before a makeup table.

"Do I look all right, fellas?"

Billy eyed her critically. "Fine. Just a dab more rouge and a little heavier on the lipstick. You lost half of it on Mike's nose."

"That man!" She bent forward, leaning between the two men to look at herself in a mirror. "He should be kept in a cage."

"He . . . he seemed to be very fond of you," Pipp said quietly.

"Well, we've known each other for a hundred years."

BILLY—the name called in a megaphone boom—YOU AND MIKE FOR THE FIRST SHOT. BREAK A LEG . . .

Billy plucked a paper bib from his neck and hurried away from the table. Mae sat in the vacated chair and searched on the table for a jar of rouge.

"Mike's a great kidder," she said.

"Yes," Pipp said tonelessly. "Quite a . . . womanizer . . . or so I understand."

"Oh, sure. God's gift, but a woman would have to have feathers for brains to fall for his line. Honestly, I don't see how he gets away with it. He acts like a cave man."

"Some women like that, don't they?"

"I guess so, but don't ask me why."

He glanced furtively at her. "I think you'd enjoy *Great Expectations.*"

"What?"

"*Great Expectations*— the book by Dickens."

"Oh, yes, I'm sure I would."

"I . . . I have a very fine copy. It belonged to my mother and Dickens wrote an inscription on the flyleaf. My mother had been quite literary.

She belonged to a society of some kind in London when she was a girl and Mr. Dickens was a guest at one of their functions."

"That's very interesting," Mae said, studying her face in the glass as she toned rouge over a cheekbone.

"Yes, quite a valuable book. Sentimentally, at least." He felt out of breath and had to stop speaking for a moment. "I'd like you to have it . . . as a . . . a gift."

"That's very sweet of you, but—"

"No, please," he stammered. "I . . . I really would like you to . . ."

OKAY, PIPP. LET'S GO!

He jumped up as though jerked by a wire and hurried away without uttering another sound.

She forgot about the book. The afternoon was long, hectic, but productive. Her scenes went like a charm and Dave Dale was more than satisfied. She had another couple of days' work on the dock location and then a week of interiors at the studio. Her career was looking up, not that she cared about that. Her life seemed to lack direction and she was content to drift, taking each day as it came. Billy lectured her about that as they drove back to Hollywood from Long Beach in the late afternoon.

"Damn it, Mae. You gotta hit while the iron's hot in this business. You heard Dave rave about you, and he may be a pal, but he's a hard-nosed director, too. If you hadn't done a good job he'd have bawled your socks off and kicked you off the set. You're a damn fine comedienne. you could be a star, Mae."

"Oh, sure," she scoffed.

"I mean it. Look, how many pretty comediennes are there? And although nobody's coming right out and saying so, Mabel Normand's career is over. The Taylor case ruined her at the box office. You could step right into that void. I bet Sennett would grab you in a minute. This picture is going to be a swell showcase for you and I'm going to see to it that—"

"Let's not talk about it now. All I can think about is a hot bath and a stiff drink."

Why not? She had everything it took to be a success in pictures: looks, talent . . . connections. All that she lacked was the drive, the hunger to get ahead. She had never had that drive in vaudeville. Ziegfeld had been after her. She could have wrapped the man around her finger and he would have starred her in a show if that was what she had wanted. Flo hadn't been able to keep his hands away from her body. Always touching her here . . . there. A pat . . . a pinch.

She raised her supine body slightly in the bath and watched the water run off from her breasts, a soapy ring of foam collecting in the deep hollow of her navel . . . smooth, shiny thighs. She touched her breasts abstractedly. The water buoyed them. They would probably sag when she got old, like mama's and Aunt Marie's. Now they were firm as hills. Nipples of the palest shade of brown. Star her in the Follies for a mouthful of tit, but she hadn't liked Ziegfeld to touch her. He had clammy hands . . . a paunchy face. So much for ambition.

She was drying her hair when Donovan let himself into the apartment with his key. He had just come from the studio and he was hot, tired and excited.

"Boy oh boy, did Dave rave about you!"

"Did he?" Her voice was cold. "You're supposed to phone first. Key or no key."

He ignored the remark and headed for the kitchen where the liquor was kept. She continued to dry her hair with a towel as he chipped some ice from the block in the icebox, clunked it into a glass and poured Scotch over it—the best. His bootlegger made regular deliveries.

"Don't be a crab," he said, slumping onto the couch. "Everything's going like a house on fire and you're tossing cold water on the flames."

"Don't be dramatic."

"This is going to be one hell of a great picture and you're crabbing about a key." He drank some whisky and placed the glass on the floor. "I wish you'd move out of this dump . . . get a little cottage up on Whitley Heights."

"With roses around the door?"

"Some kidder . . . some sweet kid." He held his arms out for her. "Come here."

She sat on the couch beside him and he slid a hand inside her robe and stroked her skin, warm and soft after the bath.

"I've been thinking about you all day," he said. "I was going to run down to see you, but got tied up." His hand moved down across her belly and rested at the join of her thighs. She bent forward and kissed him on the neck. The robe fell open and he moved his head and kissed her breasts, first one and then the other.

"I can't stay long," he murmured. "Sorry. Got to meet Doll at Buster's house for dinner."

She began to unbutton his shirt while he toyed with her nipples.

"Just fuck and run. I must be crazy."

"Don't be a crab," he said.

The small package wrapped in brown paper was next to the door when she opened it. She knew what it was. Donovan picked it up and handed it to her.

"Somebody sending you a box of candy?"

"Maybe," she said.

There was a note in a slim white envelope.

It makes me happy to know you have this.

Pipp

She crumpled the note in her hand before Donovan could see it. He kissed her lightly on the cheek.

"Popular girl, aren't you?"

"Sure," she said. "Sure."

Wind off the sea. Dazzling prisms of light as the sun caught the choppy wavelets of the harbor. A white ship with broad yellow bands painted on its funnels moved up the channel past the navy pier. Pipp waved at it.

"Bon voyage!"

He stood up in the back of the rowboat and waved his white navy jumper like a handkerchief.

"Bon voyage! Have fun!"

"Sit down," Mae laughed.

He did a handstand on the thwart and waved his legs in the air.

GOOD . . . GOOD! Dave Dale called out from a tug that trailed the rowboat. The camera turned. *FINE, GOOD. BACK ON YOUR FEET. HOLD THE JUMPER UP . . . BE A MAST. THAT SHIRT'S YOUR SAIL . . . FINE . . . GOOD . . .*

The tug churned ahead so that Dale could get another angle. The rowboat rocked in the wake.

"Over we go, me hearties!" Pipp cried.

"You *are* a fool!"

He did a hornpipe on the thwart. "Yo ho ho . . . ahoy, mates!"

He felt happy, a euphoria he had never known before. An overwhelming feeling of joy caused by nothing—the giving of a book, no more than that. The giving and the receiving thereof.

270

"Did you get the book I dropped off last night?" he had asked on seeing her that morning.

"Oh, yes," she said, "but you shouldn't have—"

"No . . . no . . . please. I wanted you to have it."

And then she had said: "Thank you very much."

And that had been that, the end of their conversation. Dave had intruded at that point with instructions on how he wanted the scene in the rowboat staged.

He watched her as she turned her face to the sun, one hand trailing languidly in the green water. He thought of London, that spring before the war. Walking across Hyde Park, seeing lovers in boats on the Serpentine; the men in blazers and straw skimmers, the women in organdy, broad hats, parasols.

"You're so terribly beautiful," he said, mouthing the inaudible words. A gull screamed. The liner blew its horn as it cleared the harbor, Honolulu bound.

LET'S HAVE SOME ACTION THERE. SET A POSE . . . COME ON, PIPP . . . WE HAVEN'T GOT ALL DAY, YOU KNOW!

My dearest Mae . . .

Was that right? He chewed the end of his pencil and stared at the three words. Would just *Dearest Mae* be better? *My dear friend, Mae?*

She wasn't really his *friend,* not in the common meaning of the word. He had only known her—outside of the briefest of meetings—for two days. They were co-workers.

Dear co-worker, Mae? Dear fellow actor, Mae?

He tore up the sheet of paper in disgust and took another from the slim pile of foolscap stacked neatly on the desk beside him. He was alone in the big house except for an elderly cook-maid who slept in an attic room. He should sell the place now . . . and yet . . . and yet . . .

Dear Mae.

That was better. Short, direct, conversational.

I wish to say to you on paper what I cannot hope to say to you in person. My thoughts become garbled and my tongue tied when we are face to face. I know that I have only known you for a brief period, and yet, surely, one must give credence to the age old belief in love at first sight.

Oh God, he thought, I'm writing a love letter! The realization made him tremble. He got up from the desk and paced the room. What would she think when she read it? Would it open her heart to him? Make her smile tenderly? Make her laugh, perhaps? The latter was likely. Could

271

she possibly take him seriously?

There was a bottle of Glenlivet Scotch on a refectory table and he poured half a tumbler full and downed it neat. The whisky helped. Dutch courage.

He could see himself in a mirror. Pasty-faced despite days in the sun. Never tanned. A sickly orange perhaps, but not a healthy glow. Short . . . thin . . . almost wizened. Hair thick but unruly, standing up on the crown like a pigeon's ruff. A love letter to a tall and beautiful woman.

"You silly twit."

He poured himself another drink and went back to the desk.

. . . I must believe in that, for it happened to me. Yes, dearest, lovely Mae. It happened to me! May I quote a verse that I know and love well? I am a tongue-tied fool around you, but if I were blessed with the expressive power of Wordsworth, I would have uttered the following lines to you. "She was a Phantom of delight when first she gleamed upon my sight; A lovely apparition sent to be a moment's ornament; Her eyes as stars of twilight fair; Like twilight's, too, her dusky hair . . ."

That's you, Mae, yes, and I, who have wandered lonely as a cloud . . .

He brought the bottle to the desk and wrote and drank, leveling the bottle by half and filling page after page. His words flowed in a hot, tumultuous stream, a torrent of prose, his handwriting wandering haphazardly across the final pages, the neat penmanship of the first few pages turning to a meaningless scrawl at the last. He signed it with a flourish.

"An' that's . . . that."

He took pains with the envelope, printing each letter, sealing it with a kiss. A stamp was found, licked, pressed on.

"An' off we go."

The night was balmy. A crescent moon. A riot of stars. Great branches swayed restlessly against the sky as he walked unevenly up Irving to Sixth Street and the mailbox. The metal slot opened to the touch of his hand . . . shiny chute to an iron bound interior. The door slammed shut. Letter gone. Irrevocable. Done.

"Where in God's name is he?" Dave Dale said, not expecting an answer from the rest of the company. The morning sun threw long, diagonal shadows across the dock and gleamed off the destroyer's upper works. They had only three more days before the navy towed the ship away to the bone yard. A lot of work to do and Pipp was late.

"Damn it. What's keeping him?"

"I hope he wasn't in an accident," Billy said.

Dale scowled at his watch. "Eddie's the best driver at the studio. Where the hell is that guy?"

At nine o'clock the phone rang in the warehouse room they were using as an office. It was the driver.

"Mr. Dale? This is Eddie. I got a problem, Mr. Dale."

"Where the hell are you?"

"Still at Mr. Pipp's house. I . . . I can't make him unlock his door. I tried, the maid here tried. He just won't do it."

"What door are you talking about, Eddie?"

"His bedroom, see. He's in the bedroom . . . solid oak door. I can hear him movin' around in there, things fallin'. I asked him to please open up and let me in. He just tells me to go away and leave him alone. Gee, Mr. Dale, I've known Mr. Pipp for a long time . . . used to drive at Sterling . . . I know the guy. I think he's off on a toot."

Dale took a deep breath and exhaled slowly through his mouth. "Jesus Christ."

"The maid said all the liquor's gone from downstairs. Said there was three or four quarts of booze there yesterday. All gone now. Must have it with him. Off on a bender, if you ask me."

"Je-sus."

"What shall I do, Mr. Dale?"

"Just stay there." He hung up and dialed Donovan at the studio.

"I'll go over with Gilboy," Donovan said. "Try and shoot around him. Don't waste a day."

Donovan tested the door with his shoulder. "Take an elephant to bust this baby."

"Step aside," Gilboy said. He raised his right leg and kicked the door, flat-footed, his heel connecting just below the lock plate. The door snapped open as though blown back by a cannon.

Donovan nodded soberly. "I bet you were one hell of a cop, Frank."

Pipp was on the carpet next to an overturned chair. He lay groaning in his own vomit, a bottle with a residue of whisky in it lying near his right hand.

Donovan grimaced in disgust. "Christ, I hate drunks."

Gilboy knelt beside the sprawled form and turned the head away from the sour pool in which it lay. Pipp groaned again.

"Gil . . . boy?"

"Yeah," Gilboy grunted. "Yeah."

273

"How bad is he?" Donovan asked, lighting a cigarette.

"I've seen him worse. Just one night's drinking. You should see him when he's had a week or two under his belt."

"I can live without it. Think you can sober him up?"

"Sure. But you can write today off."

"I can see that. What the hell made him do it? He was happy as a lark yesterday."

Gilboy picked up Pipp and began to carry him toward the bathroom. "I don't know. But he'll talk it out with me. He always does."

The smell of vomit and spilled whisky made Donovan feel queasy and he waited downstairs, chain smoking and watching a gardener mow the lawn next door. After what seemed an age Gilboy came down. He was in his shirt sleeves—shirt and pants sopping wet.

Donovan eyed him sourly. "You take a shower with the bastard?"

"Damn near. He'll be okay after he sleeps it off."

"He tell you what triggered the binge?"

"He mumbled a blue streak. I could make out some of it. He wrote Mae Pepper last night. Mailed the letter . . . then went to pieces."

Donovan squinted through a haze of smoke. "What kind of a letter?"

"He didn't say."

"Did she get it?"

"How would I know?"

"Hell, she was on location at seven. They wouldn't deliver mail at five-thirty, six in the morning, would they?"

"I doubt it."

"I'll phone Dave and have her driven up here. What the hell did he write that would make him go off the deep end like that?"

"Who knows? He does odd things from time to time."

"Christ," Donovan snorted, looking around for the phone. "He oughta be kept on a leash."

Mail was delivered to the desk at the Cabrillo Arms where a taciturn middle-aged woman sorted it each morning into the tenants' mail slots. She had her own opinion of Mae Pepper, one that she would have gladly expressed to the manager of the building if asked, and she handed over the woman's mail in chilly silence. She had seen the big, redheaded man who was with her come into the building more than once through the side door that opened onto the garden and she had her own opinion of him, too.

"Open it," Donovan said.

Mae hesitated. The envelope was bulky, with her name and address painstakingly written. Like a child's printing.

"It's personal . . . I'm sure."

"You can read it in the car . . . but I gotta know what's in it. I got a picture to finish. We can't shoot Pipp rolling on the floor with a bottle. That ain't funny."

"Don't push me."

"I'm not *pushing* you, but, goddamn it, he fell apart on me and I gotta know why."

She opened the envelope in the car, leaning back against the door so that Donovan couldn't read over her shoulder. He sat behind the wheel, staring gloomily up the street, trying to ignore the faint rustle of the pages . . . Mae's silence. After a long time she folded the many papers and pushed them back into the envelope.

"He's in love with me," she said softly.

He nodded. "I had a feeling it was something like that."

"He just poured his heart out. You won't be sore if I don't let you read it?"

"Oh, hell no."

"The last couple of pages are almost illegible. I guess he must have been a bit drunk when he wrote it."

"Then lost his nerve and went all the way."

"Yes."

"The poor dope."

"I feel terrible about it. Just awful."

"Hell, it's not your fault. You didn't lead him on or anything, did you?" He saw the answer in her eyes and looked away. "Of course you didn't. Why the hell did I say that? It's a problem, damn it."

"I'll leave the picture. Maybe if I'm not around he—"

"That's not going to solve anything. Hell, it'd just make things worse." He tapped the steering wheel with his fingers. "Maybe you could . . . well, sort of meet him half way on this. Talk it over with him. Be . . . you know, friends."

Her smile was a shadow. "And save the picture."

"Okay," he said gravely. "Yes. What the hell. Six pictures . . . six hundred grand . . . his career . . . mine. What does it take to be sympathetic? He's a nice little guy. What the hell does it take?"

"Nothing," she said, placing the envelope inside her purse. "Not a damn thing."

There was a dim light in the room when he opened his eyes, the softly jewelled glow of the standing lamp with the Tiffany shade, next to the wingback chair. He liked to sit in that chair and read. There was someone seated there now and he knew who it was without having to raise his throbbing head from the pillow.

"I'm so ashamed," he said.

"Don't be."

"Such a bloody, hopeless twit."

"You didn't have to be afraid."

"I felt so good about it . . . at first. Not later. Little doubts whispering in my ear. Had a few beakers to keep going. Then mailed it. Popped it in the letter box on the corner . . . walking back . . . saw something."

"What?"

"Can't say."

She walked over to the bed and sat on the edge of it. He seemed lost in the expanse of blankets.

"What did you see?"

He turned his head and looked at the shadowed room. "What time is it?"

"After midnight."

"Have you been here long?"

"Yes."

"Did the letter make you laugh?"

"I wouldn't be here if it had made me laugh. What did you see, Pipp?"

"Coming back from the post, you mean? A car. Roadster. Parked under a tree. Man and a woman in it. Making love." He drew his arms from under the blanket and folded them across his face. "A man should never say what I said to you unless he is able . . . unless he is capable . . . never write that to a woman unless . . ."

"You don't have to hide your face. Having sex in a roadster isn't making love."

He let his arms flop by his sides. His wrists were like ivory sticks jutting from the flannel pajama top.

"You don't understand, Mae. I'm . . . I'm not a man. Not in that sense, you see. I can't do . . . what . . . men do. It . . . it doesn't happen to me. Women expect it. A natural thing." He smiled wanly. "That's really a great expectation, isn't it?"

She bent forward and kissed him on the cheek. "You're a sweet man. Don't be afraid . . . ever."

276

Her dress buttoned down the front . . . twenty tiny white buttons. She stood up and stepped out of it, then slipped her chemise over her head. She sat on the bed to remove her silk stockings and to undo her hair that tumbled down over her naked shoulders like black smoke.

"Mae," he whispered, closing his eyes.

And then she was beside him, her hands gentle and sure, drawing his thin body from the cocoon of flannel, pressing his fear-clammy flesh against her.

"Mae . . . Mae . . ."

"Shhh," she whispered, cradling his head between her breasts. "Don't say anything . . . don't say a word."

LANTERN SLIDES

"The President is on the phone, Mr. Bolling."

"The President?"

"Mr. Harding . . . long distance from Vancouver."

"Ah . . ."

Vardon Bolling tilted back in his leather chair and enjoyed the luxury of letting the President of the United States wait for a few moments. He then picked up the phone.

"Good morning, Mr. President. How was your Alaska trip?"

The connection was poor, but even over the crackle and hum of the wire he could detect a weariness in the President's tone as he asked him to please speak louder.

"I said *HOW WAS ALASKA?* Fine . . . Good . . . Coming down here? *ARE YOU COMING DOWN HERE?* Fine. When? *WHEN ARE YOU COMING DOWN HERE?* Good . . . fine . . . Florence will love San Francisco. *FLORENCE WILL LOVE FRISCO.* Harry? Yes . . . Yes, I've seen Harry. *YES, I'VE SEEN HIM* . . . can't understand that. *I SAID I CAN'T UNDERSTAND WHY YOU CAN'T REACH HIM* . . . no . . . yes . . . yes . . . *I SAID YES WE CAN COME UP TO MEET YOU* . . . yes . . . yes . . . *COUPLE OF DAYS* . . . St. Francis Hotel. *I SAID SEE YOU AT THE ST. FRANCIS HOTEL* . . . couple of days. *I SAID IN A COUPLE OF DAYS* . . ."

He felt exhausted. Long distance telephone service needed a great deal of improvement—and God alone knew how many operators had eavesdropped on the call, not that anything of vital import had been discussed. An odd call, come to think of it. A letter would have done as well. The President, his wife and a large staff were on the tail end

277

of a speaking tour that had taken him across the midwest and then to Canada and Alaska. He was now on the homeward swing—Vancouver, Seattle, San Francisco, Los Angeles. Why hadn't he just written a note or sent a wire asking him and Harry to meet him in San Francisco? Why phone and shout himself hoarse? Probably just had politics on his mind. Elections coming up next year. The party had taken a drubbing in the congressional races last year, but the country was fond of Warren and the taciturn Mr. Coolidge. They'd be reelected without any trouble. Who could the Democrats possibly come up with? McAdoo? Al Smith? They'd tear themselves to pieces at the convention in *that* dog fight. Warren was a shoe-in. His support in the congress might be a bit less than it had been, but he and "Duchess" would still live in the White House.

He phoned Harry Ashbaugh, which is to say that he had Rose Hanover call all the numbers where the oilman could conceivably be found. He was finally located at his sister-in-law's house in Hancock Park.

"I've been trying to get hold of you," Bolling said affably.

The response was brusque. "You found me."

"Yes . . . well . . . so I did. Warren just called me. He'll be in San Francisco in a couple of days and would like us to come up there. Political palaver, I should think. He'd like to carry this state next year all the way down the ticket and I think we could manage that for him, Harry, I really do."

There was a long pause. Then: "I don't think he wants to talk about politics, Vardon."

"No? What then? You don't think he wants to go into the picture business, do you? Ha ha ha."

"No," Ashbaugh said evenly. "I don't think he wants to do that. I know what he wants to talk about, Vardon."

"And that is?"

"A private matter that's really none of his goddamn business. The man should stick to playing cards and sitting on the porch. He shouldn't start acting presidential."

"I don't understand, Harry."

"I didn't expect you would."

The sudden silence was awkward. Vardon was at a loss for words. Then he said:

"We have a few things to talk over, Harry. I want to bring you up to date on our progress here. Everything is right on schedule."

"I keep myself informed. I know what's going on." He sighed deeply. "I've been staying with my wife's sister . . . in the house where my Virginny was raised. She used to draw and do little colored pictures— flowers, dogs. She had a lot of dolls. I always made a point of buying the kid a doll. No matter where I was or how busy I was . . . bought her a doll. Dallas, Houston, Tulsa, no matter where . . . bought her a doll and had it sent postal express. She kept all those dolls, Vardon, they line the room. I remember buying every one of them."

"That's nice," Vardon said, clearing his throat. "Very . . . poignant."

"I can sit in this room and see her playing with those dolls. I can see her running down when the doorbell rang. I can see her running back up here and sitting on the floor and undoing the package and taking the doll out. They always sent the dolls in a box. Plenty of white tissue paper. Like a little bed. Always one damn place or another. Never did see her do that, but I can see her now. Let me tell you something, Vardon. I don't give piss for what I got. Lot of crap . . . all of it. Paid a fortune for all that junk. Chickens can shit on it for all I care. But, now you take those dolls. You take those colored pictures . . . dogs, flowers . . . they're more precious than gold to me, Vardon. I'll take every bit of it with me."

"*With* you? What do you mean by that, Harry? Are you going somewhere?"

"I may just do that. Yes. I might go to Europe for a spell. France . . . Switzerland, maybe. Take a look at the world from another part of the woods. I've got some deals cooking with the Limies in Mesopotamia and down along the Persian Gulf. Take a little cash with me and drill a few holes."

"I thought you were getting tired of the oil business, Harry." His mouth felt dry, but he wasn't sure why.

"It's going to hell in this country, Vardon. Let me tell you that. Just going straight to hell. Everybody's getting so damn prissy. Can't do this . . . can't do that. They pick on a man. An' that Warren-Goddamn-Harding ain't no goddamn help. That nigger-blooded bastard forgets who the hell put him in the White House. All those good boys from Ohio put him there. And a lot of my money put him there. He oughta get down on his knees and thank God he had friends!"

That conversation cast a pall on the day. He didn't know what it meant. He had never heard Harry Ashbaugh say a bitter word about anyone. He was not the type of man to express vindictiveness in any verbal way. He knew that Harry was capable of ruining his enemies, but that was strictly business. Dog eat dog. The code of the market-place. What he had listened to over the phone had been fury barely contained. Fury at what?

At three-thirty-five precisely that July afternoon the pall deepened. Giannini called from the bank. He had, he said, been analyzing that day's transactions on the New York stock exchange. There had been, unaccountably, a small wave of selling of Ashbaugh Oil near the close of the session. Institutions, mostly. The selling had driven the price down one and a half points.

"Profit taking, A.P.?" Bolling asked.

"That's what I thought," the banker said. "Then I telephoned Andrew Drexel at Morgan's and he told me they were prepared to unload two thousand shares tomorrow on orders from one of their customers . . . Columbia University, I believe. I asked him why. After all, I said, the stock can go nowhere but up, and he said that a rumor out of Washington had made some of their institutional investors nervous."

Bolling held the telephone very tightly to his ear. "What sort of a rumor, A.P.?"

"He was not specific, Vardon. Some story that someone in the Navy Department was passing around. Something to do with the Tule Hills reserves."

"What is that?"

"An oil field, up Bakersfield way. Government land, put in trust for the navy during the war. What that has to do with Harry Ashbaugh I wouldn't know, but this selling worries me. I know how rumors are. They can stampede investors the way thunder stampedes cattle. Nothing to it but noise, but when the running stops your stock has lost fifty points or more. Well, I won't lose any sleep over Ashbaugh Oil going down a point or two. It's ten points higher now than when we took it as collateral, but twenty points . . . thirty . . . fifty . . . that could be catastrophic."

"Yes . . . it would." He had trouble getting the words out of his mouth. His tongue had turned to so much dry meat.

"The cash we advanced was not my cash, you understand. If the value of the stock dips below the amount of the loan I'd be forced to foreclose to protect the bank's investment. Now, I am only thinking out loud on this, Vardon. I don't believe for a moment that that will happen. It may be nothing more than some vicious rumor that will soon be laid to rest. However, if I were you, I would call Harry, if you can. I have not been able to do so."

"He's . . . he's at his—"

"Yes, his sister-in-law's house. I know that. I called him there, but he did not come to the phone. He did not want to talk to me. That upsets me . . . a little."

A little! Sweet Jesus! What was going on?

"I . . . I don't understand that, A.P."

"That makes two of us. Go to New York, Vardon, and drag Harry with you. Hold the line at ninety-eight and three eighths!"

Fate conspired. He would believe that to his dying day. A jest of the Almighty's to teach him humility. Ashbaugh Oil dropped ten more points before he woke up in the morning. A New York newspaper wrote cryptically of secret senate hearings probing an allegation that Secretary of the Navy Denby had permitted naval oil reserve land to be transferred from his jurisdiction to that of Secretary of the Interior Albert B. Fall's. The article made no accusations, but the editor of the paper had printed a photograph taken in 1921 showing Albert B. Fall and Harry Ashbaugh shaking hands in front of a Washington hotel. Both men were smiling.

Wall Street lived by the belief that where there's smoke, there's fire. By ten o'clock in the morning, West Coast time, Ashbaugh stock had tumbled another twelve points. Hold the line at ninety-eight and three-eighths was now an impossible dream.

"Mr. Giannini on the telephone, sir." The butler's tone was bland. Unconcerned. He was an English gentleman's gentleman, a colonel's batman during the war. The son of a Yorkshire farmer, he had a feel for land and invested his savings in it (listening carefully whenever the Levin brothers came to dinner). He would die a multimillionaire in 1967 with one of the longest streets in the San Fernando valley named after him. He seemed always to sense his bounteous future.

"What did you tell him?" Bolling's voice was hoarse, his countenance haggard.

"That I felt certain you had departed for the railway depot, but that I would check and make sure."

"Thank you . . . thank you. Tell him . . ."

"That you have left?"

"Yes."

"Quite so, sir."

The trip east seemed interminable. There was a quicker way—flying by day and connecting with a train at night. The service was experimental. It saved time, but it was exhausting and dangerous. Bolling stayed safe and secluded in his drawing room, brooding as he watched the sun-parched landscape of the great plains unfold beyond the window. Thinking . . . worrying . . .

PRESIDENT STRICKEN

The headline emblazoned all the papers when the train rolled into Chicago.

HARDING TAKEN ILL IN SEATTLE

. . . crab meat, the papers said. Ptomaine. The President's train would carry him to San Francisco. The trip was being cut short.

Hold the line. Make some gains. Vardon Bolling was a charming and persuasive man, a fine orator, a booster, one of the recognized gods in the pantheon of business. Bruce Barton sang his praises in the clubs of power, before lunches with other titans.

"Ashbaugh is more than oil stock," Bolling would say after Barton's introduction, after mutton chops and peas, after assortments of cheeses and glasses of fine, old brandy. "Oh, yes, Ashbaugh means more than oil. It means motion pictures—the fastest growing industry in the United States today. Motion pictures made under the golden sun of the Golden State . . . and motion picture palaces . . . edifices of unparalleled magnificence. A new era of popular entertainment. Sterling-Bolling-Ashbaugh is but one division of the Ashbaugh complex, but by no means its most junior one. The profits to be generated by the combination of great pictures and luxurious theaters will startle even the most wildly optimistic booster of the American dream . . . !"

Hold the line. Make some gains.

"You have a message to sell," Bruce Barton, advertising genius, evangelist of the marketplace, told him. "Put a smile on your face and a shine on your shoes and sell . . . sell . . . sell."

Hold the line. Make some gains. Brokers began to advise their customers not to sell Ashbaugh. Quite a few bought the stock back again. The erosion ceased. The price began to inch up.

THE PRESIDENT IS DEAD

Just like that. A few days of illness. A touch of food poisoning—a common enough ailment in the middle of summer—and then the man was dead. Pneumonia was listed as the cause. Ugly stories began to spread in the drawing rooms of the mighty. No autopsy performed. The body quickly embalmed. A coffin-laden train coming slowly east, flag draped in death bunting. Mourning crowds. Warren had been liked. Comfortable as an old slipper.

HARRY ASHBAUGH DEPARTS

(NEW YORK) In the face of increasing speculation about "secret agreements" between Secretary of the Interior Albert B. Fall and Harry Ashbaugh, the oil tycoon left for Europe this morning aboard the White Star liner *Majestic* bound for Cherbourg. This reporter came across the controversial millionaire as he was walking up the gangplank carrying a large suitcase. As eager White Star porters abounded, I asked him why he was carrying his own luggage . . . and what did it contain. The crusty old fox winked and said, *"Falls."*

He had actually said "dolls." But no matter. He was gone, outward bound on a lake smooth Atlantic. The storm was behind him, rising like demons out of stuffy committee rooms on Capitol Hill.

SCANDAL GROWS
HOW MUCH OF ASHBAUGH OIL BELONGS TO NAVY?

Investors panicked. They had lost all faith in Ashbaugh stock. It was foolish, of course, it was sound as a gold piece, but fear drove it down to the ground and would keep it there for three years. It would slowly rise under a new corporate name and those farsighted men who bought it on the cheap would make fortunes. But no matter. Vardon Bolling was ruined, if not totally in purse, at least in reputation. The dream of great "Sterling Palaces" was riven to dust. Those few that had been completed were sold for a fraction of what they had cost to build. (The pure gold leaf that Harry Ashbaugh had insisted on meant nothing to shrewd-eyed potential buyers who knew that gold paint would have done as well— *"Who can tell gold leaf from paint on a seat in the dark?"*) The bank was selling off what it could in order to recoup fifteen million dollars, plus interest. Thin-lipped bookkeepers and accountants searched through the studio ledgers like moles through dank earth. They found no evidence of mismanagement, but they found figures that startled their frugal souls. An enormous sum of money had been spent preparing for the various epic motion pictures that were to have been previewed in the theaters that were no longer owned.

Bolling felt outraged and humiliated. He returned to the coast on the

Santa Fe's California Limited to find strangers snooping through his most intimate papers and production memos.

I would like the court ladies in Knighthood to wear nothing but the finest imported French lingerie. I believe that the knowledge that they are wearing the best next to their bodies will make them feel like the royalty they are supposed to be.

"Was that a necessary expenditure, Mr. Bolling? After all, fine ladies underwear can be purchased through Sears, Roebuck for a fraction of the cost . . ."

"The company must weigh the expenditure of every dollar. Austerity is the path back to fiscal health. No pictures costing millions of dollars to produce can, or will be made. The receivers are adamant about that. And, to be frank, we doubt if you can inspire confidence in the people whom we hope will invest in a new venture that will rise from the ashes of the old."

SBA PIC KAPUT

Variety! Bolling had always enjoyed reading it, now he shunned it with dread. Every headline he scanned was like a razor slicing at his flesh. The *Los Angeles Times* was no better, though more understandable to the general reader and, in a way, kinder . . .

STERLING-BOLLING-ASHBAUGH PICTURES DISSOLVED

And that was that. He sat in his million dollar home (more or less a million) and watched the leaves turn brown on the elms. He could not longer afford the house. It would have to be sold. Servants let go, chauffeur and fleet of cars dispensed with. A small house, perhaps even an apartment . . . a woman to come in and clean. He could see nothing but despair in the falling leaves. His lawyers were more optimistic. He was down, but far from out. The bank was not being vindictive. Of course they had to take all possible steps to recoup their unfortunate investment, but that could be done without driving Vardon Bolling into the poorhouse. In fact, all that had really happened was that a dream had died. He had failed in his endeavor to control the picture business. Perhaps Zukor would be more successful, but somehow he doubted it.

The business was growing too large for one man or one group to grab the lion's share. It was like trying to corner all the salt in the sea. The Levin brothers, who were not his attorneys but who were his friends, reminded him of a ploy that would get him back at the studio—not as its head, of course, but as an independent producer. Doll Fairbaine's contract was with *him* and it had six more months to run.

"Of course," he cried, rising from the chair he sat in, reaching for a bottle of excellent Moselle and refilling the glasses of his two guests. "A picture with Doll that will set them all on their ears! I'll go down on my knees and beg Griffith to direct it. What a stupendous combination! And not a little Hoosier picture, either. Something with scope . . . depth . . . a touch of humanity. Doll once told me that a man must go through the fire and, by God, I have been through it. I truly feel like a man reborn, revitalized. Why, by thunder, I'm better off without all the cares of running a huge film factory resting on my shoulders. I pity the man they choose to slip into my old shoes."

"Donovan," Myron Levin remarked casually. "That seems to be the number one choice at the moment. Nothing like keeping it in the family, eh, Vardon?"

Vardon Bolling said nothing. He stared into space and drank a glass of wine, then poured himself another, and another after that.

CASSETTE

There is a fine article in *Filmplay,* the January 1924 issue, which I'm sure you remember.

Yes, of course.

It must rank as one of the great laudatory pieces of all time. A totally uncritical view. Not exactly unique for *Filmplay* which always tended to give even sinners the benefit of the doubt, but even so . . .

Yes. Very complimentary, but you have to remember that they had the good of the industry at heart in that article. All that mess in Washington was coming to light, the scandals in just about every branch . . . and Hollywood was being touched with the brush because of Harry Ashbaugh's involvement. And through Ashbaugh, Vardon Bolling and Sterling. Sterling went bankrupt, but the studio was still there—all the stages and all that talent. Everything was reorganized and stock in a new company was put on the market. That stock had to be sold and they figured I might just be the guy who could give Wall Street confidence. I'd made two swell pictures with Pipp that were just burning up at the box office and I had a reputation for being a guy who could get five bucks worth of production values for every dollar spent. Being Doll's husband hadn't hurt my chances, either. She was still a big box office draw and the board of directors of the new corporation . . . Sterling Publix it was called then . . . hoped to lure her into signing a multi-picture deal when her contract with Bolling expired. But that interest waned when they saw some of the new stars I was developing: jazz babies in up-to-the-minute stories, roadhouse sex, fast cars and fast people, gangsters, bootleggers and high society high-jinks. Those pictures were as timely as the headlines.

Yes, they sure were. Still, all of these huge projects that Bolling had in the works were scrapped and that seems a pity.

It was, but no one had any faith in them. They would have cost millions to produce and the idea behind the new company was to make a great many pictures at a reasonable cost and be content with modest profits on each one. We never made a picture that lost a dime and the accumulation of small profits on many pictures added up to fantastic success over the years.

Well, I can't stop myself from playing the might-have-been game. I've seen pictures of the knight's castle set that Bolling constructed and I can visualize it in a film with a cast of thousands. All of that wasted. A shame.

I never made a picture with a cast of thousands, but I did use the castle set for the third Pipp film, *Connecticut Yankees* . . . a burlesque of the Mark Twain story. The set burned down shortly after that. Fully insured . . . which started a few tongues wagging about me, but that's another story.

Yankees was the first Pipp and Wells film, wasn't it?

That's right. *Sons of the Sea* had been a terrific hit and Billy had been so good in it that the exhibitors wanted him to have co-billing. That was okay with Pipp, so I guess you could say that the team was born then —officially.

But not to remain with you. How come?

Oh, you know, fate has its own way of propelling things along.

You were certainly being nicely propelled.

Yes, top of the hill. Although I didn't have the power I would have a few years later.

Christ, what a terrific time to be successful! Coolidge in the White House . . . the Jazz Age going into full swing . . . Valentino . . . Nazimova . . . Ramon Navarro . . . Buster Keaton . . . I don't know,

286

I think I was born in the wrong time. As a film maker . . . or, anyway, a hope-to-be film maker, I tend to see time and place in terms of light and color. Everything today has a brown tone to me. Muted shades, a lack of clarity. Plastic conformity and smog. That's Southern California to me. But looking backward to that time . . . 1924 . . . I visualize a clear yellow light. Vivid blues and greens, startling Moorish whites, like those marvelous, almost primitive lithos that used to adorn orange crates. Golden Sheik . . . California Maid . . . Azuza Sunshine . . . everything so fresh and clean. Sharply etched skylines, Catalina Island always on the horizon.

Oh, they were swell days, all right. But it was just a time . . . good and bad. It wasn't all a clear, yellow light. No, not all of it . . . not by any means.

BROKEN BLOSSOMS

The hills were so clean. She stood on the verandah in the fading light, hands thrust into the pockets of her riding breeches. Fanny sat at her feet, sniffing the evening cool. Not a sound from the hills except the call of nesting birds—her birds on her land. Not a soul for miles. Her mountains and her world. She could have stood there forever, immovable as a tree, watching the land change from the deepest green to black. Beyond the rim of the lower hills she could see the tiny cluster of lights that marked the village of Westwood and far in the distance, past great empty spaces, a thin crescent of lights following the curve of Santa Monica Bay. The breath caught in her throat it was so lovely. Beauty and tranquility. That was what made life worth living. It hurt to think that Earl no longer shared her love of the ranch. Hermits, that was what he had said . . . *"We're like a couple of hermits up here, Doll."*

She heard Juanita call out that dinner was ready and she went reluctantly into the house and had her meal alone—except for Fanny who sat begging beside her chair. She rarely ate with Earl any more. He was off to the studio before she woke up in the mornings and was never home before midnight. She didn't resent it. He wasn't neglecting her on purpose. He had a big job to do and he had to feel his way along. A day to day process, steeling himself for each new challenge. She still found it hard to believe that he was head of the studio, just as she found it hard to believe that Vardon was out.

The thought of it made her wince. Myron Levin had tried to explain to her the complicated financial problems that had led to Vardon's losing control of the studio, but it still didn't make any sense to her. After all, it hadn't been dear Uncle Vardon's fault that Harry Ashbaugh had turned out to be a crook, conniving with that awful man in

288

Washington to steal oil from the United States Navy.

"It's not fair!"

"No, Doll, it isn't. But it is life."

"Life shouldn't be that cruel! That unjust!"

But it was. Fate had ways of sneaking in and dealing terrible blows when one least expected them.

That was why she loved the ranch, although she found it difficult to express her feelings to Earl. If he had been a more religious person he might have understood, but he thought religion was a lot of bunk. That was why he didn't like Anna Temple—not that she could blame him for that. She was beginning not to trust the woman herself. It seemed to her that Anna Temple was more interested in making money than in doing God's work on earth. And she never had made contact with Niles although she had promised to do so and the many attempts had cost a small fortune—two thousand dollars a seance. Anna Temple was in the business of religion. Earl had told her that, but she had refused to listen to him. She had liked the big, dynamic blonde and could see why so many thousands of people were drawn to her.

"Mostly men," Earl had cracked. *"I bet that broad does more on her knees than pray."*

She had hated Earl for his attitude toward Anna, but all that was in the past. Anna had only been trying to exploit her, to prey on her belief in the thereafter.

"It might cost a million dollars to contact your brother, Doll," Anna had said one day. "Only God can permit the souls of the dead to return from the void and speak with the living. I've talked to God through his son, Jesus . . . sweet Jesus who has always been so close to me even when I was a tiny child and used to see him walking the dry fields of Deaf Smith County. Yes, Doll, Jesus spoke to me at ten minutes past four yesterday afternoon and he told me, Anna Temple, gird your loins for battle. There is God's work to be done on earth. There are countless souls to be saved. You can no longer preach out of a tent, even if it is the biggest damn tent ever seen. You must have a marble temple, its walls paneled with cedar from Lebanon and draperies of golden damask. And Jesus said that God would allow Niles to speak to you whenever you wanted if you would just open your coffers and let some of that gold flow up to heaven."

And right at that moment she had lost all faith in the woman. She saw her for what she was, a tent show bible thumper of the type they had run across on the chautauqua from time to time, the kind who could raise up such visions of fire and brimstone that every tightfisted

289

farmer in the neighborhood would hurl money on the stage to keep from going straight to hell.

She had not told Earl of her decision never to see Anna Temple again. That would have meant telling him why—that she had discovered God dwelling in her own hills, in the arroyos chocked with mesquite and scrub pine, in the grassy meadows and sandy gulleys. God was in the birds that nested in her trees. He was in the yucca and the swaying eucalyptus. His voice was in the wind. Not the voice of Niles. She would never hear that voice again. Niles was dead and the dead did not speak to the living. But God spoke . . . if one stood very still and listened. That was why she could never move from this place. Never, no matter how much pressure Earl put on her. He wanted to build a house on part of the land she owned in Beverly Hills . . . up the road from the hotel . . . three and a half acres. Room for a big house and formal gardens, a tennis court, pool, stables. A place to entertain, to throw parties, to get into the swim of things.

"It's a new Hollywood," Earl had said.

Perhaps it was, but did she have to be a part of it? She hated parties, and Hollywood had gone party mad . . . dusk to dawn. Jazz bands, liquor . . . No. She liked being a *hermit.* Peter had been a hermit and he, too, had found God in the wilderness.

"Hello, Earl."

"Hello, baby."

He still spoke to her in terms of endearment, but there was a rift between them. She had taken to sleeping alone since the death of Niles and he had not complained about it. For the past ten months they had been just two people sharing a house and not getting in each other's way.

"Did you eat?"

"Oh, sure, grabbed a sandwich at the studio."

"Can I fix you a drink?"

"Yeah . . . that'd be great."

He sensed a change in her attitude. And as he watched her cross the room toward the liquor cabinet he noticed another change—the candles were not burning on the mantel. The urn of ashes was gone.

"The room's different," he said diplomatically.

Her hand shook slightly as she reached for the crystal decanter of whisky.

"A man came today from the Hollywood cemetery and took the ashes away. I'm going to have the urn placed in a crypt . . . a perpetual flame burning in front of it. They'll do it properly. With taste, dignity."

"Sure. It's the best thing."

"Yes. I made up my mind this morning. I went for a long ride and . . . something, a kind of inner voice . . . told me to phone and make the arrangements."

He could understand her pain and he walked over to her and took the decanter from her hand.

"You did the right thing, Doll."

"I hope so."

"Sure you did. You have to bury the dead, go on with life."

She watched him intently as he poured whisky into a glass. When he was finished she said:

"I have something to tell you, Earl, and I hope you'll understand."

He took a drink, studying her. He'd never seen her stand so rigidly. Her body seemed to be composed of compressed steel springs.

"Shoot," he said.

"I . . . I talked to God today."

He took another drink, rolling the whiskey around in his mouth for a moment before swallowing it.

"Oh? And what did God say?"

She smiled and her body relaxed. "That's my Injun . . . just like that . . . *what did He say!*"

"If he spoke to you he spoke to you, Doll."

"I love you for understanding me, Earl. For being so . . . kind to me."

He nodded slowly and reached for the decanter. "I try to be understanding."

"And you are. Very. Can I tell you about God?"

"Sure. Why not?"

"Well . . ." She took a deep breath and then exhaled slowly. Her face was beatific. "Anna Temple was wrong. All those bible thumpers are wrong. God doesn't *speak*, Earl. He isn't a *person* with a deep *voice*. He isn't a *man*. God is . . . well, God is a rightness . . . a perfection . . . an idea. God talks to you by giving you the right thoughts. He plants it into your mind. You know how I felt about having Niles here. The ashes of his body here . . . so I could . . . touch him now and then, feel close to him. Well, today, as I was riding up by the water tower . . . and there are coyotes up there, Earl, they have a den near the eucalpytus trees . . . where the rocks are . . . and the dogs know it, Earl . . . they could sense the coyotes and they wouldn't budge a step from the road. Something told me to ride up to the tower and I did. Just Duchess and me. The dogs stayed back on the road, whimpering.

291

Maybe they sensed more than the coyotes. Do you think that's possible, Earl?"

"It's possible." He clenched the glass. The whisky was a comfort.

"When I got up there I felt something in the wind . . . a vibration I had never felt before. And that's when God spoke. My brain filled with light. In one second I knew exactly the right things to do: Have Niles' ashes interred . . . and a lot of other things."

She was looking at him with an odd little half smile that he found disquieting.

"What other things, Doll?"

"You and me . . . and what we do with our lives. Vardon telephoned me yesterday. He wants me to make a picture. Mr. Griffith would direct it. That would be my last contractual obligation. After that I'd be free to do whatever I wanted. I don't have to make a picture for Vardon, but I feel I owe it to him. It would help the man. Wouldn't it?"

"Yes. Help him a lot, I guess."

"All of that flashed through my mind. I saw the future so clearly, Injun . . . and you were there. I saw the right path for you . . . and me."

"And that is?"

"We go away." She clutched his arm and drew him toward the couch. "We go for a long trip after the picture is over. We go to France and visit Mama in Paris. And then we go to Italy and to Switzerland, to Spain and to England . . . there'll be crowds everywhere, because I am truly loved in those places, Injun. Like some kind of princess or something . . . and then we come back to Hollywood and I'll buy Joe Simberg's studio and we'll call it the Donovan-Fairbaine studio. You'll be the head of it and we'll make our own pictures. I know that Mr. Griffith would join us because he is in terrible financial trouble because of that studio of his on Long Island and nothing he's done has made a penny since *Way Down East.*"

"Times are changing," Donovan said in a flat voice. He sat on the edge of the couch and nursed his drink. "*The White Rose* was a 1916 kind of picture. A lot of people think that D.W. is over the hill. And this latest one of his . . . *America* . . . the word is that it's dull as hell, an old-fashioned flag waver . . . George Washington and Paul Revere in twelve reels. Jesus! Who'd go and see it with what's around today?"

"Sex and hipflask pictures," she scoffed, pinching his arm. "Jazz babies and all that flaming youth stuff. Don't be silly, Injun. Mr. Griffith is the master. I know his last couple of pictures have done badly at the box office, but that doesn't mean he's over the hill, as you put it. No . . . not by a long shot. He'll bounce right back . . . with me as his star. Vardon owns a wonderful story, a novel. *The Girl from Mackinac.* It's the story of a young girl who lives with her blind father in a cabin in the north woods . . . in Michigan . . . and she falls in love with a lumberjack, but her father hates the lumber company. There's a tremendous blizzard and the blind father is trapped . . . the girl and the lumberjack struggle to find him . . . swirling snow . . . falling trees . . . a really spectacular kind of picture, Injun, with a message of love and self-sacrifice that will tug at the heart."

He swallowed the last of his drink. "You sound like Vardon."

"Do I?" she said ingenuously. "Oh, I hope I caught some of his enthusiasm. I know it would be the right kind of picture for us. A great, sweeping story of love found and love lost and love found again. It would take a year to make because Mr. Griffith would like to capture the full span of the seasons . . . spring . . . summer . . . fall . . . the dead of winter . . . the cycle of life."

"Doll," he mumbled. "Listen, Doll—"

"And I can see myself so clearly in the role. That vision came to me as I stood on the hill this morning and God spoke to me in the wind. I saw myself as that girl from Mackinac, struggling through adversity to find love and happiness in the end. Peace and fulfillment. We've been happy here, haven't we, Injun?"

"Yes, Doll." He stared into his empty glass.

"And so there's no reason to change things. No reason to move away and build a house and open it to a lot of shallow, sponging people. We don't have to be hermits, Earl . . . we can have quiet little parties here with a few close friends. And we can travel . . . and have our studio and make such wonderful motion pictures . . . stories of love and faith and goodness . . ."

"I have a job, Doll . . . obligations."

Her smile was tolerant. "But you'd give that up, silly Injun. That's not the right place for you, anyway. You're not really the boss. Not like Vardon was the boss. You have to fight everything out with the board of directors . . . with the bank and all those awful people from Wall Street. You're not really your own man at all. I know what's going on there . . . people call and tell me. And the pictures you're making. Comedies, all those jazz pictures . . . fast cars and fast women with a moral tag stitched on at the end to satisfy the Hays Office. Those are awful pictures, Injun, and you know it."

He shifted the empty glass from one hand to the other. He could have used another drink, but didn't feel like getting up to get it. To have another drink would mean prolonging what had become a one-sided conversation.

"I'm very tired, Doll, why don't we—"

"Oh, there's no hurry, Injun. We can talk it over tomorrow . . . make our plans. You go to bed. I'll just sit here for a while and think about this day. Such a strange day and yet . . . such a wonderful day . . . an inspiring day . . ."

He headed for bed, crossing the big room toward the hall, glancing back at her. She was staring into space. Smiling. He doubted if she was aware that he had gone.

"Good morning, Mister Donovan."

The efficient Rose Hanover brought in the trade papers and the morning mail. She had accepted the transition from Vardon Bolling to Earl Patrick Donovan without a qualm. Bolling had tried to lure her away with nebulous promises, but being the sole supporter of a widowed mother she had a keen sense of survival. The structure of Sterling Pictures might have undergone drastic changes, but the weekly pay envelopes had not been even one second late in arriving.

"Top of the morning to you, Rose."

Donovan settled behind a desk that was overflowing with scripts, letters, budget sheets and exhibition gross statements. Bolling had taken his hunting prints and fine English furniture from the office when he left and the room was spartanly furnished. It suited Donovan because he was rarely in it. There was too much to do on the lot. He glared sourly at all the papers.

"Let's make a dent in this crap. It just tries to bury me. How long have you been in this business, Rose?"

"Mister Bolling hired me in 1913."

"It's about time you had more responsibilities. Consider yourself a production assistant. Fifty bucks a week raise . . . hire yourself a girl and get all this junk in order. I just want to know the important stuff. You can give me a daily report and take care of the routine things yourself."

Rose Hanover looked stunned. "Fifty a week . . . raise?"

"Make it a hundred. Let's get this circus into high gear, what the hell."

He stalked the lot like a restless tiger, patting heads and kicking butts. The future of Sterling, now owned by a conglomerate of indepen-

294

dent theater owners, a distributing company, a bank, a Wall Street brokerage house and ten thousand shareholders, might be in some doubt, but there was no doubt in anyone's mind who ran the show.

"What the hell do you think you guys are doing?"

"Building new sets for that college picture, Mister Donovan."

"Like hell."

"Mister Pratt's orders."

"Well, we'll see about that. What the hell does he think he's making? *Intolerance?* Drop those goddamn hammers and go repaint the set on stage seven."

"Yes, *sir,* Mister Donovan. You're the boss."

"You're goddamn right I am."

He sought out Chester Pratt who was as restlessly peripatetic as himself, his anger at the little ginger-haired man cooling off as he roamed from one end of the lot to the other. He passed the castle set just before noon to find Dave Dale in trouble with a routine and falling behind schedule.

"What's the problem, Dave?"

"Nothing I can't work out. I want Pipp to fly over the wall after sassing Merlin the magician, only the goddamn wire is too thick . . . it'll show on the screen and look ridiculous."

"Get piano wire," Donovan snapped. "I want this picture in the can by tomorrow night."

"It will be. Don't worry about it. We won't even take a break—we'll work all night if we have to."

Pipp, standing nearby in a tangle of wire, protested.

"I was going to take Mae to lunch, Earl. That Chinese place on Sepulveda."

"She can split a sandwich with you here. Sorry, Tom. No hour and a half breaks today."

He moved off before Pipp could make any further protest. A camera car rumbled past on its way to the New York street set.

"You seen Chester?" he called out to the driver. The man jerked a thumb in the direction of Stage 4.

Pratt was alone on the stage, except for fat Kewpie Dolan who was his shadow. The director was examining the skeleton of a new set while Kewpie sat on a box eating a banana.

"Hello, Chester," Donovan said.

"Hello yourself," Pratt said tonelessly.

"I got a bone to pick, Chester. You're building too damn many sets.

I pulled the crew off that sorority house dorm for *Dancing Coeds.*"

The director said nothing. He stalked the wood framework like a fox moving through saplings.

Donovan leaned against a two-by-four and lit a cigarette.

"Don't keep it bottled up, Chester. Smoke's coming out of your ears."

"Okay," he said, seething. "You want some gripes then you came to the right man. I'm sick of all this crap I'm doing. I try to get *some* value in the damn things. I don't like using one set for five goddamn pictures."

"Nobody knows the difference and they're making dough. That's all that anybody gives a damn about. Just hold on."

"I'm so fucking sick of sheiks, shebas and rouged knees I could throw up."

Donovan blew smoke through his nose. "The public loves it. You thinking of quitting?"

Pratt kicked a loose board viciously. "No, but goddamn it to hell."

"Okay. Let's not blow a cork. Things are getting rosier and I think we can expand the product. Norman Dawson Payne dropped a script off last week. Finally got around to reading it yesterday. It's gutsy as all hell . . . about some Mexican bandits. Part of Pancho Villa's army who take over a mining town in Sonora. Place is run by a couple of American engineers. It's got everything . . . battle stuff . . . shoot-outs. The damn thing's like a whip across the face. I thought it might be something Dave could handle, but I think I'll keep him on the Pipp and Wells pictures. How'd you like the job?"

Pratt stared at him intently. "You're not kidding about this, are you, Donovan?"

"Hell no. The scenario's in my office. Have Rose give it to you. It's called *Two Iron Men.* I've got some ideas on it, but I'll tell you about 'em after you read it. One hundred percent location shooting. Hell, we can hire all the real bandits we want ten miles from Yuma."

"Thanks, Donovan. I'll read it right away. I swear to God, I'm so fed up with these flapper pictures I—"

"Sure, I know. And speaking of flappers, Will Hays was on the phone this morning complaining about that roadhouse scene in *Where Are Your Daughters?.* He thought it was too suggestive."

"Too suggestive? That's the whole point. The testing of the girl's virtue, the—"

"That's exactly what I told him. I even quoted the Bible, every passage I could remember about sin and redemption."

"Did he go for it? I'd sure hate to reshoot all that stuff."

"Of course he went for it. The day I can't handle an Indiana rube is the day I give up."

A fresh wind blew in from the ocean bringing the scent of rain. Donovan cursed softly but vehemently under his breath as he walked toward the cutting rooms. That was all he needed right now with four pictures shooting out of doors, a goddamn rainstorm! He glared balefully at the sky, at thin streaks of ragged cloud. Maybe, he thought bitterly, Doll would put in a good word with the man upstairs.

He spotted the car as it came through the gate and moved slowly down the road toward him, a spanking new Templar runabout, light blue with a tan canvas top. A shiny new dime of a car, but not nearly as handsome as the woman behind the wheel.

"Hello, stranger," he said as the car pulled up beside him.

"Stranger yourself," Mae said.

"You're a sight for tired eyes." She was wearing a pale beige coat with big tortoise shell buttons down the front, a brown turban framed her face. "Yeah, something to see, all right."

She looked away from him, one gloved hand gripping the wheel. "I'm meeting Pipp for lunch."

"Not today. No lunch break for the clowns. Pipp has to fly over the castle wall before I let him have a cup of coffee."

"Tough son of a bitch, aren't you?"

"Yeah, but with a heart of gold." He leaned against the car door. "How about your having lunch with me?"

She stared fixedly ahead. "No."

He put a hand inside the car and ran a finger up the side of her neck. "Do you know the Palm Inn . . . just this side of Hermosa?"

"No, I don't." Her voice was throaty.

"You can't miss it. I'll be there at one-thirty."

She put the car into gear and rolled on, not saying whether she would be there or not—but he knew that she would be.

A SHORT SCENE

"Jesus," he said, chuckling softly, "I used to think that motion pictures were worlds apart from what I was doing."

"What were you doing?" she asked, lying on her side, her head against his chest, one hand moving slowly up and down his right thigh.

"Doing? Hell, I don't know. Shoveling elephant shit, looking in

297

looney bins for pinheads, shortchanging the rubes. What the hell *wasn't* I doing! Earning a dollar . . . a hard dollar . . . but it beat digging coal or working the docks. Then, see, I'd maybe hit some burg a few days ahead of the carny. Drum up a little business, nail a few posters, stuff like that. Dead as hell in those towns with the rubes standing in front of the feed store and the sports in the saloon. Maybe a cathouse on the edge of town, couple of washed out bints from Chicago old enough to be my mother. Well, you know, to hell with all that. Take in a flicker. Doll Fairbaine . . . Mabel Normand . . . Mae Marsh . . . Wally Reid . . . a Griffith picture, maybe. I saw *Intolerance* in Baltimore. Fourteen reels. That's how long it was. *Fourteen* reels. Of course, I didn't know that then. All I saw was the goddamndest thing I ever saw in my life. And I remember thinking . . . Christ, the guy who made this thing doesn't have to hustle up freaks. They die on you, did you know that? Find a good fat lady and she splits a gut one night and you gotta hustle like hell and get another one. Pinheads die like flies. They always smile. Simple, see . . . not right in the head. Crazy as mice, but gentle . . . sweet. Very nice people, pinheads, only they die at the drop of a hat, smiling from ear to ear."

"Are you drunk?"

"Hell, no . . . excited . . . maybe a little sad. I don't know. I feel like I'm in the middle of a long road and I don't know whether to walk back or keep on going. Ever feel that way?"

"Sure."

"Well, that's how it is with me. That's why I had to see you. I can spill things out . . . get it off my chest. You don't mind, do you?"

"No."

"Fine, swell . . . what was I talking about?"

"*Intolerance* . . . fourteen reels."

"Sure. Fourteen goddamn reels. Nothing will ever top that picture. Those huge sets . . . thousands of people . . . war . . . massacre . . . hangings. Everything flying back and forth in time. Makes your head spin. Big flop that picture . . . audiences didn't like it. Too damn much. They couldn't get it all in. Made 'em confused. I saw that picture and I knew I could never do anything like it. Never. That was in, oh, 1916, I guess. I was hoping to get the hell out of the carny business and try my luck in the West—but that picture sort of dampened my plans. I didn't know then that it was going to be a flop, I guess Griffith didn't know it, either. Hell, he's still paying for it. That picture's like a hole in one of his veins. Anyway, getting back to Baltimore, I walked out of the theater and I said to myself, Earl Patrick Donovan, you're a horse's ass. You couldn't even *think* of something like *Intolerance*. I never made the fourth grade so what would I know about Babylon? Nothing. I said, all you know about are pinheads, cooch dancers and Chinese bibles."

"Chinese what?"

"Stick to what you know best, I said to myself, but what's really funny is that I'll never know as much about moving pictures as Griffith, but I know one hell of a lot more about rubes. I know what it takes to part a rube from his money. I know what he'll pay to see. You gotta hit a rube in his guts. You can't try and educate a rube. He resents it, see. He doesn't like it one bit. He'll empty his goddamn pocket to stare at an alligator boy or gawk at a three hundred pound woman, but you can't squeeze a nickel out of him to improve his mind."

"The Donovan touch?"

"Yeah, you could put it that way."

"Picture in your mind the primeval quality of the land. Great forests run to the very edge of the lake, a lake vast as the sea, wind whipped and cold as iron. Tiny hamlets bloom in this wilderness, carved out of the woods by brute force, the muscles of men, the biting edge of a steel blade on a hickory shaft."

An actor, Donovan was thinking as he did his best to appear entranced. David Wark Griffith speaking, walking slowly back and forth as he orated his lines. The Master . . . the Great Man. Tall, hawk-faced, faultlessly garbed in the best London tailoring. Doll and Vardon Bolling couldn't keep their eyes off of him. They followed his every movement, strained forward on their chairs at every word . . .

"And in this green darkness, this jungle of spruce and pine, there dwells a simple heart. A lovely maiden . . . the *little dear one* we shall call her, chaste and loving child of a bitter man. A blind man, a man withdrawn from a world that treated him so cruelly . . . a man blinded because of the greed of the lumber barons. Our little dear one knows nothing of this. She is a child of the woods, growing to glowing womanhood surrounded by the creatures of the forest. She knows nothing of the perfidious nature of man. One day she hears a sound. She cocks her head to one side and listens. We see the deer and the squirrels, the beaver and the wolverine listen also. We then show lumbermen swinging their axes on the giant trees. There is an army of them. Many are mere brutes. Hard drinking louts, coarsened by their awful labor. A lumber baron . . . fat . . . wearing a fine suit, smoking a big cigar—greedy faced, hard-eyed. He waves a hand at the virgin forest and says 'Cut it all down.' There will be few titles. I detest breaking up the visual imagery with a lot of words. A preamble will be written . . . perhaps by Carl Sandburg . . . setting the message clearly for the audience."

"Of the triumph of love over greed!" Doll said fervidly. "That there is in each man a tiny spark of goodness and humanity no matter how brutalized he might be."

"Exactly," Griffith said. He clasped his hands behind his back and rocked slowly on his heels. "Yes. That is precisely it and my little golden doll will move the audience to both smiles and tears."

"Oh, isn't it wonderful, Earl?"

Donovan turned in his chair so that he could look out the window behind his desk. Bolling's old film factory sprawled at his feet, churning out a different kind of product than Bolling had envisioned. A score of flappers moved quickly out of the shadow of Stage 5 and hurried toward Stage 7 for the fraternity dance scene in *The Charleston Dancer*. Silk clad legs flashed. Buttocks shimmied under tight fitting dresses.

"Listen," he said. "I've got to be truthful about this, D.W., I don't want to get involved in this picture. I don't want to sound like a bastard, but I can't see any hope for it at the box office. It might have been a good idea five or six years ago, but now . . ."

Doll jumped to her feet. "That's a terrible thing to say, Earl. I think you should apologize to Mr. Griffith!"

"That's perfectly all right," Griffith said graciously. "I respect Mr. Donovan's opinion. I would not find it necessary to apologize to him for my views on *his* pictures."

"I know this is the property for me," Doll said. "I know it because . . . because *something* tells me it is. You know it's the right picture for me, don't you, Vardon?"

Bolling looked shaken. "Yes. Yes I do."

She walked quickly to the desk and knelt at Donovan's feet, hands clasped as though in prayer.

"Please, Earl, say that you like it. Speak from your heart on this. *The Girl From Mackinac* will be *our* picture. The first of so many wonderful pictures, Earl. It has to be because that was the message in the wind. That was what . . . what I was told. I explained all that to you, Earl. You know what I heard that day below the water tower. I can't go against that. You and I, Mr. Griffith and dear Uncle Vardon, the four of us with our own studio, making pictures of hope and love, showing man for what he is, a creature of God. Built in His likeness, imbued with His spirit."

He looked down into her impassioned face, into eyes that were glazed with an inner fire.

"I'm sorry," he said. "Sorry as hell, but He didn't speak to me. He didn't tell me what to do. I've got to stay here and play the cards in my hand. Can't you see that, Doll? I'm running the show here. I can't pull up and leave."

She rose slowly to her feet, never taking her eyes from his face.

"You can't do that, Earl. That isn't the way it's supposed to happen . . . the way He said. He wouldn't lie to me. Never. If you don't join with us, if you don't come with me to Michigan and then to our own studio then it's because He changed his mind. I have to find out, Earl. I have to go there and listen. Wait very quietly under the tower . . . listen very carefully . . ."

"What is she talking about?" Vardon asked nervously. "I don't understand what she's saying."

"Shut up," Donovan said.

"Because he may not want me to make a picture at all . . . ever, ever, ever. Do you think that's it, Earl?"

He couldn't look at her. He couldn't look at Bolling or David Wark Griffith, either.

"I don't think He'd want you to do that, Doll. You can make all the pictures you want without me."

She shook her head fiercely. "Never. No. I can't be that wrong. I know it. It was so clear. Such a brilliant illumination. My brain was like a crystal ball and I could see everything so clearly . . . even our names on the sign. Green and gold . . . Donovan dash Fairbaine Studios . . . the ads in *Variety* and *Photoplay* and *Film Daily* . . . D. W. Griffith and Vardon Bolling have joined forces with Doll Fairbaine and Earl Patrick Donovan to make the kind of moving pictures the whole world is crying out to see. Yes, Earl, I saw all that with great clarity." She shut her eyes for a moment. "So clean it was. But if, but if you *don't* come with me . . . if you *don't* come . . . then I must have heard it wrong . . . I must . . . wait . . . find out . . ."

"For Christ's sake," Bolling cried. "Will you please tell me what she's saying?"

"She doesn't want to make the picture," Griffith said, a tight smile tugging at his thin lips. "That's quite obvious to me. Nothing on earth would have given me greater pleasure than to be able to direct my little golden doll once again. I have no fonder memories than those long ago days at number eleven, East Fourteenth Street in New York City. Such happy times. Such wonderful hours spent with such faultless thespians:

301

Henry Walthall, Lionel Barrymore, Blanche Sweet, my dear Lillian and Dorothy, Adele de Garde. But if it is not to be it is not to be. I like the concept, Vardon. It has all the power of *Way Down East* and I know it will be as successful. I can see Lillian in the role . . . or Mae Marsh. It will be made. It's simply a question of money. Wouldn't you say so, Vardon?"

Vardon Bolling could say nothing. There was a roaring in his ears and his legs were trembling, forcing him to sit down again. He wondered if he was on the verge of a stroke. *Money!* Good God. Of course it was a question of money. *Everything* was a question of money these days. Money could be raised on Doll—not that it would have been necessary. The Levins had been willing to invest her own money in the venture. Without her there was nothing. He couldn't raise a dime on his own name . . . his own reputation . . . no, not for years. Not till all this oil scandal . . . this disgrace was laid to rest. And D.W. couldn't raise much. Not now. Not after *The White Rose* and the meager attendance of *America.* Not after James Quirk's withering editorial about him in the latest issue of *Photoplay*—a vicious, uncalled-for attack that must have hurt D.W. deeply although he never showed pain. The great face of stone . . . a sardonic smile—if he smiled at all.

"Money," he said, the word barely heard. "Yes . . . just money."

"I'll ride up there again," Doll said in a burst of passion. "I will do that. I know I'll get another sign. Don't you feel that I will, Injun? Don't you think He'll speak to me again?"

He looked out the window. The flappers were gone. All those fleshy little bottoms. All gone. Nothing between the stages but shadows. A newspaper scattered by the wind.

"Sure He will," he said. "Sure."

She was living with him, although Donovan imagined that *staying* was closer to the truth. More nurse and companion than mistress. They had never talked about it, not once, avoiding the subject by unspoken agreement. He never talked about Doll and she never mentioned Pipp's name when they met two or three afternoons a week at the cottage he had rented in Hermosa Beach. No roses around the door. Paint flecked clapboard. The wild booming of the surf. Salt marsh, sea grass and blowing dune.

It wasn't a day for them to meet, but he had to see her. He felt explosively taut. He had made a decision, rightly or wrongly, but it had been made. In the middle of that long road. Going forward on it toward some dimly perceived objective.

He parked his car in the driveway of Pipp's house and walked across the lawn toward the front door. Her car was by the garage—blue and tan, shiny in the afternoon sun. Pipp would still be out in Glendale at the airfield, the first day of shooting on *The Barnstormers*.

"You shouldn't come here," she said, opening the door herself, the maid hovering in the background.

"Let's go for a drive."

"No."

"Then let me in for a minute. I want to talk. Jesus, what a day. I told D.W. Griffith to shove a story up his ass and Doll and I are kaput. She doesn't know it yet, but I'm moving out."

"Oh?" She put a hand to her throat and toyed with a necklace of jade beads.

"Do I have to stand here like a brush salesman?" He stepped past her, into the hall. The maid smiled at him and went off about her business.

"Let's go into the library," Mae said, watching the maid go up the stairs. She waited until she heard the woman's footsteps on the upper landing and then walked down the hall and into an oak-paneled room lined with book shelves and furnished with leather chairs and a chintz covered sofa. Donovan followed her and closed the door behind them.

"I've got to get away for a couple of weeks or I'll end up in the bughouse. Come with me, Mae."

Her fingers were restless on the beads as she turned to face him. "Now? Just like that?"

"No. Not this second. A few days. Mexico. The Hotel Casa del Sol in Santa Rosario . . . about an hour's drive from Yuma. Chester's down there scouting locations for a blood and thunder so I've got to go there anyway. Bribe a general or two so we can make the picture in Sonora without any trouble. I'll stay on after Chester leaves. You can take a train to Yuma and I'd meet you."

She sat stiffly on the edge of the sofa. "God, how do I tell Pipp?"

"He's not two years old, Mae. Why don't you wean the guy?"

"Oh, shut up."

He searched his pockets for a pack of cigarettes. "I'm sorry. That was a lousy crack. He's been good to you . . . and you've been damn good for him. Hell, I know what you're feeling—that you're running out on him. Okay, if you love the kid, then stay."

"It's just that he loves me . . . very much."

"Sure he does. Who wouldn't? But that's not enough and you know it. You wouldn't be driving down to Hermosa if it was."

She winced. "Give me a cigarette." He lit a Camel and handed it to her. "I don't want to hurt him."

"Of course not, but I don't believe he's as fragile as everybody seems to think. What the hell, he's got to grow up sometime."

He began to stalk the room, glowering at the books. Leather bindings. He wondered if Pipp had read them all.

"What is this going to do to Doll?"

"That's my problem, not yours. Look, Mae. I want you with me. I'm sick of grabbing an hour or two every now and then. It's swell down in Mexico. Sun . . . wide open spaces . . . a knockout hotel. You can hear birds at night. Doves, I guess."

She puffed on her cigarette. "I wouldn't have to tell him right away."

"Oh, hell no."

"I could just tell him I was going east for a couple of weeks. New York, Montreal, and then . . ."

"Sure. Why not?"

She studied him gravely as he walked back and forth. "How badly do you want me?"

"You know how badly."

"Tell me."

He stopped in front of her and cupped her chin in his hand, raising her face.

"You're the most beautiful woman I've ever known. So damn beautiful I feel like socking somebody in the jaw. I wake up in the middle of the night sometimes because I think you're beside me . . . hope you are, anyway. You know what I mean, Mae?"

She touched his arm, feeling the power there. "Sure."

"I may not love you the way Pipp does. I love in my own way. If it's enough for you then come down and we'll take it from there. One day . . . one night at a time."

Her skin felt hot and there was a tight sensation in her throat. "I'll be there."

He let go of her and stepped back. "Take next Thursday's train . . . Santa Fe . . . get off at Yuma."

"Shall I send you a wire?"

"Only if you change your mind."

"Do you think I will?"

He tapped her gently on the chin with his fist. "Not in a million years."

304

Dusty cottonwoods and a water tower. Sand hills dotted with mesquite and queerly twisted cactus. Only two passengers left the train in Yuma, a short, powerful looking Navajo with a turquoise and silver band around his hat and Mae Pepper, svelte in a dark blue traveling suit. All eyes, male and female, had been on her since the train pulled out of Los Angeles. Tom Pipp and Billy Wells had brought her to the depot.

"Those are the actors in that picture we liked so much, Martha . . . about the two sailors. You remember."

"Why, yes, so it is. Pipp and somebody."

"Wells. Billy Wells. Tubby fellow, isn't he?"

Billy driving right up to the train in his new Apperson, chocolate brown with a thin yellow stripe highlighting the coachwork, taking Mae's pigskin suitcase from the trunk and handing it to the redcap while Pipp flustered over Mae, asking her a hundred times if she had her ticket . . . had a book to read . . . had the candy he'd bought. Just before the train pulled out Pipp had removed a small package from his pocket and handed it to her.

"Open this when you get to Chicago," he said. "Not before. You promise?"

"What is it?"

"A little something," he said, shifting his feet in embarrassment. "A token."

ALL ABOARD!

Mae compressed her lips, shoved the package into her purse and turned quickly toward the steps. A porter took her arm.

ALL ABOARD!

Dust devils spiraling toward a painfully blue sky. Nude hills. White birds stalking the sand flats of the Colorado. She shielded her eyes against the sun as she stepped down onto the platform. The train hissing, eager to be gone. Donovan stepped out of the shadows of the station house looking at home in his riding pants, open shirt and broad-brimmed hat.

"Good trip?"

"Hot," she said.

"Hot as hell here. They've built a swimming pool at the hotel . . . artesian water . . . cool as a highball."

She had to force a smile. "Sounds swell."

He sensed her stiffness as he placed an arm about her waist.

305

"Anything the matter, babe?"

"Just tired, maybe a little depressed. Pipp fussed over me. I don't know, I feel such a bitch."

"You'll get over it." He gave her a quick hug, the train pulling out behind them, several people standing on the observation platform. "You'll feel like a million dollars in no time at all."

They drove south in the back of an open Packard, a Mexican in a khaki uniform driving it, dust goggles fastened to the crown of his peaked cap.

"Compliments of General Roberto Vicente Lopez, military governor of Sonora—for *this* week at least." Donovan smiled wryly. "Every time I pay one guy they replace him with another, but it looks like we're all set now. We should start shooting in three weeks. Want a part? There's a gorgeous Spanish girl role. You could do it."

She stared through the windscreens at the harsh land. "What happens to her?"

"She gets violated by a hundred bandits."

"The story of my life."

"Seriously. She rides into the sunset with the hero . . . on the back of a white horse. Bloody but unbowed."

The driver slowed slightly as they came into Santa Rosario, a hand pressed against the horn button. Children, chickens and dogs scurried out of the car's path. Mae stiffened.

"Tell him to take it easy."

Donovan smiled. "He doesn't speak a word of gringo. Anyway, they don't believe in brakes down here." He waved a hand airily. "Look around. This is Mexico, kid."

She saw clustered adobe buildings and ramshackle hovels thrown up out of tarpaper and tin; a pink church, ornate as a wedding cake; soldiers lounging against a whitewashed wall; a row of pink and blue and ochre shacks with women standing in narrow doorways.

"The hotel is better," Donovan laughed.

They were out of the little town as suddenly as they had come into it. The driver floored the accelerator and the car roared down a well packed and oiled gravel road. In ten minutes they were through the wrought iron gateway to the Casa del Sol. Green lawns . . . trees and flowers . . . expensive automobiles parked along a crescent drive . . . the hotel's white walls . . . green shutters.

"You're going to love it here," Donovan said, giving her arm a squeeze.

There was one huge bed in the room and she sank down on it gratefully, kicking off her shoes. Donovan opened her suitcase and began to put her things away in a black oak dresser. Sunlight filtered through wood shutters and cast a neat pattern on the tiled floor. He held up a long nightgown.

"You brought a lot of stuff you won't need."

"Don't be so sure of yourself."

He folded the nightgown into a drawer and came over to the bed, bending over her and kissing her firmly on the lips. Her mouth opened and he ran his tongue across her teeth.

"Some sweet kid," he murmured. "Some babe."

She was still lying naked across the bed when he came out of the shower, rubbing his hair briskly with a towel. The last rays of the sun filled the room with a pale orange glow that made the hairs on his body look like a tangle of gold wires.

"We'll have a couple of drinks and then one hell of a dinner," he said, draping the towel around his neck as he searched a drawer for underwear. "It's informal here so you can wear what you please."

"I'll come as I am," she said.

"That'd set you up just swell with General Lopez. He'd probably make you queen of Mexico."

The house phone on the wall jingled and Donovan stepped into a summer union suit before answering it.

"Who?" he asked. "Oh sure . . . put him on." He held a hand over the instrument. "It's Chester."

"So?" she said.

He scowled at her and then removed his hand from the mouthpiece.

"Chester? Hell, I thought you'd be halfway home by now. What? Where the hell's Casa Verde? Oh, yeah . . . sure. Well, nothing you can do about it. Nice of the guy to drive you back here. I bet you and Kewpie could stand a triple highball. Sure. I'll be down in about ten minutes. Yeah. See you guys in the bar. Don't worry about it. See ya, fella." He hung up and walked over to the bed, sat on the edge of it and rested a hand on her thigh.

"That was Chester."

"I know," she said.

"His car busted an axle while he was checking out a location this morning. He's been stranded all day. Some rancher gave him a lift back here."

"That's too bad. About the axle, I mean."

"Yeah. Well . . . anyway . . . I'll have the general's driver take him and Kewpie to Yuma. They can hop the train back to Los Angeles."

"All your little problems solved."

"Sure." He stroked her petal flesh with his fingertips. "Look, Mae. I gotta get some drinks into the boys . . . and a quick dinner. They've been standing out in the sun all day. You know how it is."

"Fine with me. I like Chester."

He ran the back of his fingers across a soft moistness. "I don't want him to see you, Mae . . . to know that you're here."

She raised herself on her elbows and looked at him. "What difference does it make? The last thing Chester Pratt would do is to run to Pipp with the good news. And as for Kewpie Dolan, he wouldn't know if the sun rose unless Chester told him."

Donovan stood up abruptly and went to the closet for his clothes. "It's got nothing to do with Pipp. I don't want Chester to think that I'm staying down here to . . . well, you know."

Her eyes were cold. "To fool around? To make whoopee?"

"Don't put it that way."

"It's what you mean though, isn't it?" She sat up and drew a sheet across her body. "Isn't it?"

He didn't answer her. He pulled on his pants and then walked back to the bed and sat beside her.

"Let's not start out on a sour note. Okay? I don't want you down there because I don't want one of my directors to have one damn thing to talk about, or to think about, my personal life. What the hell, we've got two weeks to ourselves after he leaves. Two weeks to really work something out between us."

"Such as?"

"Don't pressure me, Mae. You know my situation. There's going to be all kinds of fireworks when I ask Doll for a divorce. Oh, she'll give it to me, all right. I feel pretty sure about that . . . but every gossip writer in the business will sharpen their shovels and start digging. I want you out of it . . . safely tucked away somewhere. You understand that, don't you?"

"Right down the line."

He kissed her on the neck. "That's my babe."

She watched him finish dressing, and then he was gone, blowing her a kiss from the doorway. She wanted a cigarette and knew there was a pack of Murads in her purse, but there was something else in her purse, tucked away on the bottom, and she didn't feel up to seeing it. She knew what was in the small package that Pipp had given to her— a letter would be there, neatly folded around a box . . . a velvet box with

308

a ring inside of it. The letter would be beautiful, filled with quotes from Shakespeare, Wordsworth, Byron and Shelley, words of love that he could never utter to her directly. A love letter wrapped around a love token, to be read in Chicago. He would be waiting in a few days time for a telephone call.

Long distance from Chicago . . .

"Oh, God."

She got off the bed and walked into the bathroom, still steamy from Donovan's shower. Her body looked strange in the full length mirror . . . misty . . . lush but blurred. The body of Pipp's wife—or Donovan's whore.

Chester Pratt saw her as she walked into the dining room and he half rose from his chair, a fork with a piece of steak ranchero on it still in his hand. Donovan looked quizzical.

"What are you going to do, Chester, make a speech?" Then he turned his head. "Well," he said, "if it isn't Mae Pepper. Mae, I guess you know everybody."

"Sure," she said. "How are you Chester?"

"Very well, thank you," he said with painful formality. "And yourself?"

"Couldn't be better." She patted Kewpie Dolan on the top of his head as a waiter scurried for a chair. "How's the grub, Kewpie?"

"Great," Kewpie said with his mouth full. "Couldn't be . . . better."

Donovan pushed his plate away and tilted back in his chair. His smile was expansive, if tight.

"How about this? Old home week."

The waiter set a place for Mae and handed her a menu. She studied it critically, avoiding Donovan's steady gaze.

"I thought I might test for the girl part."

Pratt nodded solemnly. "You'd be great for it."

"I don't think so. Not quite the type. I think you should get a real Mexican girl. Very young . . . seventeen, eighteen. A girl with . . . well, an obvious innocence."

Pratt cleared his throat and cut a slice of meat. "Could be."

"Don't you think I'm wrong for the part, Donovan?"

"No," Donovan said. "But then it's up to you. If it's going to make you feel uncomfortable, then forget it. You'll find something else."

"I've got something else. I'm going to stick with it . . . for better or worse."

309

He stood in the bar playing poker dice for drinks with General Lopez. He could see the lobby from the bar and he could see one of the bellboys carrying Mae's suitcase down the stairs and across the lobby to the front doors. He felt a sharp knot of pain in his gut and he looked away.

"Four queens," the general crowed. "That beats your jacks and kings."

"Any time," Donovan said.

Pratt came into the bar, his knee-high laced boots ringing on the tiled floor.

"Well, we're taking off, Earl."

"Have a good trip. I'll be back after I wrap things up with the general."

"Not to worry," the general said, scooping the dice off the bar and placing them in a leather cup. "President Calles is my uncle."

Donovan checked his watch. "You going to make it?"

Pratt nodded. "Sure. We should get into Yuma about two in the morning and flag the Sunset Limited when it comes through at a quarter to three."

Donovan saw Mae crossing the lobby with Kewpie Dolan. Heading for the car. He turned his back and reached for the dice cup.

"Take care of yourself."

He was half drunk, but the whispering and throat clearings that he could hear through the door woke and sobered him. It was dawn and a cool wind made the window shutters creak. A motorcycle stuttered into life and roared off down the drive. The whispering in the corridor became louder and he could hear the deep voice of the general. He sat up, feeling clammy and cold, waiting for a knock upon the door.

"Rose? Can you hear me, Rose? Yeah, it's a lousy connection . . . routed through Yuma . . . I'll talk louder. Rose, listen carefully. There's been a bad accident . . . car blew a tire. Mountain road . . . Chester's dead. Yeah, terrible . . . Kewpie, too . . . and Mae Pepper. *Pepper* . . . you know her . . . yes . . . God awful thing. Didn't suffer . . . no one had any pain . . . blessing. Yes, a blessing . . . now listen to me, Rose. Call Frank Gilboy and tell him about Mae . . . he'll know what to do. Chester's wife is in Santa Barbara . . . the Biltmore . . . you call her, Rose. You can handle that best. And Rose . . . listen . . . write this down. I've got a regiment of Mexican cavalry moving in here on the fifteenth for the picture. Gotta roll on this . . . be set up here by the thirteenth . . . so . . . so . . . tell Dave Dale I want him down here right away and to bring Granny Granville with him and one of the art directors—Talbot or Green—and put another director on the Pipp and Wells picture. Sam or maybe Tony King. It doesn't matter . . . it really doesn't matter, Rose . . ."

General Lopez put a drink in his hand when he hung up the phone. He drank half of it, then set the glass on the desk in the general's office and walked up to his room. The maid hadn't made the bed yet and he sat on the edge of it and ran a hand across the rumpled sheets. Her odor was still there, faint, lingering. It would probably be there forever. His fingers touched a hairpin and he picked it up, holding it gently between his fingers for a long time.

OUT TAKES

The heat struck Billy like a blow in the face as he stepped off the train. It bounced off the station platform and cannonaded from the corrugated iron roof of a baggage shed. It had been raining in Los Angeles and he wasn't dressed for an Arizona heat wave. The sun scorched him through his clothes, beat on his light brown bowler as though it were made of brass. He saw Frank Gilboy standing in the shadows of the terminal and he walked down the platform toward him, breathing slowly through his mouth because the hot, dry air hurt his nose.

"Hello, Frank."

Gilboy spat out a well chewed toothpick. "Billy."

"Is he still there?"

"Yeah. Hasn't budged."

"Is he in bad shape?"

The big man shrugged. "I don't know. He could have booze with him, but all he's ordering is tea and toast. I took the adjoining room and I could hear him walking around all last night . . . back and forth. Nearly drove me nuts."

Billy removed his hat and wiped sweat from his head with a bright blue handkerchief.

"And you're sure he wants to talk to me?"

"That's the message he phoned down to the desk. Tell Mr. Gilboy to call Mr. Wells. Okay. You're here. Maybe you can do something with the kid. I'm sick of trying."

They drove to the Mesa Hotel in Gilboy's car, the sun hammering through the canvas top.

"He's through at Sterling," Gilboy said after blocks of silence. "It's

311

now official. Out of his contract as of today. It's what he wanted. There was no kick from Donovan."

"No," Billy muttered solemnly. "Of course not."

It was cool in the hotel lobby and Billy felt his sweat congeal under the ceiling fans. Gilboy stayed in the lobby, sprawled wearily over half a leather sofa and Billy took the elevator to the fifth floor.

"Is that you, fat chap?" The voice was faint through the door in answer to his knock.

"Yes," Billy said. "Open up, Pipp."

"It's not locked. Come in."

The drapes were drawn in the room, but he could see Pipp in the dimness, lying on a fully made bed. He pulled a chair up to the bed and sat down.

"How do you feel, Pipp?"

"I don't know. I don't know how I feel. Odd . . . very odd."

He didn't look bad, Billy noticed with relief. A bit pale, but then he was always pale. His suit was clean and his shirt unstained. He didn't look like a man who had been on a bender.

"It took Frank two weeks to find you."

"Did it? Funny. I was here all the time."

Billy's smile was weak. "I guess he just looked in the wrong places."

"Yes. Whorehouses and speakeasies. All my old haunts."

"Have you been . . . you know . . ."

"Soaking it up? No. Haven't touched a drop. Whisky won't help."

Billy stared down at his hands, folded tightly in his lap.

"No. It won't help at all."

Pipp sat up and swung his legs over the edge of the bed. His feet didn't touch the floor.

"I've been standing by the window mostly. You can see the railway tracks from here. The trains going east . . . going west into California. A lot of trains come through here in a day, fat chap."

"Yes, I bet they do at that."

"Got a bit maudlin for the first few days. Imagining her on one of those trains . . . coming back from Chicago. Felt a bit sorry for myself, to tell the truth. A bit self-pitying. But all that passed. I think I'll go away, Billy. Go back to Australia . . . or maybe to London. Go back into the halls. I think I could do quite well. Oh, not the kind of money I've been used to, but that doesn't matter. I don't need much money."

A drape stirred in the wind. A window blind rattled against the glass.

"She *was* coming back, you know," Billy said quietly.

Pipp rubbed his lips with the back of his hand. "I know that. Yes.

I know all about that. Still . . . there's a pain."

"Sure."

"And so I thought . . . that if I went away . . . Well, anyway, I've half made me mind up about *that* . . . but I can't help feeling windy about it. A bit on the bad side . . . After all, you're a straight man and you might have some trouble finding another comic."

"Don't worry about me," Billy said. His voice was toneless. "I'll make out okay."

"So I felt I owed it to you to tell you. Face to face like. And . . . well . . . I'd appreciate your comment. I mean to say, do you think I'm doing the right thing?"

Billy looked into Pipp's thin, unhappy face for a long time and then he stood up and walked over to one of the windows and pulled the drape back, letting in a flood of sun.

"If you leave, you'll carry Mae with you for the rest of your life. And you'll carry her all alone. I loved her, too. I've always loved her. I feel just as much pain as you do. I'm your friend, Pipp, not just your straight man. Who would you find in London who would understand about Mae? Who would you talk to about her? Who would give a damn? Christ, get the hell out of this room . . . stop sticking knives in your chest. Do you know what's playing down the street? *Sons of the Sea* . . . kids lining up for half a block. *Sons of the Sea* and a Tom Mix picture. Let's you and me walk down to that theater and say hello to those kids. It'd give 'em a big kick. Pipp in the flesh—in Yuma, Arizona, for God's sake. Or you can stay here and watch the trains. You can watch till the day you die, but she'll never be on one of them."

The fat man walks on the balls of his feet with a peculiar mincing gait that gives him a perilous air, like an elephant balancing on a wire. The smaller man keeps pace with him, pumping his arms, a travesty of a swagger. They walk out of the lobby of the Hotel Mesa, out of the cool dimness where ranchers sit at noon and down the main street toward the Bijou theater, walking in the hard yellow sunshine of an Arizona spring into a kind of immortality.

FADE OUT

313